WEST OF YOUR CITY

WEST OF
YOUR CITY

Poems by

William Stafford

THE TALISMAN PRESS
Los Gatos, California 1960

Acknowledgments

Acknowledgment is made to the *Atlantic, Borestone Mountain Poetry Awards, 1955, Colorado Quarterly, Hudson Review, The Nation, New Republic, Pocket Books, Inc., Poetry, Saturday Review, Southwest Review Talisman Press, Western Review*, for permission to reprint here poems which first appeared in the pages of those publications, and to the corporation of Yaddo for assistance in the preparation of this book.

Library of Congress Card 60-9512

CONTENTS

Midwest

Far West

Outside

Midwest

West of your city into the fern
sympathy, sympathy rolls the train
all through the night on a lateral line
where the shape of game fish tapers down
from a reach where cougar paws touch water.

Corn that the starving Indians held
all through moons of cold for seed
and then they lost in stony ground
the gods told them to plant it in —
west of your city that corn still lies.

Cocked in that land tactile as leaves
wild things wait crouched in those valleys
west of your city outside your lives
in the ultimate wind, the whole land's wave.
Come west and see; touch these leaves.

ONE HOME

Mine was a Midwest home—you can keep your world.
Plain black hats rode the thoughts that made our code.
We sang hymns in the house; the roof was near God.

The light bulb that hung in the pantry made a wan light,
but we could read by it the names of preserves—
outside, the buffalo grass, and the wind in the night.

A wildcat sprang at Grandpa on the Fourth of July
when he was cutting plum bushes for fuel,
before Indians pulled the West over the edge of the sky.

To anyone who looked at us we said, "My friend";
liking the cut of a thought, we could say "Hello."
(But plain black hats rode the thoughts that made our
    code.)

The sun was over our town; it was like a blade.
Kicking cottonwood leaves we ran toward storms.
Wherever we looked the land would hold us up.

CEREMONY

On the third finger of my left hand
under the bank of the Ninnescah
a muskrat whirled and bit to the bone.
The mangled hand made the water red.

That was something the ocean would remember:
I saw me in the current flowing through the land,
rolling, touching roots, the world incarnadined,
and the river richer by a kind of marriage.

While in the woods an owl started quavering
with drops like tears I raised my arm.
Under the bank a muskrat was trembling
with meaning my hand would wear forever.

In that river my blood flowed on.

IN THE DEEP CHANNEL

Setting a trotline after sundown
if we went far enough away in the night
sometimes up out of deep water
would come a secret-headed channel cat,

Eyes that were still eyes in the rush of darkness,
flowing feelers noncommittal and black,
and hidden in the fins those rasping bone daggers,
with one spiking upward on its back.

We would come at daylight and find the line sag,
the fishbelly gleam and the rush on the tether:
to feel the swerve and the deep current
which tugged at the tree roots below the river.

AT THE SALT MARSH

Those teal with traveling wings
had done nothing to us but they were meat
and we waited for them with killer guns
in the blind deceitful in the rain.

They flew so arrowy till when they fell
where the dead grass bent flat and wet
that I looked for something after nightfall
to come tell me why it was all right.

I touched the soft head with eyes gone
and felt through the feathers all the dark
while we steamed our socks by the fire
and stubborn flame licked the bark.

Still I wonder, out through the raw blow
out over the rain that levels the reeds,
how broken parts can be wrong but true.
I scatter my asking. I hold the duck head.

HAIL MARY

Cedars darkened their slow way
over the gravel in town graveyards
in places we lived—Wichita, or Haven.

By themselves, withdrawn, secret little shadows
in their corners by the iron gate,
they bowed to the wind that noticed them,

Branches bending to touch the earth;
or night raised them to block the sun
with a thousand utterly weak little hands,

Reciting.   They say candle-vigilant woods
in high Arizona swirl twisting upward
out of red dust miles of such emphasis,

Like them, dark by dark by dark.

LISTENING

My father could hear a little animal step,
or a moth in the dark against the screen,
and every far sound called the listening out
into places where the rest of us had never been.

More spoke to him from the soft wild night
than came to our porch for us on the wind;
we would watch him look up and his face go keen
till the walls of the world flared, widened.

My father heard so much that we still stand
inviting the quiet by turning the face,
waiting for a time when something in the night
will touch us too from that other place.

CIRCLE OF BREATH

The night my father died the moon shone on the snow.
I drove in from the west; mother was at the door.
All the light in the room extended like a shadow.
Truant from knowing, I stood where the great dark fell.

There was a time before, something we used to tell—
how we parked the car in a storm and walked into a field
to know how it was to be cut off, out in the dark alone.
My father and I stood together while the storm went by.

A windmill was there in the field giving its little cry
while we stood calm in ourselves, knowing we could go
    home.
But I stood on the skull of the world the night he died, and
    knew
that I leased a place to live with my white breath.

Truant no more, I stepped forward and learned his death.

A VISIT HOME

In my sixties I will buy a hat
and wear it as my father did.
At the corner of Central and Main.

There may be flowers by the courthouse windows
and rich offices where those town-men
cheated him in 1929.

For calculation has exploded—
boom, war, oilwells, and, God!
the slow town-men eyes and blue-serge luck.

But at the door of the library I'll lean my cane
and put my hand on buckshot
books: Dewey, Parrington, Veblen . . .

There will be many things in the slant of my hat
at the corner of Central and Main.

THE FARM ON THE GREAT PLAINS

A telephone line goes cold;
birds tread it wherever it goes.
A farm back of a great plain
tugs an end of the line.

I call that farm every year,
ringing it, listening, still;
no one is home at the farm,
the line gives only a hum.

Some year I will ring the line
on a night at last the right one,
and with an eye tapered for braille
from the phone on the wall

I will see the tenant who waits—
the last one left at the place;
through the dark my braille eye
will lovingly touch his face.

"Hello, is Mother at home?"
No one is home today.
"But Father—he should be there."
No one—no one is here.

"But you—are you the one . . .?"
Then the line will be gone
because both ends will be home:
no space, no birds, no farm.

My self will be the plain,
wise as winter is gray,
pure as cold posts go
pacing toward what I know.

Far West

WALKING WEST

Anyone with quiet pace who
walks a gray road in the West
may hear a badger underground where
in deep flint another time is

Caught by flint and held forever,
the quiet pace of God stopped still.
Anyone who listens walks on
time that dogs him single file,

To mountains that are far from people,
the face of the land gone gray like flint.
Badgers dig their little lives there,
quiet-paced the land lies gaunt,

The railroad dies by a yellow depot,
town falls away toward a muddy creek.
Badger-gray the sod goes under
a river of wind, a hawk on a stick.

OUR PEOPLE

Under the killdeer cry
our people hunted all day
graying toward winter, their lodges
thin to the north wind's edge.

Watching miles of marsh grass
take the supreme caress,
they looked out over the earth,
and the north wind felt like the truth.

Fluttering in that wind
they stood there on the world,
clenched in their own lived story
under the killdeer cry.

A SURVEY

Down in the Frantic Mountains
they say a canyon winds
crammed with hysterical water
hushed by placid sands.

They tried to map that country,
sent out a field boot crew,
but the river surged at night
and ripped the map in two.

So they sent out wildcats, printed
with intricate lines of fur,
to put their paws with such finesse
the ground was unaware.

Now only the wildcats know it,
patting a tentative paw,
soothing the hackles of ridges,
pouring past rocks and away.

The sun rakes that land each morning;
the mountains buck and scream.
By night the wildcats pad by
gazing it quiet again.

24

IN THE OREGON COUNTRY

From old Fort Walla Walla and the Klickitats
to Umpqua near Port Orford, stinking fish tribes
massacred our founders, the thieving whites.

Chief Rotten Belly slew them at a feast;
Kamiakin riled the Snakes and Yakimas;
all spurted arrows through the Cascades west.

Those tribes became debris on their own lands:
Captain Jack's wide face above the rope,
his Modoc women dead with twitching hands.

The last and the most splendid, Nez Percé
Chief Joseph, fluttering eagles through Idaho,
dashed his pony-killing getaway.

They got him.   Repeating rifles bored at his head,
and in one fell look Chief Joseph saw the game
out of that spiral mirror all explode.

Back of the Northwest map their country goes,
mountains yielding and hiding fold on fold,
gorged with yew trees that were good for bows.

THE GUN OF BILLY THE KID

When they factoried Billy's gun
and threaded it on that string
that ended in far hearts,
the quitting bell rang.

From a gunshop with walls honeycombed
mild as church sunlight
with promises for the soul
the gun went out to hunt.

That line the gun barrel followed
wavering for years then trued
went strangely devious on Sunday,
tugging at its pool of blood.

Nosing miles of promise
the front sight could find its game
and rest at point with no doubt—
this the round world confirms,

But over the wall of the world
there spills each lonely soul,
and snapping a gun won't help
the journey we all have to go:

In the iron of every day
stars can come through the sky,
and we can turn on the light
and be saved before we die.

Now I once handled firearms
but I handed them back again,
being a pacifist—
then why do I sing this song?

Because, of all the lost,
only the sign of the cross
can bring a killer home,
and Billy the Kid was one,

And Smith and Wessen, who helped,
and singers and story-tellers,
kids in the vacant lots—
all careless hearty fellows.

I follow this, light and strong—
this belief men treat like smoke deer—
through a world like our Southwest
with its monotony, distance, and power.

Billy the Kid was game,
but his game was murder in life:
to know, to see, to save—
for these do good men strive.

And I say my story is true
and is about God and is well;
I tell it the way it came to me,
as one of the truths to tell.

WILLA CATHER

Far as the night goes, brittle as the stars,
the icy plain pours, a wolf wind over it,
till white in the south plunge peaks with their cold names,
curled like wreaths of stone with blizzard plumes.
In the highway shed at GrayBull the workers pause
and hear that wind biting their fences down,
scouring the land, as in early days the Sioux
with winter riding their backs in the folds of their robes
fled the White Father toward the Bitter Roots.

Over that shaking grass a thousand miles
where Spanish Johnny sang to the man he killed,
Nebraska, stretching, touched a continent
trying from the rock of Quebec to Santa Fe
for a certain humble manner of meeting the days:
cedars repeated themselves over the scarred ground,
surrounding with patience the Archbishop's garden;
a badger dug a den wisely; down in Shimerda's
dugout a face turned toward mesas and some still town.

That land required some gesture: conciliation.
A steady look from a professor's house
made the space of America slide into view
to press against the cheekbones all its wind
that carved the land for miles, and in the wind
an old man was calling a language he barely knew,
calling for human help in the wide land, calling
"Te-éach, te-éach my Ántonia"—
into all that silence and the judgment of the sky.

BY THE SNAKE RIVER

Something sent me out in these desert places
to this apparition river among the rocks
because what I tried to carry in my hands
was all spilled from jostling when I went
among the people to be one of them.

This river started among such mountains
that I look up to find those valleys
where intentions were before they flowed
in the kind of course the people would allow
where I was a teacher, a son, a father, a man.

Hills lean away from the loss of this river
while it draws on lakes that hang still among clouds
for its variable journey among scars and lava,
exiled for that time from all green for days
and seeking along sandbars of bereavement at night.

This river is what tawny is and loneliness,
and it comes down with a wilderness of power
now and then begging along a little green island
with lush water grass among the rocks
where I have watched it and its broken shells.

The desert it needs possesses too my eyes
whenever they become most themselves to find
what I am, among sights given by chance
while I seek among rocks, while the deep sturgeon
  move
in this water I lift pouring through my hands.

SMALL ITEM

A tumbleweed that was trying,
all along through Texas, failed
and became a wraith one winter
in a fence beyond Las Vegas.

All you fortunate in this town
walking, turning, being so sure,
and catching yourselves before ruin,
graceful and intent on your own—

In the space between your triumphs,
the tumbleweed, missing and trying,
flickered out there, haphazard, with grace too,
flared beautifully wasted at random.

AT THE BOMB TESTING SITE

At noon in the desert a panting lizard
waited for history, its elbows tense,
watching the curve of a particular road
as if something might happen.

It was looking at something farther off
than people could see, an important scene
acted in stone for little selves
at the flute end of consequences.

There was just a continent without much on it
under a sky that never cared less.
Ready for a change, the elbows waited.
The hands gripped hard on the desert.

LORE

Dogs that eat fish edging tidewater die—
some kind of germ, or too much vitamin.
Indian dogs ate copper for a cure;
a penny will save a spaniel that ate salmon.

On the shore beachcombers find a float
of glass the Japanese used on a net
that broke away deep over the side of the world
and slid blue here on the beach as a gift.

Pieces of driftwood turn into time
and wedge among rocks the breakers pound.
Finding such wrought-work you wonder if the tide
brings in something else when the sun goes down.

WEATHER REPORT

Light wind at Grand Prairie, drifting snow.
Low at Vermilion, forty degrees of frost.
Lost in the Barrens, hunting over spines of ice,
the great sled dog Shadow is running for his life.

All who hear—in your wide horizon of thought
caught in this cold, the world all going gray—
pray for the frozen dead at Yellow Knife.
These words we send are becoming parts of their night.

VACATION

One scene as I bow to pour her coffee:—

> Three Indians in the scouring drouth
> huddle at a grave scooped in the gravel,
> lean to the wind as our train goes by.
> Someone is gone.
> There is dust on everything in Nevada.

I pour the cream.

THE FISH COUNTER AT BONNEVILLE

Downstream they have killed the river and built a dam;
by that power they wire to here a light:
a turbine strides high poles to spit its flame
at this flume going down.   A spot glows white
where an old man looks on at the ghosts of the game
in the flickering twilight—deep dumb shapes that glide.

So many Chinook souls, so many Silverside.

SAUVIES ISLAND

Some years ago I first hunted on Sauvies Island.
Wide, low, marshy—it was in the way
for explorers, except when they wanted game.
Now it is held by spare-time hunters like me.

What do we gain on Sauvies Island? I can tell you
in the space of this one little block: neglect.
We don't expect or give anything—we just go hunting.
It's a wild spot, and little is expected.

Of late I have been very successful.
My friends and family count more and more on me.
On that first trip I shot one duck;
my partner was deservedly surprised when I let him eat
    half.

My life has become counted on by too many nice people;
going back I hunt little surprises, and Sauvies Islands.

WATCHING THE JET PLANES DIVE

We must go back and find a trail on the ground
back of the forest and mountain on the slow land;
we must begin to circle on the intricate sod.
By such wild beginnings without help we may find
the small trail on through the buffalo-bean vines.

We must go back with noses and the palms of our hands,
and climb over the map in far places, everywhere,
and lie down whenever there is doubt and sleep there.
If roads are unconnected we must make a path,
no matter how far it is, or how lowly we arrive.

We must find something forgotten by everyone alive,
and make some fabulous gesture when the sun goes down
as they do by custom in little Mexico towns
where they crawl for some ritual up a rocky steep.
The jet planes dive; we must travel on our knees.

THE MOVE TO CALIFORNIA

1.

THE SUMMONS IN INDIANA

In the crept hours on our street
(repaired by snow that winter night)
from the west an angel of blown newspaper
was coming toward our house out of the dark.

Under all the far streetlights
and along all the near housefronts
silence was painting what it was given
that in that instant I was to know.

Starting up, mittened by sleep, I thought
of the sweeping stars and the wide night,
remembering as well as I could the hedges
back home that minister to comprehended fields—

And other such limits to hold the time near,
for I felt among strangers on a meteor
trying to learn their kind of numbers
to scream together in a new kind of algebra.

That night the angel went by in the dark,
but left a summons: Try farther west.
And it did no good to try to read it again:
there are things you cannot learn through manyness.

2.

GLIMPSED ON THE WAY

Think of the miles we left,
and then the one slow cliff
coming across the north,
and snow.

38

From then on, wherever north was,
hovering over us
always it would go,
everywhere.

I wander that desert yet
whenever we draw toward night.
Somewhere ahead that cliff
still goes.

3.
AT THE SUMMIT

Past the middle of the continent—
wheatfields turning in God's hand
green to pale to yellow,
like the season gradual—
we approached the summit
prepared to face the imminent
map of all our vision,
the sudden look at new land.

As we stopped there, neutral,
standing on the Great Divide,
alpine flora, lodgepole pine
fluttering down on either side—
a little tree just three feet high
shared our space between the clouds,
opposing all the veering winds.
Unhurried, we went down.

SPRINGS NEAR HAGERMAN

Water leaps from lava near Hagerman,
piles down riverward over rock
reverberating tons of exploding shock
    out of that stilled world.

We halted there once.   In that cool
we drank, for back and where we had to go
lay our jobs and Idaho,
    lying far from such water.

At work when I vision that sacred land—
the vacation of mist over its rock wall—
I go blind with hope.   That plumed fall
    is bright to remember.

ALONG HIGHWAY 40

Those who wear green glasses through Nevada
travel a ghastly road in unbelievable cars
and lose pale dollars
under violet hoods when they park at gambling houses.

I saw those martyrs—all sure of their cars in the open
and always believers in any handle they pulled—
wracked on an invisible cross
and staring at a green table.

While the stars were watching
I crossed the Sierras in my old Dodge
letting the speedometer measure God's kindness,
and slept in the wilderness on the hard ground.

WRITTEN ON THE STUB OF THE FIRST PAYCHECK

Gasoline makes game scarce.
In Elko, Nevada, I remember a stuffed wildcat
someone had shot on Bing Crosby's ranch.
I stood in the filling station
breathing fumes and reading the snarl of a map.

There were peaks to the left so high
they almost got away in the heat;
Reno and Las Vegas were ahead.
I had promise of the California job,
and three kids with me.

It takes a lot of miles to equal one wildcat
today.   We moved into a housing tract.
Every dodging animal carries my hope in Nevada.
It has been a long day, Bing.
Wherever I go is your ranch.

Outside

BI-FOCAL

Sometimes up out of this land
a legend begins to move.
Is it a coming near
of something under love?

Love is of the earth only,
the surface, a map of roads
leading wherever go miles
or little bushes nod.

Not so the legend under,
fixed, inexorable,
deep as the darkest mine
the thick rocks won't tell.

As fire burns the leaf
and out of the green appears
the vein in the center line
and the legend veins under there,

So, the world happens twice—
once what we see it as;
second it legends itself
deep, the way it is.

OUTSIDE

The least little sound sets the coyotes walking,
walking the edge of our comfortable earth.
We look inward, but all of them
are looking toward us as they walk the earth.

We need to let animals loose in our houses,
the wolf to escape with a pan in his teeth,
and streams of animals toward the horizon
racing with something silent in each mouth.

For all we have taken into our keeping
and polished with our hands belongs to a truth
greater than ours, in the animals' keeping.
Coyotes are circling around our truth.

BOOM TOWN

Into any sound important
a snake puts out its tongue;
so at the edge of my home town
every snake listened.

And all night those oil well engines
went talking into the dark;
every beat fell through a snake,
quivering to the end.

This summer, home on a visit,
I walked out late one night;
only one hesitant pump, distant,
was remembering the past.

Often it faltered for breath
to prove how late it was;
the snakes, forgetting away through the grass,
had all closed their slim mouths.

LEVEL LIGHT

Sometimes the light when evening fails
stains all haystacked country and hills,
runs the cornrows and clasps the barn
with that kind of color escaped from corn
that brings to autumn the winter word—
a level shaft that tells the world:

> *It is too late now for earlier ways;*
> *now there are only some other ways,*
> *and only one way to find them—fail.*

In one stride night then takes the hill.

TWO EVENINGS

I

Back of the stride of the power line
a dozen antelope dissolved into view,
but we in the car were fading away—
we were troubled about being ahead of time.

The world became like a slow mirror,
clear at first till images welled,
as if decisions could raise the sun
or eyes build faces in the quicksilver.

II

Today toward night when bats came out—
flyers so nervous they rest by turning
and foreknow collision by calling out "Maybe!"—
we anticipated something we did not expect.

Counting the secretaries coming out of a building
there were more people than purposes.
We stared at the sidwalk looking for ourselves,
like antelope fading into evening.

ICE-FISHING

Not thinking other than how the hand works
I wait until dark here on the cold
world rind, ice-curved over simplest rock,
where the tugged river flows over hidden
springs too insidious to be quite forgotten.

When the night comes I plunge my hand
where the string of fish know their share
of the minimum.   Then, bringing back my hand
is a great sunburst event; and slow
home with me over unmarked snow

In the wild flipping warmth of won-back thought
my boots, my hat, my body go.

THE WELL RISING

The well rising without sound,
the spring on a hillside,
the plowshare brimming through deep ground
everywhere in the field—

The sharp swallows in their swerve
flaring and hesitating
hunting for the final curve
coming closer and closer—

The swallow heart from wing beat to wing beat
counseling decision, decision:
thunderous examples. I place my feet
with care in such a world.

A RITUAL TO READ TO EACH OTHER

If you don't know the kind of person I am
and I don't know the kind of person you are
a pattern that others made may prevail in the world
and following the wrong god home we may miss our star.

For there is many a small betrayal in the mind,
a shrug that lets the fragile sequence break
sending with shouts the horrible errors of childhood
storming out to play through the broken dyke.

And as elephants parade holding each elephant's tail,
but if one wanders the circus won't find the park,
I call it cruel and maybe the root of all cruelty
to know what occurs but not recognize the fact.

And so I appeal to a voice, to something shadowy,
a remote important region in all who talk:
though we could fool each other, we should consider—
lest the parade of our mutual life get lost in the dark.

For it is important that awake people be awake,
or a breaking line may discourage them back to sleep;
the signals we give—yes or no, or maybe—
should be clear: the darkness around us is deep.

51

CONNECTIONS

Ours is a low, curst, under-swamp land
the raccoon puts his hand in,
gazing through his mask for tendrils
that will hold it all together.

No touch can find that thread, it is too small.
Sometimes we think we learn its course—
through evidence no court allows
a sneeze may glimpse us Paradise.

But ways without a surface we can find
flash through the mask only by surprise—
a touch of mud, a raccoon smile.

And if we purify the pond, the lilies die.

ACQUAINTANCE

Because our world hardened
while a wind was blowing
mountains hold a grim expression
and all the birds are crying.

I search in such terrain,
face flint all the way,
alert for the unreal
or the real gone astray.

And you I greet, gargoyles—
untrue, assuming no truth,
never expecting my compass,
built from the first on grief.

ON THE GLASS ICE

It was time.   Arriving at Long Lake the storm
shook flakes on the glass ice, and the frozen fish
all lay there surprised by February.

I skated hard in the beginning storm
in order to meet every flake.   Polished,
the way rich men can wait for progress, the lake waited.

It got a real winter blanket—the day
going and the white eye losing downward,
the sky deeper and deeper.   No sound.

In deep snow I knew the fish were singing.
I skated and skated till the lake was drowned.

SAYINGS FROM THE NORTHERN ICE

It is people at the edge who say
things at the edge: winter is toward knowing.

> Sled runners before they meet have long talk apart.
> There is a pup in every litter the wolves will have.
> A knife that falls points at an enemy.
> Rocks in the wind know their place: down low.
> Over your shoulder is God; the dying deer sees him.

At the mouth of the long sack we fall in forever
storms brighten the spikes of the stars.

> Wind that buried bear skulls north of here
> and beats moth wings for help outside the door
> is bringing bear skull wisdom, but do not ask the skull
> too large a question till summer.
> Something too dark was held in that strong bone.

Better to end with a lucky saying:

> Sled runners cannot decide to join or to part.
> When they decide, it is a bad day.

IT IS THE TIME YOU THINK

Deaf to process, alive only to ends,
such are the thinkers around me, the logical ones—
the way in the yesterday forest, startled alert, a doe
would look along a gun barrel at Daniel Boone,
becoming the fringed shirt with instant recognition.

Deaf too, I stand on the peninsula of fear
remembering in their silent cars the newest hunters,
not the ones who stood with shadow faces
or stepped among the oaks and left the field,
but sudden men in jets who hunt the world.

And I think of the cold places in the river—
springs so deep it is hard to think about,
they come so wide and still into what we know.
But, thinking, I would be sudden with all cold springs,
before the blend, at once, wherever the issue.

I would sweep the watch face, narrowing angles,
catching at things left here that are ours.
There must be a trick, a little pause before
real things happen—a little trap to manage events,
some kind of edge against the expected act.

I am too local a creature to take the truth
unless and until by God it happens to me.

SUNSET: SOUTHWEST

In front of the courthouse holding the adaptable flag
Jesus will be here the day the world ends
looking off there into the sky-bore
past Socorro over sunset lands.

There will be torque in all the little towns,
wind will beat upon the still
face of anyone, just anyone,
who will stand and turn the still

Face to full dial staring out there
and then the world will be all—
the face hearing only the world
bloom from the eyes, and fall.

FOLLOWING

There dwelt in a cave, and winding I thought lower,
a rubber bear that overcame his shadow;
and because he was not anything but good
he served all sorts of pretzel purposes.

When I met plausible men who called me noble,
I fed them to the bear, and—bulge! rear!—
the shadow never caught up with his girth,
as those talkers never caught up with their worth.

And Bear and I often went wild and frivolous,
following a way that we could create, or claim,
but we had to deal sometimes with the serious
who think they find the way when the way finds them.

In their deliberate living all is planned,
but they forget to squeak sometimes when the wheel comes
    round;
Bear and I and other such simple fellows
just count on the wheel, and the wheel remembers the
    sound.

POSTSCRIPT

You reading this page, this trial—
shall we portion out the fault?
You call with your eyes for fodder,
demand bright frosting on your bread,
want the secret handclasp of jokes,
the nudges of innuendo.

And we both like ranting, swearing,
maybe calling of names:
can we meet this side of anger
somewhere in the band of mild sorrow?—
though many of our tastes have vanished,
and we depend on spice?—

Not you, not I—but something—
pales out in this trying for too much
and has brought us, wrong, together.
It is long since we've been lonely
and my track looking for Crusoe
could make you look up, calling, "Friday!"

NEVER

NEVER
K. D. McENTIRE

an imprint of Prometheus Books
Amherst, NY

Published 2013 by Pyr®, an imprint of Prometheus Books

Cover illustration © Sam Weber
Cover design by Grace M. Conti-Zilsberger

Inquiries should be addressed to
Pyr
59 John Glenn Drive
Amherst, New York 14228–2119
VOICE: 716–691–0133
FAX: 716–691–0137
WWW.PYRSF.COM

17 16 15 14 13   5 4 3 2 1

Library of Congress Cataloging-in-Publication Data

McEntire, K. D., 1980–
    Never / by K. D. McEntire.
        pages cm.
    Sequel to: Reaper.
    Summary: Torn between her duty to her friends, the Riders, and her duty as the Lightbringer, Wendy must make the ultimate sacrifice to bring the worlds into balance once mmore, even if it costs her very soul.
    ISBN 978–1–61614–771–6 (hardback)
    ISBN 978–1–61614–722–3 (ebook)
    [1. Supernatural—Fiction. 2. Soul—Fiction. 3. Death—Fiction. 4. Future life—Fiction.] I. Title.
PZ7.M478454238Nev 2013
[Fic]—dc23

2013001487

Printed in the United States of America

For Poppy.

You always understood
that the best way to bond
with a quiet seven-year-old
was over Disney, chili dogs,
and many, many books.
I miss you so much.

ACKNOWLEDGMENTS

As always, this book wouldn't exist without a truly fabulous group of people. I'd like to thank the consistently amazing Joe Monti, Lou Anders, and Gabrielle Harbowy. Thank you so much!

Thanks go to George Levchenko—not only is he an amazing photographer and web designer (Shameless Plug: http://www.glnet.tv)—but he very graciously answered 9 PM translation request texts and didn't frown too hard at my garbling his heritage. Thank you, George. You rock.

Karen. You know who you are, lady. Thank you.

Last but not least, thanks go to my husband Jake. Without you I'd never have time to write. Ever. Thank you so, so much.

PROLOGUE

SLAM.

"Huurrk!" SLAM.

The basement door creaked open. Rubbing her eyes and flipping open her cell phone to check the time, Laurie edged down the cold concrete stairs.

"Kara? Honey? It's midnight. What are you doing?" Dropping her phone into her robe pocket and wrapping her arms around herself, Laurie hesitated on the top step and squinted into the dim recesses of the basement, wishing she'd thought to grab her glasses at the first loud bang. "Note to self: need LASIK," she muttered, feeling her way down a stair at a time, following the slams and grunts and mourning her warm, soft bed upstairs. The cats had probably already stolen her spot.

"Should've put better lights in first," she grumbled.

They'd purchased the house for a song two years ago and had slowly renovated the entire place from top to bottom, doing most of the tedious bits themselves but hiring contractors for the intricate work. This room was the last to go—they planned on making it into a den eventually, but for now it was snug, remarkably dry for San Francisco, and intact. There were some leftover furniture from the previous tenants: an ancient, wavy mirror, spiderwebbed with cracks; a molding chaise; and some rusting bed frames. Junk they still needed to haul off or recycle.

Laurie yanked on the closest light cord. The faint circle at the

bottom of the stairs didn't illuminate much, but it was better than nothing. Now she didn't have to squint. Kara stood at the end of the room, by the fireplace. She was wielding a sledgehammer.

SLAM.

"Kara, why are you breaking the fireplace? Aren't we leaving the basement alone until you get a raise?"

"You want a den," Kara paused to say, readying the sledge-hammer for another blow. The soot-stained firebox was gigantic, plenty large enough that her swings didn't brush the stone arch or the firebox edges.

Kara braced her legs and let fly with the hammer again.

SLAM. "Half the price of those quotes was the demolition of this stupid fireplace."

SLAM. "Well, I've worked on the job for years."

SLAM. "If I can't knock down a wall, then I need to—"

SLAM. "—hang up my tool belt."

Uneasily, Laurie moved closer and pulled the cord on the dangling light bulb above, illuminating the remainder of the dusty room. Closer to Kara, Laurie could smell the Jack and Coke and, sure enough, there was a red plastic cup on a nearby stool, half full. "At this time of night? Really? Are you drunk?"

"Nope."

SLAM.

Kara stopped a moment and jerked her head toward her drink. "I've been sipping on that all night. It's all I had at the party. I'm not even close to drunk." She rubbed her hands together to get a better grip on the hammer—Laurie considered reminding Kara about the work gloves flapping out of her back pocket but, considering Kara's mood, thought better of it. No matter what Kara claimed, Laurie knew her love well enough to recognize all the signs of a truly belligerent drunk when she saw them.

Kara said, "I couldn't sleep. I've got, what, three more days off, right? I can pull this down in three days, no problem. Less if you help."

"Help?" Laurie squeaked, eyeing the neat line of tools laid out on the tarp. "I can't . . . I don't have any experience . . . what if it's a retaining wall?"

This time Kara stopped and gave Laurie a look of such derision that Laurie felt stupid for even bringing the worry up. "I'm sorry. You know what you're doing," Laurie said, turning back to the stairs and perching on the bottom step. "Right."

"Did I wake you?" Kara asked, wiping a forearm against her forehead, smearing sweat and dust in a dark swath across her face. "Is that why you're down here?"

"Yeah," Laurie said. She rubbed her neck and sighed, trying not to think of how filthy she must be getting. "Look, I know you've done this before. And I know you can do this alone, but . . . I don't know, shouldn't a *team* of professionals be doing this? This place is *old*, Kara. What if you inhale lead paint or asbestos or something?"

SLAM. "Fireplace—hell, the basement itself—is too old for that crap. It's all hand-hewn stone, honey. Solid. It's a real piece of craftsmanship."

"Then why are we tearing it down, again?" Laurie wrapped her arms around her knees and tried not to stare at the cracked mirror propped up on the sidewall.

The face stared out at her.

Kara had never believed her when Laurie said that she saw the face, and that sometimes it followed her, grimacing and growling from the different mirrors around the house, but Laurie was positive that she wasn't crazy. It was too bizarre to just be in her head. She knew what she saw.

Shivering, Laurie drew her robe closer. She'd never had this problem when they lived in Chicago; Laurie'd never had a single paranormal experience before she'd inherited the fixer-upper on Russian Hill. Glad to get out of the Windy City, Laurie had jumped at the chance to move. She'd gotten the job at the Stanford ER, and she and Kara settled down in San Francisco to start their new life.

Laurie never imagined the house would come with an occupant. She'd never been fond of horror movies, Laurie had no idea what to do, and it was getting worse.

It wasn't just the face, either, though the face was the worst of all. She also saw ghosts and skeletons and rambling, rotting things everywhere, even at work. But, the face . . . The face was awful; she hated it and, from the way it was glaring at her, she was fairly sure it felt the same way about her.

SLAM. "Old as this thing is, that earthquake a month ago could have turned it into a fire hazard. Even if we left it, I wouldn't dare use it. I can build you a *safe* fireplace, if you still want one down here. Besides, the way this room is right now, we wouldn't get our money back if we sold. So just go back to bed and let me tear the stupid thing down. Okay, honey?"

Laurie glanced at the face in her peripheral vision. It was showing its teeth now. Forget the bed and the cats; Kara had her grandmother's mirror hanging in their bedroom and the last thing Laurie felt like doing was hiding under the covers while the face watched her toss and turn. "I think I'd rather hang out, if it's all the same to you."

"You're the one who's gotta work tomorrow," Kara said with a shrug. Then she sighed and jerked a thumb at the duffel bag by the stairs. "Maybe you're right. Get a mask; if there's crap in the air, you shouldn't breathe it in. I'll put one on, too, in just a sec." She braced her legs and pulled the hammer back. "I'm on a roll here. I want one more good hit first."

Laurie scrambled to pull a dust mask out of the bag. It wasn't heavy duty like the ones Kara wore on the job, or the ones the contractors had worn to redo the insulation in the attic; this thing was barely a germ mask like she wore at the hospital. Still, every little bit helped.

Kara waited until Laurie had the mask strapped on and then swung at the back of the firebox with all her might.

CRACK-WHOOSH.

"Crap!" Laurie jumped to her feet as a blast of icy air hit her in the face and blew her hair back. "What the hell was that?"

Kara, dazed, tugged on the edge of the hammer and a large chunk of firebox tumbled forward, hitting the hearth of the fireplace with a sharp THUNK.

From the mirror, the face smiled for the first time. The dim figure spun, pale hands aloft, and piggy red eyes glowed with glee. Laurie felt her stomach sink.

"Kara!" she snapped. "That's enough. You're done for tonight. Let's go upstairs."

Kara didn't budge.

"NOW, Kara."

"There's something back here," Kara said, drifting forward and hunching over to stare into the hole that the large chunk of masonry had left behind. She reached down and picked up the Maglite from the corner of the tarp. Thumbing it on, Kara shone the light into the crevice. A bright silver shine reflected back, blinding Laurie across the room.

Hand shading her eyes, Laurie began backing up the stairs.

Kara was an Amazon of a woman. If Kara wasn't going to leave under her own steam, Laurie knew there'd be no way she could move her; that didn't mean that Laurie was willing to sit down here and wonder what would shine so brightly after a century or two deep in the dark, while the creepy face screamed silent laughter in the mirror.

Laurie turned to scramble up the stairs. Over her shoulder she caught one last glimpse of Kara leaning as close as she could to the hole and shining the light deep inside.

"Laurie . . . honey," Laurie heard Kara call, "I think there's a *room* back here—"

The door slammed behind her.

CHAPTER ONE

*W*hoosh-hisssshhhh. Whoosh-hisssshhhh. Whoosh-*hisssshhh.* The sea kissed Wendy's feet, curling the sand into miniature whirlpools around her toes as she picked her way along the tide line. She loved the way the sand gave under her soles; the crumbly, drier sand clinging to her left foot and the firm *squelch* of the still-wet sand releasing her right with each step. Wendy loved the salt smell and the foggy light, the way the beach stretched empty and quiet for forever in both directions; she even loved the slightly rank smell of rot and marsh that eddied around her now and again from the distant flats up ahead.

"Mom?" Wendy asked, stooping beside her mother as she bent to gather shells. Mary chose each shell carefully, lifting it to the cloud-hidden sunlight and peering for imperfections before rinsing it in the surf and adding it to the mesh bag dangling at her hip.

"Yes, sweets?" Mary's bag was almost full. The shells scraped against one another, a slight scratching that could only be heard in the lull between the *whoosh* of the waves lapping the shore and the *hissshing* as they drew back out to sea. The hem of Mary's long white cloak was impeccable; no sand clung to the underside, no saltwater speckled its length.

"I love you." Wendy reached for a shell to add to her mother's collection, but stopped when Mary shook her head. Her hair, glossy and dark red, glimmered in the light. Wendy had long since given up hope that her own carroty curls would darken to that lovely, burnished color. Her hair had a hard enough time just keeping the black dye she dosed it with on a regular basis. It always washed out far too soon.

"That one's not good enough," Mary explained, plucking the shell from Wendy's fingers and flinging it into the surf. "You must only use the best materials when constructing, Wendy. Materials made to last."

"Constructing what, Mom?" Wendy asked. Her mother dipped down again and plucked another shell from the sand. It was nearly identical to the one she'd just pitched into the sea.

"Whatever you need," Mary replied, standing and brushing her hands together. "It has to be your very best effort. Nothing else will suffice." The wind picked up, yanking tendrils of hair across her face. Brushing them aside, Mary sighed and pulled up the hood of her cloak.

"A storm's coming," she warned, jerking her chin at the black clouds gathering on the horizon. "Get ready to take cover."

Then, spying a clear spot in the sand up ahead, Mary moved on with purpose, leaving Wendy loitering behind.

"Okay, Mom," Wendy agreed to her mother's back. Mary was always saying stuff like this—a storm's coming, take cover, watch your back, do your best, you never listen . . .

No . . .

Wait . . .

That was the White Lady, wasn't it? It was the White Lady who'd said that Wendy never listened, never asked the right questions. Mary had always drummed into Wendy the importance of watching her back, but she'd never accused Wendy of being ignorant or purposefully stupid.

But . . . who was the White Lady? Wendy knew that she ought to know—the knowledge was there, itching, in the back of her mind, hovering on the tip of her tongue—but she couldn't quite touch it. There was a misty wall there, blocking her. Wendy frowned. She had an uneasy feeling that she was forgetting much more than who the White Lady was, right now.

"Hey, Mom?" Wendy asked, hurrying to catch up with Mary. Her mother had knelt down again, her cloak hanging low around her

as a barrier against the rising wind. Only her hands and arms were visible as she plucked shells from her bag and arranged them in a long rectangle in the sand. The shells touched edges, the flat bottoms pointing inward, the curved edges pointing out, buried deeper in the sand. "Why aren't there any babies? In the Never, I mean."

"Babies are too pure to stay in the Never," Mary replied, her nimble fingers picking the shells without glancing at her hip to see which was next. "Like animals, babies are creatures of impulse and flesh."

Mary sat back on her heels, tilting her head as she examined the long rectangle in the sand before digging into the bag once more. "No self-knowledge. Hardly any self-awareness to speak of. Babies know hunger and suffering but not the reason or the reckoning of it." Mary outlined a number in the top center of the rectangle, using the smallest shells for the detail work and outlined edge. "You have to sense what you are missing for suffering to exist." She tilted her head at her creation. "You must suffer to grow. But you knew that already. Didn't you?"

Her fingers are so white, Wendy noticed, *and slim*. She squinted at her mother's hands as the storm front began to move in, cutting into the soft, misty quality of the light and darkening the sky above.

Wendy eyed the sky for lightning.

"You do know that you are beautiful to me, right?" Mary finished, pale hands darting across the sand, each nearly moving independently of the other, first the left dipping into the bag for a shell, then the right. "Even in your misery, you are the most exquisite creature. Stubborn, proud, touchy. I love you most of all for your flaws, even the pieces of me that I loathe, slapping me in the face with my failures. You are *me*, made bright."

The number, 3, was complete, sitting in the top center of the rectangle, formed of white cockle-shells and outlined with tiny dark sand dollars. Mary moved on to the center right of the rectangle and fished out her last shell, a slightly larger than hand-sized conch, that she set in the center right of the rectangle. Mary spent a moment fid-

dling with the edges until the outer curve of the conch was sunk into the sand and only the cup remained. In a way, it reminded Wendy of a handle; she could easily see slipping her fingers under the smooth curve and tugging.

"Um . . . thank you?" Then, after a beat of nervous consideration, Wendy asked, "Mom . . . who's the White Lady?" The wind was really beginning to pick up now, tugging at her windbreaker and making her plaid miniskirt snap in the breeze. Her mother's cloak hardly moved at all.

"There," Mary said, satisfied. She stood and brushed her cloak with her hands; no sand fell. She was spotless. "Finished."

"Mom? Did you hear me?" Wendy asked, nervous now. She didn't like the look of the sky, of those black clouds roiling like an overboiling pot in the near distance. The rest of the sky was shading purple-black now; the friendly, fuzzy white fog-light was nearly gone. It had to be her imagination, but Wendy fancied that she saw eyes—dark red eyes—glaring at her from the clouds.

"Mmm?" Mary asked, bone-white hands on her hips. She tilted her head and examined what Wendy now definitely recognized as a door shaped of shells in the sand. The *whoosh-hissssh* of the surf had faded; all was wind and silence.

Lightning flashed across the sky—soundless, blue-white and sharp—and Wendy instinctively counted, waiting for a clap of thunder that never came. She dropped off at fifty with a sinking in her gut. The sea could make distances tricky, Wendy knew, but the storm was much closer than that. It would be on them any minute.

"Mom?" she prodded, every inch of her tingling. "Mom, who is the White Lady?"

"Can't remember, dear? Why don't you try a little harder?" Pulling her hood aside, Mary looked at Wendy and Wendy cringed away.

Mary's beloved, familiar face was a ruin, crosshatched with old scars and bleeding from fresh wounds. Her eyes were milky, one blown out completely with white, and seeping blood and pus in thin rivulets

down her cheeks. The tattoos—the exact same ones Wendy sported across her own collarbone—had shriveled and twisted with ancient age and heat, the mummified flesh split over her bones and curling at the edges like thin, weathered parchment. As a counterpoint an exquisite necklace, intricate and twisted and finely etched with Celtic markings, lay across her chest, glinting golden in the light.

"It's you," Wendy remembered dully, the white mists of memory parting. "You are . . . were . . . the White Lady."

Mary's hair snapped in the wind, the curls tickling Wendy's cheeks from several feet away. Wendy brushed the curls away and bit her lip.

She should have known it was a dream. How many years had it been since Mary's hair had been that long? She'd cut it when Wendy was still young, and their ritual of brushing each other's hair every night before bed had ended a quiet death.

In the before time.

Before . . .

Before Eddie's dad died.

"I'm still . . . I'm still sick, aren't I?" Wendy remembered; the realization was like those soundless flashes of lightning, cutting across the pleasant, hazy fog of her memories in one sharp, brilliant blaze.

"I'm in the hospital right now. This is . . . this is just a dream. I'm dying." Wendy pressed her hands to her lips, felt how dry they were, and how hot her flesh was. She was burning up from the inside out.

"You're working on it," Mary—no, the White Lady—agreed. She crossed her arms—not simply pale like Wendy thought, but bones hardly clad in flesh—across her chest and gazed at the coming storm with a strange, shallow peace that Wendy envied. "However, you don't have to."

"I don't think I've got a whole lot of choice in the matter," Wendy snapped. The White Lady was a sick and twisted mockery of everything her mother had been, and Wendy felt foul even being on the same beach with her. But . . . the White Lady knew things.

Knew things Mary had never gotten around to teaching Wendy, or had actively kept from her for Wendy's own safety.

"It's not like the rest of the Reapers are going to let me keep walking around," Wendy pointed out bitterly. "I'm in the way. I'm meddling with their oh-so-mysterious plans. Elise doesn't like it. Or me." Wendy smirked. "Or you, really, now that I think about it. She, in general, just doesn't seem to like much except listening to her own gums flap."

"Even after all this time you're still not asking the right questions," the White Lady said—not mockingly, Wendy realized, but sadly. "Why do the Reapers have any say in what you do or how you go about it?"

"Um," she said, "well . . . you? Them? I don't know! We have this whole family I didn't know about—that you *kept* from me, I'd like to add—and they've got rules and regulations and *a handbook*, and the best you can do is to tell me that they don't have any say in what I do?"

"The only power they have over you is what you grant them, Wendy. You are the one who let them grow close," the White Lady reminded Wendy mildly, turning to face the incoming tide and thickening storm. "You trusted Jane with your Light, she twisted it, and now you are burning with, and dying from, fever."

"If you'd warned me about the Reapers before getting yourself shredded, maybe I wouldn't've trusted them," Wendy snapped, coloring angrily. Her hands balled into fists. She wanted to punch the White Lady in her ruined-beautiful face, to crush the remains of those familiar features until any semblance of her mother was nothing but blood and bone on the sand. "Thanks for the 'I told you so,' by the way."

The White Lady shrugged, careless and cool. If she sensed Wendy's fury she didn't make much note of it. "It is not a bad thing to trust. It speaks highly of you, in fact. You take people at face value unless given a reason not to. I find that an admirable trait."

"The fact that you think *anything* about me is worthwhile is . . ." Wendy faltered. "Wait. Wait a second. You *can't* find any part of me admirable or not. You're dead."

The White Lady turned; raised a mangled eyebrow. "Your point being?"

"No," Wendy said, shaking her head sharply. "No, I mean you're really, really dead. Not, 'oh hey, Mom's in a coma and her twisted soul is running around town kidnapping kids and visiting my dreams' kind of dead, but the 'we *buried* you' kind of dead. I sent your soul into the Light myself! And souls . . . souls don't come back from the Light, not that I know of at least. I killed you."

"Yes, you did, didn't you?" the White Lady said mildly, a thin smile twisting the corner of her lips. "You opened yourself completely to the Light and let the power flow through you. All my disguises, all my taunting, washed away in the waves of Light."

"Can I . . . can I be like you?" Wendy asked abruptly, remembering how the other Reapers, like the White Lady, had been able to twist their shape in the dreamscape. "Can I? Can you teach me how to alter my dream-skin? You're not my mother or the White Lady. They . . . she . . . is dead. You're someone . . . else. So what do you want to teach me? Will you? *Can* you?"

Laughing, the White Lady abruptly flung up her arms to the crackling, furious sky. "And, at long last," she bellowed to the heavy, laden clouds, "she finally begins asking the right questions!"

The clouds opened up. A freezing, punishing rain pounded down. Wendy was instantly soaked; icy water steamed off her blazing skin, evaporating where it hit. The world was water and noise; Wendy couldn't see more than an inch in front of her face.

"Who are you?" Wendy shouted through the thick downpour, fumbling forward, hands outstretched toward the White Lady. Blinded by the rain, Wendy quickly stumbled and fell—the White Lady, or whomever she'd been, was gone, leaving only the door of seashells behind and the faces in the clouds, the red-rimmed eyes in

the darkness, peering down. How she could see them through the downpour was beyond Wendy's ken. All she knew was that the red eyes were getting closer, the rain icier, and soon even the heat of her fever wouldn't keep her safe.

Grabbing the conch-handle, Wendy yanked on the dreamscape door.

It opened . . . and she slipped through.

CHAPTER TWO

"A GAIN!" The paddles hummed and zapped. For a brief moment the room was silent and then . . .

Beep. Beep. Beep.

"Got her," the ER doctor said, stepping back from Wendy's body. Only Piotr, hovering close by, noticed the trembling of his hands. "Whew. That was a close one, huh?"

"You ignored her DNR," growled Jenna, the intake nurse. "I'm reporting you."

"Go ahead," the doctor said, wiping his brow and turning his back. "Do your job. I did mine."

"DNRs exist for a reason," she hissed, fingers pressed on the thin tattoo peeking over the edge of her scrubs. "I hope you enjoyed playing the hero." With that, she turned and flounced out.

"Don't mind her, doc," the head nurse said, piling gelpacks around Wendy's legs; now that she was stabilized, the ER staff could relax. "Do-Not-Resuscitate or not, no one in their right mind would've let this kid die. Not over a fever."

The spirits in the room glanced at one another as the nurses and attendants filed out. Soon only Wendy, the dead, and the doctor remained.

Wendy's salvation had been a close one, but only the ghosts knew *just* how close.

"I can't believe that worked," Eddie finally said to Piotr, breaking the taut silence. "I can't believe you pulled that off. But . . . *how*? How did you manage to make him change his mind?"

Piotr's fingers burned where he'd been knuckle-deep in the

doctor's neck—he could still feel the ghost of the doctor's living bones, sense the thrum of blood and energy cupping against his palm as he'd ordered the doctor to save Wendy, despite Jenna waving the DNR paperwork and demanding otherwise. It shouldn't have worked . . . and now a whole world of strange and uncomfortable questions needed to be answered.

"Eddie is correct," Lily murmured, joining Piotr at Wendy's side, watching the measured rise and fall of her chest and avoiding the doctor making notes at the end of the bed. "This sudden inter- action with the living is troubling, Piotr. Discerning how you man- aged such a feat—"

"Does it matter, Pocahontas?" Elle demanded, patting her pin- curls. "He got the job done, didn't he? Case closed!"

Eddie shook his head sharply. "Are you kidding me? Piotr shouldn't be touching *anyone* until he knows what he's doing. He could be hurting people!"

"This point is quite valid," Lily agreed, tapping her fingers on her elbows. "Piotr's new ability—"

"Is a blessing!" Elle protested angrily. "And you two dunder- heads want him to just forget he even—"

"Shh," Piotr hushed them. "Look."

The gray of the room slowly lit up, until Wendy's spirit—pale and not nearly as luminous as her Lightbringer form, but still much brighter than the other spirits—sat up in bed.

"Turns out," she said, rubbing her chest with one hand and scowling, "that getting a ton of electricity pumped through you hurts. Oooowww."

Eddie, startled, jumped aside, passing through the new IV drip and ending up halfway in and halfway out of a small stack of chairs beside the bed. "You're alive . . . dead . . . you're okay!" He leapt toward Wendy and grabbed her in a bear hug, hauling her off the bed in his exuberance. "Oh man, Wendy, don't you ever do that to me again! I . . . we . . . look, lady, we almost lost you, okay? Just . . . just don't do that."

Sniffling, he pulled her close and held her, rocking back and forth on his heels. Wendy hugged him tightly, smiling. She looked happy that Eddie was so happy. She glanced over his shoulder, and Piotr, only a few feet away, shifted from side to side and looked uncomfortably at the floor, the ceiling, her body on the bed . . . anywhere but at Wendy's spirit.

"Eddie . . . Eds, I'm okay. I promise. See?" Wendy untangled herself from her best friend's embrace. "Strong like ox, I am. Tough like bull. Grrrr." She flexed an arm and then jokingly punched him in the shoulder. "No worries."

"Always worries with you these days," Eddie replied, cupping Wendy by the back of the neck and drawing her forward so that their foreheads were touching. "You scared . . . all of us. Seriously."

Piotr cleared his throat and Eddie pulled away, squeezing Wendy's upper arms as he drew back.

"I don't know what the fuss is all about with you two. I'm hotter than he is by far," Eddie said loudly, flashing Piotr a cheeky, taunting grin. "I'm still not giving up on you and me. Just sayin'. But why don't you give Rasputin over there some lovin', just to be fair? Give the sucker a chance to compete against my awesomeness and all that."

"Eddie, you're impossible," Wendy said with mock seriousness, bussing Eddie on the cheek. Then she turned to Piotr.

"Wendy," he said gravely.

"Piotr," she replied, approaching him and brushing the hair off his face, exposing the scar beneath. Then her other hand snuck up on the other side until she was cupping his face in her hands.

"No hello, Piotr?" she asked. He shuddered.

"*Net*," Piotr said, licking his lips. He couldn't meet her eyes.

"You know," she said absently, "hugging Eddie and then touching you . . . it's so different. Eddie's skin is kind of familiar-feeling, like regular flesh but slightly more flexible. Thinner to the touch, maybe? But you . . ."

Piotr held stone-still as Wendy ran her hands along his face. He knew that touching him must be incredibly strange for her, an entirely different experience from the tentative way they'd been forced to touch before—under her hands he realized for the first time that his skin was smooth and firm, cool, and he knew that the only flaw her fingers would find was the ridge of scar tissue and the stubble along his jaw line. Over the past few months Piotr had begun to accept the fact that, amid the other souls, he alone was different, solid and firm, unbending, and ultimately unbreakable. He was a statue in a world of fluttering tissue paper.

"I merely wished to give you time to acclimate to the Never," he whispered to break the tension of her examining touch and the confusing emotions that were always coupled with his semi-permanence in a universe designed to tear souls down. "It is . . . difficult at first."

Wendy rolled her eyes. "Are all dead guys so decorous? Come here, you skinny lug." Dropping her examination, she flung open her arms and hugged him tightly. "I missed you, too. Don't let the Walkers make a pincushion out of you next time." She rested her head on Piotr's shoulder and Piotr tried not to notice that Eddie's expression had gone from pleasure to chagrin.

"We can touch," Piotr marveled, threading his fingers through Wendy's, palms pressed flush, neither of them too hot or too cold. For the first time in their relationship, Piotr and Wendy were finally on equal terms.

"Wow," Wendy said. "No worries about me reaping you, either. I know I have to get back in my body sooner rather than later, but you gotta admit, this is kind of awesome."

"Wrap up the kissy-face crap and let's blow this pop stand. I'm not getting any deader here," Elle demanded.

Wendy drew back. Eddie stood near the door, his face turned away, and Piotr had a moment of dismay. As annoying and amusing as he found Eddie, he knew that it was impossible for Wendy to not worry about him—about his feelings or otherwise. Wendy was a

generous soul; Piotr had come to terms with the fact that Wendy loved Eddie just as much as she did him . . . just in a different way.

Piotr forced some emotional distance. Eddie was a big boy; he could make his own decisions. He wanted to wait for Wendy, fine, Piotr wouldn't stand in his way. It might not be fair to allow such unbending devotion, but that was Wendy's choice to make, not Piotr's.

"Agreed," Lily said, rising to her feet. "Reapers are about, as well. We must be cautious."

Wendy pulled her hair back into a loose ponytail as the ghosts headed for the doorway. "Reapers? Are you sure?"

"There's a tatted-up nurse floating around the floor. Maybe she's not a Reaper per se, but she pushed *hard* to follow your DNR and got pretty pissy when Pete got the doc to ignore your paperwork."

"A DNR?" Wendy paled. "I don't have a DNR. What person in their right mind—" She broke off abruptly, furious. "Oh, those *bitches*. Seriously? How the hell do they manage to pull those strings so *fast*? Doesn't paperwork like that require a notary or something?"

"Elise?" Elle asked, examining her fingers and picking idly at the ragged edge of one thumbnail.

"Elise," Wendy confirmed, sneering. "Or Jane. Though it's mind-boggling that they'd go to such lengths to get me out of the way. Mocking up a DNR? It's just . . ."

"Then, for your protection and our own, we ought to leave," Lily reminded them, glancing out into the hallway. Her body was one taut line, her fleeting expression grave and tense.

"Speaking of your family," Eddie added as Lily eased into the hall to make sure the coast was clear, "did you know that Jon and Chel can see us?"

Wendy frowned. "Jane . . . Jane said as much. Before. But I didn't believe her."

Eddie patted Wendy on the shoulder. "Well, she's telling the truth. Sorry, hun."

"No. No. It sucks," Wendy sighed, "but it makes a sick sort of sense."

Lily let the way to the waiting room where Wendy's younger sister crunched up on a small loveseat, dozing uneasily. Her bleached blonde hair was tangled in a sweaty mass beneath her head and a jacket had been slung over her torso, the sleeves dragging the floor. Chel's twin, Jon, slouched in a chair beside the loveseat, paging half-heartedly through a *Life & Style* magazine, and examining the recipe section with only a modicum of interest.

"Healthy or not, those cookies look awful," Wendy said, leaning over the back of the chair and purposefully murmuring directly into Jon's ear. "Kind of like baked gravel, right? Clean that colon!"

"Could be worse," Jon replied without glancing up from the magazine. "They could be . . . oh. Um. Hi, Wendy?" He reddened as if he'd been caught paging through something dirtier than *Life & Style*. "I, uh, didn't see you walk in." Jon chewed his lip, having trouble looking at her, and Piotr knew that he wanted to say something about her current incorporeal state but wasn't sure how exactly to begin. Polite but scared; Jon to the core.

"I'm not surprised," Wendy murmured, gingerly patting her brother's shoulder to put him at ease. "There are a *lot* of ghosts wandering the halls tonight. It's kind of weird, actually."

"You're telling me," Jon grumbled, finally looking her over. He nodded once, face grave. "This place has been spook central the past hour or so—people walking through walls left and right. It's just creepy. I'd give anything to go back to normal. A gunshot grandma gushing everywhere just ain't right, you know?"

"You get used to it," Wendy sighed. "Wake up Chel and we'll bail, okay? Let's go home."

"Righty-roo," Jon agreed amicably, leaning over and poking his twin in the shoulder. "Yo, sleeping buffy! Arise and greet the day! Or the rest of the night. Whatever."

Chel opened her eyes and glared. "Is she dead?"

"Nice, thanks," Wendy snarked. "Good to see you, too."

"What happened?" Chel asked, yawning.

"I did die, but they brought me back." Wendy knocked a loose fist against her breastbone. "Pumped me with enough voltage to become a supervillain, though. Bzzzt."

Chel, grimacing, sat up on the loveseat, Jon's coat falling to the floor. "Great," she yawned, grabbing her purse with one hand as she rubbed her eyes with the other. "Glad you're not dead anymore."

"Wendy wants us to boogie," Jon added. "Let's go."

They gathered their things and were preparing to leave when a monster of a man—well over six feet tall, with a thick head of gray hair and a trimmed beard—bounded into the room. His shoulders filled the frame and the reflection of the ceiling lights on his glasses hid his eyes. According to the card dangling around his neck, his name was Dr. Kensington. He was smiling; his teeth were huge and white, straight and sharp.

Wendy watched Piotr, shivering, cover his neck with one hand.

"Ah, there you are!" the doctor said. His tone might be called jovial but his eyes were not pleased; they glared. "I'm glad I caught you!"

"Um, good?" Jon said, glancing at Wendy.

Dr. Kensington clapped a hand on Jon's shoulder, shifting him away from the door. "Please, Miss Darling, Mr. Darling, take a seat. I need to speak with you."

"How about 'no'? We're tired and going home," Chel said. She bared her teeth in an expression that tried to be a smile, but like the doctor, her mouth didn't match her eyes.

"Now, now, no need to be rude." the doctor said, guiding Jon firmly by the shoulder back to the loveseat, and then pushing with one meaty hand until he sat.

"Sort of stressed out," Chel replied, looking everywhere in the room but at him. "Not really caring about how rude I am at the moment."

"Ah yes. About that." The doctor turned on his heel and walked to the doorway where the dark-haired nurse from the emergency room, Jenna, was waiting. Smirking, she handed the doctor a clipboard.

The doctor rifled through the papers. "Now, I'll need you to clear something up for me. This is your sister's second visit to the hospital in how many weeks?"

"Well she's been here—" Jon started, pausing when Chel kicked him. "Wait," he said slowly, "why do you care?"

The doctor flipped to a printout several pages in, and prodded the lines streaking down the page. "This is measuring your sister's heart rate and her blood pressure. Notice anything off?"

Jon's lips tightened. "Her heart is beating too fast."

"Correct. Blood pressure this high . . . unmanageable fever . . . she is a prime candidate for an aneurism—or a heart attack—at this rate. Her brain is cooking in there, sizzling like breakfast bacon, but your *father* is nowhere in sight. His daughter is dying and yet . . . nothing." Dr. Kensington tapped the file, expression grim. "Do either of you happen to know where he is?"

"He's on business," Chel said stiffly.

"Wendy isn't eighteen—do you three have any alternate guardians?"

"That's none of your—"

"Because your father leaving you alone in a house, no way to contact him if there's an emergency . . . that's illegal. I doubt the State of California will look pleasantly on a man who leaves his three children to fend for themselves while he gallivants off for weeks at a time."

Jon glared at the doctor. "Hey! He's at work, ya'know, *working*, and we're not kids, we're plenty old enough—" Wendy wanted to kiss him for his gumption. Normally Jon backed down at any sign of authority but he was well and truly riled now, unwilling to bend.

"Excuse me, Dr. Kensington?" The head nurse poked his head

into the room, a tablet held out in front of him as if it were a shield. Behind the nurse, in the hallway, a familiar figure stood with crossed arms, her blue hair shining in the stuttering fluorescents. Jenna, who had been waiting silently, took the clipboard and left the room, pausing by the blue-haired visitor only a moment. They spoke, and then Jenna turned toward the main desk, the squeak of her shoes fading as she hurried away.

"Do you see her?" Piotr hissed, backing up to crouch in the far corner of the room. Lily and Elle pushed behind him, gripping their weapons.

"I do," Wendy muttered, hands in fists as she ducked down, Eddie bent low behind her. "Jane's got some nerve coming here now! What, is she trying to finish me off?"

"Can't you see I'm busy?" Dr. Kensington demanded of the head nurse, glancing over his shoulder at Jane, his index finger flicking out in a "wait just a sec" gesture. Wendy could see the left half of Jane's body—mostly her leg and shoe as she shifted in and out of view—behind the doctor. Jane's foot was tapping impatiently. The doctor grabbed the tablet out of the head nurse's grip. "What is it?"

"There's a code coming down the pike from Russian Hill—some drunk lady passed out and cracked her . . . head . . . open in her basement."

"Aren't there—"

"You're the only free doctor on the floor, sir," the nurse said pointedly. "We need you in there."

Sighing in irritation at the unavoidable delay, Jane nodded once at the doctor, tipped a wave, and turned on her heel, vanishing down the hall. Dr. Kensington growled and ran a hand through his hair. When he did so, the sleeve fell back, revealing an intricate tattoo twisting around his wrist. Piotr, Wendy, and Eddie exchanged startled glances and, as one, backed further away from him.

"Fine," he snapped to Chel and Jon. "You two! Get out of here. Go home. Expect a call from CPS tomorrow. Answer truthfully,

unless you want your daddy doing jail time." Then, as fast as Jane, he was gone, speeding down the hall and yelling for scrubs.

"Yeah whatever, doc. Screw you," Chel snapped as soon as he was gone.

Once his footsteps had faded, Jon and Chel hurried for the exit; they had to dodge as an EMT team pushed through the emergency doors. The medics were guiding an ambulance stretcher between them. A crying, robe-clad woman in bunny slippers and glasses rushed behind.

The injured woman gasping on the gurney lifted her arm and pointed to Wendy as she passed, twisting her head to keep Wendy in sight as the EMTs shoved her through a set of swinging doors.

Wendy shuddered. The whites of the woman's eyes were threaded with red, the pupils so huge they blacked out her irises. There was bright red all around her mouth, dripping down her chin and neck. Her face was malformed, stretched angularly out, and the bones in her forearms punched through the skin, spiky and white and pulsing. Yet still, despite the massive amount of pain she had to be in, it was obvious that she could see Wendy.

The robed woman dodged around Eddie as she shoved through the swinging doors, losing her left bunny slipper as she passed. Wendy knelt down and tried to pick it up to return it to the woman. She'd forgotten she was a spirit, and her hand went right through it.

The robed woman didn't notice; she was already gone.

"I have a bad feeling about all this," Eddie said. The door opened and the head nurse and a CNA rushed past, dropping off more buckets of icepacks just outside Wendy's room as they raced after the EMTs.

"So do I," Wendy said grimly, as Lily and Elle shifted to stand beside Wendy and Piotr, all of them frowning at the swinging door. "So do I."

CHAPTER THREE

The parking garage was startlingly cold, even in the Never. Wendy drew her threadbare hoodie close and zipped up the front, glad that whoever had taken her to the hospital had thought to bring it with them. Wendy knew that spirits could shape objects in the dreamscape, but Wendy had no idea if she'd be able to shape a coat out of her own essence in the Never the way she could in a dream. She shivered.

Catching Wendy's gaze, Elle slid a hand from her shoulder to wrist. Where Elle's hand touched a lightweight jacket appeared, formed from her own essence. Wendy momentarily considered attempting to manipulate her hoodie the way Elle had, but she didn't want the flapper laughing at her if she failed.

"Geeze, I'm dyin' here," Jon complained, rubbing his hands up and down his arms. "It wasn't this cold earlier, was it? Because we living in frickin' California, not Santa's worksho—" he broke off and craned forward. "What the heck is that?"

Wendy turned and stilled. There was a shadow—no, not quite a shadow, a shadowy figure—at the far end of the parking garage. For a moment she thought it was Jane, but the shadow was too dark to be Jane or any Reaper. The figure existed in the Never, not the living lands, and thin, icy fog nipped at their heels.

"Who is that?" Eddie whispered at her elbow.

"I have no idea," Wendy whispered back. She didn't know why she kept her voice low. It shouldn't matter if the figure heard them, but something about its extreme stillness and curling mist raised the fine hairs on the back of Wendy's neck.

Lily stepped forward, hands at her hips, fingers deftly drawing

32

her thin bone knives. "You are not welcome here," she called boldly. Elle, arrows drawn and already notched at her bow, joined Lily's side. "Be gone, beast!"

"Wendy," Piotr had a hand on her elbow, insistent fingers drawing her back. His other hand firmly rested on Eddie's shoulder. "You and Eddie are not safe here."

An unexpected wind began blowing through the parking garage, howling around the pillars and flinging litter from the closest trashcan into the air. A sauce-stained Taco Bell bag snagged on Chel's purse, catching at the corner. Cursing, she shook it free.

"What's going on?" Jon shouted over the wind. His hands shook and his keys clattered to the ground, landing half in a wet dip in the concrete. He reached for them and stopped. Impossibly, the puddle was freezing over as they watched, the thin rim of ice crackling across the dip in mere seconds.

"That's impossible," Jon mouthed to Chel and Wendy, the words snatched away by the rising wind.

"They are Walkers," Piotr shouted to Chel and Jon. "Their touch is draining. Be careful! Do not allow them to approach you!"

Though Wendy had faced down Walkers without her abilities before, she didn't think she'd be able to bravado-bluff her way out of a fight this time. The unexpected surge of panic this realization brought left her stunned, reeling against Eddie as over a dozen Walkers slid through the walls of the parking garage, their tattered cloaks fluttering around their calves.

The closest Walker turned to Piotr and grinned; the edge of his hood slid back, revealing handsome, chiseled features and a mouth full of gleaming white teeth. Rather than the rotting horror most Walkers were, this Walker's face was exquisite—features elegant and even and flawless—except for the oozing Celtic knot burned into the center of his forehead.

"*Ostorozhno*!" Piotr cried as the Walker's arm, whole and heavily muscled, shot forward and scrabbled at Wendy's front. "Wendy! DUCK!"

Instinctively Wendy stumbled back, yanking Eddie with her, as Piotr darted between Wendy and the Walker, jamming a fist into the Walker's midsection.

The wind died down enough for Wendy to hear the scuffles erupting all around her. Across the garage Elle and Lily had taken on the biggest Walker by themselves. He was twice the size of the girls—easily towering over seven feet and packed with rippling muscles. The Walker brushed the top of the archway with his head as he lumbered between them.

Elle, perched on the roof of a solid Hummer, was peppering the Walker with arrows at every turn, while Lily spun around the brute, stabbing forward and dodging back, arms and elbows and knees jerking into the line of fire and out again as she forced the towering Walker into a corner.

Jon and Chel, on hands and knees, ignored the Walkers and were stabbing at their frozen car keys with pens from Chel's purse. One pen had already busted—black ink was smeared all over Jon's left hand and across his left cheek—and the remains of the pen had already stuck, frozen solid, to the parking garage floor.

The rest of the Walkers, Wendy realized with a sick, sinking feeling, were headed in her direction.

"Wendy," Eddie said calmly, rising from his half-crouch and edging around the whirling mass that was Piotr's fight and the approaching mass of Walkers. "I doubt that these guys are here for me, and the Riders aren't slowing them down. You need to go. Now. Run!"

Startled, scared, Wendy shook her head. "What? No! I can't just—"

Eddie jerked Wendy to her feet. "Stop being stubborn. Shut up and RUN! GO!"

"REAPER!" bellowed the gigantic Walker Lily and Elle were battling. It became a chant, picked up by the other Walkers. "REAPER! REAPER! REAPER!"

Stumbling through the wall, Wendy ran.

Instinctively Wendy sought out the thinnest spots of the Never,

the walls she could easily pass through, and within seconds she was back in the hospital, shoving aside wandering Shades and passing through the burning heat of the living as she fled. Wendy didn't have the slightest clue where she was going or even if those Walkers were truly after her; all Wendy knew was that she was leaving her friends and family behind to face terrible odds and here she was, fleeing like a coward.

Her mother, Wendy knew, would be furious with her.

Torn, Wendy glanced over her shoulder. The Walker Piotr had been fighting was following her, hood thrown back and dogging her heels. Piotr, or maybe Eddie, had cut him across his cheek; he bled sluggish essence down the front of his robe. Bright splatters of it hit the hospital floor.

"Reaper!" he cried in a broken, sing-song voice, half-laughing, half-yelling. "Reaper, wait for me! Reaper, all I want is a kiss!" Then the Walker realized that Wendy had slowed. He sped up to compensate.

Terrified, Wendy turned to duck through the next wall and bounced off it instead. She staggered away, slipped, and fell flat on her back, cracking her temple as she went down. All thought fled; Wendy was pure, stunned sensation.

The Walker was on her before she had the sense to stand, pinning Wendy by the wrists, thrusting his knees between hers and grinding his shins into her own.

"Hello, meat," the Walker whispered and leaned forward. "You smell good."

Up close, despite the gash gushing down his front, he was stunningly attractive. His eyes were brilliant blue, shot through with flecks of silver, thickly lashed and wide. The Walker was heavier than she expected; his hands were smooth and strong. He smelled like cinnamon and musk, myrrh and old, smooth leather.

"Why?" Wendy asked. He leaned in so close that she could make out every detail of the thinly-etched knot burned into the flesh of his forehead.

"Because you are too much like your aunt, poking your nose in where it's not needed." He chuckled, low and deep. "Because even now, trapped and dying, you burn too brightly to resist." His head darted forward, jamming his tongue past her teeth and into her mouth until Wendy thought she'd choke on it.

His outsides might be attractive, but his tongue was thick and cracked and dry as dust, filling her mouth and tickling the backs of her tonsils, poking her esophagus with its impossible length. Even then, there seemed to be more and more and more tongue, filling every space in her mouth and pressing against her teeth with its heavy weight, its terrible spicy dryness, until Wendy suspected he was trying to suck out every drop of moisture in her.

Like a bug pinned to the floor, Wendy thrashed on the tile, but he was too strong; those lovely eyes were cold and dark and amused as she jerked below. Wendy tried to get a knee up, to stab him in the groin, something, anything, but his robes were too voluminous, his legs too long. The most she managed to do was alert herself to the fact that he was enjoying this encounter far, far more than she was.

The Walker's eyes glinted.

Wendy knew what he was thinking; she was down, pinned, and strangling on his tongue. The Lightbringer, scourge of the Never, brought low beneath *him.* The Walker would either end her or do whatever else it was that the Reapers had sent him to do, but he was planning to enjoy this moment first.

The Walker was used to his victims struggling, that much was clear, so Wendy, seeing her chance, went limp instead. The Walker's amused expression above her faded, and he stilled, confused. She could tell he was trying to decide whether he'd won or not, whether he should draw back or surge forward and do his worst. She'd given up, hadn't she? He clearly had orders, but she was the *Lightbringer—* shouldn't there have been more of a fight than this?

His attention wasn't on her, not really.

Wendy bit down. The Walker jerked back and Wendy went

with him, twisting her wrists up and around his wrists, using the one bit of leverage she had to force the thick part of her lower hands through the opening of finger and thumb and then to snap her fingers in a loop around his wrists, turning the tables on his hold. Now Wendy grabbed *him* around the wrists; she held tight and, still biting down, snapped her head forward and then side to side, worrying his tongue like a pit bull might worry a bone.

His bloody essence filled her mouth; it tasted like sour dirt and salt, like sand gone fetid and rank. Wendy wanted to spit him out but she couldn't, not yet. This wasn't over yet.

The goal wasn't to wound him, it was to startle him into scrabbling away, which he did, dragging Wendy to a standing position with him. Leaning against the wall next to a rolling medical cart filled to overflowing with supplies, Wendy released his tongue and, horrified, watched as the mutilated thing wagged at his collarbone, indented and bleeding from her teeth.

"You bith," the Walker said calmly, plucking up the end of his horrifically long tongue as casually as Wendy might have plucked at a scarf, "you bith mah tongth off."

Wendy spat beside the cart. "Not really," she said, rubbing her arm against her lips and wishing fervently for anything to wash the taste away. "It's still there. Next time, ask a lady before going in for that first kiss. By the way, I hear baking soda will do wonders for that dead-for-a-decade taste in your mouth."

"No madda," he said and winked as his tongue slipped back into his mouth like a magician's trick—one moment there, the next gone. "The Reaperth taketh care of their thervanth."

Grinning, the Walker drew out a slim golden chain from around his neck, thumbed the links a moment and then slid it back into his robe. A pulse of cold poured out of him, an icy wave of heavy air that slapped Wendy in the face.

"And for my next trick," Wendy muttered under her breath, shivering violently as ice formed on the cart at her side. "Watch me

pull a freaky-ass rabbit out of my hat."

"Just wait," he said, patting the place where the necklace had gone. "Your smart mouth will be the death of you." He giggled, the shrieking, eye-watering pitch of it making the hairs on her arms rise and sending a deep shiver down her spine. Wendy watched as the cut on his face slowly sealed shut. "Or maybe it already has been, hmm? Didn't think to leave someone guarding your body in the hospital room, did you?"

Another stab of panic. Wendy hesitated, torn between running straight to the room she'd just left and punching this arrogant ass in the face.

He's bluffing, right?

But what if he wasn't?

The Walker grinned again and Wendy, tired of his face, grabbed the most solid things at hand off the cart. Luck was with her; in her left hand Wendy had a scalpel, in her right she held a pair of scissors. Grinning, Wendy popped the scalpel's safety sheath off with her thumb.

"You know," she said, stepping forward and waving the scalpel in the air, "you don't look all that tough now."

He patted his chest again and smirked. "Try me."

Wendy darted forward, into his grasping arms. He hugged her, pinning her elbows against his chest, and laughed close to her ear, his breath like a gust of icy wind against her cheek. "Pitiful! What sort of attack was that for the—"

Then the Walker broke off. "Oh. Oh no."

His arms drooped, releasing her, and the Walker stepped back. The front of his robe had been sliced neatly open with the scalpel; the chain at his throat had been severed with the scissors.

Smirking at the distressed Walker, Wendy rubbed her thumb along the chain in her palm. It was warm and wet to the touch; like a string of hot, clammy flesh curled in her hand. The scissors and scalpel both *tinked* as they clattered to the tile at her feet.

"You healed with this," she said, plucking the golden chain up by one end and dangling it in front of him. "You obviously don't even *care* that I saw you healing, so what I'm wondering is this . . . do *all* of the new Walkers have—" she broke off. "Oh come on! Honestly?!"

The Walker, stripped of his trinket, was falling to dust. His skin peeled away, drying like a mummy in front of her, cracking along the eyes and corners of his mouth, and then *poof*, sifting down in a cloud of grit and sand. With him went the terrible, fierce joy Wendy felt at having beaten him, despite enduring his dry tongue between her lips, his erection against her knee, and the painful, pinning pressure of his shins and hands.

Just like that, only a little *poof*, and all of it was gone. All of *him* was gone.

"You have got to be kidding me," Wendy complained, waving a hand in front of her face to fan away the Walker dust. "Not that I'm sad your pervert ass is gone but . . . ew! Gross!"

"Wendy!" she heard faintly, from far away. "WENDY!"

She thought of calling to them—it was Piotr and Eddie yelling, she could tell, even from here—but that pile of dust was still settling, and the hot, wet curl of chain in her palm throbbed like a heartbeat against her skin.

"The Reapers take care of their servants, huh?" Wendy muttered, lifting up the chain and examining it. The golden links were etched with unfamiliar letters from some sort of spiky alphabet, and interspersed with Celtic knots like the tattoos all the Reapers sported. Uneasily, Wendy ran her thumb along the necklace; she'd seen this chain before, she just knew it, but she couldn't place where exactly. Troubled, she searched her memories. Nothing.

"Elise," Wendy whispered, tightening her grip on the chain until the throb slowed, until the heat faded. The voices calling for her were very near now; Lily and Elle had joined the worried chorus.

"Elise," Wendy said the name like a curse, glaring at the pile of dust as the ice around her melted in thin streams. "Elise. Elise."

CHAPTER FOUR

Fingering the Walker's mysterious healing chain, Wendy found her friends near the parking garage elevator. Thankfully, no one appeared to be terribly hurt—Piotr was dripping with either essence or sweat and sporting a rapidly swelling black eye. Lily and Elle were both pale and weary, sagging against the sides of solid cars nearby. Eddie had a scrape on his chin and another high on one cheekbone. Jon and Chel were nowhere in sight.

"Get him?" Eddie asked as Wendy approached.

"Sort of," Wendy hedged. "Where're the twins?"

"Chel had to use the pot," Eddie said, gingerly prodding the scrape on his cheek. "But after the ambush she didn't want to go alone. Jon went with her; they're going to swing by your room and make sure you're okay—well, that your body's okay—before we head home."

"Oh, good." Wendy sighed, fingers tightening involuntarily on the necklace in her grip. She thought about handing the chain to Eddie, but was worried about the implications of the action—the chain might carry some cost to use. Why else would a Walker be the one to carry it instead of a loyal Reaper?

"The Walker who chased me down was sort of mouthy. I was going to go check up on me, too."

Piotr straightened, prodding the swelling around his eye experimentally, and asked, "Mouthy? What did this Walker say?"

"Nothing much." Wendy rested one hand on the trunk of the sedan and hoisted herself onto the back of the car, tucking her left leg beneath her. "But I know who sent this group after us."

"Let me guess. Reapers?" Elle asked, eyeing Wendy imperti-

nently. Her voice was dripping with sarcasm; it wasn't really a question. "It's Reapers, isn't it? Do I win the kewpie doll?"

"Reapers," Wendy confirmed, choosing to ignore Elle's sarcastic tone and unspoken challenge. Wendy's hand dipped into her pocket. Getting to the bottom of whatever Elise had planned was more important than quarrelling with Elle, no matter how on-edge and guilty the flapper made her feel.

"Your family is beginning to make itself quite tedious," Lily said, pushing off from the rusty Chevy she was leaning against and striding toward the elevator doors.

"Whoa," Eddie cried, hurrying after her. He grabbed her wrist, stalling her. "Lily, hold up! Where are you going?"

"To check on the Lightbringer's body, of course," Lily said, raising an eyebrow at Eddie's question and, very gently, pulling her wrist free of his grip. "If the Reapers have chosen to make this an all-out war then we must make sure that Wendy's shell is protected."

"Jon and Chel—"

"Do not know what to look for," Lily reminded him. "They are new to the Never, babes in the woods. Believe me, I have thought much on this. The Reaper Jane was still in the hospital only a few short minutes ago. It would be child's play to hide from Wendy's siblings and, once they have left, to slit Wendy's throat."

"Hey!" Wendy protested, cupping her palms protectively around her neck. "Listening over here!"

"Oh, like we haven't all thought of a dozen ways to do you in already, Lightbringer," Elle snorted. "My personal favorite is throwing you off the Top of the Mark. I always imagine you'd make a lovely splat."

"Elle," Piotr sighed. "That is enough."

"Geeze, Elle, thanks," Wendy replied dryly.

"No problem, Lightbringer. Just doin' my part," Elle said cheerfully as Lily, shaking her head, turned heel and hurried back into the hospital, Eddie at her side.

Wendy yawned. Perhaps it was some lingering effect of her illness, but she felt so *tired* all of a sudden.

"Here," Piotr said, as Eddie vanished through the far wall. He pulled her close as they settled in the backseat. "Rest on my shoulder."

"I don't think I should . . ." Wendy muttered but it was impossible to keep her eyes open. Would it really be so bad to lean against him and rest for once? To let Piotr take the burden for a bit?

"Shhh, Wendy," Piotr murmured, stroking her hair. "You've run yourself ragged for days. Sleep now. Take a break. I will watch over you."

Wendy nodded and allowed her body to sink into the curve of his arm, to let her muscles relax until all the tension had drained away.

She yawned again . . .
    closed her eyes . . .
        and drifted into dreams.

Her last thought was: *Elise.*

When she opened her eyes again, Wendy was alone on a playground, a vast soccer field stretching out to her left and a rusting, abandoned swing set to her right. Behind her a tall, Rubenesque fountain spat water into a rippling pool so deep Wendy couldn't make out the bottom. The splashing filled the air with warm mist and a burbling hush—not silence exactly, but the waiting of a world about to erupt into discord.

Wendy began to walk, looking left and right for another soul. She knew this was a dreamscape—the entire place just had the *taste* of a not-quite dream—and Wendy whoever lay in wait for her, she wanted to find them quickly. The ground beneath her feet rumbled.

"Hello?" Wendy called. "Hello?"

"I was wondering if you'd have the nerve to show up here," Jane called. She stepped out from behind the fountain, naked as a twisted, tattooed Venus save for an ornate golden chain that hung to her collarbone. Her voice, snatched by the wind, sounded tinny and harsh. Wendy had to strain to hear it over the bubbling fountain.

"What do *you* want?" Wendy demanded. "Haven't you done enough damage for a lifetime in the last few days? Do you really need to do more? Is it a compulsion with you, or what?"

"You are so combative," Jane sneered, striding closer. Her hands were bare but Wendy warily backed away. You could be hurt in dreamscapes if you weren't on your guard, and after the past few days Wendy wasn't willing to trust Jane any farther than she could throw her. "Always being all . . . quippy."

"Right, like you're up for Miss Congeniality," Wendy replied snidely, trying to keep her eyes at collarbone level and above. "What do you want, Jane? We last talked, what—three, maybe four hours ago, and I don't think much has changed between then and now. Or are you just here to rub salt in the whole 'Wendy's dying' wound?"

"While I suppose that's an option, in actuality I'm here on official business."

"Official business?" Wendy snorted. "What was all the crap from before, then? Unofficial business?"

"Do you care to hear me out or do you wish to maintain your petulant child act? I can wait."

Wendy raised an eyebrow. Jane had the same swagger and verve as normal, her snide expression was spot-on, but the way she was speaking . . . it didn't fit with the sassy, fast-talking Jane that Wendy had grown to both like and loathe.

Something about this entire scenario felt . . . wrong.

"After everything you two have put me through? I ought to tell you to go to hell."

"Perhaps."

Wendy crossed her arms over her chest. "Fine. I'm listening. Go."

Jane's hands fluttered to her midsection. "Your friend Edward. His cord has been . . . altered, correct?"

Snorting, Wendy straightened. "You should know. The Reapers were the ones who 'altered' it."

"It was a necessary action," Jane growled. Her hand darted up to her face, fingers prodding the classy gold stud in her earlobe. "He was collateral."

The precise, nearly prissy way Jane rolled the earring tipped Wendy off; she rolled her eyes and bared her teeth briefly, glad to have figured out why the situation grated on her so. "Cut the act, Elise. You wear Jane's skin like a bad sweater. At least when you were pretending to be Emma you could *almost* pull it off. You're far too . . . wordy to be Jane."

"My erudition betrays me?" Jane asked, raising an eyebrow and smirking. Then she sighed in relief and shook her entire body. The Jane-flesh fell away in a shower of silver glittery dust, leaving Elise—thankfully fully clothed—behind. "So be it."

"So I get that you wanted to be Jane to catch me off guard, but why prance around naked?" Wendy asked, grimacing. "Cuz that's all shades of kinda gross, old lady."

"I chose Jane because you seem to have a stronger rapport with her than you did with Emma," Elise said stiffly, smoothing her hair. "You were entering the dreamscape too quickly for me to improvise an ensemble and it would not be out of character for my grand-daughter to . . . test . . . your sensibilities with nudity. She would find it amusing."

"Hilarious. Word to the wise, the next time you want to dress up like Skanky Smurf," Wendy said, grinning, and tapped her ear-lobe. "Jane sports flashy, long earrings, the kind you can grab and yank out in a throwdown. Not discreet gold studs. And she always stinks of grape bubble gum, even in dreamscapes."

"Noted," Elise said dryly. She cleared her throat. "So, what shall it be, Winifred? Will you treat with me? After all, the potential

payout is so very enticing. Edward's soul, freed, just like that. Is it such a great trouble to spare me a little time?"

"You just sent a truly nasty Walker after me," Wendy pointed out flatly. "I'm thinking a big, fat 'hell no, you crazy bitch' is in order here."

Elise raised one eyebrow. "I assure you, I did not."

"Sure you did!" Wendy retorted with false joviality. "I can't believe I'm describing him like this, but a hottie with a flashy necklace? Big ol' burn right in the middle of his otherwise perfect forehead? Kinda overly-grabby? Sorry, but he's gone now. So sad, too bad, he shouldn't have been making with the hands."

"No." Elise shook her head. "While there is an . . . associate of our family fitting that description who is serving penance, Winifred, I assure you, I did not 'send' anyone after you." There was something about the firmness in her expression that made Wendy, uneasily, believe her. "Not yet, at least."

"Elise," Wendy said, watching Elise's face closely, "what is going on? Seriously. No lies. No hedging. What's the deal?"

The older woman's thin lips pinched together, the edge of her teeth just barely visible against the pale pink of her lower lip. "Am I so transparent?"

Wendy ignored the question in favor of asking her own. "If you didn't send the Walker, who did?"

Elise swallowed and Wendy took quiet joy in seeing her squirm. "It is . . . possible . . . that Jane did." She straightened, glaring at Wendy, every inch of her radiating regal disdain. "We do not allow rogue Reapers in our ranks, Winifred. A fact you are well aware of, I am sure."

"Let's see here," Wendy drawled, "last I checked, both my grandma and my aunt were killed for not toeing the family line. I'm kinda aware of the penalties. Is Jane?"

"Jane knows cost of betrayal far better than you do!" snapped Elise, the line of her body blurring with taut, furious energy. Wendy watched fascinated as Elise, taking a deep breath, forced herself to

solidify in the dreamscape, smoothing the jagged edges of her body through force of will alone. "She, unlike you, *earned* her Light. She drank from the Good Cup. She memorized the—"

"She crossed her heart and pinky swore, yada-yada-yada," Wendy interrupted, sneering. "I don't know if you remember this, Elise, but I'm stuck in the hospital right now. I'm burning up—I'm *dying*—because of you and Jane and your little games. I don't give a rat's ass about any of this. Tell me why I should care that you've maybe got an AWOL Reaper. Tell me why this matters."

"Because she is after you?" Elise asked. The pulse in the hollow of her throat was pounding so hard Wendy could easily make it out. "Because she holds a great hatred of naturals and all you stand for?"

"Um . . . nope. Not good enough." Wendy crossed her arms over her chest and casually scuffed the earth at her feet. "Why don't you tell me what these 'plans' are that I'm distracting you all from and maybe, just maybe, I might give a crap about your problems."

Elise's lips clamped together. Her entire body stiffened with disapproval. *At last*, Wendy thought, doing a mental jig, *after all this time and all you've put me through, at last I'm finally getting under your skin.*

"I have my . . . suspicions that Jane has been . . . in contact with the Lady Walker," Elise replied sharply, each word clipped and terse. "As for the necessity of leaving you in the hospital's care—"

"Ahem. You mean trying to kill me?" Wendy pointed out dryly.

Elise's hands spasmed into fists. Wendy enjoyed watching her forcibly uncurl her fingers. "Binding you! Nothing more!"

Keeping her tone purposefully bored and drawling, Wendy waved her hand lazily and said, "Binding me so my Light burns me alive from the inside out. But, please, do go on."

"As I told you before, Winifred, if you do as I say, if you follow the tenets of our family, then I will not allow the binding to kill you," Elise said, voice flat. She tapped a short rhythm on her thigh with her fingers. "You do not comprehend how dangerous the Lady Walker is! You haven't a clue what she's doing!"

"I've been face to face with the Lady Walker before, remember?" Wendy said, keeping her voice perfectly even and reveling in Elise's twitching response. "Nothing happened."

"Nothing happened *then*. The time was not right. Now it is! I assure you, Winifred, as soon as the Lady Walker has been dealt with you have my word that I will free you. Both of you! I will free your Light from its bindings. I will unwind the weave we have wrapped around Edward's soul. You will be . . ." Elise grimaced but forced herself to go on, "temporarily welcomed into the fold and given a chance to prove yourself."

"Prove myself?" Wendy snapped, dropping the calm act. She'd had enough of this; Wendy began eyeing their surroundings more closely, looking for a familiar, rectangular outline. "How? And why *should* I, Elise? Or don't you remember that *you asked me* to hunt down the Lady Walker? Two days ago!"

"Again, that was then! Before I knew . . ." Elise clenched her fists together and, grasping her necklace firmly, forced a tight smile. "Winifred, we have gotten off on the wrong foot. I have been . . . I am still treating you as if you have the training the other girls have. That is my mistake. You do not know the reasons *why* we do the things we do. For this you have my apologies."

"I don't want your apologies, Elise," Wendy replied dryly. "I want to know what's going on."

"Do not approach the Lady Walker, Winifred. Your body is, thankfully, safe in the hospital. Please, return to your body. Stay there. I shall send Reapers to guard you."

Wendy pretended to consider this option for a moment. "You know what, Elise? If your idea of 'keeping me safe' is to stay in the hospital then I think I'm probably safer *out* of the hospital, thank you very much."

Elise faltered. "Winifred, I do not understand. Why—"

Wendy found herself shouting but she couldn't control the surge of anger that left her screaming at Elise at top volume. "You don't

understand? You don't understand?! Jane was just in the hospital not half an hour ago 'talking' to the staff, Elise!" Wendy made sarcastic quotation marks with her hands, waving them roughly in Elise's face so that the older woman was forced, glaring, to step back or be struck.

"Meanwhile a bunch of folks with *very familiar* tattoos tried to convince my doctor to let me die over a DNR. *My* DNR, as a matter of fact," Wendy sneered, "one that I don't, you know, actually have. Know anything about that, Elise?"

There. There it was at last. Wendy spotted the dreamscape doorway in the redwood bordering the soccer field, a short distance away. The way out was almost hidden amid the thick and gnarly bushes and trees. The door handle was a branch but if Wendy looked at the area obliquely she could just make it all out, how the door had been neatly obfuscated, the shape of it formed between blinks.

"Jane was in the hospital recently? Are you sure?" Elise's voice was thin, reedy.

"Yeah. Positive. You two came to gloat at me and then, not an hour later, Jane came back. This time she made chatty-chat with some pushy doctors trying to off me with a faux DNR and then bailed. Sound familiar?"

Mouth drawn in a thin line, Elise refused to rise to Wendy's taunts. "Winifred . . . there are . . . factions of our family that do not agree with—"

"You?" Wendy asked nastily.

"What I . . . what we are trying to accomplish in this life. With the rules set down for us, to guide us, to shape us," Elise retorted primly. "In our recent history some Reapers have attempted to reach out to . . . creatures . . . such as the Lady Walker, in the hopes that doing so will grant them power or . . . a sort of sick immortality. The kind only a twisted being such as the Lady Walker could offer."

"So just being stupid-rich while you're alive isn't good enough for you people? You want more in the Never? Why am I not surprised?"

"Idiot girl! Shut up and *listen*!" hissed Elise. "I did *not* give

orders to mock up a DNR. That would be bringing outsiders into our family business, an unacceptable action. We deal with our own. We always have! However, if there are Reapers at the hospital who are pushing such an . . . ignoble and backhanded manner of dealing with your shell, then they most certainly have left the fold!"

Her voice dropped and Wendy realized that Elise was either a very good actor or actually showing her real emotions for once; she sagged like an old woman. She looked crushed. "If Jane is dealing with them, then my . . . suspicions are confirmed. She most certainly has met with the Lady Walker."

"Sucks to be you," Wendy said, and rubbed her finger and thumb together. "Note the world's tiniest violin playing 'My Heart Bleeds For You.'"

Elise straightened. "You think I am awful, yes? You believe me to be the pinnacle of evil?"

"Yep," Wendy said, examining her nails, miming boredom. "Or pretty close to it."

"Then you know nothing!" Elise's fist slammed into her thigh with a meaty thud. "There are creatures beyond our world, beings that exist only to feast upon the Reapers and the souls in the Never! This is why I fear naturals, Winifred! If you lose control of your power you could rip a hole into the space between worlds, letting these . . . abominations into the Never, only a gasp away from the living lands! Beside these creatures, a Reaper is weak—our power, our wonderful *Light*, is only a candle in the darkness! All the Lady Walker wants is to let them roam the Never, obliterating all that we have worked for! Devouring. Gnawing. Feasting on the Reapers themselves!"

"Oh really?" Wendy rolled her eyes, though something in the way the whites of Elise's eyes grew wide when she spoke of the creatures made Wendy faintly queasy. "Afraid you might get your comeuppance for once? A little bitty beastie got you scared, Elise? Shame. If I knew that before, maybe I'd have dropped a mouse in your drawers."

"Maybe this might surprise you, Winifred," Elise said stiffly,

"but I don't want the Never to go anywhere. I happen to believe that
the cursed dead-land serves a *purpose*—the sinners are flung there to
suffer and work off their sins so that they might be granted the
release of Heaven! In return we reap both their souls and the bene-
fits of their labor. I may have benefited, true, but their labors are fair,
their duties not onerous."

"But if the dead don't work off their debt to your satisfaction,
they're punished further, right?" Wendy sneered. "Just like if I don't
march to the beat of your drummer you put me in the ER." Wendy
had had enough; it was time to go.

"I am arbiter only of the dead, Winifred," Elise replied coldly. "I
do not answer to a living abomination such as yourself. I laid you
low to *protect* this family, to protect the Never, that is all!"

"Yeah, I'm done with you and I'm done here." Wendy turned
away from Elise, striding into the copse of trees holding the dreamscape door. "Jane's run rogue? Sorry. Tough for you. I know how to
handle her if she wanders my way again and, honestly, I really
couldn't care less about poor, pitiful you and your family troubles.
You say there are Reapers chatting up the Lady Walker? Well maybe
you need to think a little harder on why they'd turn their back on
the fold, Elise. What does she have to offer them that you can't?"

Elise tried one last time. "Winifred, you would truly allow
Edward to suffer? All I ask is—"

"Screw off, Elise, and take your crappy bribes with you. I'll fix
Eddie myself. I don't want or need your help to fix the problem *you*
caused. I can handle it on my own."

"Don't you turn your back on me, young lady!" snarled Elise.
"Don't you walk away!"

Wendy knelt down and grabbed the handle in the tree-door. It
opened easily beneath her hand, the door swinging open into soft,
warm light.

CHAPTER FIVE

When Wendy opened her eyes she found Elle's knife trained against her jugular. Beside Elle Piotr was scowling, his hand curled over Elle's shoulder as if trying to pull her away.

"Good morning to you too, Elle," Wendy yawned and stretched, inwardly relaxing as Elle pulled the knife away and sheathed it. "After everything we've been through together, I thought we were getting to be friends."

"Oh no worries, Wendy," Elle cheerfully retorted, running her fingers through her pincurls and rearranging one near her temple. "We're copasetic. I just had to be careful—you talk in your sleep and I don't trust the Reapers not to pull a fast one somehow. How's Elise doing? Still crazy?"

Wendy grimaced. "She wanted a trade. My help with Jane—who's gone rogue, by the way—in exchange for Eddie's cord back in one piece."

Eddie, sitting in the front seat, leaned through the passenger side. "They have it?"

"It took me a while to figure it out before, but the truth is that *you* have it," Wendy said shortly, reaching out and pressing her hand against Eddie's gut. "Here. It's been there the whole time. They just . . . squished it up and hid it in your essence. It takes a Reaper who knows what they're doing to pull it free and shape it back into a cord."

Eddie poked his navel. "I don't *feel* any different. I feel like I could start fading away again at any time." He glanced at Lily as he said this and Wendy felt a strange, tight pang in her gut as the dark-haired girl's lips twitched into a brief smile. She knew that Eddie and Lily had been spending a great deal of time together lately; they'd had to drag a raving Piotr to the Treehouse by themselves less than a day prior.

Eddie was her oldest friend and Wendy was intimately familiar with that look; Eddie had a crush. On Lily.

Wendy wasn't quite sure how she felt about that.

Forcing a smile, she shrugged. "Sorry Eds, I told her to stuff it. I'll get you free as soon as I'm back in my own body. Pretty soon all this will be a . . . what, Elle? Why are you making that face? Keep it up and it might stick like that, young lady!"

Elle yanked her tongue back into her mouth and ceased her overwrought genuflecting, patting the knife on her hip. "Fine, fine. Anything else from Elise?"

"Not much," Wendy admitted, frowning and trying not to brood on the wild way Elise spoke of the darkness and the stink of desperation when she realized that Jane had left the fold. "Elise mostly wanted to wax poetic about creatures from between the worlds and bitch about Jane."

"Jane?" Eddie asked, his interest piqued. "She really went bad? Like, badder? Kind of hard to imagine."

"Creatures?" Lily asked.

Wendy rolled her eyes at Eddie and turned to reply seriously to Lily. "Nana Moses told me, before, that they can sense naturals . . . that we're like a gourmet buffet to them," Wendy said so softly the others strained to hear her speak.

"These creatures then," Elle said, "what happens if they scent you?"

"They would rush here, to the Never. If they found a weak spot they'd punch their way through and once they got here . . . if they fed on me, on my Light, then no one would be safe. No one. So if . . . if that were to happen, you would need to put me down. Like a dog." She lifted her head, staring at Elle directly. "I'd need your word on it."

"I'll do it," Elle said flatly, her hand resting on the bone knife at her hip. "You go crazy like that and you've got my weapons and my word." Challengingly, Elle glanced at Lily. "What about you, Pocahontas?"

"Of course, if such actions are necessary," Lily replied, unper-

turbed. "The Lightbringer has an important duty in the Never. I shall always do my best to support her in any way that she needs."

"Now that we've all agreed to stab my best friend in the face," Eddie interrupted, frowning at them, "I'd like to point out that Jon and Chel are back." He was right; the elevator doors to the parking garage had opened and the twins were heading in their direction.

"I assume I still have all my parts? Neck, hands, the like?" Wendy asked her sister as Chel reached the car.

"We had to sneak past that awful doctor again," Chel grumped, jiggling the passenger door handle as Jon fumbled for the keys. His hands were still smeared with black ink; at some point he'd rubbed some along his jaw, giving him a swarthy swath like a bruise under his chin. "He was helping haul that bunny-slipper chick into a wheelchair for some kind of transfer, so it took us a bit to get past him. Looked like she fainted or something. The DNR-bitch was pushing her toward the usual exit, so we had to go the long way around."

"I get such a nasty feeling off him," Jon mumbled, "and they've got you on some kind of secondary drip. We didn't get to really hang out with you and give you a good once over but I heard one of the nurses say it was some kind of sedative. You . . . your body . . . was thrashing around." He paused, tilting his head, one hand on the car door. "She . . . wait . . . do you guys hear that?"

Clink.

Jane appeared as if from thin air. Knife flashing, eyes blazing, she slashed forward and spun, felling Jon with a precise kick between his legs. He staggered back, gasping. Chel snarled and Jane was on her, all nails and fury.

"Jane!" Wendy yelped, reaching for her Light. Once more, it was as if she were scrabbling at a smooth, blank wall. She could feel the heat of her power—burning hot!—behind the barrier, but after all the attacks of the evening Wendy was too worn to even attempt to pry open a hole and free her Light to fight her cousin.

"What the hell!" Eddie yelled, staggering back a step before

hurrying to Jon's side. "Stop! JANE! STOP!" He knelt down to make sure Jon was okay, but looked to Wendy for orders. "What do we do?"

"We can't touch her while she's in the living lands," Wendy snapped. She swung at the Reaper but her hand swept ineffectually through Jane's shoulder. Even now, in the midst of chaos, Wendy had to admire the girl's ironfisted control. Keeping herself entirely solid while fighting was next to impossible; Wendy's spirit would have bled into the Never by now. "If she switches over, we can attack her between her physical and spiritual states, but until then I don't know what to do!"

"PIOTR!" Elle yelled, drawing her bow. "Use those magic hands of yours and poke her in the brain!"

"*Net!* I dare not!" Piotr snarled. "I do not know if it works on Reapers! She isn't Wendy. Jane will draw power from me, from my memories, and use it against us!"

"Hell yeah, I will!" Jane cried, kicking out.

"SOMEBODY DO SOMETHING!" Chel demanded, grabbing fistfuls of Jane's hair as the Reaper spun past, slamming the older girl into the corner pillar of the parking garage. Then she forced Jane to the ground, grinding her knee into Jane's hand. Chel had spent the last six years as a cheerleader; plenty of time to learn that fighting dirty was imperative when facing other irate gymnasts with boyfriend issues. If given a chance, Wendy suspected that Chel could bust open watermelons with her thighs alone.

"Dropit-dropit-dropit-DROPIT," Chel chanted until Jane let the knife go. Chel kicked the blade away; it skittered under a nearby truck. "Jon get your ass over here! NOW!"

Jane screamed and raked nails down Chel's arm, shoving upward with all her strength until they were both on their feet again, staggering in circles, Jane's hair still gripped tightly in Chel's fists. "Bitch," Jane snarled, "let go!"

Twisting left, then right, Chel struggled to wrestle Jane into a headlock. "You're gonna stab me! Hell no, I'm not letting go!" Then

she groaned; Jane was pushing them backward, pressing Chel roughly into the pillar behind them. Using the leverage of the wall to pin Chel, Jane twisted her right arm between them and *heaved*, freeing herself. Wendy saw both their gazes dart to the ground but the knife was gone.

"Jane! Stop!" Wendy cried. "Why? Why are you doing this? You let me go in the dream!"

"That was so yesterday," Jane spat, keeping Chel on her left, trapped at the wall but also unable to reach the knife. "Before I met with a Lady who put the right sort of spin on things. I was blind before, Wendy, but now . . . now I see the Light!"

"You could always see the Light!" Eddie grunted, circling her from a distance.

"Can it, Eddie. I'm under new orders now. If Grandma's Pretty Boy Walker couldn't take you out, even as a sad little ghost, then I'll just have to finish you off." Jane grinned; her teeth gleamed white in the faint garage lights. "The Lady Walker's on the move, Wendy, and she needs weirdo naturals like you to stoke the engines. Consider it . . . fighting the good fight by being Walker-chow."

Chel, taking advantage of Jane's brief distraction, darted forward and, grabbing Jane by the arm, spun her into the wall, scraping her face against the rough concrete.

"You're gonna regret that, blondie," Jane growled, running the back of her hand against the bloody corner of her mouth and spitting a gob of blood on the pavement. "Bet your soul on it."

The outer edges of Jane's shape began to glow.

"Is she gonna regret this?" Jon asked and swung the baseball bat.

"Geeze, Jon," Chel said, getting down on all fours to retrieve Jane's knife beneath the car. She was bleeding sluggishly from where Jane had clawed her, but was otherwise unhurt. "When did you grow a pair?"

"Mom said never to hit girls," Jon said uncomfortably, stowing his baseball bat back in the trunk. He started toward the emergency

station at the end of the garage—one slap of the big red button would bring hospital security and handcuffs. "I figured she'd understand if I was protecting you."

"Did he kill her?" Eddie asked nervously, kneeling beside Jane. "She's not moving."

"Don't touch her, Eds," Wendy warned as Chel, giving up on reaching the knife beneath the car, flopped in the passenger side of their vehicle and fumbled the first aid kit out of the glove compartment. "She's a viper, okay? Stay away."

"Don't be such a Mrs. Grundy, Lightbringer," Elle said, stashing her bow. "Didn't you hear that *thunk*? Jolly Jane's not jiving anytime soon."

"Elle, be reasonable," Lily said as Piotr and Eddie left Jane laid out on the concrete several feet away. "Even unconscious, a Reaper has power."

"Wish we had a Lost," Wendy muttered, stepping around the edge of a nearby van. Only Jane's feet were visible from here but Wendy still felt like a cat, as if every hair on her body was raised. Even behind the cover of the van Jane was still too close for comfort. "Specs ripped my Light right out. I bet another Lost'd shred her to pieces. Or, hell, feed her to a Walker. Maybe then Elise'd lay off."

"Wendy!" Eddie admonished.

"Eddie, Jane landed me in the hospital and just tried to shish kabob my little sister. I'm allowed not to like her, you know."

"It is only that such bitterness is unlike you," Piotr said softly, drawing Wendy close. He kissed her temple. "Do not worry yourself, Wendy. Jane will soon—"

"Escape," Elle said flatly.

"What?!" Wendy straightened and peered around the back of the van. Jane's feet were gone, the rest of her along with them. Wendy rubbed her eyes in disbelief. "How did she—"

"No one is answering the guard desk," Jon griped as he approached. He looked around. "Hey, where did the crazy chick go?"

"Screw this noise," Eddie snapped forcefully, startling them all.

"Concussion or not, Jane managed to make a jump for it, bully for her. Let's not stick around while she calls any other Reaper buddies for backup, okay? We're getting out of here. Now."

They piled into the car and pulled out, leaving the shadowy recesses of the parking garage behind.

"So. That happened. Story to tell the grandkids for sure, but what do we do now?" Jon asked once they were several blocks away. His stomach grumbled and Jon blushed as red as his hair.

"Pull into that Jack in the Box," Wendy decided, worrying a thumbnail nervously. "Grab some grub and we'll figure out what to next." She hesitated. "Unless you want to go back inside to the ER and get your hand looked at, Chel."

"Are you kidding me? That hospital is dangerous," Chel snapped. "Besides, I haven't eaten lately either. I could just murder a side salad."

"Only a side salad?" Wendy asked, regretting the words immediately. The last thing her sister needed was Wendy drawing attention to Chel's ongoing struggle with diet pills.

"One disorder at a time," Chel said defensively. "I'm only popping Advil for my aching hand, Jon won't order fries. You happy, princess?"

"Lay off, Chel," Jon said in a *soto* voice, guiding the car into the drive-thru lane. "Wendy loves us, she worries about us, and she didn't mean anything by it, so we'll all just . . . lay off. Okay?"

"Fine," sniffed Chel, poking through the glove compartment until she located the Carmex. "But if the gothette back there thinks I'm giving her a bye over her attitude at Thanksgiving she's got another thing coming. Dating a dead dude and then getting pissy when the spook dumps your ass? Ew. Gross!"

Lily pointedly cleared her throat.

Chel flushed and glanced over her shoulder. "No offense, Peter, or whatever your name is. But you were the cause of a lot of family bullshit. Just sayin'."

Wendy glared at Eddie. He smiled genially back, innocence

pouring off him in waves. Chel had no way of knowing that Eddie had been against Piotr and Wendy being together from the minute he'd learned about it. It was just a coincidence that she agreed with him.

The speaker beside the car blared. "WELCOME TO JACK IN THE BOX. CAN I TAKE YOUR ORDER?"

CHAPTER SIX

Jon, true to Chel's promise, had a salad with his cheeseburger. Chel, to Wendy's surprise, ordered a shake with her salad. They were, she decided, doing their best in a bad situation . . . which was why it pained her to have to make it worse.

Leaving to chuck the trash, Jon slammed the door behind him. Wendy watched him walk away, wriggling after a few steps to ease his pants out of his butt. Wendy tried to ignore the concern nibbling at her gut but was unable to calm her mind. He was dieting, yes, but Jon was still . . . so, so big. How had she let his eating issues . . . and Chel's . . . get so bad? Everything had been such a mess since their mom's accident! All she wanted was to get a handle on her life and everything was still spinning out of control.

Jon reappeared a moment later and slid into the driver's seat. "So where to next, sisters-o-mine?"

"Actually," Wendy said, clearing her throat and leaning forward into the front seat. "I kind of have a favor to ask."

The twins exchanged a look. "Okay, shoot," Jon said.

"Call me crazy, but I really, really want to go to San Ramon," Wendy said, resting her head on her arms. In her periphery she saw Eddie stiffen.

"You're crazy," Eddie said, leaning forward and slapping the headrest. "The *Reapers* live in San Ramon!"

"Which is why we need to go!" Wendy snapped defensively. "Jane has a point—a couple days ago Elise asked me to help take care of the Lady Walker and I did fail there. And, later, when I was dying from the fever, I called Emma and she said she was on her way but she never showed up. Doesn't that say waylaid to you?"

"It says 'trap' to me," Eddie said flatly. "This is a terrible idea. What if Jane escaped to San Ramon?"

"I kind of hope she did," Wendy retorted bitterly. "I'm going straight to Nana Moses, like I should have the first time Elise came to me and demanded that I toe the Reaper line. Instead I heard her out and ended up in the hospital because of it. No more. I'm going to the matriarch and if Jane or Elise wants to stop me, I'll make them pay for it."

"I don't know," Jon drawled, hesitating. "It's just . . . Eddie kind of has a point. I mean, Wendy, we can't help you if you cross them. We can't help out; Chel and I know nothing about reaping."

"See?" Eddie said, throwing his hands up triumphantly. "Jon sees sense here."

"Look, guys, I swear to you on Mom's gr—" Wendy flushed. "I mean, I'll teach you as soon as I can. I promise. Scout's honor. But in the meantime I *need* to go to San Ramon. It's important. I have to talk to Nana Moses about Elise and Jane, I have to find out what the Lady Walker's been up to, I have to hunt down Emma, and it's not like they've got cell service in the Never."

"But—"

"Wendy has the right to see the Reapers," Piotr snapped, his voice slicing through Eddie's muttered protests. "They are her family, it is important that she speaks with them. Why do you not see this, Eddie?"

"Why don't you see that they're going to be gunning for her?" Eddie demanded. "Or are you hoping that she kicks it so you—"

"Ada is gone, possibly captured by the Reapers," Lily interjected sharply. "We might yet be able to rescue her. After what she has done for us, it is our duty to do so, if possible." Lily looked Eddie firmly in the face and Eddie, after a moment, wilted.

"Yeah, sure," he muttered. "Fine. You're right."

Wendy glanced between Eddie and Lily. Eddie'd hunched up his shoulders and turned his face away. He was blushing. Eddie never blushed.

"Umm, thanks," Wendy said to Lily, who met her probing stare with her standard stoicism.

"Rescuing Ada is the right course of action," Lily said simply, laying her hands in her lap, fingers lined in a neat row against her kneecaps. "Eddie knows this in his heart."

Chel flipped around in her seat to stare pointedly at Lily. "Who is this Ada chara—you know . . . yeah, never mind, I don't even care at this point, I really don't." Chel flopped back and poked Jon in the elbow. "Do you ever get the feeling lately that you stumbled into the theater three-quarters of the way through the wrong movie?"

"All the time," he sighed and jammed the key into the ignition. "Fine, we can take a run up to San Ramon. BUT. But you owe us one hell of an explanation. And gas money."

"Anything you want," Wendy promised fervently.

Jon waved an arm at the street. "Buckle up, then. Let's go visit a bunch of crazy Reapers. Top off the night nicely."

Filling Jon and Chel in on the details of the past few months took longer than Wendy anticipated. They were more than halfway to San Ramon when she finished.

Jon changed lanes and yawned. "So what's the deal?" he asked. "What did you all do that landed you in the Never? Kill people? Kick puppies? What?"

"Nothing," Lily said, serene and still beside Eddie, gazing out the window at the passing streetlights overhead. "We have done nothing to deserve our fate."

"Nothing at all?" Jon scoffed. He missed Piotr's scowl. "Cannibal ghosts? Dark demons from between the worlds? The Never doesn't sound like limbo, it sounds like Hell. If that doesn't say 'being punished' I don't know what does."

"Turn here," Wendy directed and Jon slid into the exit lane.

Looking out the window at the passing streetlights, Elle's reflec-

tion grimaced. "The Never might be purgatory, but it's not Hell. Trust me on this."

Chel snorted. "What's the difference?"

Elle chuckled bitterly. "I've been dead almost a century and I haven't once seen an angel with a flaming sword blocking a soul from the Light. We do that to ourselves, no intervention required."

Jon smacked the steering wheel with his palm. "Angels like Wendy?"

"Oh no you don't," Wendy protested. "I am *not* an angel. You are not an angel, Chel is not an angel, and Jane and Elise are *certainly* not angels. No angels here. Nada. None."

Sneering, Jon made a rude gesture. "Fine. Whatever. Deny it all you want, but you're *some* kind of supernatural being. You send the dead into the afterlife! If that's not the job for an angel, I don't know what is."

"Hmm," Chel mused.

"Oh for . . . what?" Wendy demanded. "What now?"

"Welllll . . . can't Reapers make weapons out of their Light? Blazing swords, maybe?"

"*Not an angel*," Wendy reiterated flatly. Eddie snickered.

"I'm done with this topic. You're not an angel, whatever," Jon said, pulling up to the stoplight two streets away from Emma's place. "Here. Despite this piece of crap, we're nearly there." He flicked the GPS, hard, and turned enough so that Wendy could see his deep scowl. "Ta-frickin'-da."

"What's next?" Chel took a deep breath. "You gonna go tattle on Elise and Jane to this Nana Moses lady?"

"That's the plan," Wendy said. "With any luck Nana Moses will know where Emma is, too. Or Ada. Elise was pulling Jane's strings and now she's not. All this drama . . . it has to stop. Let's call down the long arm of the matriarchal law and get the hell out of Dodge."

"What if Elise or Jane is there?" Elle asked, playing absently with the ornate edge of Lily's skirt. "Will the head honcho really listen to you then?"

Wendy laughed. "I kind of hope Jane or Elise *is* there, to be honest. If she actually *knew* what's been going on, I'm positive that Nana Moses would put her foot down and get Elise's crazy under contro—"

"Um," Eddie said quietly as they turned onto Emma's street. "Wendy?"

The flicker-flash of red-blue-red-blue bathed Emma's house and the surrounding homes in eerie light. The neighboring houses were dark but Emma's place was lit up like an airport runway; every window was bright and several women stood in the front yard, talking among themselves. Several dead corgis—their spirits curious-eyed and bushy-tailed—darted around the yard, yapping.

An ambulance and a black van sat at the end of the driveway. Two paramedics were loading a gurney into the van. Two more were loading another into the ambulance.

There was a matte body bag on the gurney.

"Do you know who might be in the body bag?" Wendy asked Eddie. "You were here for weeks, can you see *anything* that you recognize?"

"No," he whispered. "But I recognize the one they loaded in the ambulance." He buried his face in his hands. "I guess we know what happened to Emma now."

"No. This isn't happening," Wendy said, gripping Piotr's hands so tightly her knuckles bled white. "Are you sure, Eddie? Lots of us have red hair, maybe it wasn't—"

"It was," Eddie said apologetically. "Sorry."

"But I never meant for Emma . . . I just . . ." Wendy whispered. Piotr squeezed her hand gently and then disentangled their fingers, taking Wendy by the shoulders and pulling her closer for a hug. "Emma wasn't supposed to get hurt," she told him. "She's not like the others."

"It's a little late, Lightbringer," Elle sneered, hands bunched

into fists as she glared at the women gathered on the lawn. "In for a penny, and all that. So that miracle doctor of yours is down for the count. What's next?"

"Shhh, Elle," Wendy muttered, desperately trying to organize her thoughts. It was hard going; her mind kept replaying the sight of the bundled body being fed into the back of the black van. "Let me think."

Of the half-dozen or so women loitering in the yard, she recognized not a single person. Eddie, who'd spent more time with her extended family than she had, was luckier.

"Hey," he said, pointing out a young, plump woman in a pair of yellow pajamas smoking a cigarette on the sidewalk. "There's Annabelle."

"Jon," Chel ordered, "park across the street."

"What? Are you mental? No!"

Chel smacked her twin on the shoulder. "Park the car. We drove all this way. This opportunity goes nowhere, got it?"

"What are *you* going to do?" Jon demanded, hands clenching and unclenching on the wheel. "March up to them and ask them to take you to their leader?"

"Wendy goes nowhere until we find out who passed," Chel hissed. "I'll make sure it's safe for her to talk to Nana Moses and while I'm at it I'll get the skinny on why the doc is down. Park the f'ing car, Poindexter. They've never seen me, it's safe for me to make nice."

"Whatever. Go ahead and try your braindead plan, see if it gets you nailed," Jon snarled, pulling into the spot Chel indicated. "I'm too tired for this. Get out."

The door slammed and Wendy watched, guilty thoughts running crazy circles in her mind, as Chel approached Annabelle and plopped down on the sidewalk beside her. After a moment Annabelle shrugged and held out a hand. Chel pulled a thin silver flask out of her purse and took a swig, then handed the flask to Annabelle.

"Go ahead, booze it up. Great idea," Wendy grumbled, latching on to her annoyance like a life preserver. "I thought only alkies kept flasks in their purses."

"She quit everything else cold turkey, and we didn't know if you were gonna live or die in the hospital or what," Jon growled, rubbing the back of his hand against his eyes. "Wendy, just . . . lay off, okay? For once? Stop pushing everyone so hard. We're not you."

"Excuse me?" Wendy snapped. The surge of irritation was too much, and she knew she was vastly overreacting, but letting the anger pound through her kept her hands steady and sharpened her thoughts. "Dude, Dad thought *I* was the one with a drug problem. He thought *I* was the one with issues, thanks to her."

"Oh you have issues," Jon replied, yawning and ignoring her quiet fury. He sagged in his seat suddenly, and looked lost. "Everyone in this family does. Yours just aren't the type that can be fed over-the-counter." Wendy thought Jon glanced at Piotr in the rear view mirror as he said that, but it could have been her imagination.

"All that . . . crap will kill her," Wendy retorted, deciding to not touch the Piotr point, annoyed that Jon, ever the peacekeeper, was stubbornly refusing to rise to the bait. He knew her too well, damn it.

"Well, apparently in this family dying really isn't such a downer," Jon said levelly, rubbing his eyes. "Besides," he added in a quieter tone, "you've spent years be-bopping around town hanging out with the dead. That's healthy?"

"Shut up, you two! Chel's actually getting info off Annabelle," Eddie said suddenly, leaning his face as close to the window as he could without sliding through the glass and exposing himself to the Reapers. "Can anyone hear what they're saying?"

They all strained in silence. Nothing.

"So, who is this chick?" Wendy asked, leaning over Piotr's lap to peer out the side window. She felt him still beneath her, his hand briefly brushing her thigh and hesitating against her hip before settling on her lower back where her corset rode up.

"Cousin of a cousin or something," Eddie replied dismissively, sitting back and flicking a glance at Piotr's hand with a tiny frown. He reached over and patted her shoulder familiarly, fingertips resting at the nape of her neck.

"You don't know for sure?" Annoyed with their subtle pawing, Wendy shrugged both of them off.

"I didn't bother tracking who was related to who after a few days," Eddie said. "There are just too many of you. It's all a big hive, really, with a Nana Moses queening it up at center stage." Wendy didn't miss the momentary smirk Eddie shot Piotr when he thought she wasn't looking. She sighed inwardly. Now wasn't the time.

Behind them the ambulance pulled away, the headlights washing across the car and illuminating the interior. Jon ducked.

"With Emma out of the picture, even temporarily, it's all a crazy show now," Elle murmured, fists still clenching and loosening in her lap. Lily patted her shoulder and Elle shrugged her hand away, disdainful of the offered comfort. "We have no idea if even one of them other than her and Nana Moses is going to be on our side. Bunch of loose cannons. That's just fabulous."

"Heads up, Chel's done," Jon said sharply, straightening in his seat. "She's got company."

Behind them, Elise stood at the top of the driveway, outlined by the light pouring from the opening garage, pointing and shouting, gesturing wildly at their car. The women on the lawn were turning in their direction. Annabelle's hand was at her chest; the edges of her body were beginning to glow.

Elle turned in her seat. "What's happ—"

As Chel yanked the passenger side door open, one of the nearest Reapers, a middle-aged woman with a no-nonsense haircut, grabbed her by the ponytail and pulled hard.

"CHEL!" Jon yelled reaching for his buckle.

"Don't you dare!" Wendy snapped at her brother. "Give her a sec! She might be able to twist free!" She turned to Piotr, hissing, "If

Chel can't get free on her own you need to do something! Poke that bitch in the brain! Please, Piotr? Please!"

"We need to help her *now*!" Eddie cried, trying to crawl over Elle to help Chel. Elle and Lily both grabbed him by the arms and pinned him down.

"Living against the living!" Elle shouted in his ear as Eddie fought and bucked. "You can't do anything against Reapers, you dumbo! They'll burn you up!"

The Reaper was persistent. Chel managed to half-claw her way into the passenger side seat.

"NOW!" Wendy demanded and Piotr nodded once before he shoved past the tangled, struggling mass of Eddie and the girls. Careful to avoid Chel's wild punches, Piotr leaned between the two front seats.

The middle-aged Reaper was paying no attention to the ghosts; Chel was flailing like a dervish, all arms and elbows and nails made worse for the close quarters, and the Reaper, half-sprawled over Chel's hip and back, had her hands full just keeping a hold of Chel's hair. The other Reapers were coming at a run. Wendy tried to guess their odds and realized that Piotr only had one chance.

Then Piotr rammed his fist straight into the Reaper's skull.

"Let. Go."

The Reaper did and Chel, twisting on her back, kicked the woman hard in the stomach, driving the Reaper onto the sidewalk where she sprawled, stunned.

"NOW! GO, JON!" Wendy and Chel yelled simultaneously. Chel yanked her legs into the car and slammed the door. She slapped the door locks as another Reaper, running full-tilt, crashed into the trunk, fingers scrabbling at the window. Another pounded on the back door.

"GONE!" Jon yanked the wheel and peeled out, swerving around a Reaper in the street, leaving the Elise and brilliantly lit house behind.

"Chel?" Wendy asked as they merged onto the highway. "What . . . what happened? What did you find out?" She craned for a moment over her shoulder—no one appeared to be following.

When she turned back, she saw that Chel was bent over, head resting on her knees, her breath coming in sharp, harsh gusts. Her sister was trembling like a stricken violin.

"Chel?" she asked. "Chel, are you okay? I didn't even see Elise show up. Did she hurt you?"

"No, no, I'm fine," Chel said, gripping her knees and slowly uncurling in the seat until she sat up straight. She wiped a hand across her mouth. "You know how you were planning on getting Nana Moses to straighten everything out?"

Wendy shivered; her stomach suddenly ached. "Yeah?"

"She's dead." Chel's fingers tangled together as she tried to get herself under control. "She's dead, your friend Emma's in some kind of coma, and Elise is blaming you for both. The whole family, coast to coast, thinks you set out to kill Nana Moses. That you wormed into her good graces and got to her somehow. She even claims that you did something to Jane's mind to make her bail on the clan. The Reapers are looking for you, Wendy, and they are *pissed*."

CHAPTER SEVEN

"**S**hould we go home?" Jon asked Wendy, nervously glancing in the rearview mirror. They weren't being followed.

"Not right now," Chel said before Wendy could answer, angling the makeup mirror and shifting side to side in the passenger seat, trying to get a good view of the highway behind them. She'd finally finished shaking. "Maybe later, but not right now."

"Okay, fine, so where do we go?" Jon asked. He rubbed his eyes with the back of his left hand. "If we can't go home, we don't want to drag anyone else into this mess. We can't go back to the hospital—Dr. Mc-I'ma-call-CPS is probably still on duty."

"Maybe I'm flappin' my gums here," Elle said, leaning forward so that Jon and Chel recoiled to the sides from her cold, "but maybe it's time to take a little visit up Nob Hill way."

Beside her, Lily frowned, uncrossing her legs and drawing them up, tucking her knees beneath her chin as she regarded Elle warily. "The Council? What do you expect to happen should we attempt a meeting with them?"

"Nothing much, but Frank did say he wanted a word with the Lightbringer, right? And the Top of the Mark's solid." Elle tapped the side of Chel's seat to make her point.

Just then, with hardly a grumble of warning, the street bucked and rolled, the car rocking like a boat as the earth trembled beneath them. Jon, screaming, slammed on the brakes, and the car fishtailed across two lanes of highway, finally butting up against the breakdown lane barricade, facing backwards. The shockwaves shook the car like a dog with a bone. Wendy's teeth

clamped down painfully on her tongue as the ground rolled and rolled and rolled.

After long seconds the earthquake slowed and stopped.

"I wonder how solid it's gonna be now," Eddie muttered, shaking his head like a dog so that his hair hung raggedly in his face. "That quake took *forever*."

"Is it just me or did that quake seem . . . I don't know, to have a direction?" Chel asked, rubbing the center of her forehead with the heel of her hand. Wendy could see that her sister had slammed her head into top of the glove compartment during the worst of the quake. One side of the compartment had cracked and was leaking old napkins and straws, the curled and yellowed edge of the insurance paperwork barely poking through. "It didn't feel like it . . . normally does. It felt like . . . like it was coming from the west. Like a wave, rolling only one way."

"Chel's right," Wendy agreed, peering out the window. Lights flickered, illuminating the buckled pavement in strobing shadows. "I've been in some biggies and that one was . . . weird. Different."

"What's the radio say?" Chel asked, spinning the radio dial. All was music, even the station normally reserved for emergency broadcasts. "How big do you think it was? Four? Four point five?"

"The dial's gonna catch on fire if you don't give it a rest, Chel. Let the world have a sec for people to get up to speed," Wendy said, forcing herself to stop chewing her lower lip nervously. "I bet everyone who's awake is still picking their butts up off the floor. It's New Years, most of them are probably too drunk to realize it's actually the world spinning around them."

"So . . . are we headed into the city then?" Jon said, gesturing for Chel to keep an eye out on the road as he carefully maneuvered the car around. He pointed ahead to where part of the highway was broken and buckled. "We can't go that way. There's the exit but it's blocked off with debris. Thank heavens this car is built like a boat. We're going to have to go around the mess up ahead through the breakdown lane and over some of the torn up sections."

"That could shred the tires," Chel warned. "Dad'll be ticked off."

Jon shrugged. "Or we can wait for the city to get around to this stretch of road."

Wendy shook her head. "No. Take the breakdown lane and see if you can get all the way to the end of the exit. The next road is a main street so we *should* be able to pick up on an unbroken stretch at the next entrance."

"That breakdown lane is damn near coated in broken glass," Chel muttered, biting the side of her thumb and scowling. "I can even see rebar! Can you make it? Safely?"

"He'll have to," Wendy said. "That earthquake came from the north. The Council is west. So we go west, rebar or no rebar. Jon? Hit it."

They could make out the dim shape of Angel Island amid the thick mists pouring across the bay. Eddie leaned over and prodded Wendy in the shoulder. Wendy, too tired to respond, dozed against Piotr's neck, his arm slung behind her and holding her lolling head steady. Eddie stretched to poke Wendy again, when a bump on the Bay Bridge woke her. Blearily she looked at her best friend and yawned.

"What's up, Eds?" she murmured, uncaring for once that he was witness to whatever-it-was she had going on with Piotr. "You okay?"

"Me?" he asked, directing her attention out the window. "I'm fine. I was just wondering . . . do you see that?"

Wendy blinked and rubbed her eyes. The black, heavy clouds in the distance did not change shape or move. The purple-red flashes of light glowed steadily at the center of the cloudbank, the edges lined with blinding white glimmering Light.

"Yep," Wendy said, forcing herself to take a deep, calming breath before she hyperventilated. Every single nerve in her not-quite-a-body was singing in a high, terrified pitch. "I do."

"Holy . . . what is that thing?" Chel hissed, rolling down the

window and craning her head into the chilly wind to get a better look.

Gut rolling, Wendy couldn't tear her eyes away. It had to be her imagination, but it looked like there were shapes, shadows, moving amid the clouds. It was like something plucked straight out of her nightmares . . . or dreamscapes.

"I believe that that is a crack in the sky," Wendy murmured, remembering the door in the sand, the ruined-beautiful face of her mother saying words her mother would never say, pointing Wendy in directions her mother would have let her stumble upon herself. That dream-Mary, wearing her mother like a mask, had warned Wendy that a storm was coming. She hadn't been kidding—this one looked like a doozy.

"Just checking," Eddie said. "Cuz I thought I was going crazy for a second there."

"Join the club, then," Elle said, sounding simultaneously bored and aggravated. Then she made a strangled sound Wendy realized was something caught halfway between a laugh and a sob. "Does anyone else wanna play spot the weird?"

"What now?" Lily demanded, twisting so she could look out the opposing window. "Oh . . . oh, my." She pressed a hand to her mouth and visibly paled.

Startled at Lily's expression, Wendy's eyes fluttered closed for a moment. She didn't want to open them, to face whatever mon-strosity could cause Lily of all people to grow so distressed, but then Jon hissed between his teeth.

"Am I supposed to just drive through that? What'll it do to the *car*?"

"Keep going," Piotr demanded and Wendy's eyes snapped open. She leaned over Eddie and there it was, a huge white cloud of shifting, shimmering webs covering the entire skyline of San Francisco. The spirit webs were caught in the wind, tendrils as thin as fine white silk snapping like kites in the sky, sucked by the power of the storm hovering over the bay toward the rip in reality at the core.

"But the car—" Jon protested.

"It is solid," Piotr insisted. "The spirit webs cannot harm the living much—they suck energy and life, yes, but the vehicle should protect us."

"Should?" Chel demanded, yanking her head back into the car and rapidly rolling up the window as they reached the outer strings of the spirit webs. "You're not certain?"

"Nothing is certain here," Lily said darkly. She held out her hand and Elle absently rested her palm in Lily's, fingers twining as they frowned at the waving webs together.

"You called what the spirit webs grew into . . . you called it a little forest," Wendy said softly to Lily, "but I had no idea it was this bad. That's not a little forest, that's the whole city!"

"It wasn't," Lily confessed. She leaned forward and Elle released her hand, curling her fingers back in her lap. Elle's shoulders hunched and the loose curls at the front of her face hid her eyes in shadow. Lily, sparing a worried glance for her friend, gestured out the window, pointing as she explained, "Twenty-four hours ago, the webs stretched not far at all. You could bypass it with a half hour of steady walking but this . . . this is a new aberration."

"This is craziness," Elle snapped, head jerking up, and yanking her fingers through the tangled curls lying haphazardly against her forehead. "How could it grow like this overnight?" She tilted her head back and tried to see out the side window, shuddering as the tips of spiritual toes, obviously Shades, caught by the webs, slid through the roof above them.

All of them cringed and ducked low, angling themselves so the Shades didn't touch them as they passed.

"Those are bodies," Chel said flatly, titling her head back to take in the full height and width of the mass. "Cocooned bodies wrapped in . . . what is that? It's foul."

"Spirit webs," Piotr replied, voice and expression dull.

"Piotr?" Lily asked. "What is it?"

Piotr flicked a glance at Wendy and she nearly flinched from the raw pain in his eyes. Wordlessly he took her hand in his and pressed her hand flat against his chest. Worried, Wendy took a deep breath and then . . .

Piotr.

It was like she was inside Piotr's head, inside his body, feeling the shift of his rough clothing against his back, the way the hairs on Piotr's arms caught against the fabric and the tug of his pants across his thighs. She could feel the echo of his mind, his thoughts a beat ahead of her own, a hot tingle racing through her skull as Piotr fought to keep his mind to himself.

Piotr's chest was aching, the pain ramping up the closer they got to a thicker mass of the webs. He . . . no, they . . . pressed a hand to his/their ribs, silently willing the pain to disperse. The last time he had felt this kind of pain had been before Sarah, the Lost girl, had healed the Lady Walker's poison coursing through Piotr's system, before Sarah'd buried her fingers in the diseased, overcome shell that acted as a body and blessedly burned the pain away.

But . . . when Sarah had healed Piotr, had she destroyed the spirit web seed growing within? At the time Piotr had assumed so—there'd been no niggling pain, no ache in his gut to tell him otherwise—but now the outcome wasn't so certain. Piotr's insides, where they didn't ache, tickled . . . as if something small was growing there.

Wendy, gasping, yanked her hand free. Lily, frowning, brushed her palm against Wendy's elbow and Wendy twitched away, terrified for an instant that she'd be yanked into another soul's body, but Lily's touch was calming and cool. Nothing like the quiet havoc of Piotr's malfunctioning body.

Troubled, Wendy tucked into her little corner, rebuffing all attempts at conversation as the spirit webs grew thicker and wilder around them.

They left the bridge, headed for the hotel at the top of Nob Hill.

The going was slow—even at this time of night, the streets were flooded with people staggering from place to place. Most were laughing, raucous, unaware of the spirit webs wrapping around their bodies and digging thin, pointed tendrils into their hearts, heads, and guts.

One rip-roaring drunk woman stumbled up to their car and pounded on the hood, laughing and demanding a ride. Her face was coated with a thick mesh of web; the tendrils had worked their way past the corners of her mouth and were snaking down her throat. Her low-cut dress couldn't cover the fine weave of web that curled around her entire body—she wore the web like a bodysuit, from head to heels, and the web was growing thicker by the second, feasting on her years and willpower.

Chel cringed away from the window. "Can't you hurry?" she hissed to Jon.

"I'll run someone over," he snapped back, hunching over the wheel and trying to see past the mass ropes of web dangling down. The closer they got to Nob Hill, the heavier and thicker the spirit webs became. "I'm having a really hard time differentiating between living and dead as it is. Don't make me add to it."

A long, undulating howl cut through the air, originating deep in the heart of the forest, near the Palace. Even the living stilled as the howl rose and broke on a high, rough note, only moving again once the echoes had faded away.

"I don't like the sound of that," Elle murmured suddenly, breaking the utter silence in the back seat. "I think our Walker-eating beastie buddy's back, Pete."

"You may be correct," Piotr replied, palm pressed flat against his gut. He would not look at Wendy but she found that comforting. She needed a little space after that intense dive into his head. "But we can't concern ourselves with the monster at the center of the forest. It is a dog, *da*? So long as we do not breach its territory—"

"You mean like we're doing now?" Eddie asked. He'd taken

Wendy's hands in his own, their fingers wound together as they sought familiar comfort. Wendy saw Piotr's face twist as he spotted their linked fingers and she felt a stab of sadness at his quickly smothered dismay but she wasn't willing to let Eddie go. They'd been friends forever; Piotr had to accept that.

"We should be fine," Piotr insisted, but Wendy knew that he wasn't so certain. Wincing, he gripped his chest again. No one else seemed to notice his increasing distress but Lily. She said nothing but Wendy noted the knowing look in Lily's eyes, the drawn frown that darted across her lips. Piotr's pain had caught her attention, she wouldn't be willing to pretend everything was fine for much longer. Wendy was thankful that Lily was a good friend. She would hold her tongue for now, but Wendy knew that if Piotr didn't disclose the cause of his pain quickly, she'd call him out. Wendy wondered if she should beat him to the punch but it seemed . . . invasive, rude, to tell the others of his worries.

Piotr could sense Lily and Wendy watching him obliquely, gauging his every move. It was simultaneously aggravating and soothing, knowing that if he collapsed they both would leap to action. His best friend and his love. How did he get so lucky? Then, as if taunting him, the niggling pain gnawed at his gut, nearly bending him double with the intensity of it, rippling through his core. As the pain blossomed, working its way across his torso, Piotr felt the memory unfold around him, soft and pervasive as fresh-fallen snow . . .

The snow was as deep as his thigh in places and his hands were fading to brown, tacky as the blood dried. The breeze picked up; downy feathers spun, lifted high and drifting down again, sticking to the drying blood on his forehead, to the tears and sweat cooling on his cheeks. Keeping the frozen river to the right, Piotr slogged through the snow, heading for where the village sat, nestled in the vee where the banks of the river split, protected on three sides by the frozen water.

Piotr took another step, fur-clad foot breaking through the ice atop the snow beneath. The Reaper's cloak was dragging the snow beside him, leaving thin, oddly patterned trails splattered with faint pink as the feathers dragged in the drifts. Great black flocks of crows and gulls and ravens weighed down the overhanging evergreens all the way to the end of the forest but not a peep was heard; the forest was unnervingly quiet.

"Mother will know what to do," Piotr thought, fingers reflexively tightening on the cloak of feathers, ignoring the tickle of blood trickling from his face onto the cloak, absorbed by the feathers and wetting the snow.

The forest was a mottled mass of white-green-black as far as the eye could see, and then, from the corner of his eye, Piotr spotted a flash of red, of silver-grey, and the whip-quick motion of the long braid only a hint of the shape shifting in the tree's shadow, gone before Piotr was sure he'd spotted it.

At first Piotr was confused—this snow was deep, no one he knew could move that swiftly and silently in snow this deep—before Piotr remembered who—what—he was dealing with.

REAPER.

Piotr was yanked out of his memories when Elle stiffened and pushed Eddie aside, pressing her face against the side window. "SHHH! Do you hear that?"

"I can't hear anything," Eddie grunted, wincing and shifting beneath her weight, "with your knee crushing my junk!"

"LISTEN," Elle demanded. Eyes narrowing, she looked left and right and Piotr followed suit, trusting Elle's instincts implicitly. They'd only traveled a short distance due to the forest of webbing; there were still several blocks to go before they reached Nob Hill. Were they on California Street? It was so hard to tell in the mist and amid the dangling webs, but the street was tilted at a crazy angle here, steep and slick.

Snuffle. Loud and wet.

Snuffle-snuffle-snort. Loud and wet and *close.*

"Go-go-go," Wendy growled at Jon. "Move-move-move!"

Jon hit the gas, the car struggling against gravity, but it was too late; the beast filled the road in front of them, shoulders as high as the car, teeth as long as Wendy's forearm.

It was like a dog, or a wolf, but not, and a cat, but not. It was furry and huge, filling the front windshield with its bulk, and its legs were corded with strangely-shaped muscles, but it had five legs and bizarre, bulbous knots poking out, eye-like appendages blinking at her, amidst the fur of its chest and legs. Foam, white and stringy, dripped from its jaws as the gigantic dog-wolf-cat-thing dropped its head low and examined the occupants of the car.

"Can dogs have red eyes like that?" Eddie asked in a breathless, high voice, as if the air had been knocked out of him. "All slitted like that?" His voice cracked. "And tails? Tails that snap back and forth like that? That's not possible, right? Right?" He pressed a hand against his mouth. "What. The. Hell."

Lily laid a hand on Eddie's thigh. "Hush," she whispered, voice steady but sharp, cutting through the panic in the car instantly. "Be calm. Do not draw its attention."

"But it's looking at us," Eddie hissed.

"It may yet be only curious," Lily replied evenly and Piotr envied the way she held perfectly still. His every muscle screamed at him to flee but Lily was like a predator herself, poised and waiting for the perfect moment to move.

"Be still," she continued. "Be calm. Whatever this beast is, it senses our fear, it smells your panic."

The monster growled low in its throat and Piotr groaned in pain, hands reflexively jerking up to his torso, pressing hard against his ribs and belly.

"Piotr?" Wendy asked, untangling her fingers from Eddie's. "Piotr, are you okay?" Her voice dipped down. "Is it the . . . ?" She gestured to her gut.

"Push past the creature, go slowly but faster than this," Piotr gasped, writhing on the seat as if his very guts were going to come

spilling out his belly. "It . . . it's not from this world, it doesn't understand . . . it doesn't understand what we are yet. It's . . . it's . . . from the space between the worlds . . ."

"What? How do you . . ." Jon hesitated. "I don't—"

"Listen to the man!" Chel snapped and shoved Jon over. Before he could protest Chel lifted her left leg high and jammed it down on the accelerator, missing Jon's foot by half an inch. The car shot forward, swerving as Jon tried to steer around his sister and the beast, confused, darted to the side, sliding against the steep slope and scrabbling for an instant for better purchase on the street.

"You're gonna hit someone!" Eddie yelled, but the way, miraculously, had cleared before them. Cars honked, dimly, from the living lands, but the Never was so thick here Wendy could only just make out the outline of the living world. All around was nothing but death and decay, the spirit webs draining the vitality from every living thing. Here, in the heart of the forest, nothing moved except them, and the Never itself seemed twisted, wrong, like it was bleeding out into the living world.

How had Wendy lived like this, juggling the sight of two worlds laid atop one another, for so long? The double-world vision always made his head ache violently.

Using Piotr's shoulder as leverage, Wendy lifted up in a crouch and twisted to stare out the back of the rear window. Piotr followed her lead and saw that the beast had vanished into the foggy mist, the ropes of spirit web obscuring it from view. They were alone—them, the webs, and the Shades being devoured like flies above them.

"How much longer?" Chel whispered, voice trembling. "I can't see anything but the Never right now."

"*Pahzhalstah*," Piotr commanded. "Stop. Here."

Shrugging, Jon obliged, no questions asked. Piotr could tell that Wendy's brother was unnerved but was attempting to act tough. The spirit of her family impressed him; they were a tough lot,

that was for sure. Once upon a time he would have been proud to call all three of them Riders.

"There," Piotr said at last, when movement in the mass caught his attention. "Look."

The Lady Walker was backlit against the fog; her cloak a dirtier shade of the same heavy white that crept across the world, curling through the streets on eddies of breeze.

Wendy swallowed thickly. She hated the tremble in her voice as she said, "Okay guys. It's go time. What do we do? How do we want to handle this?"

"We can't run her over," Jon said. "At least . . . can we?"

"We could try," Chel said grimly, but Wendy shook her head.

"No. Use your eyes," Wendy said, hearing her mother's arrogance creeping into her tone. It was a tone she loathed, a know-it-all texture to every word she said. Wendy tried to temper the urge to imperiously demand that they look closer and instead gently explained, "See how she's—oh, I don't know how to describe it—see how she's firmer than the landscape around her? She's more solid than the car here. We'd slide to either side of her at best."

"Wendy?" Chel's voice was high and tight but pitched soft, speaking as quietly as she could manage. "Dreamspace stuff can affect the real world, right?"

"Yeah," Wendy said, not taking her eyes off the Lady Walker. She reflexively ran her tongue against her teeth, missing the comforting *clink* her tongue ring would have made if the White Lady hadn't ripped it out. "Why?"

"What about stuff that happens in the Never? Can that affect the real—the living—world?"

Wendy thought of her answering machine, the only voice recording she'd had of their mother, and how it'd been crushed in the hands of a Walker—a Walker who'd been sent to fetch Wendy by the woman in the mist before them.

She shivered. "Yeah, Chel," Wendy whispered, allowing herself a moment's mourning for her mother's mutilated message. "Sometimes . . . sometimes, yeah it can."

The Lady Walker beckoned, one long, bony hand curling in their direction, an open invitation. Then—so close it raised the hairs on the back of Wendy's neck—the wet snuffling-sniffle of the beast broke the silence. Its gargantuan head parted the mist and webs to the right of the Lady Walker. It sniffed the air.

"Lovely," Chel said, the despair creeping beneath her words. "Well, it's been nice knowing you all. I'd say have a nice afterlife, but we all know how that turns out."

The Lady Walker's hand slashed down, a cutting motion, and the beast stilled beside her. Then it growled, but only faintly, and retreated back into the mist.

"That thing listens to her?" Eddie moaned. "Just fabulous, she's got the hell-Fido trained up good and proper. I wonder if it piddles on the paper, too?"

"Okay, enough! Stop being so damn negative. I'm going out there," Wendy said, forgetting her ethereal state and reaching for the door handle.

"No!" Eddie said, grabbing her wrist. "What is meeting up with the rotting wonder going to accomplish?"

"Anything is better than this . . . this dread, Eddie," Wendy replied, shaking him off her arm. "Stay here."

"I shall go with you," Piotr said.

Rolling her eyes, Wendy shook her head. "Stay here. Protect the twins."

"Hey," Chel protested, "we don't need our big sist—"

"Shut up," Wendy said kindly. "Listen to Piotr. Understand?"

Chel, mutinous, tried to look away. Wendy poked her sister hard in the shoulder, ignoring the sizzle from Chel's living flesh. "Michelle. Do you understand me?"

"Yeah, fine, whatever," Chel grumped, rubbing her shoulder. "Hurry it up, Suicidal. We don't have all day."

Wendy waited until Eddie, scowling, sat back and allowed her to pass without further incident. Then she was outside, leaving the mud-splattered car behind, lost amid the swirling fog and facing the Lady Walker down in a world like a washed out western. Wendy, amused, paused to picture tumbleweeds blowing past as the Citibank clock struck midnight. Even in the Never it was hard to walk up the steep slope of the street. Wendy hid her struggle by walking sedately toward their meeting, smirking the whole while.

The Lady Walker, seeing her smile and sensing her amusement, hesitated. "You find this funny, Reaper?"

"Not even close," Wendy assured her. She sighed and thrust her hands in her pockets. "Do you have anything to do with that rip in the sky, by any chance?"

The Lady Walker grinned, the sagging and rotten half of her face sliding loosely over her bones, exposing yellowed teeth and shredded tendons. "If I did? What would you do about it, girl?"

"Nothing," Wendy said, shrugging. "But I hear that the Reapers are ticked off over it. Elise even tried to bribe me to 'take care' of you a few days ago."

Surprisingly, the Lady Walker began to laugh, a broken, rusty sound, as if she'd spent her entire life with a three-pack-a-day habit. "Did she now? Good."

Smirking, so that Wendy could see the wriggling things moving behind her terrible smile, the Lady Walker wiggled her fingers at Wendy. "You Reapers amuse me. You are family, a clan, yet you fight among yourselves, attacking from the shadows, and laying blame on nature running its course. And all the while I taste your tears and laugh and laugh and laugh."

"Nature . . . do you mean that vortex thing up there?" Wendy glanced over her shoulder. They were deep in the spirit web forest— Wendy had no idea why she kept expecting to see clear sky above the rip in the distance—but all she could see was the sagging of cocooned Shades twisting in the breeze.

"I mean the old woman, and the fretful way they fuss and blame you," the Lady Walker said. "It was simply her time. It comes to us all. Except Piotr. Except me."

"Because you're the Unending Ones," Wendy said, wondering how the Lady Walker already knew about Nana Moses' death. "How'd you two manage to land that gig?"

The Lady Walker patted her hip and for the first time Wendy realized that the Lady Walker had a swatch of fabric hanging there, a thin curl of cloth that hung nearly to her ankles. "The how of things is of no matter. It is the *why*."

"Are you going to let us keep going?" Wendy snapped, suddenly tired of this rotting woman and her horrible riddles. She reminded Wendy unpleasantly of the White Lady, not because she was rotting and awful to look at, but because even the cadence of her voice had a lilting, tortuous rhythm to it. Every conversation with them both was nothing but riddles and rhymes and Wendy was sick to death of it. "Or is that animal *thing* going to block the way?"

"I contracted with Jane to bring you to me. She failed and yet, poof, here you are." The Lady Walker's fingers played with the rotting hole in her face, drifted up and brushed the horror that had once been her eye. "I am lucky."

"Maybe," Wendy said, resting her weight on one foot, prepared to run like a rabbit if she needed to. "Maybe not. Why did you want to talk to me?"

"I have heard . . . many things, girl. Many whispers make their way to me. I have heard that you do not reap the unwilling spirits anymore. Is this true?"

"Yeah, it's true," Wendy said, narrowing her eyes. The way the Lady Walker was swaying back and forth was giving her the heebie-jeebies. "What of it?"

The Lady Walker tilted her head far too far to the left, looking at Wendy quizzically through her ruined face. "Why? Do you hope to gain from the remaining spirits the way Elise and the Reapers do?"

"Because I think maybe it's not my job to force souls to do what they don't want to do." Why was the Lady Walker asking these questions?

The Lady Walker laughed shortly. "Oh, flesh, how you amuse me! The words that spring from your mouth dance in the air as if they were butterflies and yet . . . they are meaningless and dead." She spat on the ground. "They are filth."

"Look, creepy, all I want is to get to Nob Hill."

The Lady Walker pursed her ruined mouth. "I see."

"Everyone wants something, Miss . . . Lady." Wendy squared her shoulders. "What do you want? What will get my friends and me out of this forest and up the hill? Jane says you want to gnaw on my bones or something, but I'm thinking that if that was your deal you'd already be chewing. So what's the plan? What do you want?"

"My greatest desire is within my grasp, scratched out of nothing with my own two hands. I want for nothing . . . except one thing," the Lady Walker said, fingering the curl of fabric. She pulled it off her dress and flung it at Wendy's feet.

"What is this?" Wendy asked, kneeling down and picking up the fabric. It was a sensible gray swatch, shiny satin but durable, frayed only where some dull blade had sheared it from a larger bolt.

"Give it to your boy," the Lady said, grinning her snaggle-toothed smile. "With my compliments. Then return and hear my price for your passage."

Flipping the foul woman off and tucking the odd fabric away, Wendy turned and realized why the Lady Walker was so amused. The spirit webs had dropped down behind the car, draping the road completely in a curtain of writhing white. There was no way to push through them, even in the car. They'd all be stripped of will and essence within seconds.

Close . . . so close . . . Wendy could hear the wet snuffle of the ˙ as it stalked through the weft of webs.

ʰat was suspiciously fast," Jon joked as Wendy, balancing

carefully and ruing her already aching shins and calves, returned to the vehicle. "How much was the toll?"

"She gave me this." Wendy handed off the swatch of fabric. "She wanted me to give it to Piotr and then go back." Wendy ran her hands along her arms. "The forest . . ."

"Closed in behind us while you were jabbering," Elle said, taking the swatch. "We noticed." She examined the fabric before handing it over to Piotr. "I have no idea what this is. Do you know, flyboy?"

"Da. This is . . . this is Ada," Piotr said running a thumb along the frayed threads. "A part of Ada's dress, I am certain of it."

"Your scientist buddy? What's she got to do with it?" Chel asked.

"She is still in one piece," Lily murmured, taking the swatch from him. "This is part of her essence; it has not faded so Ada still exists. The Lady Walker is telling us that either she has Ada, or she knows where Ada is being kept."

"Like kidnappers sending a finger to prove the victim is still alive," Eddie mused, sticking his tongue out and grimacing. "Twisted."

"I will go," Piotr said. "Wendy ne—"

"Bull*shit*, you'll go!" Wendy snapped. "We don't negotiate with crazy, Piotr. She wanted me, I'm going back out there. Not you."

"Without weapons? Are you nuts?" Eddie demanded. "She put up with your bravado once, but if you tweak her nose again that dog'll eat you whole!"

Wendy rolled her eyes. "Please. I'm the Lightbringer—"

"Without abilities! Without Light!" Eddie crossed his arms over his chest. "Are you trying to get yourself killed? I know the way you work, Wendy. Is this a guilt thing?"

Surprisingly, Piotr took her side. "Let her go say her piece," he said. "Wendy is competent."

"Are you kidding me?" Eddie demanded. "You're her . . . sort of her boyfriend! You should be yelling the loudest! Don't you care?"

Lily laid a calming hand on his arm but Eddie flung it off. "No'

If he really loves her he shouldn't be shoving her out the door to piss on that lady's parade! Especially with Hell-Fido out and about!"

"What Wendy and I are to one another is none of your concern," Piotr retorted pointedly. "She is the Lightbringer. She is aware of her own capabilities. And the Lady Walker will not harm Wendy. If she were going to, Wendy would be gone by now."

"You know an awful lot about this chick, *Pete*," Eddie snarled. "Got anything to share?"

"I knew her in life," Piotr said, not bothering to disguise the disgust in his tone. "My lost memories are slow in returning, but when they do they come in full. The Lady Walker destroyed my family and laughed as they died. Do not claim I do not wish her terrible suffering."

Eddie stilled. Wendy knew that he was struggling with what to say, that he was tempted to simply turn away and drop the fight but instead he humbly said, "Man . . . man, I'm sorry. I didn't know." Her heart swelled with pride for him.

"How were you to know? Your body still lives and my bones are as dust." Piotr smiled bitterly. "A word of advice: choose your flailing words wisely. You might cut yourself with them."

"Look, guys," Chel said, "not to break up the machismo marathon, but the webs are getting thicker. Will *someone* go out there and pee in her Cheerios already?"

Wendy patted Chel on the shoulder and pushed past Piotr and Lily, shaking off Eddie's half-hearted grab at her wrist, wordlessly sliding through the door.

"Lightbringer! Take this and be well," Lily said, slipping through the door and hurrying after Wendy. She paused to draw a bone knife from its sheath.

"This is your favorite knife," Wendy said as the girl pressed the ~~ndle~~ into Wendy's hand. "I can't—"

"~~B~~ring it back in one piece. Make it taste the essence of the ~~r~~ such honor, I shall lend you my blade."

Wendy nodded, feeling like she and the ancient fighter were finally seeing completely eye-to-eye. "I'll do my best."

"Do better," Lily instructed, and stood back.

Wendy nodded and, ignoring Eddie's muffled yells from within the car, she strode into the middle of the street.

CHAPTER EIGHT

"**Y**O! HALF-FACE! COME OUT, COME OUT, WHEREVER YOU ARE!" Wendy wiped her mouth with the back of one arm; she couldn't shake Piotr's words—he'd known this woman when he was alive. She was the reason he was dead. The Lady Walker had killed members of his family. And now Wendy was going to talk with her again, this time with the knowledge that whatever she did might affect how Ada was being treated.

Wendy couldn't help wondering if she'd lost her mind. What sane person actively sought out someone capable of not only surviving centuries of death and destruction on their own, but seemed to flourish from it?

She did, apparently.

The Lady Walker stepped from the nearest clump of webs and approached Wendy, her cloak sinuously sliding along the littered ground as she walked.

She smiled her sharp smile and Wendy felt a burning flutter in her gut, as if her Light were flaring brighter as the Lady Walker approached. "You taste . . . like death," the Lady Walker whispered, leaning in. Her breath puffed out in a sickly-sweet wave.

"Well, you smell like death," Wendy retorted. "Guess that makes us even."

A single finger brushed down Wendy's cheek, cold and sharp as honed ice. "Proud. So proud, and yet unaware that you have done me a great favor. The Reapers would have tracked me down, and pulled up the spirit webs ages ago, but instead they waste their time on the likes of you! Elise thinks I wish to devour you, to take your strength in and make it my own. She is . . . a fool, girl. A foolish, stupid woman."

The Lady Walker held out a hand that was mostly bone and sagging, blackened flesh. She took Wendy's hand in her own and Wendy fought the rising of her gorge at the feeling of the ungloved flesh sliding beneath her fingers.

"I don't want your power. You can offer nothing to me that I cannot claw out for myself, girl! You've seen what I can do. Leave this city, death-dealer. Turn your face east and do not stop. That is my price to allow you to visit the Council. When you are done I want you to run. Run fast. Run far. Leave the Reapers—leave Elise—to me. I will free my hosta— I mean, your *friend* Ada—after I am done with the Reapers." Snickering at her fake verbal slip, she released Wendy's hand. "After Elise, your new matriarch, kneels begging at my feet, then you shall have your scientist back."

Scrubbing her palm on her thigh, Wendy swallowed several times. Her mouth was sour with bile, her entire body ached from holding herself still until the Lady Walker leaned back, giving her space. "Why? Why let me go?"

The Lady Walker shrugged but her good eye glittered in the light. "Perhaps I see in you something of what I once was. Perhaps it is a . . . matter of a debt repaid. What does it matter? The Reapers are no part of you; your mother saw to that. Let me have my vengeance upon them." She tilted her head up to the canopy of spirit webs. "Let the sky burn."

Circumspectly, Wendy's hand dipped into her pocket. She pulled out the handsome Walker's healing necklace and, while the Lady Walker's head was still flung back, Wendy slipped the necklace over her neck and beneath her hoodie.

"No dice," Wendy replied. "The Reapers suck, yeah, but I like my sky intact, thank you very much."

The Lady Walker smiled. "So be it." Then she waved a hand toward the car. "Enjoy your slow death and know you begged for it by name. I gave you a chance to flee." She smirked and turned away, leaving Wendy alone in the mist.

A thump to the left startled Wendy into skittering right a step. There, on the pavement, lay a woman Wendy had only briefly met, but recognized immediately.

"Ada!" Wendy gasped and hurried toward the older woman, arms outstretched to help Ada to her feet. The street was growing cold and slick beneath her feet, aggravating her footing upon the already steep slope.

"No!" Ada gasped, thrusting out a hand to keep Wendy at bay. "Do not touch me! I am contaminated!"

"What?" Wendy asked, faltering. "I don't—"

Ada stumbled to her feet and Wendy's words died in her throat. "Oh . . . oh, Ada . . . oh, Ada, what . . . what happened?"

"This." Ada's free hand pressed against the gash in her gut. Spirit webs snaked out of the wound, curling up around her torso and down around her thighs, pinning her voluminous skirt to her legs. One long and nasty tendril curled twice around her throat like a thin, deadly choker. The tip of the tendril flirted with her lips, curled in a spiral at the edge of her mouth and probed the corner.

"Ada believed she could play in the realm of gods," whispered the Lady Walker's voice from the fog. "She thought she could meddle with what she didn't understand. To explain the way things had become instead of simply accepting the way things are. Foolish, idiot child." The laughter rolled from the fog, rough and rotten and grating. Wendy fought the urge to cover her ears with her hands.

"The spirit web poison," Ada explained. "They injected my own concoction into me." She smiled and Wendy flinched at the sight of her shattered, jagged teeth. "It works . . . quite fast. Mary would have been pleased; the vials would have protected you. Even a Reaper . . . would be helpless."

Wendy turned her face away, ashamed at what her mother had wrought. "Yeah. She would have been so proud."

"Do not worry yourself," Ada said, coughing so hard her body shuddered. "I reap what I've sown."

"I can't access my Light," Wendy cried. "I can't burn the growth away, I can't help you!"

"I know, I know," Ada soothed. "Piotr managed . . ." She pressed a hand to her belly, leaned over, and gasped. "How he managed to hold off . . . the infection . . . the seed's growth . . . for so long . . . amazes me."

The Lady Walker appeared behind Wendy, her hands cupping Wendy's shoulders in an icy grip. A Shade lay at her feet, drained nearly dry by clinging spirit webs. It still had the faintest will, and moved feebly beneath the webs, reaching for Wendy's ankles and moaning.

"Piotr is like me," the Lady Walker whispered. "Unending. No mere poison could fell him—only slow him down. Drive him insane, husk him out . . . but not kill him. He is unending. He is eternal. Just. Like. Me."

She sighed, her lips too near to Wendy's cheek, her awful, rotten breath gaggingly close. "Last chance, girl, I grant this to you. Your mother paved the way for my rise. Take what I offer. Leave now. Or suffer."

"What about Ada?" Wendy demanded, shifting so the Shade couldn't clutch at her feet. She hated to be so cold but Wendy knew that she had to be reasonable; if she had to run the Shade might trip her up. "You claimed you'd free her if I did what you demanded but . . . you're killing her!"

"You can't kill what is already dead," the Lady Walker said, nudging aside the skeletal Shade. "Case in point. However, I *will* free her, after the Reapers have been dealt with. You have my word."

"Will there be any of her *left* to free?" Wendy asked. She didn't let her gaze skitter to the Shade though it was a strain not to. The Shade was so thin and wasted as to be beyond age, beyond gender. It was nearly a walking skeleton, just dusky flesh stretched tight over bones. The Shade's eyes were gone—only the gruesome thorns and buds of the spirit web's seeds remained.

"If her will is strong enough," the Lady Walker replied care-lessly, waving a hand idly as she smiled at Wendy, her remaining teeth gleaming in the pale, gross light. Her waving hand then rested, butterfly-light, on Wendy's shoulder. "She may yet survive."

"I am so tired of this crap," Wendy growled. "No. No, okay? No-no-no. No deals. No bargains. No bullshit. I'm done! Okay? I'm . . . I'm done. With you. With the Reapers. With all of this! No more!"

"If you will not kneel or run, then you leave me no choice." The Lady Walker's hand tightened for a fraction of a second. Then, moving quickly as a scorpion striking, the Lady Walker kicked Ada's ankle; it broke with a terrible crunch. Ada crumpled to the ground.

"You bitch!" Wendy yelled, dropping to a knee beside the downed spirit. "Ada, can you walk? Hop? Anything?"

"She won't need to. If you will not deal with me then I am done with her," the Lady Walker said, leaning down, her hands curling over the top of Wendy's shoulders roughly; one dipped down to cup Wendy's left breast, to slide over her ribcage, the other probing Wendy's hip. Where the flat of the Lady Walker's hand pressed against her chest, a flat, icy chill crept across Wendy's skin, numbing her body and sapping her strength.

"She is useless. Ada suffers and will continue to suffer . . . unless you kill her now. Kill her, Lightbringer. Prove to me that you are unlike your brethren. Kill her."

"Wendy," Ada said, shaking her head. "It's a trap. Don't. Don't . . . listen to her—she's trying to . . . distract you. Leave me. Go! RUN!"

"Yes, Lightbringer," murmured the Lady Walker. "Run."

"Why are you doing this?" Wendy asked, hating the begging tone creeping into her voice. "Why can't you just leave everything be?"

"Why should I? I have the Reapers in chaos, biting one another's tails." The Lady Walker drew a shining knife from the folds of her

cloak and leaned down, casually grabbing the Shade by the hair and hacking its head from its body with three hard swipes. "Thanks to your mother, I have the Never itself at my mercy."

"Wait, what about my mo—" Wendy began.

The spirit web dissolved like black ink in water and the battered remains of the Shade burst into a blaze of brilliant, black-threaded Light.

Above them there was a wail and a huge sensation of pressure, of sucking, like the three of them were being pulled out to sea by an insistent riptide. Wendy and Ada grabbed the torn and twisted pavement beneath them. Wendy was glad that they weren't further out in the road, where the ice was thickest and the sloping street the most severe. The Lady Walker stood firm, laughing wildly as, with a gigantic *whoomph*, the ground began buckling and seizing frantically, the soil vibrating and pounding beneath them.

The earthquake pulsed for several seconds as Ada and Wendy rode the wave, both screaming.

At long last the earth stopped spasming and the Lady Walker reached down and helped Wendy to her feet. "There are over a hundred Shades within a four block radius," she said, smiling. "Every Shade I destroy calls another of my . . . pets . . . into this world. For every Shade that sees my blade, another terror is born. Tell me your Reapers can deal with *that,* Lightbringer."

"Wendy . . ." Ada whispered. "Wendy . . . help . . . me . . ."

Yanking free of the Lady Walker, Wendy turned on her heel. She had taken only two rapid steps away when she heard the thick, snotty snuffle to her right. She managed a third step before the beast slid out of the closest building and dropped its head low, eye-level with Wendy. It growled, red eyes lighting, and a wave of fetid breath nearly knocked Wendy over.

Wendy turned aside, shaking, doing her best to ignore the beast though every nerve trembled at the sight and smell of it. "Stop playing with us. We're not mice."

"In the eyes of the creatures from between," the Lady Walker said, drawing a compact out of her cloak and flipping it open, "we're all mice."

Wendy briefly spotted her reflection in the small mirror within before the Lady Walker, grinning, leaned down and slammed the compact across Ada's face. The compact cracked against Ada's cheekbone and the broken mirror scored her flesh, leaving a trail of seeping essence. Ada, stunned, crumpled to the ground.

"What—" Wendy began, but was cut off as the hellbeast beside her surged forward, darting for Ada's prone body. It seemed to fall apart as it drew closer to the mirror; for a moment the beast was insubstantial as smoke . . . and then it was gone.

"What happened?" Wendy asked before she could stop herself. She glared all around, demanding answers. "Where did it go?"

But the Lady Walker was gone. Wendy was alone with Ada.

Slowly, Wendy gathered Ada by the elbows and supported her up to her feet. Falling to the ground had knocked Ada's bun loose, and her hair lay in a messy tangle about her face. She leaned on Wendy heavily.

"What was all that about? Here," Wendy said, glad that the Lady Walker had left without further confrontation. She pushed a hank of Ada's hair off her wounded cheekbone. "I think I have a spare scrunchie in my—"

Ada bit Wendy's hand.

Screaming in surprised pain, Wendy yanked her hand back while Ada, growling, dropped to all fours and swelled, doubling in size in seconds. Her proper dress split at the shoulders and arms, the nipped-in waist tore to shreds as Wendy, dumbfounded, watched.

"Oh hell," Wendy whispered and staggered several steps back. She hit a patch of ice and nearly tumbled, catching herself at the last second. In the moments she spent struggling with her balance, Ada's body twisted 180 degrees, torso spinning so that her arms snapped backwards to support the convolutions. There was an awful cracking

noise as joints appeared in the middle of her biceps and calves. Ada now hung upside down, arched like a spider, and her fingers lengthened, nails digging into the street. Wendy watched in mingled horror and pity as Ada's skirt, stretched to splitting, fell aside, leaving Ada's body naked and slit apart, her skin ripped and bleeding, essence streaming off her in rivulets.

"A . . . Ada?" Wendy whispered, arms outstretched at her sides. "Are you . . . oh, ick, are you in there? Ada?"

The Ada-beast, now jammed into its new skin, took a step forward and then another. The mouth opened up, the jaws expanding far too wide, and Wendy could make out the spirit web pulsing as it wriggled its way past the corner of Ada's mouth and dipped down her throat. Wendy gagged in sympathy.

Testing the treacherous street with her foot as best she could, Wendy took a step back. The Ada-beast took a step forward. One back. One forward.

Then, just as Wendy had decided to make a run for the car, the spirit web surrounding the Ada-beast's torso shivered and glowed bright. The beast charged forward, skittering like a spider on four horribly jointed arms.

A burning at her chest was the only reminder Wendy had of the necklace as Ada's fingernails scraped across her cheek, slicing her skin. It only took a second for the wounds to close—Wendy had a moment to be glad that the necklace seemed to be working independently of any action she took. The Ada-beast scraped and clawed in circles around Wendy, jabbing hands and feet outward and slicing her repeatedly. The necklace worked its magic and healed her over and over again. Even Ada's quickest touch, like the Lady Walker's, was like a stroke of ice against her skin. Wendy trembled in cold and pain under the onslaught.

Trying to crawl away time and time again, only to hit steep slicks in the street and sliding backward, Wendy, battered and briefly bruised, realized that the creature was *playing* with her. It

either knew or sensed that she wasn't as hurt as she could be, as she
ought to be, and was choosing to test her limits, to see if she'd break
for it and run. The necklace was like an icy brand around her throat
now, burning her with the intensity of its cold; it hurt more than the
wounds it was healing.

Hissing in pain, Wendy reached up and hooked a finger around
the necklace, lifting it off her skin. The moment she did the beast
stabbed forward and hooked a hand-claw around the links, yanking
them free and flinging them to the asphalt. The overuse had made
the necklace weak; the beast's icy touch was too much. The necklace
shattered on impact.

No more healing.

"Shit," Wendy hissed, scanning frantically left and right for anything she could use as a weapon, before she remembered that Lily's
knife hung in the loop on her belt. She'd been so caught up in
arguing with the Lady Walker that she'd forgotten it was there!

Pulling Lily's knife off her belt required Wendy to take her
attention from the Ada-beast for a moment; the blade was honed to
a distressingly sharp edge and Wendy feared for her fingers. By the
time she had the knife in hand the beast had circled around behind
her, cutting off her escape to the car. Long ropes of drool dripped
from Ada's mouth, pooling on the ground. Wendy's thighs burned
as she crouched deeply down.

"I have no idea what I'm doing," Wendy said and gripped the
knife. As if it understood what she was saying, the Ada-beast swiped
at her and Wendy reflexively jerked the blade forward, slicing into
its elongated hand. The creature hissed and yanked back, shaking
the jointed fingers. It bled, but only momentarily, sluggishly, before
the wound closed.

"No," Wendy whispered. She'd not been expecting that.

The Ada-beast chuckled, dipped low, and a long shiver raced
down its spine, reminding Wendy of a cat wriggling just before it
pounced.

It never got the chance.

An arrow embedded itself in the side of Ada's face, releasing a gush of noxious fluid and essence, milky and sour, that ate immediate holes in the asphalt. Wendy stumbled back, searching for the source of the missile.

"Move, Lightbringer!" Elle yelled, notching another arrow as the Ada-beast, annoyed, roared and swelled, batting the arrow free from its cheek. The hole closed up in seconds, completely healed. "Get out of the way!"

"It's Ada!" Wendy yelled. "Don't shoot, it's Ada! Maybe we can save her! Stop! Stop! It's Ada!"

"Get out of the way, ducky! She's gone!"

Lily was at Wendy's side in a moment. "Wendy, Ada is lost," she said, snatching her knife from Wendy's loose grip. "We will distract the creature as best we can, but it heals too rapidly. You must find another way to destroy it! Go!"

"I—"

"LISTEN for once in your misbegotten life, Lightbringer! GO!"

Wendy fled to the car. Piotr and Eddie were just outside, near the trunk of the vehicle, brandishing makeshift torches from Mary's camping supplies at the waving tentacles of spirit web that were encroaching on the car, crawling and dangling and dropping down.

"Get to safety!" Piotr yelled at her and swiped one of the torches just above Wendy's head as a long sticky stream of web thumped down. "In the car! *Beest rayeh*! Hurry! Move!"

Wendy dove inside. "Crap-crap-crap," she groaned, sliding across the backseat. "Chel!"

"What?!" Chel's voice was high and thin, her sister was shaking and terrified. "What's going on? What the hell happened to that lady?"

"Wendy, what do we do?" Jon demanded.

CHAPTER NINE

The beast howled, and the essence pretending to be Wendy's flesh crawled at the eerie sound.

"Okay . . . okay, um, I have no idea—NO IDEA—if this will work," Wendy gasped, running shaking fingers through her tangled curls. "But . . . I mean, what the hell, it's all I can think of right now. I need you. One of you. Both of you. Maybe. But I need you to come with me! Chel!"

"Me?" Frantically, Chel shook her head. "I don't—"

"CHEL! Look, I won't let you get hurt! I mean, I'll try not to, okay? It's the best I can do."

"But why do you need me?" Chel demanded, clearly panicked. "I don't know what I'm doing!"

"I can't access my Light!" Wendy snapped. "I can't and you, maybe, probably, I don't know, I have no idea . . . but it's worth a shot, right? Trying to access your Light?"

Still, Chel hesitated and Wendy wanted to smack her sister upside her cowardly head. She smothered the urge. It was something their mother would have done. It wouldn't help. "Will it hurt?"

"The first time? I . . . I can't remember, to be honest," Wendy admitted. "But even if it hurts, it doesn't last long." Wendy leaned forward so that her younger sister could see her face, how serious she was. "You can do this, Chel. I know you can."

Swallowing thickly, Chel nodded. "Okay. Show me."

"This way," Wendy said and slid out of the car, waiting to hear the car door slam behind her before she drew off to the side, closer to where Elle and Lily were darting in and out of the fray like dancers, dealing deathstrikes that only aggravated the Ada-beast.

98

"Okay, Chel, listen," Wendy instructed tensely. "You're looking into the Never."

"Duh," Chel said. "I can't even see the living world right now, the Never's so thick."

"Don't remind me," Wendy muttered. "Come over here to the sidewalk. Careful, it's icy out." When Chel joined her, Wendy pressed her palm against her sister's chest, just above the sternum. "Here is where your Light lives," she explained, wishing she could feel the bright burn beneath Chel's flesh. "When you feel it, you'll feel it here first."

"WENDY!" Elle yelled from the top of a nearby mailbox. "WHATEVER YOU'RE DOING, HURRY IT UP! I AM RUNNING OUT OF ARROWS OVER HERE!"

"I can't—" Chel began, looking past Wendy to Elle. "Is she . . . is she going to be okay? Shouldn't we—"

"Pay attention to me, not her!"

"But I can't do what you're telling me to do. There's no . . . no burn or whatever. I can't!"

Wendy slapped her. "Yes," she said coldly. "You can."

"Hey!" Chel snapped, hand pressed against her reddening cheek. "That hurt!"

Wendy slapped her again; it was a flat crack, an almost professional sound, like the bang of a gavel or the clack of handcuffs closing. Suddenly she understood how her mother must have felt, all those times she'd protested her ignorance, her fear of the unknown in the Never. "Did it?"

"Look, bitch," Chel warned, "you might be a ghost or whatever but I can still—"

SLAP. "Can still . . . what? What can you do to me?" SLAP. "I mean, after all, I'm essentially dead, right? You can burn me a little with your touch, sure, but even then you're like a warm bench on a spring day compared to other Reapers." SLAP. "You know what? I'm actually kind of digging this. I've always wanted to beat the crap out of you. You and your buffy friends—"

"Fucking hell! That's it, if you do that one more—"

SLAP.

"BITCH! You asked for it!" Chel swung at Wendy and Wendy neatly stepped back, dodging. Then she sidestepped and slapped Chel again.

"Too slow," Wendy taunted. "Too slow, too weak. Not watching your back. Letting me in because you're scared." SLAP. SLAP. SLAP. "Afraid of hurting me. Afraid of hurting yourself." SLAP. "Except you're not afraid of screwing yourself up, right? You'll down a bottle of pills a day if it'll make you popular." SLAP. "Why is it *I'm* the one who's practically dead, when *you're* the one with the fucking death wish, you pill-popping—"

"DAMN IT, WENDY! STOP IT! I'm not MOM! I'm not the one you're mad . . . mad at!" Gasping, furious and scared, Chel tried to block the next slap but Wendy was too fast; she darted in and under, poking Chel hard enough in the center of her chest that Chel dropped her guard. Then Wendy shoved her sister. Chel, not expecting the attack to escalate, stumbled back. There was a patch of ice behind her.

Coming down hard, Chel cracked her elbow on the concrete trying to avoid tripping over a straggling loop of spirit web and slipping on the ice instead.

"No wonder your boyfriend dumped you," Wendy said—the cruelest cut she could think of.

There.

Wendy felt it happen. The fear vanished with an audible *pop*, sending a small shockwave through the close space of the Never. Chel's rage peaked in a sharp spike, pulsing in a wave out from her core. Light, bright and brilliant, bloomed in Chel's chest, growing too almost quickly for Wendy to track with her eyes alone.

Chel's breast vanished under the encroaching wave of Light, her torso, her legs and arms and head, until she was nothing but a glowing figure . . . and then her shape was lost amid the expanding corona of warm Light and sweet, lilting siren song.

"Good," Wendy whispered, expecting the fear of the Light to overcome her any moment, the same way Piotr had described all spirits felt around the Light, but she wanted to point her sister in the direction of the Ada-beast first. If Wendy had to sacrifice herself to wake Chel to the Light, so be it. So long as Piotr and Eddie and Jon were safe—that was all she cared about.

"That way, Chel," Wendy said, reaching into the Light's fire and taking her sister by the shoulders. She turned Chel toward the Ada-beast, but Wendy needn't have bothered; the creature had heard the siren song and was barreling toward them.

"I've got this," Chel said and Wendy shivered at the tinkling cadence of Chel's voice. She didn't feel attracted like a moth to the flame, the way Piotr described the Light to her, but it would probably come at any moment. Wendy sat back to wait.

The creature, growling, flung itself forward. Wendy thought that the encounter would be over in moments—it was a ghost, twisted and terrible, but just a ghost nonetheless.

Instead, the monster, snarling, nearly tore Chel's face off. It shot forward, snapping at her head, and Chel fell back and grabbed the beast around the torso. Tendrils of Light spun out from Chel's body—Wendy hadn't had time to describe how to control the ribbons of Light, but Chel managed to feel her way soon enough—and stabbed down, impaling the beast through the eyes and mouth, stripping the spirit webs from Ada's flesh with a wet ripping noise.

The web came away and Chel's tendrils darted forward again, cauterizing the exposed tendons in one fast swipe. There was a stink like burning fur and spoiled meat, all overlaid with the coppery smell of spilled blood and the too-sweet scent of dripping essence.

The beast howled and jabbed a sharp-fingered hand out. Chel yelled in pain—Wendy found even her pain sounded startlingly musical—and staggered left, half-supporting herself against a thin and twisted tree planted in the sidewalk.

"Ada is burning away," Lily gasped, joining Wendy and taking

her by the shoulders. She held her side and staggered with each step, as if hurt. "We must step back . . . Lightbringer, please, being this close . . . it hurts. It is dangerous. Please . . . we must flee . . ."

Startled, Wendy looked at Elle and Lily. Both wore highly pained expressions; Elle had wrapped herself around the mailbox to keep herself from moving toward the Light. Both were shaking with the urge to fling themselves into the Light.

"She . . . she's calling to you?" Wendy asked stupidly, unbelieving what was right before her eyes. If Lily and Elle were so affected, why wasn't she?

"Worry not for us. Ada is . . . being . . . saved," Lily replied, shivering and clinging to Wendy now, using the Lightbringer as support, rather than holding Wendy back. "We . . . we must go now. We can stay no longer. It's growing . . . hard to con . . . concentrate."

"But Chel . . ." Wendy shook her head. Chel was holding her own, but not winning. "It's not dying. That thing . . . this isn't what I was expected. Give me your knife!"

Lily, shaking, managed to free her blade and hand it to Wendy once more. Wendy slid the knife to Chel's side.

"CUT THE THROAT!" she screamed. "BEHEAD IT!"

Chel didn't take the knife. Instead the tendrils of Light, the sweet ribbons Wendy was used to handling, spun into a tight rope of Light in Chel's hands. She used the Light in ways Wendy had never thought of, looping the Light rapidly in a controlled spin that she slipped over the Ada-beast's head.

"What is she doin—" Wendy broke off, gaping, as her sister snapped the Light closed like a garrote, slicing Ada's head off her body in one rapid yank. The beast's body jerked twice and fell over, bleeding sluggishly all over the sidewalk.

Her Light shut off as if Chel had cut it closed with a switch and Lily, sagging beside Wendy, giggled like a drunk woman and shook her head. "That . . . that was unexpected."

Blooming with the remnants of Light, like a distant after-

image, Chel bounced on the tips of her toes, grinning. "That thing almost killed me! And I kicked its ass!" she yelled giddily, laughing like a loon. "I wanna do it again!"

"Wooboy," Wendy sighed, taking Chel by the shoulders and wincing at the heat. Her sister had most certainly unlocked her Light; Wendy could now feel the heat of it just beneath Chel's skin, like coals of a banked fire. "Well, don't go crazy with it yet, cowgirl. There's a ton you still have left to learn, and I don't even know half of the stuff I was supposed to learn either. We're still nothing close to a match for a normal Reaper."

Piotr and Eddie limped up to the side of the car. The spirit webs were backing away from the vehicle now, giving them enough of a berth that Wendy was positive they'd be allowed to continue on. Piotr, though pale, did not seem to be in as much pain as before.

"It is the webs . . . and the beast," he explained when Wendy, without speaking, strode to his side and pressed her hand against his chest. "They are connected to one another and I . . . I am somehow connected to them."

"We are going to talk," Wendy said pointedly. "Not now, no time. But soon. You and I. And we're going to talk about keeping your mouth shut when you're in pain—i.e. how you're NOT to be all silent and manly if you're hurting. And . . . and about that mind-meld thing. Understand me?"

Sheepishly, he nodded.

"Great," she said. "Now . . . um, about Ada."

"She's gone," Elle broke the news bluntly. "Sorry. At least Chel here did the deed and not the Lady Walker. Chel was . . . surprisingly efficient, actually."

"I knew that Ada had passed into the Light," Piotr said, squeezing Wendy's hip as she slid through the car door into the backseat. Wendy absently swatted at him but smiled as Eddie, sagging and tired, slid into the seat behind Jon.

"How's that?" Jon asked, peering into the Never in front of

them. Wendy could see thinner spots now, places where the webs
had retreated, leaving them enough space to squeeze through.

"The fabric of her dress has faded," Piotr said. "As Specs' glasses
did when he passed into the Light, and Dunn's cap." Piotr brushed
a hand across Wendy's wrist. "She did not turn to dust; her soul was
set free. I wish her well on her journey."

"So, wait," Chel said, turning in her seat, "I sent a ghost to
Heaven?"

Wendy sighed. "What happened to being an atheist-maybe-
agnostic-at-best?"

"Screw that noise," Chel declared, bouncing in her seat. "That
was amazing! I'm totally calling myself an angel now! Angel of . . .
dumdumdum . . . DESTRUCTION!"

When Chel laughed again, Wendy shook her head and met Jon's
eyes in the rearview. Chel needed time; she was hurting, and reacting
poorly to what they'd just seen. They knew their sister—she was not
like this.

"Soon," Wendy mouthed, and Jon nodded, revving the engine
and pulling slowly forward.

The spirit webs parted before them, allowing them passage.
They were on their way to the Top of the Mark and the Council once
again.

CHAPTER TEN

When they reached the Mark Hopkins Hotel, Jon dropped Wendy off at the front door. The spirit web forest hadn't stretched this far yet, but at the rate of growth it would overtake Nob Hill in a matter of days at best.

"Wait, I shall go with her," Wendy heard Piotr say as Jon began to pull away. Jon obligingly stopped the car a second time and Piotr hurried after Wendy, leaving the others behind. Wendy waited for him at the foot of the hotel, watching the people milling within. She knew that she ought to feel *something*—anger, or perhaps joy that these people were untouched by the spirit webs—but all she could feel was a heavy, encompassing weariness.

The storm clouds seemed to pulse on the horizon.

"Think I can't handle the Council alone?" Wendy asked pointedly, trying not to let her mind circle back to the way Ada's skin had ripped, the way her teeth gleamed in the dim Never-light.

"*Net*, never," Piotr said, and held open his arms. "I just wished for a moment alone with you."

Leaning forward so that his lips brushed the curve of her ear, Piotr's breath fanned her cheek and his hands curled around her upper arms as if he were cupping delicate glass. His thumbs ran idle circles against her flesh and Wendy fought to keep herself from shivering. How did Piotr always know just the right place to touch to soothe her when she was stressed?

"Thank you," Wendy said. "Thank you."

Piotr drew her close and hugged her, tucking Wendy's head into the curve of his neck and shoulder, patting her back, relaxing her.

Snuggling into his hug, Wendy took a deep breath, inhaling the

clean scent of him—the evergreen and smoke, cool tang of ice and snow, all underlain with an earthy scent like rich loam and soil, like the fields of fresh-turned dirt warming in the sun Wendy passed when she drove through Napa Valley.

Wendy snatched the moment of peace and calm and rubbed her chin against his shoulder. "I am not looking forward to being skin and bone again. Being like this, here with you, is really nice."

"I am not . . . Edward," Piotr said softly, looking over her shoulder, "I am not alive. But know this: I cherish every moment I have left with you. Every. Single. One. And one day, when you return to your flesh, you will remember this night and know . . . that I care."

Wendy flicked a glance in the direction of the disappearing car and groaned; Eddie's face was a pale smear against the darkness. Wendy was too tired and on edge to deal with any sort of jealousy between Piotr and Eddie, perceived or otherwise, but before she could grouch at Piotr for putting pressure on her at a really inopportune time, Piotr's head dipped down.

All was, for one brief and glorious moment, still.

"Wendy," Piotr murmured as Wendy sighed and, regretfully, stepped away from the hug, "I . . . I wonder if you would do me a favor."

"For you, Piotr? Anything." She said it without thinking, without hesitating and, Wendy belatedly realized, she meant it. She would do anything for him.

"I . . . think I may remember why I can do . . . why I can touch some of the living and have them do as I desire." Piotr held out his hand and Wendy instinctively rested her palm in his. He smiled. "Will you allow me to show you something? Something important?"

"Show me?" Wendy frowned. They were at the edge of the long curved driveway, the car idling at the end of the drive, near the corner. How was he going to show her anything here?

"Show you," Piotr said. "Do you trust me, Curly?"

Wendy smirked at the nickname. "Of course I do. Fine, fine . . . show me."

Taking her other hand, Piotr leaned forward and pressed a small kiss on the tip of her nose. "*Spasiba*. Close your eyes."

Still smiling, Wendy did so. She felt Piotr's hands grip tighter . . .
        tighter . . .
            tighter . . .

There was a pulse, like heat, followed by an overwhelmingly chilled flush of air. Opening her eyes, Wendy found herself standing on the edge of the forest, the icy wind whipping her hair into a tangled knot. Piotr, beside her, sighed and took her hand. Wendy wanted to ask him what was going on. It was like what had happened before, where she had been briefly in his head, but this was . . . more. More vivid. More realistic. More disconcerting. More.

Where were they? Was this a dreamscape or something? But Piotr's expression was so drawn, so grave, that she didn't dare break the silence with questions.

The dreary, gray snowscape grew brighter as a small band of men, in the distance, trudged down a hill toward them. Piotr's hand tightened on hers. As they neared, Wendy realized that they carried a bloody man on a travois, two in the front, one behind. Despite the startling splashes of red, he was handsome and wiry, strong of jaw with a shock of blue-black hair.

He looked like Piotr.

When they passed close, Wendy waved a hand in front of the closest man hauling the travois. He did not alter his path or look at her.

"This is a memory," Piotr explained, voice pitched low. "Not my memory—I did not exist yet—but a memory given to me. As I am giving this memory to you, now. With a touch." He held up a hand. "This is my real strength, Wendy. This is my real power . . . I can feel so many memories, many of them not my own, thrumming under my skin . . . given to me so they might carry on. That is what we experienced before . . . except that you were living a memory then as I made it. In my mind."

"Memories . . . given to you?" Wendy asked. "How is that even possible?"

Piotr smiled. "My memories . . . my recollections of my time on Earth and in the Never . . . they've been coming back so slowly. Too slowly, I thought. Lily, she said to me, Piotr, be patient, they will come in time."

He sighed and pressed a hand to his chest. A terrible looking flower was blooming from his ribcage, very much like the one that had been curling out of the deep wound in Ada's side, and Wendy realized that the spirit web really was still inside him. Piotr had been grabbing his chest not just because it hurt but because it was eating him alive from the inside out. His flesh moved as the sprouts beneath shifted beneath his skin.

Piotr rubbed a hand across his ribs, grimacing. "I think . . . I think whatever we just went through jarred more memories loose. I think . . . no. No, I remember . . . so much now." A tear tracked down his cheek. "Perhaps too much now. Isn't that always the case, though? What you most want is the thing that is worst for you."

"Piotr . . . your chest . . . it's so bad . . . why didn't you tell me it was this bad—" So many questions—hopefully the right ones—sprung to Wendy's mind but she wanted to remain respectful of this strange place and Piotr's odd, withdrawn expression. She broke off. This, she realized, was the wrong question.

Piotr pulled her close, half-hugging her, and pressed a soft, sad kiss high on Wendy's cheekbone. The spirit web bloom shivered at their closeness but did not hurt her.

"This was my father," Piotr explained, eyeing the men. "These men are my uncles. The man you waved your hand in front of is . . . was the youngest in the family. My father was second born."

"He's . . . was . . . hurt," Wendy said, knowing how dumb, how feeble she sounded, but incapable of not saying anything at all. "Why are we here, Piotr? What is this place?" Then, remembering that he was dead, she added, "*When* was this place?"

"When I was alive," Piotr said quietly, "when my parents were . . . alive . . . we lived upon the vast and snowy steppes. I suppose I could find these ancient rocks on a map if I studied hard enough, if I had the proper coordinates and GPS and whatnot that the living lands are rife with, but even so I could not tell you exactly which year this was." He chuckled quietly. "Over two thousand years, I think."

"Really?" Wendy stared at Piotr but his face was impassive. "You're . . . you're over two thousand years old? Dead. Are you kidding me?"

"I've been taking care of the Lost for so long," Piotr murmured, resting a palm against the bloom working its way up his chest, "that the only way I know how to tell tales is to begin with 'Once upon a time.'"

"Hey, however you gotta do it," Wendy said, shrugging and stepping away. The way he was stroking the flower disturbed and worried her. Piotr was already so pale, so thin . . . what if it devoured him the way it had devoured Ada? What if it opened him up to one of those creatures?

"Ah so. These stories are so predictable—once upon a time a girl met a boy, *da*? That is how these tales go."

As if the vision were waiting for Piotr's words, suddenly a young woman appeared beside them. She appeared so unexpectedly that Wendy almost struck her. Only the realization that this wasn't real—that it was nothing more than a memory—kept Wendy from attacking. Wendy felt Piotr's chuckle feather the hair at her temples, sensed the cloying, noisome touch of the bloom brush her side.

"Who is she?" Wendy asked, studying the girl—she was tall, wiry, copper-haired and pale-skinned, with almond-shaped eyes and a full mouth. Her arms and hands looked tough and strong, corded with muscle, but what amazed Wendy was her garb.

"Leather armor, no helmet, basic wooden shield," Wendy murmured, impressed, stepping closer to the girl. "No sword that I'm seeing, either. Nice, not many ladies can pull that off. I wouldn't want to walk up to those guys dressed in much less, especially in the middle of woodsy nowhere."

Piotr smirked. "The armor is for show. It changes with each person she visited—for a rich man she would have come clad in chainmail. For my father leather was the best she would wear. But that is not what is important here, Wendy. Look at her cloak."

Wendy squinted. "It's a cloak? I don't know what I'm looking at here, Piotr. It's covered in . . . what? Jay feathers? Maybe crow feathers? Is that important?"

"And she rode on the wind's back, and came to him, and kissed his lips," Piotr said, his voice lilting strangely, in a lyrical cadence that sent shivers down Wendy's back. "In her cloak of feathers plucked from the crow-tails of Huginn and Muninn, gathered from ravens and swans and other beasts of the sky, the lady Eir flew from battlefield to battlefield, attending to her orders. She was a shield woman, a warrior, a Valkyrie sent to collect souls from snowy battle-fields . . . but they weren't known as Valkyrie in that time, in that place. She was a Reaper. She was Death's handmaiden. And she was on a mission from Freyja herself."

The girl beside Wendy smoothed her hair and straightened her cloak. Her cheeks were crimson with the cold, her eyelashes rimmed with frost. Piotr moved to stand behind her and reached a hand out, not quite touching the imposing figure, his fingers a scant inch from her mane of shining hair. "As the sun reached the apex of the sky, the Reaper Eir lit upon the snow-driven hill, and heeded the blood on the snow, and bided her time, for the soldier was not yet dead."

"Piotr?" Wendy whispered but he didn't answer. A tear tracked down his face and Piotr's lips twitched, his brows drawing close; he swallowed thickly. The bloom at his chest pulsed, petals opening and closing, as if it were drinking.

The Reaper beside Wendy bit her lip, frowning at the young men below who had paused to build a fire as the youngest, the one Wendy had nearly touched, sorted through their bag for dried meat.

One of the men—Wendy assumed he was the oldest—scooped snow into a cup of bone and set it near the slowly smoking fire to

melt. Curious, Wendy drifted over to them, marveling at the way she didn't even have to move her legs—a thought alone took her from place to place. Wendy just appeared as if she, too, were like the strange, copper-haired maiden.

"Wait a second. He's our age," Wendy realized, leaning over the travois, getting a closer look at Piotr's father. "He's not even eighteen . . ."

Wendy flicked a look at the copper-haired Reaper, Eir, and paused. The shape of her lips, the arch of her eyebrows, the way she tilted her head as she moved to kneel beside Wendy, beside Piotr's father on the travois, and examined his battered face . . . it all struck a cord deep inside Wendy.

"Piotr?" Wendy whispered, forgetting about the flower, about the car wreck, about her worry for her family and the hole in the horizon in the sudden, stunning realization that Piotr was far beyond what she'd originally thought him to be. She'd always known he was special, but never imagined *how* special. "Is this . . . is this Valkyrie, this Reaper, whatever . . . is she your mom?"

"Unlike my mother, my father was a farmer," Piotr said, smiling ruefully and kneeling on the other side of Eir, still examining his mother rather than looking at Wendy. "Not a soldier. He was very bad with a sword."

"Looks like," Wendy agreed, eyeing the dried brown stain on the cloak spread across the young man's gut.

The three of them knelt there, in the snow, for what seemed like ages.

Wendy was long past nervous and edgy. Getting used to the idea that Piotr was half . . . strange . . . allowed herself to return to wondering what was going on in the Never without them, hoping that Jon and Chel were okay, when the brothers, coughing and grumbling, rose and cleared camp, preparing to gather the travois to travel on.

"Piotr—" she whispered. "They're moving."

Piotr's father opened his eyes. "Oh," he whispered, looking at Eir leaning over him, her long glimmering hair surrounding his face like a protective cocoon, "so you are the one I was waiting for."

The red of Eir's cheeks deepened. "Hush," she said. "Save your strength, stay as comfortable as you can. Your time is soon."

"You hear these words from the lips of all dying men, I'm sure, but if I can hold your hand," Piotr's father replied seriously, reaching up one bloodied hand to stroke her pale cheek, "I would willingly travel to the black places and back. For the touch of your lips, I would do even more."

Eir flushed. "Hush," she said again, but her color was deep, and Wendy could see Eir's pulse throbbing at the base of her throat. Eir shifted in place and it dawned on Wendy that Eir wasn't playing hard to get . . . she was actually overwhelmed by his compliments.

"He's raving," the youngest brother said. "We should help him to meet our great-grandfathers in the quiet fields. This . . . what we are doing has no honor—carrying him back on his enemy's broken shield. Grandfather would be most displea—"

"Quiet, Kirill," the oldest commanded, flicking a contemptuous glance at his younger brother. "If it weren't for your foolish bravado in battle, Borys would not be so wounded. And Grandfather was not a man to worship so. Shut your mouth or I will shut it for you."

Kirill rolled his eyes and, despite the gravity of the situation, Wendy smothered a smile. Their bickering was just so much like the way she and Jon and Chel . . . Wendy felt her smile fade. Jon. Chel. It was starting to really bother her now, that she was trapped in this memory with no easy seashell door to escape through. The concern slammed into her again, leaving her breathless. She turned to ask Piotr if they could leave, if he could share this memory some other time, but beside her, Piotr's expression was startlingly grim.

Wendy decided to bide her time for at least a few minutes more.

"And now it comes," Piotr said as the begrudging silence between the brothers was broken by a whinny.

The men who topped the rise were just as bedraggled and bloodied as the brothers. Their clothing was just as mended and worn, their weapons just as dinged, yet Wendy got a sense from them that these newcomers were not farmers. These were desperate men.

The one in the lead, holding the corded strip of leather that was serving as a bridle, greeted them first.

"Ho, travelers! We are weary and wish to rest. May you spare a bit of room around your fire?"

"You may have it," the eldest brother said curtly. "I am sorry, we have snuffed the embers, but the clearing is still dry, the ground still warm from our fire. It should not be hard to light again, and there is a cache of deadwood just over there, in the shade of that fallen ash."

"May I give you a kiss?" Borys whispered to Eir as she, standing beside his travois, reached down to grip his hand, comforting him. "Such a little thing, from a kind lady as lovely as yourself."

He winked and Eir, flushing, rolled her eyes and chuckled. "You are a flirt, sir," she said, fingers plucking at the necklace at her neck. "The Winged Ones do not kiss flirts."

"Oh, would you prefer me to be proper?" Borys asked, smiling wider, sensing that he'd caught her attention. "To woo you as a lady like yourself deserves? To fly to your palace in the sky and beg on bended knee for just a touch of your hand, a single press of your lips? No, no, you are wilder than that—I can see it in your eyes. You know the truth of things. You know the way a true heart beats, with passion, seeking to sink into the earth and, raining salt-tears, become one with the sky."

She blushed brighter red, nearly scarlet from temple to collar now. "Hush! You have a flapping mouth."

"Then my lips have had much exercise," he joked. "Perhaps you'd like to test their strength?"

Wendy, so caught up in their flirting, missed whatever was said between the brothers and the newcomers. Suddenly weapons were drawn and the two groups were hacking at one another violently.

Kirill, stabbed through the shoulder, stumbled into the brush as his attacker turned and spotted Borys, still holding on to Eir's hand.

"One kiss," Borys whispered quickly. "Please, lady, before he has my head split apart."

"All these Westerners are madmen," the soldier snarled and, flinging his sword to his feet, drew the dagger at his hip. "They even haul their dead home!"

· Eir, sensing his movement, paled and, in one fluid motion Wendy could hardly follow, struck out with a spear of Light so bright that Wendy's eyes gushed water; she was temporarily blinded.

When her sight returned, Wendy was stunned to find that Eir had killed all the attackers—smoking holes pierced their centers through. The older brothers likewise lay strewn on the ground; all the soldiers were dead save for Kirill. Kirill crawled from the bush with his shoulder still streaming blood and another rivulet dripping from his dark, bruising temple.

"Wow," Wendy said, mentally stumbling for the right phrase to describe what had just transpired. "That was . . . amazing. She's got moves like Emma. Or Jane. That was just . . . dude. Wow."

"This just . . . I'm such a silly fool," Eir sighed, resting her hands on her hips as she surveyed her handiwork. "I've made a mess of things, haven't I? And for what? A man? My sisters are going to mock me for months."

"You saved me," Borys whispered to Eir, holding up his hand, reaching for her. "I may be only a man, but thank you. Thank you so much."

"No, I really didn't," Kirill groaned, staggering to the eldest brother and resting his head on his brother's chest. "He's dead. They're all dead." Kirill coughed. "Borys, what happened?"

"Kirill, it was fantastic! It was—" Eir pressed a finger to her lips, *shhh*ing Borys, and shook her head. Borys, understanding, shook his own head.

"Well, Borys?" Kirill asked impatiently. "What happened?"

"Mykola was overwhelmed with an insane, protective fury," Borys improvised, gesturing to the oldest brother. "He ran them all through, spinning wildly and screaming like you've never heard, and then collapsed himself."

"He's dead," Kirill said again and flopped back into the snow. "Oh, Borys. What are we to do?"

"Well, hell, that's a good question," Wendy said. "What do you do when your invisible girlfriend straight up assassinates a bunch of dudes just to keep you breathing? I mean . . . was she supposed to kill them?"

"Save for Kirill, they were all due to die in that battle," Piotr said, examining his mother's face. "My mother did nothing untoward but cut their lives a few minutes shorter. Unusual—Reapers generally collect souls, not end lives—but in this case it is allowed. Their time was up either way."

"We go home," Borys answered Kirill as Eir knelt beside him and whispered in his ear. Her left hand hovered over his stomach, her hair dangled against his cheek, copper-bright against the bluing-pale flesh. "Or as close as we can manage. And then we rest, Kirill, in the bier where our ancestors sleep in the quiet fields."

Using the cleanest cloak he could find, Kirill tore strips off to bind his shoulder. He spat in the snow. "For a madman, you make good sense."

Rolling over so the cloak spread over him fell free, Borys struggled to smile, though Wendy couldn't believe that the man could move at all. He'd been split from gut to ribs; she could see shiny loops of intestine peeking through the flayed flesh. She fought to keep her gorge down.

Borys coughed. "They say the mad and the dead speak with the gods. I think I have good council."

The fog crept in and Piotr was at Wendy's side once more; expression flat, eyes tired. Wordlessly, he pulled her to him, crushing the bloom between them, and kissed Wendy's eyelids.

She closed her eyes.

CHAPTER ELEVEN

Ten minutes later, still shaken, Wendy was guided upstairs to meet Frank. He was playing poker for a pile of dead guns and shining silver knives, surrounded by his Council cronies. A battered cardboard box, once the packaging for tiny Japanese stuffed pigs, held a smaller motley of items—single bullets of all shapes and sizes—and Frank had a huge haul in front of him. He, unlike most of the elegantly clad spirits around him, wore a simple blue chambray work shirt and a pair of khaki pants over heavy boots. His dark hair was smoothed back and, unlike the others, Frank was not drinking.

"Hello Frank," Piotr said, as Frank set down his cards and led them to an employee break room off the kitchen, away from the throbbing music and crush of ghosts dancing in the dining room. The side wall had an impromptu bar set up in the Never. A long stretch of the outside wall was glassed in; the San Francisco lights glittered in the darkness, brilliant and shining against the black expanse of the bay. Only the barely-visible edge of the spirit web broke the beautiful expanse. "As requested, I have brought Wendy to meet you."

"I'm not blind," Frank chuckled. "So you're the Lightbringer."

Frank scratched his chin, eyeing Wendy, and gestured to the woman barely wearing a collection of sparkly red scraps who followed closely behind him, acting as a bodyguard. "Here, honey, neither of these two mean me any harm. Do me a favor and go finish up for me."

Turning fluidly, the scarlet-clad lady returned to the table, picked up his cards, chuckled, and flashed the rest of the table a smirk. Then she confidently reached for the line of knives Frank had assembled before him.

"I'm out," said a tall black man in Navy whites, folding his

cards on the table. "Damn." The others scrambled to follow suit. The slinky woman grinned as she collected Frank's haul and wiggled her fingers in Wendy's direction, waving coquettishly.

"Frank! You want me to deal again, or is it break time?" The dealer was a weedy-looking man in an ill-fitting tux. He had to raise his voice to be heard above the din.

Leaning in the doorway of the breakroom, Frank ignored him and addressed Wendy. "You're lookin' a little dead to me, kid. Are you feeling well?"

"Coma," Wendy replied coolly. "It won't last. I'll wake up in no time."

Chuckling, Frank straightened and flapped a hand at the nearby waiting spirits. "Council's adjourned for the night, folks. Close up shop and we'll meet up again tomorrow, sort out the territory issue down out in San Jose. Danny! Don't forget bullet inventory."

Surreptitiously, Wendy's fingers snaked to her side where one of Elle's knives sat snugly hidden. To her quiet relief, the Council spirits didn't approach. They—and all the other spirits hovering nearby with drinks at the ready—filed out the walls and doors, vanishing rapidly from the room as the dealer and the sparkly-dressed woman guided them quickly away.

"Neat trick," Wendy said, forcing a smile and dropping her hand from her hip. She was still shaky and on edge—Ada's face, Piotr's memories—all of it tangled together in her head and made concentrating on Frank difficult.

"Hmm," Frank said, threading his fingers over his chest and tilting his head back, not even bothering to hide his slow, intense perusal of Wendy from head to toe. After long moments he settled in a nearby chair, flopping down and crossing one leg over the other. "You're a looker, but even a blind man could see that you aren't your mother. Not by a long shot."

Eyes narrowing, Wendy pulled out the chair across the table from Frank. "Piotr tells me that you knew her."

Frank rubbed his chin and smirked. "You could say that. We were business associates."

He shifted in his seat, expression soft and hazy, his gaze somewhere past Wendy's left shoulder. Frank's lips twitched and Wendy was struck with the sudden and unwelcome realization that he had *had feelings for her mother*. It was all over him, the way he said her name, the pleasant crinkling of the fine mesh of lines in the corner of his eyes. Square-jawed, broken-nosed Frank wasn't a strictly handsome guy, but when he spoke of her mother it was like a light lit up within him; reminiscing about Mary made Frank almost glow.

Chewing over this new information, Wendy almost missed Frank clear his throat and snap back to the conversation. "Mary was . . . a nice lady. A real class act."

"Whose idea was it to team up?" Wendy asked archly.

Frank's smirk faded. "It was hers," he said. "No spirit's crazy enough to seek out a Reaper, kid, even one rumored to be pissed at her *familia*. Not even the sickest Walker gets close to a Reaper unless they have to."

"So, if no ghost gets close to Reapers unless they're loco," Wendy glanced at Piotr who smirked and waved back at her with two fingers, "how did my mom get you all to partner up?"

"With guile." He snorted. "You know about your ex-aunt, correct?"

"Tracey, yeah," Wendy said. "I know she existed. Mom never talked about her much. I also know the Reapers had her killed."

"Not the Reapers, Lightbringer. *Elise*. Elise had Tracey killed."

"What? Elise wouldn't . . ." Wendy paused. "Actually, no, she totally would." Rubbing a hand across her eyes, Wendy sighed deeply. "Why? Why did Elise have my aunt knocked off?"

"That I can't answer for sure," Frank said, shrugging. "Who knows the reasoning behind what Elise does? All I *can* say is that she forced your mother to do the deed."

Piotr spoke then, quietly, so that Wendy had to strain to hear.

"All my information is secondhand, but Tracey had begun to question the Reapers, the way Elise was running the family while Alonya—your Nana Moses, as Eddie calls her—was gone. She . . . she had great concerns that the Reapers . . . for whatever reason they were granted their powers . . . that the reason had grown perverted over the centuries."

"Does questioning the status quo sound familiar, Lightbringer?" Frank asked lazily. "Sound like anyone you happen to be by any chance?"

"Tracey was like me?" Wendy asked, turning that news over in her head. "You're saying that she didn't want to reap ghosts just because they were dead . . . she wanted something more? She wanted to know *why* they had to reap ghosts?"

Frank tapped his fingertips against the tabletop. "Bingo! Award the lady a kewpie doll!"

"Elise must have been pissed," Wendy murmured. It all sounded distressingly familiar. "Tracey messed up somehow, right? She crossed some mysterious Reaper line way past just asking annoying, inconvenient questions."

"Keeey-rect!" Frank took a deep swallow of his drink. "So Tracey died, per orders, but before she kicked it Tracey made Mary promise to stay strong and lay low. Mary didn't want to at first, but eventually she went along with it. Revenge kept Mary ticking. She wanted to see Elise suffer."

"That doesn't sound like my mother," Wendy protested, though a niggling voice in the back of her mind disagreed. *It might not sound like Mom, but it sure sounds like the White Lady.*

The Lady Walker had said something similar, hadn't she? That there was more to Mary than met the eye?

As if sensing Wendy's disquiet, Frank shrugged nonchalantly, rasping a hand down the stubble on his cheek. "Mothers have a way of presenting themselves, don't they? Everything has to look smooth and effortless-like. It's only when things start heading south that

people notice that Mom's too busy to bother. I don't see why Mary'd be any different from any other momma ever."

That, at least, did sound like her mom. Wendy frowned. "For you guys it must have come out of the blue, Mom leaving the fold like that. Did you think she was spying for Elise, at first?"

"Of course. Wouldn't you?"

"What made the Council give Mom a chance, then? I mean, if I thought someone was spying for Elise, I'd tell them to hit the road."

"Ada convinced us to give her a shot. She was head of the Council back then, and she ran the city like one of her labs: tight and secure." Frank moodily looked out the window. "Mary must've come here every day for a month before Ada'd even speak to her. If it were me, I would've reaped the lot of us out of frustration, but Mary was a persistent little thing—patient, determined. She kept coming back."

Frank rose and poured himself a drink. "Can I offer you a beer? It's crap on tap, but it's the best we can salvage."

"No, thank you."

"Suit yourself." Taking a long, deep draught of his beer, Frank grimaced at the taste. "More for me."

"Why did Ada finally cave?" Wendy asked. "Persistence is one thing but . . . it doesn't seem like her to let sheer stubbornness win the day."

Drinking the dregs of his beer, Frank closed his eyes and grimaced. "You. Mary convinced Ada that she was on our side by introducing Ada—and later the Council—to you."

"I don't like the look of those clouds," Eddie said, leaning against the trunk of the car and crossing his arms. The cold was biting, and a sharp wind scudded across the driveway, bringing with it the scent of wet decay and spoiled vegetation. He shivered. "And that . . . stuff . . . that's buzzing around the hole up there. What the heck *is* it?"

"If we had the answer to that, I doubt any of us'd be hanging out around here, now would we?" Elle replied.

They'd been waiting for Wendy and Piotr for fifteen minutes already and Eddie could tell that Elle was restless. She'd slid through the car door and perched, kneeling, on the roof, bow drawn and arrows lined in a row by her knee.

A gull wheeled overhead. Elle notched an arrow and aimed.

"Be still, Elle," Lily said, resting a hand on Elle's elbow and settling beside her on the roof of the car. Lily's hair, loose for once, was whipping in the powerful wind. Eddie was tempted to reach out and let the ends brush the palm of his hand but he didn't want to be a creeper and besides, he and Lily still hadn't a chance to talk about the kiss they'd shared before. Eddie loved Wendy with all his heart but he wasn't stupid and he wasn't going to be the pathetic, clingy friend-zoned dude that hung around and waited for his chance—if Wendy's choice was definitely made then he needed to reassess . . . well, everything. Lily might be a part of that.

"It's probably a spy for the Reapers," Elle protested, but relaxed her draw, allowing the arrow's tip to point down.

"Perhaps," Lily murmured, drawing one of her blades and eyeing the honed edge, testing the sharpness with the edge of her thumb. "But we have other troubles."

"Walkers!" Jon yelled from the driver's seat, the sudden noise from below making Eddie jump. His door slammed as he rushed around the side of the car and pounded the roof with one hand. His eyes were bloodshot and puffy; Jon had taken the opportunity to doze while they were parked. "Walkers, six o'clock! Where's Chel?!"

"She went in to the ladies—probably powdering her nose," Elle replied coolly. "This is more like it!" Elle crowed, sighting the first Walker. "Good, old-fashioned monsters. I was getting so sick of thinking Walkers!" Eddie could see the bright glee in her eyes as she fluidly straightened and drew. Her arrow whizzed past Jon's left ear and embedded itself in the closest Walker's chest. The Walker staggered back a few steps but then continued forward, dragging a mutilated leg behind. Its face was sloughing off, its right arm was half-

gone, but still the Walker shambled toward them with a mindless efficiency.

"Nice to know you prefer a zombie over a dude you can reason with," Eddie growled, wondering if Piotr had left a knife or stick or *something* he could defend himself with.

"You can't reason with Walkers," Elle retorted, letting the arrow fly. It drifted due to the wind but still shot the Walker through the left eye with a slick, wet pop. "All you can do is put 'em out of their misery!"

"These are not entirely mindless," Lily noted, dropping down from the roof of the car, her knives drawn. "They are still traveling in packs."

Moving to take her place, Eddie hauled himself on the trunk to get a better view. "There's like a dozen of them," he moaned, squinting through the dark. "Jon! Go get Chel! Hurry!"

Jon only got three steps toward the front door of the hotel before the Walkers closed rank. There was no way to get past them without one of the Walkers grabbing him.

"I can't!" Jon yelled, weaving side to side on the balls of his feet like a forward looking for an opening. "They're too close!"

"Here," Lily said, slapping Eddie on the shin. She held up a blade. "Take this."

Glad that she had his back, Eddie nodded and took the weapon, holding it inexpertly. Lily's blades were heavy and sharp; he felt as if he were going to slice his own fingers off. "Thank you."

"Be careful. Our business is not complete," Lily said and with a flash of heat Eddie remembered the brief feeling of her lips pressing against his, the pulse of her essence pouring into him and healing him. Lily's aid had been temporary—Eddie knew he'd already begun to fade at the edges again—but it had been given freely.

"Thank you," he said again, meaningfully.

Lily spared him a bare nod, but the closest Walker was upon them and she had no time to talk. Lily leapt forward, knife slashing,

and Eddie felt a chill bloom behind him. He spun and spotted the Walker who'd snuck up on them, using the bushes of the hotel's landscaping as cover. This one was not nearly as ugly as the others; the Walker had been young when he'd died—no more than twenty, possibly twenty-two—and through the rot Eddie could make out the ghosts of acne the Walker had died with spattering across its cheekbones and chin.

He stabbed it in the face.

"I'm sorry?" Wendy frowned. She hadn't been alive during the time period Frank was referring to. "What do you mean, Mom introduced the Council to me?"

"Mary had a brain, a beef, and a baby on the way." Frank looked Wendy meaningfully up and down.

Wendy flushed. "She was pregnant with me when she came to see the Council."

"There was this crotchety old ghost on the Council back then—some Chinaman brought over when they built the railroads—who refused to listen to Mary unless she could prove she had something to lose by teaming up with those of the dead persuasion. She let him stick his face into her gut. He went in up to the neck."

Wendy shuddered. "You're kidding me."

"Not in the least little bit. It was enough to get that old coot's attention. Ada's too. So we listened to the plan . . . and it was a good one."

"So the Council gathered every ghost they could get their hands on and hid," Wendy said. She knew this part by heart. "Mom made the entire city a—pardon the pun—a graveyard. No one to do Elise's dirty work, no one for the other Reapers to send into the Light."

And, Wendy thought, smirking, *if there were no Shades to send on, no ghosts to banish into the Light, then all the Reapers in the city would start to have a nasty buildup of Light, just like the one that landed me in the hospital. The Council would have no way of knowing that side effect of reaping,*

but Mom would have, certainly. What better way to send the Reapers run-
ning for greener pastures than to hide all the cows?

"Every mother-born-and-died of us. If you think herding cats is
hard, try organizing Walkers." Frank stood and walked to the bar.
Slipping through a thin space, he reached down and pulled out a
shot glass. "Sure I can't convince you to join me?" he asked, waving
the glass. "The beer we scavenge is terrible, but there's fantastic
harder hooch. Lotta bourbon and wine snobs in this town."

"No, thank you," Wendy replied.

"More for me," he said amicably, and gathered up his glass and
a tall, amber-colored bottle from beneath the bar before returning to
the table. Though she itched to keep the conversation flowing,
Wendy waited for Frank to pour himself two fingers of the spicy-
scented liquor and down it. His Adam's apple bobbed as he drank;
when finished, he set down the glass and poured himself another
glug, but instead of drinking this shot he held the glass and swirled
the liquor.

"Tell me about Elise," Wendy urged as Frank stared into the
glass. "Tell me about the Reapers."

Jon, lost and scared, had closed himself in the car. He frantically
texted Chel but the 'No Bars' signal blinked at him. Blink. Blink.
Blink.

Hitting the side of the phone with his hand, Jon turned the cell
off and on again. It took forever to power on and then . . . blink.
Blink. Blink.

"Come ON!" Jon yelled, pounding the phone against the
steering wheel. "Come on! Come on! Please? Please! COME ON! I
HATE YOU! I HATE YOU, YOU PIECE OF SHIT, FUCKING
WORK!" The screen cracked on the last yell, sharp shards jamming
themselves into the meat at the base of Jon's thumb. Cursing, Jon
yanked his hand back, letting the cell fall to the floorboards, and
sucked his wound reflexively.

His head felt strange—hot and heavy and pounding. Jon licked his lips, his tongue rasping over the dry, cracked flesh, and wished that he'd eaten more with dinner, gotten a shake, a larger soda, something. He felt shaky, weak, his heart was thudding painfully in his chest, and Jon could actually *feel* the thrum of blood rushing through the byways of his body.

That's when he noticed it . . .

His hands were glowing.

Jon raised first his left hand and then his right, holding them up at face level. White light glimmered at the edges of each fingernail.

"Wendy?" he whispered, forgetting that his big sister was upstairs playing politics with a bunch of dead guys. "Chel?"

No answer. Jon was on his own.

Holding his hands out as if they were dangerous weapons, Jon twisted in the driver's seat and shoved the door with his shoulder. He was a big guy and the latch on that side had never been much good; the door popped open.

On the ground near the trunk of the car Eddie, wrestling with a Walker at least a foot taller than he was, was the first to spot Jon's glow.

"ELLE! LILY! Back up!" Eddie let go of the Walker, Lily's knife embedded deeply in the creature's chest, and the Walker fell back a step and then turned, facing Jon, arms hanging against its sides.

Jon couldn't see what the girls did but he was surrounded in seconds, his butt pressed against the car door and his hands outstretched. The Walkers stumbled toward him, forming a sloppy half-circle. Many of them were utterly silent but two or three were sobbing.

Above the sad sobs the air began vibrating with the strangest, sweetest sound.

"RUN!" Eddie yelled to the girls and Jon saw, out of the corner of his eye, both Lily and Elle take off in the direction of Lombard Street, hands pressed over their ears.

"Eddie?" Jon said. He could hear his voice cracking somewhere beneath the siren song and Jon loathed himself for his weakness. Chel hadn't been shaking when wielding the Light. Chel had been fully aflame by now, laying waste left and right. "Eddie, please don't leave me."

"I'm here, Jon," Eddie said, voice steady and soothing, somewhere to the left and behind him. Jon felt rather than saw Eddie climb back up on the car. His welcome voice whispered from above. "I'm not leaving you."

"I . . . I don't know what to do . . ."

"I don't know what to tell you." Eddie's voice caught on the last words and he coughed. "Wendy says . . . Wendy says to just let go."

"But . . . I can't . . ." Jon wanted to. His hands were burning now, his entire body felt like it was alight; his fingers were splayed, his palms open, but still . . . nothing. Just the slow, painful heat growing hotter by the second.

"Eddie?" Jon whispered. "I can't turn it off. It hurts, Eddie. It hurts."

The Walkers were in his personal space, crowding close. The nearest was inches away from touching him, the rot overpowering, the gaggingly sweet-sour scent of death permeating every breath.

Jon shuddered when the Walker touched him.

Its arm blazed white fire. The Walker didn't scream or cry or writhe. It simply stood there, the brilliant blaze eating up its arm, over its torso, engulfing its head and licking down its legs, cooking the rotten skin in a charred, sickening corona like burned bacon and melting plastic. Within seconds it was a shining skeleton, lit from within and without.

Then, and only then, it did a shuddery dance, the last remnants of scorched sinews and tendons jerking in an epileptic jig until the bones alone remained.

The Walker crumpled to the ground and the next nudged forward to take its place.

"I'm gonna puke," Eddie whispered. "Jon . . . Jon that thing's not dead . . ."

Jon, horrified, looked down. The bones of the first Walker were shivering as if whatever spark of life that connected them together still existed in the pile of broken bits.

Then the next pair of hands descended and the next Walker lit up.

"Tell me about Elise," Wendy urged. "Tell me about the Reapers. Tell me what Tracey had planned and what my mom did for her. Everything you know."

"What do I get in return, kid?" Frank's eyes crinkled as he took another sip. "You don't seem to have a lot of salvage laying around."

Wendy's hands closed into fists. "My undying gratitude?"

He chuckled. "Undying. Funny word choice there. You know, considering."

"Reapers can concentrate on an item in the living lands," Piotr pointed out from the doorway, "and make it appear in the Never. Given time." He gestured at the table full of guns. "Like gunpowder, perhaps. Flint. Or more useful items of salvage . . . say, tents? Items that the living take for granted but don't pour much energy or thought into. Crowbars. Hammers."

Smile widening, Frank leaned back in his seat and steepled his fingers. "Now we're talking."

"So it's a deal?" Wendy said, trying not to think too hard on the repercussions of arming the Council with working weapons in the Never. "I promise to make a couple items solid for you when I get back and you tell me what's up?"

Frank nodded and ran one hand through his hair. "Keep in mind, Lightbringer, that Mary kept most of her plans close to the vest. She learned a lot but she didn't share much."

Scowling, he poured himself a third shot and tipped the booze back. "You, girl, have your mother's eyes, you know that? It's nice,

seeing those eyes . . . sane. Er. Saner." He laughed. "In the end, Miss Mary quite contrary turned out to be crazier than a . . . a . . . bunkhouse rat, didn't she? Nuts, the both of you. Deep down where it counts, where the crazy can save you."

"I don't think being unbalanced can save you," Wendy replied stiffly.

"Oh yeah?" Frank slammed the shot glass on the table with such force Wendy was surprised it didn't shatter in his hand. "You're here, aren't you? Here, but completely powerless. At our mercy, if you will. A Reaper just busting with Light all locked up so she can't get at it. Some people would call that downright stupid—right now you're essentially walking Walker-chow, yeah? But me? Me, I think you're just whackado enough to be brave. Elise isn't stupid. She knows you're here, visiting me. Eyes and spies, Wendy, eyes and spies. Back then, now, always, that lady's got *people* everywhere."

Wendy nodded, shivering at the idea of being fed to the Walkers. "I know."

"What I know about the Reapers," Frank mused aloud. "What do I know, what do I know . . . well, Elise likes to get her fingers in something important of yours and *squeeze.*"

Grimacing, Frank tipped the bottle again. It clattered, empty, against the glass. He strode over to the bar and grabbed another bottle. "Reapers don't have to send you on, you know that? They can just burn all of your essence away until you're a pile of quivering bones. You're not in the Light. You're still in the Never. But you're . . . raw. Bare. *Exposed.* I'm told it hurts like a bitch. And then, if they've a mind, they can build you up again. If they're talented enough."

"I . . . I didn't know that." Wendy looked to Piotr and he nodded. The idea of it made her ill.

Frank poured a shot from the fresh bottle, downed it, and glared at the booze. "No matter what your shape, in the end you beg for the Light. Like a junkie. We'd do anything for a chance to finally die. Elise takes advantage of that. She'll use the Light like it's napalm.

Just carpet-bomb whole areas until every soul comes out of hiding, no matter how it drains her. No matter how weak she is in the end. Because even if she's physically weak, if the Never is bowing down and singing her praises, well, then Elise still wins. Elise hurts. She heals. She breaks you down and then raises you up, over and over again until you're utterly hers."

He pounded the table with a fist. "You're in a coma but you're still *alive*. You've got no idea what the Light is like for us. The smell, the song . . . you're still kicking so you can't know how it grabs you by the gonads and *yanks*."

Was that why Chel's Light hadn't called to me, Wendy wondered. *Because I'm still alive?*

"I'm . . . I'm sorry," Wendy whispered. She hadn't done any of the things that had made Frank so twisted and jaded, but yet she felt responsible for her family and their transgressions. All this, everything Elise had been doing, *had to change*. "I'm not like her. You know that."

Frank touched his cheek and smiled bitterly. "No, Elise only has ghosts *working* for her. She isn't *dating* 'em."

Piotr growled quietly from the doorway. Grinning, Frank tipped the glass in Piotr's direction and sipped it. "Oh, pipe down, comrade," Frank told Piotr. "No offense meant. Look," Frank leaned forward and slung a companionable arm around Wendy's shoulders, holding up his glass in the other hand. He tilted it left, right, swirling the liquid and watching the play of droplets on the side of the glass. "As for Tracey, what she might have done to sprint past that line . . . let me lay it out for you, Lightbringer. The only truly old souls in the Never have regular contact with the Lost. And I'm not talking Riders."

"You mean Walkers." Wendy bit her lip. The news wasn't as painful as she would have expected. So much about her mother was starting to add up, and Wendy wasn't sure she liked the final sum very much. "She dealt regularly with Walkers."

"First Tracey, then Mary," Frank said, pulling away from Wendy and tapping his glass on the table. "Though Mary's decision to dabble on the rotten side had more to do with her sister than any real desire to make nice with nasties, if you catch my drift."

"You're saying my mother asked the Walkers about the Reapers, about where they came from, for Tracey. She saved up all of Tracey's inconvenient questions and kept asking them. Probably made deals to get them to talk to her, right?" Wendy crossed her arms over her chest protectively, hugging her elbows close, and grimaced. "I wish I didn't believe you."

Raising an eyebrow, Frank touched his index finger to his nose and grinned, tipping back his cup and swallowing in one smooth motion. "You don't have to," he said. "The truth exists whether you believe in it or not." Frank shook his head. "Mary didn't enjoy it; she put up with them for a purpose. Just like any good Reaper. Duty over all."

"Did the Walkers tell her anything?"

"Must've. Elise's been prying around town for weeks now, trying to trace back the places Mary went to, the spirits Mary communicated with." He paused. "Or, at least, she was. Right around the time the Lady Walker walked into the spirit web forest and took it over, Elise stopped nosing around."

"You think she found what she was looking for? *Who* she was looking for?"

"It's possible. Probable, actually—a lot of Walkers'd tell Elise anything she wants for a chance to look lovely all over again, let her fix their faces right up. Can't fix the sin, but at least you can hide it."

Wendy wondered what the beautiful Walker who'd attacked her had given Elise and she was glad he was now dust all over again.

"Thank you, Frank. You've given me . . . something to think about." Chewing her lower lip, Wendy rose to go, but was stopped short by the sight outside the window. The Top of the Mark was

high enough that she could see the rent in the sky, brooding sullenly over the ocean. "Frank?" Wendy hesitated. "Do you . . . do you know anything about that thing?"

"What did you do, Jon?" Chel asked, toeing the quivering bones. "Are they still . . . alive?"

"Not alive," Elle said, squatting down and examining the pile. "But there's will in there, you can feel it. If you left 'em long enough I bet they'd eventually come back. It'd take awhile. It'd hurt. But he'd be back."

"What are you waiting for?" Chel demanded, punching her brother in the shoulder. "I know they're monsters and all, but put them out of their misery."

Jon swallowed heavily. "I . . . I don't know how. I don't know how I burned them in the first place." He knelt down beside the closest pile and held a hand out over the shivering bones. There was a clattering beneath his palm but his hands didn't light up. Jon had lost his glow.

"Can you do it?" Lily asked, crossing her arms over her chest. A multi-colored bruise swelled high on one cheek; one of the Walkers had landed a lucky blow and a ragged cut now gaped from temple to temple. As Jon watched, the seeping wound slowly closed, leaving a long, irritated red scab behind.

"I don't know," Chel said, pressing her hands to her chest and staring hard at the piles of bones. "It's . . . warm . . . but it's like . . . like when you're trying to grab something just outside your reach and your fingertips keep brushing it but you can't get a grip." She scowled around the empty parking lot. "We can't do this by ourselves! How much longer is Wendy going to *take*?"

"The Lightbringer will finish in due time," Lily murmured, brushing her hair away from the nasty cut. "But the wind smells . . . wrong. Prepare yourselves."

And, as if her words had called to them, more Walkers appeared

from the mist. Chel, scowling, raised her hands to her chest, but the blaze of Light did not appear.

Jon's fingertips burned.

Frank glanced over his shoulder at the gigantic pulsing mass pushing against the edges of the crack in the sky.

"No one knows for sure, but we've got a good idea who's behind it." Approaching the window, he jabbed a finger toward the encroaching mass of spirit webs. "The webs are collecting any bit of spiritual debris they can get their sticky strings on. Living or dead. It's impossible to get in there unless the Lady Walker wants you to. Most of the city is cut off."

"Yeah," Wendy murmured. "We figured that one out on our own. We got here after a . . . thing . . . attacked us in the webs."

"Lucky you, traveling in a pack. Safety in numbers and all that." Frank's hands spasmed. "I hear tell that Ada was dragged into the forest yesterday, by her hair. There hasn't been a peep from her since—I'm sure she's as good as gone. Those cocoons will suck the will out of a person in hours, even someone as stubborn as Ada is."

"We saw her consumed in the webs," Wendy admitted, deciding to not relay the whole story. "I'm sorry. I couldn't save her. I tried."

"It's not your fault. You just . . . you've been dragged into something far bigger than you are." Frank rested his forehead on the glass, glaring at the rent in the sky.

"The Lady Walker opened the hole in the sky, didn't she?" Wendy asked. It was just a guess, but it *felt* right.

"It's something, ain't it?" He shuddered. "Yeah, I think she did. The Council has people all over town who report back to us, ya dig? Earlier tonight, the crazy bitch and her Walkers made a trip out to the hospital. They dragged some poor soul bursting with energy . . . with Light . . . into the spirit web forest. Just like they did with Ada." He shot a calculating look at Wendy. "The sky opened up after and, right along with it, there was one hell of an earthquake."

Suddenly all the Lady Walker's demands that Wendy walk away made perfect, disquieting sense. She'd been bragging that her desires were within her grasp . . . what did she want with a tear in reality? What lived beyond the hole?

"You think she . . . used the soul somehow? To pry open the crack in the sky?" Wendy asked in a low, quivering tone. She couldn't help wondering if the soul the Lady Walker dragged into the spirit web forest been Emma's.

"Must've. There was too much Light, but none of it was . . . contained . . . the way you all do. It was shapeless. It had to be one of yours . . . Reapers, I mean. Maybe a young one? Someone who didn't know what they were doing, or how to fight back." Frank said, hand trembling as he picked up the bottle. His eyes were bloodshot now, his lips cracked and raw at the edges. Wendy wondered what was in that moonshine and thought that it was better that she didn't know. He took another sip.

That disqualifies Emma, Wendy thought. *There's no way she'd go down to the likes of the Lady Walker without a fight. And her Light is far from shapeless.*

"If Ada's definitely gone then the Council has no one smart enough to figure out what to do with that *thing* . . ." Frank let the sentence drift into uneasy silence. "I'm sorry, Lightbringer. We can't help you. We're helpless."

As one they stared out the window. The crack was bigger. It expanded and contracted as they watched, the edges shifting against the backdrop of grey sky. It looked like . . . Wendy berated herself for thinking such a ridiculous thing even for a second, but it looked like the crack in the sky was *breathing*.

CHAPTER TWELVE

The ride home was spent in somber silence; the ghosts squeezed in the back, sitting on one another's laps while Jon and Chel shivered in the front, the heater going full blast to counteract the frigid chill pouring from all the dead in the backseat. Every now and then Wendy would catch one of them slanting glances at one another from beneath lowered lids.

A large pile of Walker bones clattered in the trunk, reminding Wendy that Jon and Chel's abilities were still too uncontrolled to be counted on. Jon hadn't meant to strip them down to bones and faint will, but since he had, what remained of the Walkers might as well be useful. Wendy had plans for the piles of shivering Walker bones.

"Home sweet home," Wendy said as Jon pulled into their driveway. He sagged with relief and Wendy decided not to tease her brother over driving with only a learner's permit. Jon parked the car and turned off the engine. It ticked as it began cooling; for several seconds no one moved an inch.

"Okay guys, you know the drill," Wendy said, yawning and scrubbing the grit out of her eyes. "Keep it short and sweet. It's a risk spending the night but we've got nowhere else to go so we're crashing for the night but getting up at dawn. You're not up, you get left behind."

"Home sweet disaster zone," Chel grumbled, her voice heavy and exhausted; she rubbed an arm across her eyes, wiping the grit away as she pushed open the passenger side door. Wendy noticed that Chel, curious, waited for the ghosts to begin exiting the vehicle and watched each of them slide through the doors before asking, "By the way, do you know anything about what went down in the kitchen?"

"The kitchen?" Wendy stopped, standing in the trunk of the car, visible only from mid-torso up. "Yeeeeaaaah. I forgot about that. I'm so sorry, guys. In my defense, though, I *was* trying to escape with my skin and soul intact."

Yawning, Jon slammed the driver's door shut. "Wait a sec. You're the reason the fridge is toppled over? What'd the fridge ever do to you?"

"Haha," Wendy said.

"Answer the man," Chel ordered playfully. "Because, no offense, you can't lift a wet noodle on a good day. How'd you manage to flip it?"

"Yeah," Jon insisted. "Did you Hulk out? Is this a Reaper power thing?"

"It wasn't me," Wendy sighed. "It was . . ." she hesitated, glancing at Elle and Lily and Piotr, the trio standing off to the side and observing the exchange with her siblings with unconcealed interest.

"It was a group of Walkers," Wendy grumbled.

"Walkers?" Elle gasped. Then she laughed, a peal of mirth like bright, brilliant bells that sent her pincurls shaking. "You joker, Wendy, you had me going! Walkers can't touch objects in the living lands!"

"These Walkers could," Wendy replied darkly, her expression stilling Elle's laughter. "They destroyed my answering machine, too."

Eddie grimaced. "The one with your mom's voice on it?"

"Yep," Wendy confirmed, dejected. She wished Eddie hadn't reminded her why she'd kept the ancient answering machine around in the first place. Now that was just one more reason to be depressed over the day.

"This is a troubling thing," Lily said. She was gazing around the front of the house impassively, arms crossed low over her belly, examining the shadows in the neighboring yards. The way she glided with each step reminded Wendy of a cat, or a ninja, the silent shifting of her weight an impressive display of sinewy leg strength and subtle grace. Lily moved like purposeful, patient death.

One day, Wendy thought, turning to go inside, *I need to get her to teach me how to do that. That is too badass to pass up.*

"Are we sure we want to risk the Reapers finding us here?" Eddie asked Wendy quietly as they approached the front door. "What if they come after us while we're chilling?"

Wendy yawned. "Sleep in shifts. Something. We circled the block three times, Eddie, and Lily's doing another check right now, see? I'm sure it's fine." Wendy chose to keep her other worry to herself: that if she fell asleep, Elise or Jane might be waiting for her in a dreamscape.

Chel reached for the door handle, but the door swung open soundlessly on its own. The foyer was too dark to see more than a foot inside. The nightlight in the hallway was out, leaving the archway into the kitchen black.

"Jon?" Chel asked is a soft, breathless voice, "Did you forget to close the door when we left for the hospital?"

"Um, no. I know I locked it, too," Jon replied, hovering just behind Chel. He rested one hand on her shoulder. "That can't be good."

Chel reached just inside the door and flicked the light switch on and off. Nothing. "It's dead," she said, brows drawing tightly together. "Maybe a breaker blew?

Nervously, Jon said, "I can check. One of those crank-jobber flashlights is in the . . . um . . . the trunk, right?" He reached out and flicked the switch up-down-up in a quick staccato rhythm, as if trying to turn it on again might do the trick.

"Isn't this the part where you're supposed to walk away and call the cops?" Eddie asked from behind them, causing the twins to jump in startled unison. "I mean, I love a good horror movie as much as the next guy, but when your cast of characters is already pretty much ninety-percent dead, you don't really wanna go killing off the only living guys in the flick, right?"

"No one's going to die!" Jon retorted in a high-pitched, thin

voice. "It's just a power outage or something! Everyone's probably having troubles!"

"But next door still has the Christmas lights on," Wendy pointed out. The lights from their neighbors were dim, but she could see them even in the Never.

"Shut up," Chel snapped, hunching her shoulders up and turning her back away from the lights. Wendy knew that her sister was purposefully not looking next door.. "We don't need your stupid logic." She crossed her arms over her chest. "Damn it, I just want to go to bed! What the hell?"

"Eddie's right. I'm calling the cops," Jon said, reaching for his phone.

"On New Years?" Chel retorted. "With the mess the earthquake made of the highway? Great idea. It'll be dawn by time they get around to us! We might as well have slept in the car!"

"Well, what do you want me to do, Michelle?" Jon growled, hands on his hips as he glared at his smaller sister. "I distinctly remember locking the front door, okay? You lock a door and watch a bunch of ghosts go sliding through it, well that tends to stick with a guy. Plus, I had to go searching for my keys. I *remember.*"

"Guys?" Wendy said.

"I don't know," Chel snapped back, mimicking his frustrated stance by jamming her own hands on her hips. "You're supposed to be the smart one! Why don't *you* tell *me* what to do? I mean, more than you already do!"

"Guys," Wendy said again, a little louder this time.

"Nice, Chel," Jon sneered. "Real nice. I'm not ordering you around. You're the bossy bitchy one these days. You think I'm not tired? All I want is to go pick up the kitchen and take a shower! I don't want to call the cops either!"

"GUYS!" Wendy yelled. Startled, Jon and Chel shut up.

"You've got at least three people here who can't die because they're already dead, right?" Wendy pointed out. "If you two are

going to be looking into the Never and dealing with the dead then you have to learn to—"

Wendy faltered into silence. She had been about to say, "*learn how to use them properly*" but that sounded suspiciously like something Elise or Jane would say. "You can just ask one of them for their help," Wendy finished lamely.

"Wendy is correct, I will go," Lily said, sliding past Elle and Piotr, pausing to squeeze Piotr on the shoulder as she passed. Wendy hid her scowl but could feel her lips turning downward. Lily, oblivious to Wendy's frown, knelt down and examined the mat on the stoop, brushing her fingers along the edges. "If you are to be Lightbringers then you must learn to better take in your surroundings. Can you not feel it? There is a tinge to the air—"

"Well, Pocahontas, hurry your tiny butt, then," Elle said, lifting a foot and gently prodding her friend on the hip with her toes. "Or let's find another sort-of-maybe safe spot to hunker down for the night."

"Oh for— screw this," Wendy grumbled, pushing past Lily and her siblings, storming into the house as loudly as she could, stomping her feet and flinging her arms about as if she would scare any Walkers away by puffing up like a frightened cat.

"Olly-olly-oxen-free!" Wendy yelled. "Come out, come out, wherever you are! YO! LADY WALKER! I know you're in HERE!" She didn't; Wendy was goading Lily for lecturing her siblings, but the words tripped naturally off her tongue.

Lily growled behind her and Wendy smiled into the dark. The dead girls might know everything there was to know about stalking Walkers and moving soundlessly from place to place, but Wendy had them both beat in sheer nerve. It wasn't much, but considering how close Lily and Piotr were, how long they'd been the best of friends, how he depended on her guidance, it was enough to warm Wendy's slightly worried heart.

Wendy peered into the kitchen. "No Walkers here," she announced, amused at the way her siblings crept in the front door

behind her. Wendy strode into the living room. The shades and curtains had been drawn on the back patio door. The only light was a thin crack of streetlight outlining the edges. "No Walkers here," she continued. "Let's go upstairs."

Wendy had taken only a step or two in the direction of the stairs when a skeletal hand shot through the doorway of the half-bath beside the stairs and grabbed Wendy by the neck, jerking her off her feet and through the door. She heard Lily's startled shout behind her, Elle's curse, and felt the biting cold of the Walker's fingers dig into her windpipe as the tall monstrosity yanked her through the back wall of the bathroom and into the crawlspace beneath the stairs.

"Lady Walker knows your taste," the Walker hissed in her ear, rotting hands delving under the hem of Wendy's corset and pressing upward, the remains of its fingertips skittering across her ribcage and brushing the undersides of her breasts as it pushed her against a solid spot in the Never and dipped its head down. "Now I do, too."

Wendy, stunned, struggled to wriggle free from the loathsome touch but then it began speaking—no, chanting—in a slow, sibilant language she vaguely recalled hearing somewhere before. What was left of its fingers were frigid, the voice hissing in her ear sent shivers down her spine, thin crackles of frost forming where its breath—where its words—brushed her skin.

Its tongue flicked out, long and rough as sandpaper, and the Walker licked a trail from Wendy's jaw to her temple, tracing a pattern against her flesh.

"The Lady Walker seems to know a lot of things," Wendy managed to gasp, pushing against the frigid press of the Walker, jamming the heels of her hands into its festering collarbone and forcing her face away from its chilly, gritty tongue.

"She knows the end," hissed the Walker. "She knows the why and when. For you, she offers a truce once more. Return to the house of webs. Claim allegiance to the Lady Walker and know the future. Know her very thoughts."

"Yeah, screw that noise. I'm swearing allegiance to no one, much less your creepy boss." The bones beneath Wendy's hands creaked, the flesh gave a little more, and Wendy heard a high, thin ripping noise, like parchment being slowly shredded. It took her a moment to realize it was his *skin* beneath the robe, slowly giving under the pressure of her blocking hands. Despite her pushing, the Walker moved even closer. More of its flesh ripped.

Wendy, gagging at the spicy stench of cinnamon and pepper that puffed in her face, tried to make light of the situation for her own sanity. "Also, if the Lady Walker wants to talk, I'd really prefer a note, maybe passed during Algebra. Slobbering, rotting courier is just so *yesterday*."

The cold was making her dizzy and slow. Wendy tried to slide back through the wall, to sink into the rest of the house and escape, but the Walker had picked his spot well. The wall was as solid as steel behind her; there was nowhere Wendy could escape to.

An overhead light burst on in the dusty crawlspace beside them. Someplace distant, Wendy could hear Chel demanding that Jon flip the next breaker.

"I really must insist. She wishes another word. You spoke so briefly before," the Walker continued, fingers scraping along her sides. Now that she could see it, the Walker was twice as nasty as it'd been in the dark. It was smaller than other Walkers, but still terribly tall and painfully strong, and the bulk of its face was long gone, warped and wrapped and sagging beneath the eyes and over the cheekbones.

The one saving grace was that the Walker's fetid embrace, horribly invasive as it was, was direct and to the point, unlike the Walker from the hospital. The way the fingers skittered across her flesh suggested that it seemed to be looking for something; what, Wendy couldn't imagine. "So be it. Should you refuse, she leaves you with a word."

"That word had better be 'goodbye,'" snarled a voice behind

them. Piotr charged forward and bodily yanked the Walker off Wendy, dragging it by its hood down to the ground and shoving his knee into its chest. Wendy clearly heard ribs crackle and snap beneath the pressure.

"You dare!" Piotr snarled in its decomposing face. "You dare touch my *solnyshko moyo*? This is not to be allowed!"

The Walker grinned nastily up at Piotr. Most of its teeth were long gone, leaving open, festering holes in its jaw, some crawling with worms and maggots or yellow with pus, and others just seeping black, gaping decay.

"This is not for your ears, Rider," the Walker said and looked over Piotr's shoulder to where Wendy, still reeling from its frigid touch, rested against the wall.

"She wants to say to you, Lightbringer, one thing: '*Mother.*'" The Walker said the word so softly that Wendy was forced to strain to hear him.

Flummoxed, Wendy glanced between the Walker and the Rider, hoping that perhaps Piotr knew what the Walker was talking about. "'Mother'? I don't—"

The Walker threw back its head, laughing. Then, before Piotr could do more than gape in surprise, the Walker drew out a long, sharp dagger and, shoving Piotr's hands aside, jammed the dagger between its own ribs.

Unimpressed, Wendy expected nothing to happen. This was a Walker, after all. She'd seen a Walker get nearly beheaded before and nothing had happened. She was stunned when the Walker's body began smoldering. Piotr, yelping, pushed away and grabbed Wendy by the arm, yanking her over the Walker's corpse as Light began eating holes in the Walker's shape. Thin tendrils of smoke poured out where each pinprick of Light punched its way through the flesh and fabric, searing holes in the walls of the Never around them.

"What the hell is happening?" Wendy asked Piotr, panting, her heart pounding in her chest. "Where did he get a knife like that?

And why would a Walker go *kamikaze*? They like sticking around, not offing themselves."

He could only gape and shake his head. "I know not."

Moments later, it was done. The Walker was nothing but a dry pile of dust. The knife it had used was blackened from bolster to butt. The blade had been seared away by the Light.

Slowly, carefully, Wendy knelt down and picked up the remains of the knife. The handle was marked with fine lines—swirls and whorls and delicately etched knots. Wendy held the knife up in the dim overhead light, squinting.

"I've seen something just like this," she said at last, stunned. "This . . . I think this knife belongs to the Reapers. Look."

Frowning, Piotr took the knife from her, peering at the handle. He ran his thumbs along the etchings, and where Piotr touched the marks his skin turned momentarily more translucent. After several seconds, Wendy could just make out the faintest scent of burning. If it hurt Piotr, though, he kept his complaints to himself.

"I believe you are correct," Piotr said and began to say more, but a shout from outside their enclave cut him short. Pocketing the knife, Piotr led the way through the side wall into the bathroom, and from there into the hallway where Eddie crouched on the floor at the foot of the stairs, bleeding essence and sporting a gash in his forehead.

"Eds!" Wendy gasped, hurrying to her friend, only to be shoved aside at the last moment by Elle. An icy figure darted past them, swiping at Wendy's face as it went.

Despite the attack, Wendy was startled to realize that Elle and Lily, bone weapons drawn, were chasing another figure from the house. Face grave, Piotr knelt beside Eddie. Wendy, trusting that Eddie was in good hands with Piotr, followed the girls out of the house, her heartbeat pounding in her throat.

The intruder sprinted away beneath the streetlights and Wendy realized it was a girl, heavily tattooed, and painfully skinny beneath

a thin spaghetti-strapped shirt. Her blonde hair was silvery beneath the halogens; her tattoos were familiar.

"Reaper!" Elle snarled, reaching for an arrow.

"No!" Wendy yelled, "Don't!"

"What the hell, Lightbringer?" Elle asked, clearly perplexed. "Why not?"

"She can't hurt us or she already would have," Wendy explained. "She's in training. None of that ink is heavy-duty, it's all just the early stuff. Like mine, see?" Wendy pushed down the neck of her hoodie to show Elle her tattoos. "If she were dangerous, she'd have ink like Jane or Emma . . . intricate as hell, all over her arms and legs, not just around her neck. There's nothing. She's nothing."

The girl stopped at the end of the street and flipped the bird at the house before pounding on the back door of parked minivan. The headlights blazed alight and the door slid open. The girl darted into the backseat as the engine caught and the van peeled out.

"She can't see us," Wendy marveled. "They sent her to break in, probably to go through our stuff, but Jon and Chel came home . . . Elise wasn't expecting that. The girl ran rather than face them."

Cursing an impressive stream of flapper *patois* that Wendy struggled to make out, Elle impetuously shot a bone arrow after the van. It arced through the back window and disappeared, but the Reaper didn't reappear. The vehicle turned the corner and vanished beyond the dense, bushy trees at the end of the street.

"That Walker had a Reaper-to-be only rooms away—one that had no clue it was there—and it didn't even try to eat her. Wow . . . the Lady Walker really has them marching to her beat," Wendy murmured. Beside her Elle was still shaking and yelling at the departed van.

"Calm, Elle," Lily urged, sheathing her knives and resting a hand on Elle's shoulder. "Peace."

"I'm getting tired of being waylaid," Elle sneered, shaking with rage. The minivan was long gone at this point, but Elle shook her

fist in the direction it had turned and spat after it. "Walkers! Reapers! More Walkers!"

"Be still. We will soon be on our way," Lily agreed, taking Elle's shoulders in both hands and guiding her back toward Wendy's house. "We will find a location where we cannot be found so easily."

"The Reaper-wanna-be dropped her cell," Wendy said. It was a cheap flip-phone, dotted with glitter hearts and sparkling under the streetlights. Wendy knelt down beside the phone and poked it. It did not move. She was disappointed; part of her had expected to be able to feel it in some way, maybe even shift it a little in the living lands.

"It's after midnight," she said, standing up. "Since it's New Years, the highway is going to be crawling with cops looking for drunk drivers come home after parties, and probably CDoT crews to deal with the earthquake fallout, too. An hour there, an hour back, minimum, and both the toll roads and I-80 are closed right now, thanks to stupid drunks."

"Are you certain, Wendy?"

"Pretty sure, yeah. Hell, even if the wanna-be Reaper borrowed a cell and called home base *right now*, the chances of getting another Reaper out here in less than a couple hours are pretty slim. They'd probably have to take the back roads the whole way."

Lily raised an eyebrow. "Even so, a few hours is not a great deal of time."

"It's enough," Wendy said. "Enough time to . . ." she drifted off, biting her lip in concentration. The sky was dark. Dawn was maybe five or six hours away, and yet Wendy fancied that there was an unsettlingly bright light burning on the horizon, a thin strip of scarlet color that she had to squint to make out. Had the rent in reality gotten so big already, that it could be seen as far south as Mountain View? Wendy thought of the heavy clouds in her dream, the baleful eyes in the storm.

Premonitions? Or something more?

"Enough time to?" Elle prompted.

"Enough time to blow this pop stand." Wendy sighed and hopped to her feet, trudging toward her house. "Let's go share the good news. No rest for the less-than-wicked."

CHAPTER THIRTEEN

Piotr was waiting for Wendy in the side yard as the girls approached. Wendy felt her heart flutter at the sight of him standing still and pale in the moonlight.

"Piotr?" Lily asked. "May we be of aid?"

"Go inside if you will," he said, smiling at the girls. "I would speak with Wendy but a minute."

They waited for Lily and Elle to vanish through the wall before Wendy said, "Okay, what's u—"

Piotr stopped her question with his lips. Wendy guiltily sank into his embrace and enjoyed the stolen moment. When he pulled away she was flushed and happy, despite her reservations.

"What was that for?" she asked.

"I wanted . . . I wanted to show you another memory," he admitted, threading his fingers through hers. "Will you go with me? Will you see what I have to show you?"

Wendy was tempted. The last memory had been so intense, so personal, so very Piotr. But she knew they didn't have time to dally.

"If you fear the time," Piotr said, correctly interpreting the desire and concern warring within her, "I assure you, it will be but a moment here. Shared memories . . . move more swiftly. All of them do, this I promise you."

"No time lost?" Wendy asked.

"No time lost," he promised her.

Wendy bit her lip. Upstairs she could see Eddie, standing in the window.

"Okay," she said as he drew back and out of her sight. "Just . . . just for a minute."

"Take my hand," Piotr said, rubbing her knuckle with his fingers. "Close your eyes."

Wendy did.

Wendy found herself once more in the vast world of white with Piotr beside her, holding her hand. The terrible bloom encasing his torso was back, but this time it had worked its way up his chest and had wrapped tendrils around his throat and curled around his ears.

Wendy wondered if he even noticed it was there.

Piotr chuckled and ran his thumb over her chin, tilting her head forward so he could kiss her forehead. "Since we have this brief moment, Wendy. I wanted . . . I need to show this to you. These memories are important to me. I don't dare lose them again. I need someone to hold them for me . . . just in case. Someone special."

Uncertain, Wendy bit her lip. "Are you sure, though? It just seems so personal."

Piotr raised an eyebrow. "Of course I am certain. If not you, with whom would I share these things?"

Wendy flushed. "I don't know. Lily?"

Chuckling, Piotr hugged Wendy close. "Jealousy from the Lightbringer? It does not become you. *Net*, Wendy, Lily may one day learn these secrets, but today . . . today only you shall know the inner workings of my past. Of my heart."

Swallowing deeply, Wendy nodded. That Piotr would express so much made Wendy uneasy, as if he were preparing to say goodbye. Roughly, she shoved that thought out of her mind. "Okay, so last we left off on MemoryTV, your mom had gone home to Valhalla or wherever, right? To do the honorable 'I failed' thing? So what happened then?"

"What do you expect happened? My mother was supposed to gather every soul that afternoon—the bandits, the brothers except for Kirill and Borys, my father—to take them all in one swoop. Kirill was supposed to live and the soul of my father . . . well, he was

different. Freyja had requested him specifically. His gift in the fields was known even so far as Fólkvangr and Freyja wanted him to till her land, to make merry with the other chosen soldiers, and wait as the rest of the host gathered and prepared themselves for the final upcoming battle."

"So the boss-lady was pissed."

Piotr's lips quirked. "That is one way of phrasing it. She gave my mother another chance to collect my father's soul. He had, inexplicably, survived his wounds, as did my uncle Kirill. Together they toiled in the fields, tilling the land and providing sustenance for the village in the vee of the river. But, despite the itch of healing and the long, hard days without two of his brothers, my father could not forget my mother's face. Many girls of the village were intrigued by him, but his brush with death—or, rather, Death's handmaiden—had left him uninterested in their attentions."

"Well, seeing as they're your mom and dad, and not 'that bird-lady' and 'the dead dude,'" Wendy said dryly, "I'm guessing Eir failed her second chance at collecting him."

The mists in front of them cleared, exposing a long row of vegetables. Borys was on hands and knees in the dirt, pulling an onion from the earth and examining it closely. The ground was clear now, free of snow, and the scent of the fresh-turned soil warming in the sun was intoxicating.

Just as suddenly as before, Eir appeared, stepping from thin air and striding swiftly across the field to where Borys sat back on his heels, squinting at the green onion roots and frowning. Wendy was interested to note that her armor was gone. She was dressed as a girl might be, in a long tunic and a pair of simple sandals, her hair drawn back in a long, glossy braid. She held her cloak loosely over one arm; a thin and familiar chain glittered at her throat.

"If I am not mistaken," Eir said, leaning over his shoulder from behind, "you peel it first."

Borys wasted no time in leaping to his feet and grabbing Eir up,

hugging her close. She tucked her head into the curve of his neck and shoulder, dropped her cloak in the dirt, and wrapped her arms around him. If she noticed Borys treading on her cloak to lift her up, Eir didn't seem to care.

They kissed.

The mists closed again and Piotr turned to Wendy, drawing her close, crushing the spirit web blossom between them. He pressed a chaste, sweet kiss to her forehead. His hands on her shoulders were trembling.

"She gave up immortality to be with him," Piotr said, lips ticking her temple, "she hardly knew him, but whenever we would ask her, 'Momma, why did you marry Papa?' she always said, 'He had the kindest eyes.'"

Piotr laughed, but it was not a joyful sound. It was broken and tired and forced. "For him my mother removed her cloak of feathers and magic and buried it deep. In time, away from the fields of the host, Eir bled like a mortal woman, drank Borys' liquor and tasted his salt, and devoured deer meat killed with her own hand. All this she did to stay by his side. Eir became mostly flesh.

"Time . . . time moves differently in the Bright Lands than it does here. My mother had many, many years with my father before Freyja realized that Eir had not returned to Fólkvangr with the farmer as requested."

"How many years?" Wendy asked, pulling away and wrinkling her nose. The flower felt wrong beneath her hands; fetid and soft, like limp, sweaty skin pressed against her collarbone, clinging with tiny, tiny burrs to her flesh.

Piotr stepped back. His eyes crinkled as he mimed counting on his hands and toes. "Oh, about twenty-one, maybe twenty-two?"

Wendy glanced left and the mists were gone now, obliterated by the hot streaming sunlight and the intense green-gold of the meadow. She could hear the nearby river rushing by, see the edge of the meadow clearing meld with the tall trees of the forest, and there,

striding across the thigh-high grass was Piotr, four young girls trailing behind him and one older girl, no more than twenty, bouncing a babe strapped to her hip at the back of the pack, following along at a more sedate pace. The girls were mostly dark-haired except the oldest and youngest. They were true carrot-tops, though the baby's hair was bright, glossy auburn.

"Keep up!" Piotr-in-the-memory demanded, stopping to scoop up one of the youngest, a child of no more than six. He balanced her on his hip and waved a hand toward the sounds of the burbling river. "Mother says the nest is this way!"

Wendy was startled to realize that Piotr's twisting scar—the one that ran from his temple down the side of his face all the way to his jaw—was conspicuously absent in this time and place. His face was clear and smooth, his eyes bright with playful older-brother bossiness.

"Piotr, put Þrima down! There's no need to rush, we have all day!" laughed the oldest, jiggling her baby to make the infant giggle and squirm. "Uncle Kirill and Yuri won't be back from the trading until closer to sunset at best. And there's no guarantee they'll even be here today!"

"And won't he be a dear, hungry for dinner and none on the table, Róta?" Piotr replied tauntingly, sticking his tongue out at the older girl.

It took Wendy a moment to realize that this easy familiarity was a shade too easy, their camaraderie a bit too relaxed. She didn't know why, but Wendy had initially thought the girl was perhaps Piotr's wife and that the baby was his child—they were the right age and the girl was very pretty—and Wendy had been sitting very firmly on her emotions, worried that her animosity toward the lovely girl would show.

Now her petty jealousy suddenly felt very silly.

"Piotr . . . are all these girls your sisters?" Wendy demanded, disbelieving, as the older girl cheerfully flipped Piotr a foreign ges-

ture Wendy instinctively knew was rude. "How many brothers and sisters did you *have?*"

"Three older sisters," Piotr chuckled. "Five younger."

"EIGHT siblings?! No . . . are you kidding me? Were they all girls?"

"All but me." His eyes twinkled. "Nine children in all, and every one of us survived past infancy. My mother was a very patient woman. In the village she was lauded as being a very healthy woman, and a lucky one, for never having to bury a babe."

"I'd imagine," Wendy murmured wryly. "Today the grocery bill would've been insane. Good thing your dad was a farmer, huh? But in that day and age, I bet he wasn't thrilled about the over-abundance of girls."

"On the contrary," Piotr said as his past-self guided the girls to a shady, marshy area where several large geese and more than a few goslings trundled amid the high grass.

"My father adored all of us. He didn't begrudge Róta the dowry we could scrape together for her, even when her husband died hunting shortly after the wedding and she was forced to return home. We all took turns cooking and tilling, weaving and scrub-bing, hunting and fishing and fowling. We did not begrudge one another any success."

"How very modern of you," Wendy said dryly. "You're telling me that you scrubbed pots just like your sisters did and they went off and stabbed furry animals?"

"I did no more than my sisters and no less. Wendy, we were a family on the farthest edge of the village, the closest farm to our nearest enemies. We had to work as one in order to survive, even the youngest among us. Every one of us was taught how to weed the garden as soon as we could walk, how to sweep the floors and how to tan the leather of whatever animal we could catch and kill."

Piotr looked at the memory moving around them and laughed. The blossom's petals shivered at the sound. "For example, Þrima's

about to learn how to catch dinner on the wing, if I'm not mistaken."

Past-Piotr waved to one of the middle girls. She approached and knelt down, pulling from her pack a large, closely woven net made of fine, shining thread. Wendy's brow furrowed. "Is that . . . is that hair?"

"Mother was an adept seamstress," Piotr said, shrugging. "She could take any material and weave it into . . . well, into something like gold for us, since her wares sold highly in the village market. An hour in her hands could turn forest spider webs into a cloak for the chieftain's newest bride or simple willow fronds into the sturdiest fish snares you've ever held. But for items around the farm—practical items, or useful, everyday things—she always incorporated my sisters' hair, especially Róta's or the other redheads, and these items were always stronger than similar items, more durable or flexible. My sisters knew to never cut their hair if they could help it. Every night the eight of them would sit in a circle brushing one another's hair, with Róta combing her own as well as Þrima's. At the end of the evening my mother would sweep the floor and pick clean the brushes, setting aside the hair for her projects."

"That is both fascinating and disgusting," Wendy murmured, watching the scene before her.

Beside them, past-Piotr and Þrima snuck up on the closest goose, little Þrima doing her best to mimic her older brother's every deliberate step. Downstream the other girls and Róta sat on large flat rocks and let down their elaborate braids, pulling their skirts up to their thighs, sunning themselves and finger-combing any debris out of their long, long hair.

Piotr sighed. "It is a beautiful day, *da*? It is warm, the fields are growing, and we are a family."

The tableau before them darkened as he spoke; a fast-moving storm cut across the sky, clouds rolling over the sun and cooling the girls sunning themselves within minutes. Róta, scowling, gathered up her ankle-length hair in one arm and lifted her baby from her lap

with the other. Piotr and Þrima had captured their dinner—a pair of fine geese with freshly-broken necks—and as a group, glancing up at the threatening sky, they hurried across the meadow as fast as they could, back toward the forest.

"What happened?" Wendy asked.

"Eir," Piotr said, the blossom on his chest drooping along with him, "was remembered. And since she was Freyja's favorite Reaper, Freyja decided to give her one . . . last . . . chance."

The three warrior women rode horses as tall as houses.

Unlike Eir, who'd simply stepped into being wherever she needed to be, these three were intent on making a scene as their horses pounded across the sky over the village, setting dogs to howling and roosters to crowing at the wrong time of day, feathers and chaff dusting the air.

The girls, to their credit, did not scream or fuss. Instead they tripled their pace, legs pumping as fast as they could as they sped past the village, aimed directly for their father's fields. Piotr, carrying Þrima on his back and the geese tangled in the net at his hip and Róta, supporting her baby's head and snagged up by her long, long hair, both fell quickly behind and took the fork in the forest that led home instead.

"I . . . feel like I know that one in the front," Wendy said as they reached the dooryard of Piotr's home and found Eir there, blocking the way into her home from the three larger women. The leader of the three, curling locks framing her face, poked Eir in the shoulder repeatedly as she made her point. Wendy wondered what she was saying but the memory here was curiously silent.

Eir looked so small and fragile compared to the Valkyrie—without her armor, without her cloak of feathers, Eir was just a normal woman with a brood of children who needed protecting and a homestead targeted by an enraged goddess.

"Of course you know her," Piotr said, his voice pitched in a low, harsh growl. "This is Sanngriðr. The Lady Walker."

"No!" Wendy could hardly believe it, the difference was so dramatic. But, as she looked the Valkyrie over, she began noticing all the similarities that had drawn her eye before. "She's prettier with a whole face," Wendy noted. "Though I think I like her better as skin and bones; she seems more formidable this way, all muscles and bullying. But why is it quiet now? I can't hear anything but you."

"These memories are only cobbled together," Piotr explained, glaring at the Valkyrie. "Some from me, some from my mother, and others from my sisters who could act as my eyes in times when I was elsewhere."

"Oh, geez, I barely noticed that you weren't actually here." Wendy looked around the yard. "So who gave you this memory?"

"Bolya." Piotr gestured to a dark-haired girl carding wool on the porch; her eyes expression was open and startled as the three Valkyrie surrounded Eir and began gesturing pointedly.

"What's wrong with her?" Wendy asked curiously, amazed at the intent way Bolya watched the tableau. "I thought you said you were all healthy growing up?"

"Born healthy, yes, but even a Reaper can be wounded. My mother never buried a child to illness, but we didn't all leave childhood completely unscathed."

"She's deaf," Wendy realized, feeling idiotic for not putting that together before. She was going to ask more but Sanngriðr was curt with her demands; while Wendy and Piotr were talking Sanngriðr and the others mounted their mares and took dramatically to the skies. Moments later Piotr, Þrima, and Róta arrived at the homestead.

They found Eir shaking with anger and crying furious tears as she scrubbed the hearth. In the distance Wendy spotted Bolya rushing toward the fields and the rest of Piotr's absent family, waving her arms wildly to get their attention, her mouth open in a silent scream.

"Pay attention," Piotr said, taking Wendy by the wrist and gesturing toward his mother, his past self, and his remaining sisters. "This is important."

"Remember," Eir said suddenly, the memory breaking into sound again as Þrima knelt beside Eir at the hearth and buried her thin face in their mother's strong shoulder, "remember that hearths are the best places to hide things."

Then, looking pointedly between Þrima and Piotr, she lifted up a heavy fieldstone that appeared to be embedded in the floor at the base of the fire. Instead it lifted easily and beneath was the cloak of many feathers, the golden chain, and a thin shift of white—all the clothing that she'd worn when she abandoned the heavens for Earth.

Past-Piotr and present-Piotr, both standing in the doorway, said, "We'll remember, Momma. Please don't cry."

"These are not tears of pain, or of sorrow, Piotr, but of rage," Eir said, wiping the wetness from her cheek and holding the drops up to the light, cupped in her palm like diamonds. "These are tears that must be shed. Now, listen to me and listen well, for we have only a short time before my sisters will return."

"We're listening, Momma," Þrima promised.

"Every spring," Eir said, "I must travel to the river to wash my cloak. This cloak." She held her hands out at arm's length and flapped, miming shaking out a great swath of fabric. "This must happen every single year. No matter the weather, the cloak must be washed."

"Why?" Þrima asked, leaning forward.

"Because without the cloak I cannot return home," Eir said. "And feathers must be kept clean to fly."

"You want to leave us?" Piotr asked, voice low.

"Oh, Piotr, no! It is nothing like that!" Eir hesitated and then added, "Piotr . . . Þrima . . . for your father I have taken on human flesh. I have weighed myself down with meat and broth and blood and babies, but always I keep in mind that someday my husband will die, that my children will pass and I will live on."

Piotr frowned. "You can't die, Momma?"

"Son, my sisters and I . . . we are long-lived. So long-lived we

might seem immortal to humans. And, as my children, you are strong and healthy and will be long-lived as well, but you will never reach the years my kind will reach. Þrima here may live to be a hundred, or possibly two hundred years old, but no more. Even weighed down with this heavy human life I could easily—easily!—live on for two thousand years or more."

Smiling, Eir reached out and stroked Piotr's cheek. "Already Róta is of an age as the day I stepped onto the snow and soil and took on a physical shell for your father. I have hardly aged since then and people in the village are beginning to . . . talk."

"Who cares what they say?" Piotr demanded, pounding a fist on his thigh. "They're a bunch of busybodies anyway, and—"

"Piotr! Peace, Piotr, peace! Their rumors are not unexpected, sweet boy. I know that one day, when my children and grandchildren have passed from this place, that I will need to return to the Bright Lands and present myself for punishment. The necklace allows me to go there, the cloak is my badge, my proof that I am one of the Reapers."

"Punishment? Momma, no!" Þrima shook her head, her red curls bouncing against her cheeks. "You haven't done anything wrong!"

"She disobeyed an order," Piotr corrected his little sister. "She did it for Papa. Because he had kind eyes and she loved him."

"Piotr has the way of things," Eir said pressing her hand on the hearth. "I know that I will need, one day, to do the right thing, to face Freyja and explain myself. Thus I kept my cloak and I need to keep it safe."

"Can we help, Momma?" Þrima asked. "I'd do anything to help you so you're not in trouble."

Eir chuckled and ruffled her daughter's curls. "You are helping, my fierce, lovely girl. Now that I know that I may not, in fact, be granted the time I originally thought, I want you two to know that my cloak is here, and how to keep it. Can you promise me that,

Piotr? Þrima? Will you swear to keep my cloak safe, my necklace safe, so that I may return home and explain myself?"

"I promise, Momma," Piotr said. "I'll keep your cloak safe. The necklace too."

"Þrima?"

"I promise, Momma," Þrima parroted. "I'll keep your cloak safe too. Better than Piotr will!"

Laughing, Eir drew her children close as, in the distance, Wendy could hear the sound of pounding footsteps approaching. She glanced through the open doorway and spied a much-older Borys sprinting across the far garden at the edge of the homestead's clearing, his children trailing behind.

With that, the world around them faded to white until there was no floor, no walls, and no roof above them, just an endless wash of white.

Wendy opened her eyes.

CHAPTER FOURTEEN

"That was . . . intense," she said. "Piotr, how do you stand it? How can you stand getting all the memories back like this? In this . . . this huge painful flood?"

He shook his head. "I share them. With you. Only you make . . . this . . . bearable." Piotr leaned forward and brushed a finger against her cheek. "Come. We will be missed inside."

Wendy followed Piotr through a thin spot in the wall into the kitchen. Chel, Jon, and the others were examining the kitchen with dumbfounded expressions.

Wendy winced. The lead Walker who had visited the previous evening to fetch her on behalf of the Lady Walker had overturned the fridge one-handed; the kitchen was a mess. Wendy poked at a water bottle with a toe. It didn't move and her foot slid through with no resistance at all. She thought of the Walker upstairs, how he had crushed her belongings with just one hand, bullying her into going with him. How had the Walker *done* that? "I'm really sorry about the mess."

Jon flipped the kitchen light on and tossed the car keys on the counter. "You can't control everything, Wendy. Okay, Chel, you get this corner," he said, kneeling by the toppled fridge, "and I'll get this one. We'll lift together. One-two-three-HUP!"

Together the twins uprighted the fridge, plugged it back in, and between the two of them, managed to shimmy it into place. Chel knelt down to finish cleaning the floor while Jon found old towels to wipe the walls.

"Aw, man, I forgot about the cookies." Jon said, lifting a paper towel off the counter and scowling at his burnt cookies underneath.

158

"Guys," Wendy said, "we need to pack and go. The intruder was definitely a Reaper. A baby Reaper, a Reaper-in-training, but a Reaper nonetheless."

"Reaper, schmeeper," Jon said negligently, almost vibrating with energy as his second wind took over. "We can handle some chick breaking into the house, that's what 911 is for. You know what really has me creeped out? The Lady Walker. What's her deal, Wendy? How'd the Walkers manage all this?" He waved a hand at the pile of obliterated cookies and the broken bottles on the floor. "You know what sucks the hardest? I wasted a can of organic cocoa on these. That stuff is not cheap."

"Color me sorry, Jon, I'll spring for more when I've got a wallet I can actually open," Wendy said testily, reaching down and trying with all her might to pick up the overturned water bottle. *It's just plastic*, she angrily thought. *Why can't I budge it? What made those Walkers so special?* "Walkers, Walkers everywhere, only bony asses to kick."

"That's it?" Jon asked, examining each cookie individually before dumping them one by one into the trashcan. "That's all you've got? Just 'Walkers'?"

"That alone ought to be enough of an explanation," Wendy replied, grouchy and not bothering to hide it. Giving up on moving the bottle, Wendy leaned forward, resting her elbows on the counter. One elbow rested firmly on the Formica, the other slid through. Frowning, Wendy straightened. *Fine*, she decided, angry that even here, in her own home, she couldn't rest against counters that should be solid, and had been trapped behind walls that shouldn't be. *Fine, whatever. I'll just stand.*

"Why aren't you scared of the Reapers?" she demanded of her brother, glaring at the counter.

Scowling, Jon dumped the last of the cookies en-masse, saving aside the least-burned cookie to try. He nibbled the edge before grimacing and, without looking, chucked the cookie over his shoulder into the can. "We handled Jane easily enough."

"You got lucky," Wendy said flatly. "Jane and the other Reapers won't let you sneak up on them again."

"Fine then, Wendy-Wan-Kenobi, please teach this ignorant one the ways of the afterlife so that I can act all smug, too."

"I'm not smug!" Wendy protested, stung. "It's just that there's more to the Never, more to Reapers, than you think, Jon."

He crossed his arms over his chest. "Okay. Educate the plebeians. Make this whole afterlife thing worth our while. Because there's a pile of not-so-living bones in the trunk that is making me a touch schizoid, you know? I'm feeling all guilty on one hand and like a super-hero on the other hand. It's not a pretty feeling."

"Jon, shut the hell up. You're acting like several flavors of wad, man," Chel said, clambering to her feet and disappearing into the laundry room. She reappeared a moment later, ratty old towels overflowing from the rag basket now balanced between hip and forearm.

"Flavors of wad?" Eddie asked, bemused. "That's new."

"Yeah. Jerkwad. Dickwad. Asswad. That's just my opinion, of course. Listening to you two is giving me a headache. Let Wendy talk and stop with the pucker-face." She glanced at the ghosts. "And don't even get me started on you guys. You're guests. I don't care if you are dead or whatever; pipe down and be polite."

Eddie belched, long and loud, before grinning at Chel. "What, I'm a guest now? I'm not family?"

"Okay, that's it, I'm done with all of you," Chel grumbled, dropping the rag basket on Eddie's foot. He jerked back before realizing that the basket couldn't hurt him. Elle snickered and Eddie colored.

"Chel, come on," Wendy said, feeling bad for smirking at Eddie's reaction and embarrassment. He deserved it though, the big flirt. "What do you want out of me?"

"More training would do for a start," her sister grumbled. "Especially if other Reapers might be on the way."

Scowling, Chel dropped back to her knees and grunted as she swept a hand under the counter, cursing beneath her breath. Curi-

ously Wendy crouched down at Chel's level and saw that a ketchup bottle had spun out and lodged itself beneath the counter and against the wall. Loose hanks of her bleached blonde hair swung against Chel's cheeks as she shifted her head this way and that to try and get the best angle to wedge beneath the counter. "You did promise," she grumbled. "About training."

Wendy glanced at Jon. He seemed unhappy with the idea. "What about you, Jon? Are you certain?"

"Might as well, right?" Jon muttered as he picked up the ketchup bottle, examined it for cracks, and wiped it down with a sani-wipe before setting it in the fridge door. "I need to know how to control the Light, too. So no one else . . ." he swallowed thickly, and Wendy knew he was thinking about the Walker bones piled in the trunk. ". . . gets hurt."

"Okay," Wendy said, clapping her hands brusquely. "You two want to see the big time? Fine. Great. Time's short. Let's go out back."

CHAPTER FIFTEEN

Five minutes later Wendy met Jon and Chel shivering in the backyard, clothed in nothing more than their underwear and shoes. Leftover batons from Chel's cheerleading days were on the ground at their feet, silver and sparkling. Jon's was tasseled.

"Is being in our frillies really necessary?" Jon asked. Wendy pointedly ignored the way he flushed as Jon glanced at Lily and Elle sitting on the bench in the side yard. Both girls were being polite, keeping their eyes at chest level and above, but Elle's smirk told Wendy that she'd been a lot less polite when Jon'd first stripped down.

"It's no worse than the beach," Chel said, teeth chattering as she tilted her head back and looked at the moon hovering high above. "Colder than the beach by quite a bit, but it's not like we're nude."

"Exactly. When Emma put me through *my* paces, I was nude . . . and armed," Wendy said, gesturing to the batons. "I learned that your clothing can come with you if you concentrate hard enough. Pick up the sticks. They aren't hoity-toity sacrificial knives passed down through generations of Reapers, but they're pointy enough for poking."

"Batons," Chel corrected, reaching down and hefting the one near her left foot. "Not sticks."

"Your clothing remains when you are the Lightbringer?" Elle asked, leaning forward and waving her hands in an S shape, indicating Wendy's curves with the swaying of her fingers. "We can never tell. You're too painful to look at."

"It does," Wendy replied. "Ghosts can't look straight at you, but other Reapers can if they concentrate. But that's not the important part. The part that really matters is the fact that you can bring stuff from the real world into the Never and from the Never into the

living lands. Also," she paused for effect, "from the dreamscape into the real world." She'd only done that a couple times herself, but her siblings didn't need to know that.

"No!" Chel gaped. "We can bring stuff out of our dreams? Like a horror movie?"

"No," Wendy said. "Not out of dreams, out of a dreamscape. Your dreams and a dreamscape are *not* the same thing. You'll learn more on that later. For now, we're going to work on you shifting from the physical world into the Never and back again. We need to build up your speed, right now that's the most important part. You're weakest in the in-between space between the physical body and the incorporeal, and the Walkers know that and will take advantage of it. Trained Reapers are scary-fast at switching, so you must get fast as quickly as possible. Otherwise, when we come up against Jane again you *will* get your ass handed to you."

"What about you? Are you fast?"

Wendy thought about how their mom had purposefully kept her from any sort of useful application of her skills and snorted. "No. I'm not. I might have been, given enough time, but I didn't have enough practice before I landed in the hospital. I was fast enough to tag Emma a few times by the time we were done training, but Jane is faster than Emma by a long shot, and I have no clue how speedy Elise is. It's safest to assume faster than Jane. Do you get where I'm going with this?"

"Go back and forth asap, got it," Chel said, bouncing from foot to foot and shivering in the cold. "But how?"

"Face off," Wendy ordered. "Have the batons ready?"

"Seriously? Ugh," Jon groaned. Behind him, crouched in the lemon tree's lowest branches, Piotr snickered.

"Tassel side up, Jon," Wendy said coolly. "The other end is the counter-weighted one. Speed is of the essence here, not strength. Chel, whichever end is weighted on yours, put it in your palm."

"This one's balanced," she said, flipping hers up with her toes

and snatching it out of the air. In the background Elle golf-clapped, chuckling.

"Chel already knows how to call the Light, Jon, and to sort of control it. You won't need to—"

"Are you kidding me?" Chel demanded. "You think Tubby McFatso here is going to get away scott-free when you were such a complete asshole to me?"

"Hey!" Jon protested as Wendy snapped, "I *beg* your pardon?!"

"You heard me, Chunky," Chel said, glaring at her twin. "You got to cower in the car like a little girl while I went outside and did the *real* work."

Jon flushed, scowling. "I was keeping the car running! Wendy told me to stay put! Unlike you, I *listen* when the person who knows what's going on talks!"

"Right, because you can't think for yourself," Chel sneered. "I forgot."

"You're being a real bitch," Jon growled. "What's the deal, Michelle? You get a little bit of power and now you're crazy with it? And besides, what do you call burning those Walkers to just bones?"

"I call it torture. They still know what's going on, they just can't do anything about it," Chel snapped. "And, I'm not power-mad, I'm just sick of having to haul your heavy ass around, Dumbo. Do you know the sheer amount of shit I have to put up with every single day at school because your pathetic, loser ass is my twin brother?"

Sneering, Chel leaned forward and poked Jon in the gut with the baton. "'Wendy's wrong about me, Chel'; 'I'll go on a diet, Chel,'" she mocked him in a high, sharp falsetto. "Some diet, Jon. I saw you sneak a cookie out of the trash. Gross, man. Just disgusting."

"Chel—" Wendy began, and started to step in between them, to play the peacemaker as always, when she caught a flash of Piotr gesturing at her from the corner of her eye.

Oh, Wendy realized. *Jon has no idea how I woke Chel up to her Light, she was hidden by the mists. Chel's baiting him on purpose. She knows Jon*

better than anyone else. Chel's betting that the reason he couldn't control the Light with the Walkers was because he just wasn't mad enough.

Wendy glanced at Eddie and the girls, and then jerked her head in the direction of the house. Piotr nodded, understanding her concern, and dropped from the tree. He snuck up on Eddie and within a minute had the other spirits out of the backyard and traveling as far away as possible. If Jon accidentally reaped one of them while learning to wield the Light, he would never forgive himself.

Come on, Jon, Wendy rooted for her younger brother. She'd been harsh to him a time or two in her life, but Chel knew her brother the way she knew the contents of her makeup bag. Chel was a master at pissing her twin off; she could work him up in seconds and, Wendy was both pleased and irritated to notice, Chel's pointed accusations already had Jon at a high, blazing pitch. Her brother was trembling in rage; for a moment Wendy worried that he'd sock Chel across the jaw before he succumbed to the blaze within. She needn't have worried.

The furious flash of Light was blinding.

When Jon finally wound down, the heat coming off him was impressive. Wendy could feel it as far back as the kitchen door, where she'd settled to let the Light and Jon's struggle to draw it back inside run its course.

"What now?" he said, staggering toward Wendy, sagging from the energy expenditure required to call the Light.

Before she could call for him, Piotr appeared at her side, Eddie just behind him. They both had armfuls of old, rustling bones.

"Now," Wendy said, resisting the urge to tussle her little brother's hair, "you send these guys on to their rest." She gestured and the boys laid the bones at Jon's feet in two neat piles, turning their face away from the fiery glare burning in his palms.

Wendy was about to show Jon where to put his hands when the ground shivered beneath them. This time the earthquake barely shook the leaves. Mountain View was far enough away from the spirit web forest for the shockwaves to be minimal.

"There goes another soul," Eddie grumbled, faster on the uptake than Wendy was. She had still been wondering where the quake had come from but knew as soon as he spoke that Eddie was right on the money. "Yay, another creepy beastie brought through. Welcome to the world."

"What now?" Chel demanded as Jon knelt down and set the bones ablaze. The heat was immense. "Now that . . . more earthquakes are happening?"

"It changes nothing. As soon as he's done you two work on getting faster," Wendy said, gesturing to the baton still dangling from Chel's fingers. "Face off. Go at each other as fast as you can, tapping as hard as you can. You have half an hour. Make it count."

Forty minutes later found them back in the kitchen, Wendy eyeing the clock. There were maybe four hours until sunrise. It seemed so much later, like she'd been awake for weeks. She wasn't the only one suffering from sleep deprivation, though. Dressed in a pair of their father's old, warm sweats, Jon was finishing the cleaning. He had large purple circles beneath his eyes. Switching back and forth between the Never and the living lands had drained him.

Chel, on the other hand, was twitching with unspent energy. Despite her annoyance with the situation, Wendy was proud. The twins had managed to hit one another in both the living lands *and* the Never several times. Both were sporting long, baton-shaped bruises all over their bodies. Jon's left cheek was swelling and Chel had a particularly nasty bruise spreading from her right shoulder over her collarbone and snaking down her ribs. Their mom, if she could see them, would be so proud.

"Okay," Chel said, bouncing on her toes as she scrubbed down the kitchen counter with a bleach wipe, "since that Reaper was poking through our stuff, it's obvious that we can't stay here. Time to pack and bail." Chel threw the bleach wipe at the trashcan. "The thing is, though, where do we go? Without Nana Moses to keep the

other Reapers from gutting us, anywhere we run is going to be dangerous. Especially if naturals glow so brightly that ghosts can sense them anywhere."

Everyone fell silent, pondering Chel's point.

"There may be one place you can hide," Piotr said slowly, long after the silence had stretched to an uncomfortable pitch. He looked to Wendy for confirmation to continue. "But I do not know if it is wise."

"What're ya thinking, flyboy?" Elle asked, leaning comfortably against one of the high stools at the counter.

"Clyde," Piotr said, wincing. "He may be willing to set aside his animosity toward visitors for a short time. If properly compensated, that is."

Lily bit her lip. "Oh."

"That's a polite way of puttin' it," Elle agreed, tapping her fingernails against the metal back of the stool. "But if anyone can stash a baby Reaper so no one could find them, it'd be ol' Clyde." She licked her lips and looked first Chel and then Jon up and down. Her expression was so searching, so dark, that Wendy wondered what she was seeing. "He'll want salvage. Special salvage, knowing him."

"Salvage is never a concern," Piotr replied. "A short trip to the Treehouse—"

"Will get you gutted by waiting Walkers, most like," Elle said, cutting Piotr off with a sharp wave of her hand. "Naw, dealing with Clyde you have to be smoother than bribing him. He's old-school."

"Not that old," Lily murmured. "I have been dead far longer. Most of the Riders have."

"Old enough," Elle said, rolling her eyes. "Old enough to take affront if we try to pay their way straight up. Nah, we have to barter with the man. See what he wants first, and then pander to that."

"I don't like the sound of this," Eddie said in an undertone to Wendy. "This Clyde guy sounds like some kind of mobster or something."

"Even if he is, so what?" Wendy replied, not bothering to keep her reply quiet. "What choice do we have?"

"And that," Elle said, straightening and lifting her arms above her head so that her skirt rode high on her thighs, "is the smartest thing anyone's said all night. Come on, let's go."

"Wait, you really want to leave?" Jon said. He was white-knuckled, holding himself up with the counter, Wendy realized. The training session really had taken it out of him. "Really? They're just Reapers, Wendy."

Troubled, Wendy refrained from glancing at Piotr or Lily for support. She knew that tone—Jon had reached some internal breaking point.

Compared to Chel's overdramatic, exuberant nature, Jon was mellow to the point of catatonia at times. After years of treating Chel gingerly, Wendy was used to thinking of her younger brother as rough and tumble, unflappable, but every now and then Jon would prove that he was more frail emotionally than she gave him credit for.

This was one of those moments; Wendy knew that after the things Chel had said to rile him up, Jon had to be treated delicately or else he might fly off the handle. He was sensitive about his weight at the best of times; the way Chel had ripped into him must have been difficult to bear, even if he now realized that there was an ulterior motive behind her unrelenting cruelty.

Flicking a glance at the way Jon was sagging, Chel pointedly cleared her throat beside Wendy, and Wendy had to force herself not to kick her sister in the shin. *It might not connect anyway*, Wendy consoled herself, *just keep talking*.

"We don't have a choice, Jon," Wendy said as kindly as she could. "We have to go."

"Yeah, I don't think so," Jon snapped, yanking his leg back and kicking the stool Elle had been leaning against hard enough to send it clattering across the kitchen floor. It hit the stove and rebounded, crashing to the tile and making Chel jump aside.

"Screw you," he told Piotr. He pointed to Elle. "Screw you."

"Excuse me?" Elle said dangerously, stepping beside Wendy, her hands balling into fists.

"Shut up, Elle," Wendy hissed softly. "Just let him talk. He'll vent and it'll be done. He needs this."

"Screw you and you and you," Jon continued, pointing in turn to all the others in the room. "Screw all of you. I'm not dying for this family. I'm tired. Screw that, I'm *exhausted*! I'm not leaving my house, my stuff. I'm not going into hiding. I'm not going to run around town because some crazy-ass relatives of Mom's—"

"Jon—"

"—I've never even heard of think I'm some kind of 'threat.' I've called the Light, it's not that great, so I'm not going to be using it, okay?"

"Jon—"

"I'm just not, they'll figure that one out on their own, I'm sure. So I'm done. I'm out!"

Jon pushed past Chel and pounded up the stairs, yelling over his shoulder, "And, Chel, if you're smart you'll be out, too! Stop glamorizing death! It sucks!"

His door slammed.

"Smooth," Chel said dryly, sitting at the kitchen table and rolling the peppermill between her hands so that pepper flakes sifted down across her knees like black rain. "Real smooth, Gothette. Way to make him see the light. Or the *Light*, as the case may be."

"Shut up," Wendy snapped. The stool lay on the ground and she was desperate to pick it up and right it but knew that she could do nothing about it. And all Chel was doing was sitting at the table and bitching? Wonderful, just great! Chance of getting burned or not, Wendy was tempted to take a swing at her sister. "This isn't on me. Did you have to be so *cruel* earlier?"

"Hey, the truth will set you free," Chel protested, stung. "I love the butterball more than anything, I just—"

"Right, *you* care about Jon's feelin—"

"Excuse me? Of *course* I care about Jon's—"

"Sure you do. Sure you do! That's why you led off with calling him a fatass loser and then rolled right into—"

"BOTH OF YOU, SHUT UP!" Eddie yelled, slamming the counter with both fists. Thankfully, Wendy noticed, Eddie had picked a solid place in the Never to do his slamming; half an inch over and his fists would have gone through the countertop, ruining the effect of his anger.

"Eddie, come on," Chel grumbled, "do you really thin—"

"I don't care," Eddie interrupted. "I don't. You cannot even measure how little I care. You can't count the fucks I don't give with a microscope, okay? All I care about is—"

"Wendy?" Chel said, raising an eyebrow. No one missed the way Piotr, standing beside Lily, stiffened.

"Nice, buffy, just keep flapping that mouth," Eddie said, crossing his arms over his chest. "It's getting you so far in life."

Chel rolled her eyes and flipped Eddie the finger. "Like yours is getting you so far in, what, your unlife? How's your body handling, Eddie? Feeling thin?"

"We're going upstairs to fix this," Wendy interjected, stepping between Eddie and Chel. "You," she told Eddie, "sit here, cool off. You," she said to Chel, "are coming with me. We've got to get Jon out of this house. That Reaper-wanna-be was just the first in line."

"Let him stay," Chel said. "What're they going to do to him, really? You can't just kill a person in this day and age, Wendy."

"Oh really?" Wendy jammed her arm through the thin spot in the countertop that Eddie had barely missed, pushing it in up to her elbow. "They sure did a good job with me. Not to mention whatever happened to Emma."

"Fine," Chel groused, hopping to her feet. "But I'd like to point out that you're not technically dead."

"Not yet," Wendy said quietly. "*Yet.*"

"Whatever," Chel sneered and wiped her palm against her

cheek, whisking away angry tears. "Semantics at this point, right? You've been hanging out with the dead so long that you might as well be, right? You and Mom, dead together. Woot and frickin' yay."

"Chel, this is important," Wendy replied, not ready to address her sister's inexplicable jealousy. It wasn't like Wendy would have *chosen* this life for herself, whereas Chel seemed to be reveling in it. Maybe the White Lady had been right—maybe Wendy had been the wrong daughter to wake to the Light all along.

"You might—*might*—get away with staying here, Chel, but *Jon has to go*. I'm not fooling around; the Reapers will hurt him if they get a chance. Boys don't call the Light. It's a rule. Do you want to risk finding out all the things they'll do to him? Because if they did this to *me*, a chick, just what do you think they're going to do to *him*? Not only a natural but a *boy*?"

"Fine," Chel sighed. "Let's go make nice."

CHAPTER SIXTEEN

Scowling, Chel stomped all the way upstairs, stopping at the door to Jon's room.

"Jon?" Chel tapped on her brother's door with one fingernail. "You okay?"

"Go away."

Chel knocked louder. "Come on, Poindexter. Unlock the door. You can't hide in there forever."

"Says who?"

Wendy pressed her face against the door to be better heard on the other side. "You do realize that we don't need your permission to come in, right? Not me and definitely not Chel."

Trying the knob, Chel blinked. It was locked. "I don't?"

A moment later the lock clunked and the door cracked open. Jon warily looked out. "She doesn't?"

Sighing, Wendy rolled her eyes and poked a finger through the solid door. "The Never is very thin here, any spirit can come in easily. Mom's room is the only solid one."

"Yeah, yeah," Jon grumbled, stepping back to let his sisters pass into the room. "Just go, okay? I'm done."

"Have I told you lately how big a dumbass you are?" Chel asked, storming into his room and slapping her hand down on Jon's desk. Several of his fiddly anime figurines toppled over, arms and legs akimbo. She grabbed up Jon's most prized action figure and held it by its articulated elbows. "Hur-dur, I'm Jon! Watch me sit here and sulk like a big baby until a bunch of crazy ladies and their pet zombies come kill me!" She made the figure dance around and waggle its rear at Jon.

"Give me that!" He snatched the figure out of Chel's hand. "This is a collectible!"

"Whatever," Chel sneered. "These bitches put our *sister* in the *hospital*. Doesn't that bug you at all? In the least little bit? Or are you all, 'herpaderpaderp, lalala, Wendy's hospitalized again, oh well, I guess I'll sit on my ass until Dr. McCreepster calls CPS on Dad'?" She pounded a fist on the desk again. "One of them, whats'er'name . . . Jane! She nearly cut me apart tonight, Jon! With a . . . a really, really big knife! Doesn't that twist you up even a *little*?"

Scowling, Jon crossed his arms and glared at Chel. "What kind of asshole do you take me for, Chel?! Of course it bothers me!"

"Guys," Wendy protested, startled at the unexpected rancor simmering between the two of them, "take it down a notch. Chel's fine. I'm fine. We'll get out of here and we'll be even more fine."

"Yeah, you're fine. You're just fine and dandy . . . at least your soul is," Chel mocked, jutting her chin out. "Until Dad comes back to take you off life-support. Or the insurance company does. Or the interns get too busy to keep your temperature down. Or that creepy doctor trips a breaker. Or your brain crisps up like onion strings—"

"I don't—"

"And some med students crack your skull like an egg—"

"That's just—"

"And they go digging inside to see what running a long-term super-high temp does to the ol' noggin. You know, for *science*."

"Okay, okay!" Wendy grimaced and shuddered. "Thank you so much for that visual, Michelle. What the hell is with everyone picturing me in pieces tonight?"

"Maybe it's all the people who've *tried* to rip you into pieces tonight," Jon muttered, sulking as he straightened his action figures and posed them carefully into their original positions.

"My point is that we don't know how long your body can hold out," Chel snapped. "That doctor was a jerk but he did have a point. Your heart is working triple-time, Wendy." She waved a hand

around Wendy's head. "You're dying. You even *look* like you're dying. Or can't you feel it?"

Chel had a point. Wendy decided to try a different tactic. "Chel, you're worried about me. Jon is too. I get that both of you are feeling lost right now and maybe—"

"Don't psychoanalyze me," Chel snapped. "You're dying and he's a coward. What I don't get, Jon, is why you're not gunning for these bitches hardcore! Everyone's all, 'Let's run away like a bunch of scaredycats, drrr.'"

"Run away today, live to run again another day," Jon said, chewing a thumbnail. He was starting to really sag, Wendy noticed. Jon staggered like he was punch-drunk.

"What do *you* suggest we do then, Chel?" Wendy asked. "If you were in charge?"

"I don't know! Attack *them* for once! Make them see that naturals aren't anything to mess with! Maybe sick the Riders on them. Piotr and the girls can fight."

"Like *spirits*," Wendy stressed. "They fight like spirits. Flight versus fight is an intimate part of their daily existence. The thing is, Chel, if you put any ghost—*any* ghost at all—up against the weakest Reaper, they're going to lose. The Riders know that."

"Everyone seems to just *know* this laundry list of crap that Chel and I don't," Jon grumbled, resting a hand on his desk. His fingers played with the edge of a sheet of pale purple paper. At first Wendy thought the note might be a love letter but a closer glance revealed that the script on the page was no-nonsense and crowded. "That's what's got me pissed, Wendy. Can't you see that? We're flying blind and all I want to do is curl up in bed and *sleep*."

Wendy, frowning, strode to Jon's side. The way he was fiddling with that paper was setting off all sorts of nosy, big-sister signals in her brain. "For fuck's sake, Jon, grow up. Stop feeling sorry for yourself and smell the burned cookies. If you stay here someone will come for you—either to kill you or to use you to get to me. You

don't have to fight but you *do* have to tag along, unless *you* want to be the one we're visiting in the ER."

Wendy leaned over and glanced at the lilac letter; it wasn't addressed to Jon, it was addressed to her. Scowling, Wendy pulled back. "What the hell is this?" she demanded pointing. "Just what. The hell. Is. This?!"

Jon flushed. "Um . . . a letter?"

"*My* letter!" Wendy growled, vibrating with anger. "My letter from Emma, unless I'm mistaken." She slapped the desk. "This letter was supposed to tell me where EDDIE was, Jon! It was supposed to tell me about the Reapers WEEKS AGO! I was worried SICK, Jon! I thought Eddie was going to DIE and you had the damn letter THIS WHOLE TIME?!"

"I didn't mean to keep it!" he protested. "Before I read it, I thought it was something of Mom's! I was saving it! I wanted to have something of hers no one else did!"

Wendy buried her face in her hands and breathed deeply through her nose. She held it for one minute . . . two . . .

"Wendy?" Jon asked nervously. "Look, it was in a pile of papers I picked up off the counter downstairs on Friday. It was a bunch of stuff that got jumbled together while you were in the coma and right after. Hospital bills Dad hadn't paid yet and stuff. Most of it was trash, it only needed a quick go-through to make sure before chucking it. I only opened it yesterday afternoon, okay? I didn't know. I'm really sor—"

"Shut up, Jon," Wendy said, laying one hand across her eyes and forcing herself to breathe long and even, calming herself. "Just . . . just shut up."

"Wendy?" Chel whispered, automatically coming to Jon's defense the way they always did when facing outside anger. Wendy was touched by it; even now, no matter how they ripped at one another, when the chips were down they were always family. "Wendy, he didn't mean it."

"I get that. I'm not mad, I'm just . . . just . . . ah, screw it. I'm done. We're fine. Go," Wendy said heavily, waving her hand, not daring to look at the twins.

She might try to punch one of them.

"Just . . . just go to your room. Grab your backpack, nothing bigger. You'll want comfy, durable clothing. Jeans. Heavy t-shirts, thick socks. No holes. Think light layers: a couple long-sleeved shirts, sports bras, cotton undies. Nothing that rides up or chafes. No thongs, Chel."

"Ew, Wendy, gross!" Chel sneered.

Wendy ignored her. "Well-worn boots or sneakers. Nothing new, nothing with a heel, and nothing that can rub or cause blisters. No makeup. You will want lots of hair ties. A small toiletries bag— deodorant and stuff—but make sure you leave room for a first aid kit. I had to raid it yesterday when I was burning up but it should still mostly be in the usual spot. Two kits, if you can fit them both in the bag. Mom kept emergency cash in a baggie taped under her bedside table drawer. There's, like, five or six hundred bucks there. Get that too."

Chel rolled her eyes. "Sure thing—"

"I mean it," Wendy snapped. She glared at both of them, hands fisted at her sides. "I'm going to teach you two everything I learned in three years in three or four days. That means you need to shut up and listen to me. Go. Pack. Now."

"Geeze," Chel grumbled, turning and heading for her room. "Was Mom such a hardass?"

"She was worse," Wendy said under her breath, but Chel was already through the doorway of her room, slamming the door shut.

"I don't think my sports bra still fits," Jon joked nervously, shoving the extra flesh at his pectorals together to form cleavage. "How about a push-up instead?"

"Same essential kit," Wendy replied dully. "When you're done, run out back and grab the camping supplies. The tent and camp

stove are next to the broken mirror in the shed. Make sure you snag the sleeping bags from the linen closet and the water purifying tablets from the eart— hell, just grab the whole earthquake kit. Better safe than sorry. But no bottled water. We'll snag a case at Safeway on the way to the highway."

"Are you serious?" Jon asked, groaning. "We're not going to be spending the next few years dancing in the desert, Wendy. It's just getting out of the way for a few days until Dad gets back and we can sort this whole Reaper thing out, right? Don't you think this is a bit overkill?"

Wendy, irritated, reached forward and tapped the lilac-colored paper on the desk. "No," she said coolly, "I don't. Do what I say. Mom taught me—she taught me to cover my back, to be prepared for every contingency, and most of all she taught me that if you have to run, you *run*, okay? If you don't want to listen to me, listen to Mom through me. Okay? We run. We run hard, we run far, and we don't come crawling back until this whole thing is settled. I lost Mom. I'm not losing you guys, too. Okay? Okay, Jon?"

"Okay," Jon whispered, head and shoulders sagging with shame. He swallowed thickly. "But . . . I mean, we're coming home, right? This is just short term? Hiding from the Reapers and the Walkers and all the other stuff?"

"I have no clue. This could all be over tomorrow, or we might not be coming home ever. Emma was supposed to take over when Nana Moses passed, but she's not exactly in the running right now, is she?"

"Think she's still alive?" Eddie asked, voice high and reedy. "Emma, I mean."

"No clue. Probably not. For all we know the soul the Lady Walker used to crack open that hole in the sky was Emma. Now move. I'll meet you downstairs in ten."

"Time's a-wasting," Jon agreed, opening the door to his closet and pulling out a large and battered backpack.

"Wait," Wendy said and tapped the letter again. "Pull it out so I can read the whole thing."

"Sure thing," Jon muttered, tugging Emma's note out and flipping on the desk lamp so Wendy could better see. "It's only one page."

"Pack," Wendy ordered flatly and leaned over the desk, eyes scanning the page.

Winifred,

I have no time to be coy and no desire to play games. I know that you, like your mother Mary before you, can see and speak with the dead. Please know that though Mary has been working separately from our family for some time you, as her daughter, still must meet with our matriarch, my great-grandmother Alonya, and be embraced back into the fold. Your mother was a remarkable woman but San Francisco is a very large town, rife with the dead, and has far too much territory for one Reaper to hold on their own.

Please know that I have nothing but respect for Mary and regret not knowing her personally. She shall be greatly missed and we are all very sorry for your loss. You must understand that Mary was a legend to the Reapers growing up in her shadow and I can only imagine what she has taught you, the tricks and techniques she must have passed down. Only Mary could get away with giving you the Good Cup without Great-Grandmother's blessing! Please don't find me too forward, but I hope you will share these secrets and your training with me. If Great-Grandmother's permission is granted, it is my plan to stay in the SF area and help you maintain the amazing status quo. We could – and should! – work together.

In closing, as I was leaving the hospital earlier today I encountered your friend Edward. You can imagine my surprise to see him wandering outside his body! I attempted to ascertain what separated him from his shell but was unable to do so on my own and in the time allowed. To keep him safe I insisted that he come home with me. My address is included, please come retrieve him at your earliest convenience and meet the rest of us. I swear that I will use all the knowledge at my disposal to keep your friend safe and help

him back into his shell – I am so very glad I spotted him before a Walker did! Only a fool would miss how much he means to you.

I am looking forward to seeing you again!

Emma

Mind whirling, Wendy pushed past Jon. It was hard to ignore the uneven wave of heat coming off her brother; Wendy made a note to work with him again on his control as soon as they'd settled down somewhere safe. He'd learn to manipulate the Light and heat and keep himself safe if it killed her.

Wendy had barely stepped into the hallway when Eddie grabbed her by the wrist.

"We need to figure out a plan," he said, urgency underlying his tone. "Some sort of way that I can help or get some weapons or—"

"No," Wendy said, taking Eddie by the wrist. "Absolutely not, Eddie. Hell no."

Eddie dropped her wrist and stepped back, frowning. "Wendy, what's—"

"I want you to stay here," Wendy said bluntly, stepping forward and enfolding her best friend in a tight hug. "Not here-here, not at this house, but I want you to go home or to find someplace—any place—that seems safe enough, boring enough, to lay low at for a few days. Eddie . . . so much has happened . . . I couldn't stand it if anything happened to you. Not to you, too. I can't. I can't do it."

"Is this about Piotr?" Eddie asked bitterly. "It is, isn't it? You're ashamed. You want me out of the way."

"Ugh, Eddie!" Wendy drew back long enough to sock Eddie in the shoulder as hard as she could before hugging him again. "I care about Piotr, yes, and I love him, yes, but you're *Eddie*! Don't you understand that yet? I need you to be safe, you dumb butthead."

"Butthead?" Eddie muttered. "Thanks."

"Shut up. You know what I meant. I can't—repeat CAN NOT—keep going on the way I have. I can't. I'm worried about you

all the time, Eds. Please, please, please for my sanity . . . lay low, okay? Hide. Find a safe place and just hunker down." She thought of Emma, the way the doctor had kept Eddie in San Ramon, safe and sound from Walkers and the other Reapers, and how the first thing Wendy'd done on seeing Emma was accuse Emma of kidnapping him. Wendy's cheeks burned with shame.

Eddie sighed. "Are you *sure* you're not just getting rid of me so you can go smooch Piotr without feeling guilty?"

"After the way you dumped me to go spend time with that Gina-chick for weeks and weeks, if I want to smooch Piotr, I think I'd do so without any guilt," Wendy reminded him, smoothing a lock of silvery-blond hair off his forehead.

"Yeah, yeah," Eddie said, rubbing the back of his neck and obviously embarrassed at being called out on his jealousy. "Gina Biggs . . . so, so hot. She dumped my ass but good, too."

"They usually do," Wendy replied lightly.

"Only when they find out how much I care about you," he said, cupping Wendy's chin and tilting her head back. They locked eyes. "But they never listen when I explain that you don't feel the same way."

Wendy laid a cool palm against his cheek, drawing forward to brush her lips in the hollow of his cheekbone and poke him in the chest. "Now's not the time, Eds. We can talk about . . . whatever thing we have and whatever is going on with Piotr and me later. When we're both back in our bodies. Okay?"

"Just promise me that you won't do something stupid like let them pull the plug just so you can be with Piotr," Eddie said, staring hard into Wendy's face. "Or have him tell that doctor to do it with his weird mumbo-jumbo hands. I know you, Wendy. You act tough but you're a romantic at heart. Don't do anything dumb, all right?"

"Scout's honor," Wendy promised. "No plug-pulling."

"Why don't I believe you?" Eddie asked.

"I have no idea," Wendy said. "But I wouldn't lie to you, Eddie. Not about that. Now you, good sir," she hugged him once more, a

quick embrace but warm nonetheless. "You go find a place to hide out and rest. A nice, safe place to hunker down."

Eddie pressed a sweet, brief kiss to her forehead. "Be safe, Wendy. I love you."

"I love you, too," Wendy replied as he turned and headed downstairs. She pitched her voice low so he couldn't hear her and wrapped her arms around herself, hugging her elbows close and fighting frightened tears. "More than you'll ever know."

CHAPTER SEVENTEEN

ocking the house and leaving was one of the hardest things Wendy had ever done. Their grandmother would have no clue where they were, neither would their dad. None of the neighbors were awake to see them leave. So much had happened but it wasn't even four yet. They piled into the car and sped south, to San Jose.

The Winchester Mystery House grounds were well lit even in the middle of the night, and as Jon pulled into the lot and parked the car, the soft sounds of traffic lulled them into a sense of momentary peace.

Wendy was surprised at how much of the Mystery House was rock solid in the Never. Even the fences and bushes looked firm— there would be very little sliding through walls in this place. The ghosts would have to move around like the living did, though how they'd manage to open the doors or windows to get from place to place was beyond her.

The rest of the city pressed in disconcertingly close to the house and grounds, but facing the house, back to the overcrowded city behind her, Wendy could close her eyes and briefly imagine what it must have been like when this house had been the only thing for miles around, just an estate and an orchard and a crazy old lady waiting for death at the edge of nothing. Wendy tilted her head back, gazing at the shadow of the tall red roof rising four stories above the two stories remaining in the living lands. Here in the Never the colors of the house were brighter than the surroundings, and the grass was verdant and green.

"So who's this Clyde guy?" Chel asked, rolling down the window as Piotr, Lily, and Elle slipped through the sides of the car

and joined Wendy in the parking lot. "Do we know that we can trust him?"

"Groundskeeper or something. He's a recluse," Elle explained, gesturing for Jon and Chel to stay in the car. Shrugging, Jon reclined the seat and stretched out, covering his upper body with a hoodie and shielding his eyes from the streetlights with the hood. "He's got no love for Reapers and is impossible to bully, which'll work in our favor *if* we can convince him to hear us out."

"I wonder if he's the reason why Mom wouldn't let me come out here once I saw the Light," Wendy mused, drifting over to the small tourist information hut built close to the parking lot and poking the plexiglass with a finger. The glass was chilling, and for a moment Wendy worried that her fingers would stick.

"You have not visited this area since you became the Lightbringer?" Lily asked, surprised. She'd braided her hair back in an intricate bun at the nape of her neck, the glossy strands woven so elegantly that Wendy's eyes strained to follow the weft of the locks. Lily'd dropped her normal, traditional garb and had formed her essence into slim jeans and a loose, long-sleeved blouse similar to the one Chel was wearing. The modern look suited Lily's angular features too well. Wendy wished she'd go back to her suede and leather look.

"I came out to San Jose," Wendy explained, poking her corset, wondering how much energy it would take to shift the color to red or possibly silver. It seemed like so much effort, but Elle and Lily shifted form so *easily*. "I just didn't come here. Mom wouldn't allow it when I was working under her. I didn't think her spirit would wander out this way if she didn't want me coming here when she was, you know, whole."

"Knowing what we do now of your mother's actions, it is possible that she and Clyde had made an arrangement," Lily theorized, joining Wendy at the information hut. She pushed a hand against the wall; it did not give under her pressure.

"Sounds like Mom," Wendy agreed, giving up on changing her

look. People liked her corsets anyway, especially Piotr and Eddie. Why change what wasn't broken? "So what's the deal? Do we scale a fence and go looking for this Clyde guy?"

"That won't be necessary," Piotr murmured, squaring his shoulders and brushing his hands down his shirt. "Here he comes."

Clyde turned out to be a lean middle-aged man, dark-haired and dark-eyed, sporting a fantastic mustache and a set of clean, pressed overalls. He strode toward them, hands thrust into the pockets of his overalls, and stopped just on the other side of the hut, eyeing them each in turn. "Riders, huh? What can I do for ya?"

Lily opened her mouth to reply but Clyde suddenly pushed past her, standing toe to toe with Wendy. He scowled and crossed his arms over his chest, large hands gripping his upper arms. Wendy could see the individual lines creased with dirt on his fingers. His overalls were clean but his hands dirty. Interesting. "A Reaper? Here?! We had a deal!"

Taken aback, Wendy stammered, "I . . . I don't—"

Clyde grabbed Wendy by the front of her corset, yanking her hard. The bones lining the fabric gave him good leverage; he was able to jerk her roughly enough to snap her head back and forth. "When we have a deal, you and yours need to listen, damn it!"

Wendy, startled, quickly jammed an arm between the two of them as Clyde, surprisingly strong for such a thin man, lifted her almost over his head and shook her like she were a rag doll. "I am getting sick—SICK—of your kind on my property!" Clyde shouted into her face, spittle flying and sliding down Wendy's left cheek.

"I don't know what—"

Clyde shook her roughly again and her teeth clicked painfully together.

"You dare—YOU DARE—come back around here, peddling your papers? I ought to rip your soul to shreds! I ought to take that cord of yours and rip it in two! How's that sound, huh? Sound like something your bosslady—"

"I DON'T KNOW WHAT YOU'RE TALKING ABOUT!" Wendy yelled and, twisting, elbowed Clyde right between the eyes. She felt the cartilage of his nose give way and Wendy pressed her advantage, scrabbling her feet up his thighs for purchase and pushing off, shoving him away with such force that Clyde stumbled back and fell, scraping his hands on the pavement as he tried to catch himself. Wendy also fell back but was quick enough to tuck and roll, coming up to her feet with hardly a scratch. The abused bones of her corset jammed into her ribs and Wendy once more wished that she'd taken the time to learn how to shift her shape like the others.

Clyde, rubbing his nose, glared at her. As Wendy watched he jerked it once and his nose clicked back into place.

"That hurt," he growled. "What do you want, Reaper?"

"Be calm!" Piotr snarled from where Elle and now Lily were holding him back. "We did not come to fight with you! The Light-bringer comes in peace!"

Clyde glared at Piotr; Piotr glared back. For several seconds the air seemed to snap with repressed words and an inexplicable icy chill. Wendy was startled to realize that there was an aura around Clyde very similar to the glow around Jon's hands—a faint glow, green this time, an aura that hovered just above his skin.

"Wendy?" Clyde asked. He frowned. "Lightbringer?"

"Hang on," Wendy said suddenly, interrupting the staring contest. "I'll be right back." She turned on her heel and rushed toward the car, knocking on Jon's window with one knuckle, glad that the heavily splattered mud only existed in the living lands and not in the Never. The whole car was downright filthy.

Jon, sleepy and irritated, rolled down the window. "What?" he demanded. "I was mostly out!"

"Show me your hands," Wendy ordered. Jon did and then Wendy examined his fingers closely. "Can you call the Light?"

"You need me to—"

"Just call the Light, Jon. Make it snappy. Not all of it, we don't

want to reap anyone, just enough to do that glowy-thing from earlier." Shrugging, Jon did so, and Wendy was amazed to see that her brother had a green haze surrounding his body. Jon was concentrating hard so it wasn't as faint as Clyde's glow, but the haze was still noticeable when you knew where to look.

"Thanks," she muttered and hurried back to the gathered ghosts. Clyde had calmed down.

"You're the Lightbringer, huh? I've heard about you, girl. Everyone's heard about you."

"Look, I'm really sorry to bother you," Wendy said, taken aback by this abrupt, direct ghost. "No, I'm not from Elise. I don't even like Elise . . . my mom didn't either, but I didn't know you existed until tonight, and—"

"Your mom?" Clyde asked, bored. "Who is that?"

"Um, her name was Mary," Wendy said, feeling like a toddler who'd spilled grape Kool-Aid on the parlor rug. Maybe it was the fact that he'd been able to shake her above his head, but Clyde made her feel very small and uncertain of herself. "You've probably never heard of her—"

"Mary?" Clyde snorted. "Mary?" He broke off, thrusting his fists on his hips and frowning. "Little Mary had a kid? What year is this again? No, wait, never you mind answering that. If you know the year, it ages you. Dates you. Saps the ol' willpower. I'm having none of that now."

"Mum's the word," Elle drawled. "But we're here for a reason, you know, not to take the tour."

"Yeah, yeah, I figured," Clyde replied, shaking his head and flapping a hand as if to say, *It's no matter.* "No one ever comes to visit ol' Clyde without hands open."

"We wouldn't have come if it weren't important," Wendy hurried to assure him.

Clyde shrugged. "It's the way of the world. My apologies—I've had a long night and you looked like someone I've seen recently.

Light's dim, shadows and all. Come inside, we'll sit and have a natter. But leave your blades. Arrows and whatnot, too. No weapons allowed in the Winchester Mansion."

"Will the twins be safe?" Wendy asked, gesturing to the muddy car.

"They've put in cameras all over," Clyde said, flicking his eyes at the tourist hut and then gesturing to the house. "The kids have to stay in the parking lot or the police will come, but it's safe enough."

"Maybe we should talk out here," Wendy said, eyeing the parking lot, looking for telltale flashes of white. The last Walker attack in her own home had left her edgy and unsure about every corner now.

"You stay where you like, I'm going inside," Clyde said dismissively. "Make up your mind, though, I can't take much time to talk. I've got work that needs doin' and the moonlight's a'wastin'. I can't work in the day anymore, not after they started up the basement tour." He shook his head. "How they expect a man to keep things runnin' smoothly when they're traipsin' all sorts of know-nothings through my coal chute is beyond me. Last train outta the station, leaving now."

"Fine," Wendy sighed. "Lead the way."

Wendy expected him to guide them to the carriage door entrance, tracing the path she vaguely remembered the main tour took but instead Clyde led them through the exit toward the gift shop. He stopped at the far door and Wendy prepared herself for the older man to show them some thin spot in the Never to walk through. Instead Clyde reached out and jiggled the door handle.

It opened.

"It's more peaceful back here," he explained, holding the door open as Lily edged through the open doorway with Piotr and Elle at her heels. "We'll go sit a spell in the dining room to chat."

"You . . . you're opening a door in the living world," Wendy said, pushing against a knickknack table to test the solidity of the area. Her hand went straight through.

"Yep," he replied. "And it's not easy work, girlie, so move your tuchus. These doors are touched all day, every day by excited, spooked folks. They're heavy."

Wendy slid through the opening and turned, staring amazed as the fire door wheezed closed behind them.

"Since management changed hands, all the opening and closing is driving those security experts batty," Clyde said, not bothering to hide his amusement, as a thin red light began flashing in the gift shop overhead. "They've had four electricians out this month. The old guides and guards knew it's nothing, but the new team gets a guy out here at least once a night to check on me, make sure I'm not a thief. I was feeling ornery earlier tonight and set off the alarm three times movin' about. Those security folk got tired of chasin' ghosts and ain't coming back before dawn." He waved a hand at a dark spot on the wall; Wendy noted the camera mounted behind the mostly-wooden display panel. "What can I say? It passes the time."

Still chuckling to himself, Clyde led them through the back entrance of the gift shop and into a long, large room, paneled with wood from floor to ceiling and sectioned off with red velvet ropes. "Sit," he ordered, waving a hand at the ivory chaise against the far wall and the small dining table behind the ropes. "I've got things to check in here. You sit, I'll work, and we'll talk."

Wendy and Piotr rested on the chaise while Lily and Elle each chose seats at the table. Piotr's hand snaked out and gripped Wendy's, their fingers twining together in the space between them. Wendy shivered at his touch, the feeling of Piotr's calloused thumb running an idle circle along the sensitive flesh of her inner wrist, sending goose bumps up and down her spine.

Satisfied that the Riders were settled, Clyde moved to the fire-place and began examining the intricate tile around the edges of the mantle, running his hands expertly over the corners.

"This place has around forty-seven fireplaces," he lectured, kneeling down and poking his head into the well of the fireplace

examining the firebox. "Years of disuse means only about half of 'em work now but they still need to be kept nice for visitors. The missus would want it that way—she was a stickler for keeping things nice." Clyde pulled back. "There are good hiding spots around fireplaces," he said. "'Specially in this house. The missus liked her funny little details."

Satisfied with whatever he was looking for, Clyde lovingly patted the panel; it shifted, moving in the living lands under the pressure of his hand in the Never.

There was something hidden behind it.

"This is good workmanship," he said, catching her eye. "Solid. I laid some of these panels myself, though I spent most of my days toward the end working on those easy-step stairs for the missus' arthritis. She needed 'em and I wanted to make sure she could move around. You do what you can for those you love, those you respect, and if you love 'em enough, you keep on doin' even after they're gone." He paused, looking pointedly at Wendy. "You follow me?"

Nervously, Wendy licked her lips, that called-to-task feeling sitting heavily in her gut again. "Um, yes?"

Clyde looked at her hands clasped with Piotr's and sighed. "Maybe you do, maybe you don't. The point of the matter is that I'm no stranger to the Reapers—the good and the bad, yeah? Every family tree has a few rotten twigs and bug-eaten leaves, but there are big ol' branches that are not welcome here."

Wendy opened her mouth to ask if he meant her as well, but Piotr squeezed her hand hard and shook his head minutely. She stopped, waiting.

"Your momma—Mary, really?—came here with her sister a lot, growing up," Clyde continued, rubbing his hands against his overalls and leaning carefully against a the corner of the mantelpiece. "They'd sneak in after hours and wander the grounds, scaring off the animals. Good girls, Mary and Tracey. Twelve years apart but still thick as thieves, they were."

"You sound like you miss them," Wendy murmured.

"I'd be a fool to claim I didn't. It gets lonely out here, only hearin' from folks when they want something from you." Clyde scowled and pushed off the wall. "Elise, as I'm sure you've sussed out by now, has been sending girls 'round, making threats. Threats about you, about the Lady Walker. I don't like being meddled with. I don't like people coming into my missus' parlor making threats one minute and promises the next. Same fluff they're telling all the long-timers: big reward for bringing you in, bigger punishment for harboring you. It don't sit right with me."

"Oh," Wendy said weakly. "I . . . I didn't know."

"Did Elise promise you treasures if you turned Wendy in to her?" Lily asked, hands balling to fists atop the dining table. "Flesh of your own?"

"Mayhap," Clyde replied. "But don't fret. You've noticed by now that I can do what most ghosts can't. There's precious little the Reapers can give me that I can't get for myself with some effort and patience."

"They try anyway," Elle said, pitching her voice low and quiet. "They're persistent. They keep coming around, right?"

"That they do." He spit. "Patient as the grave, Reapers are. No matter though—I didn't like 'em much when I was alive and they'd come round to check up on my girls—sisters and daughter both. They had to make sure none of them showed that special 'spark,' didn't they? Never found it though, thankfully."

He paused, thoughtful. "I downright hate 'em now that I'm dead."

Wendy, startled, twisted to look at Piotr. He smiled thinly at her as if to say, *You heard that right. You and Clyde are distantly related.*

Clyde spotted the look; he hooked his thumbs in the straps of his overalls and then addressed Piotr directly. "Do you recollect me, comrade? Maybe remember seeing me around a time or two when I was alive, maybe after I died once or twice?"

Nodding, Piotr's lips twitched; he was hiding a smile. "I recall that you and I have met before."

Clyde tapped the wall brusquely. "Your memory's lost a few of those extra holes, then? Filled 'em up some?"

"Repaired," Piotr clarified. "Regenerated. Though they are still growing back."

Wendy frowned; was she the only one who saw the flicker in Piotr's expression just then?

"Reaper do that for you?" Clyde sneered. "Elise?"

"Seeing as it was the Reapers that caused the damage in the first place, *net*, it was not. And even if she offered, I would not deal with Elise for *any* reward."

Clyde shook his head. "I sincerely doubt that, son. I really, really do."

"Then you do not know me as well as you think," Piotr replied evenly.

"Or you don't know the situation as well as *you* think," Clyde retorted, idly rubbing his knuckles against his chin.

"You know why we are here," Lily said, rising from the table and approaching Clyde. She held out her hands, placating the older man, and smiled. "No Reaper or Walker can reign here, where the walls are as thick in the living lands as in the Never. Wendy would be safe here."

"Yes miss, I know I look a bit of a bumpkin, but I'm not dumb." Clyde scratched his chin and sighed. "This pains me to tell you, kiddies, but I can't help you. I can't and even if I could, I won't."

Dismayed, Wendy bit her lip. She could feel the angry tears burning at the corners of her eyes but she'd be damned if she let Clyde see her cry at his decision.

"Why not?" Elle demanded, leaping up from the table. "It's just for a day. It ain't like us staying here a peck will bother the visitors. We can have 'em out of your hair by nightfall, soon as we find a better place to stash 'em. No fuss, no muss, no bother."

"Lotta bother if the Reapers find out," Clyde pointed out mildly.

"Seeing as how I promised Elise's ambassador that I wouldn't let you stay, just earlier tonight." He shook his head. "In the right light she looks just like you, girlie. Pretty little thing if you don't mind that crazy colored hair and all those tat—"

"Stop!" Piotr demanded, quietly furious. "Despite your hatred of them, you have met with Wendy's family? Why?"

"Sometimes there are important reasons that trump a man's personal vendettas," Clyde said simply. "You've been around forever, kid. Surely you know that."

"I cannot imagine any cause that would allow you to resign your moral mores in their favor," Lily said coolly.

Clyde pushed a thumb against the brim of his hat, scratching his brow. "You have to think long term. Elise's only one woman and an old one at that. She won't last much longer, and I like the idea of vanishing into nothing even less than I like the idea of Elise bossing around the ghosties of the Never."

"Whoah, whoah, wait up a second," Wendy snapped. "'Vanishing into nothing'? She threatened to reap you if you didn't listen? Because you have to know this place like the back of your hand. I doubt she'd even be able to find you here, much less—"

Clyde's laugher cut her off. "Reap me? No, no, nothing like that! You think I'm scared of the likes of Elise? Nothin' can touch me here, on my missus' land. The Reapers couldn't find me if they spent a hundred nights trying."

"Then why—"

"You been up city-way lately?" Clyde asked, all business now, arms crossed over his chest. "You feel those tremors?"

Piotr and Wendy shared a tight glance. How much had the Reapers told Clyde?

He spotted their look and shook his head. "Foolish, all of you. I'm talking about that great big hole in the horizon, kiddies. The one spitting out nasties and quakes so big I can feel 'em all the way down here."

"We've seen it," Wendy said grimly. "But we don't know for a fact that every quake is a new creature. That's just conjecture."

"Guessin' or not, girl, if that rift opened further then we'd be up to our eyeballs in monsters! Creatures from the deep. Nasties. And the Lady Walker aims to set 'em all free." Clyde glared and Wendy belatedly realized that a glint of red was glowing in the reflection of the mirror above the mantle. Wendy glanced over her shoulder, trying to make out where the red was coming from, when the red *blinked* at her.

Following the direction Wendy was looking, Clyde flicked an angry glance at the mirror and frowned. "Used to be you needed a special spot for a nastie-beastie to mosey on through. A place of power. Now all you need is a cracked mirror and some sad soul as a sacrifice. You're a Reaper, girl, can't you feel how *thin* the Never's getting in places? How worn out? Can't you sense the spaces in between now?"

"I . . . I don't know. Maybe. Sort of," Wendy said, frowning at the mirror. Surely that blink was her imagination . . . wasn't it? Did Clyde see what she was seeing?

"San Francisco . . . this land . . . it was always a weak spot in the Never," Clyde said. "Stop for two seconds, girl, and even the likes of you can feel it. There are holes here, tiny cracks into something like the one above the ocean, the space between the worlds, and if you look close enough, the webs are causing more and more damage. Who knows how much longer it's all gonna hold?"

"Is this why you agreed to work with the Reapers?" Lily asked archly, flicking a warning glance at Elle and Piotr. "You fear these monsters from the deep?"

"You would too, if you had a lick of sense," Clyde growled. "Riders. Useless, the lot of you." Clyde looked as if he might spit for a moment, but recalled at last instant that they were in his beloved Sarah Winchester's dining room. He refrained.

"The longer the Lady Walker is left to roam around, the worse

this is going to get. The hole is only going to get bigger. More beasties are going to wriggle their way through, because she's doing everything she can to pry that hole as big as it's going to get."

Wendy bit her lip. She didn't want to remember the awful way Ada's body had twisted, the nasty ripping sound of her body rearranging itself. "Those creatures . . . I talked to the Lady Walker. She said that all she needed now was a soul and a creature could be summoned."

"She wasn't lying. There are still plenty of regular-Joe spirits up in the city to munch on. People die every day, kiddies, especially with weather like this to hobble the homeless. There's no shortage of fresh-off-the-boat souls wandering around." Clyde grimaced. "The more will a spirit has, the nastier the beastie ends up. I even heard tell that they don't have to eat a ghost. They can," his voice dropped to a nervous, gossipy whisper, "take over your body. *Invade* you, turn you inside out and wear you like an ugly sweater."

Wendy closed her eyes, the sound of Ada being torn apart from the inside out rippling through her memory. "Yeah. You've got that right."

"There are no Lost in town but one," Lily said softly, patting Wendy on the shoulder. "We have taken the buik of their meal from—"

"You didn't make off with all the Walkers, did you?" Clyde sneered. "I'm stuck here, but even I know that the Lady Walker has been promising the Walkers all sorts of goodies if they follow her for, oh, the past few weeks at least. Elise's been struggling to keep her Walkers on her side. Bribing them, I hear tell. Fixing their faces up and more with her Reaper tricks."

Wendy chewed her thumbnail nervously. "Bribing them?" She thought of the awful Walker with the handsome face and the neck-lace that fixed his flesh. Elise had sworn that she hadn't sent him, but Elise was known to lie, right? Or had the Walker waited until he'd gotten what he wanted out of her to go to Jane?

Who could she believe?

"Walkers-schmalkers. That can't be the only reason why you're so worried," Elle demanded of Clyde. "It's not like they're knocking on your door."

"Not tonight, no, but these things—like that spirit web—have a nasty way of spreading, if you catch my drift. Today the city, tomorrow they'll be sucking all the juice out of my gates." Clyde jerked his thumb toward the end of the formal dining room and the elaborate archway leading to the rest of the house. "All the thirteen shades of pretty glass and spider web lovelies in the world can't keep that sort of ugliness out forever."

"How do you know all this? Did the Reapers bring you this news?" Lily demanded, slapping the table so that the ethereal teacups clattered in their saucers. "For surely you cannot trust everything they say."

"No, girl," Clyde sneered. "I know all this because this was Tracey's *plan*." He turned, meeting Wendy's eyes. "Your momma's too. They wanted to destroy the Never. They wanted to bring it all down."

CHAPTER EIGHTEEN

Jon yawned. He was so tired, he felt almost sick with it. Sleep had been hard coming but when he'd finally succumbed it had washed over him in a great wave. He didn't know what had woken him but Chel, in the passenger seat beside him, was snoring quietly, curled against the fogged up window. Despite his tender feelings over all the crap she'd said to him before, Jon was tempted to reach out and hold his sister's hand. Chel was spiky and cruel at times, but overall she meant well. She just didn't know how to handle people.

She didn't know how to handle him.

It was growing stuffy in the car. Taking care not to wake Chel, Jon unbuckled his belt and eased out of the driver's side, shutting the door behind him as gingerly as he could. It felt weird to be standing here in the orange light of the stuttering parking lot lamps high above, the winter breeze scudding litter across the parking lot and slapping his cheeks. Jon hunched further in his hoodie, hoping that the deep shadows of the hood would keep his face covered.

Did Wendy mean it, he wondered. Would she really drag them out to the middle of nowhere to camp out? It seemed sort of extreme-

Movement, flashing quickly across the street. Not in the Never, either. Here in the real world.

Jon froze. Was it a cop? A bum? San Jose wasn't a bad part of town, not exactly, but even tourist traps like the Winchester had pockets of unpleasant activity at this time of night.

Slowly, straining his eyesight to catch the movement again, Jon reached for the door handle.

With a slow, ponderous groan the back end of his car dipped down. The handle slipped away beneath his fingers.

Jon turned, neck creaking.

The creature, only inches away from his face, clicked its teeth in warning.

Clyde turned his back on Elle and Lily and strode to the wall again, this time pushing harder until, with a sharp click, the section of panel slid open, revealing a hole in the wall, dim and lined with cobwebs. "I can see you with those angry eyes but I ain't fibbing to you, girl. Your aunt wanted to end the Never and your momma agreed with her. They made a deal with the Lady Walker toward those ends."

"I don't believe you," Wendy said through numb lips. Her eyes felt painfully dry, her heart seemed to be thrumming in her chest. Carefully she lifted a hand and marveled how the shock of what he'd said had actually affected her spiritual form. She was definitely more translucent. The Riders were right; willpower mattered a great deal in the Never.

"Why?" Elle demanded. "Why would she do that?"

"Revenge," Clyde said offhandedly, squinting into the darkness. "Elise made Mary kill her sister. Anyone's bound to be a touch tetchy after all that."

Beside her, Piotr froze. Wendy, slowly, turned and faced him. She could feel the strangest sensation—it was as if blood she didn't have was draining from her face, leaving her not-flesh cold and tingling. "I'm sorry?"

"Didn't you know?" Clyde asked, cocking an eyebrow and looking between Wendy and Piotr. "Mary was forced to kill her own sister for breaking the rules."

"You didn't tell me that," Wendy said slowly to Piotr. She slid away from his side on the couch, trying to wrap her mind around the idea and doing her best to squash the hot, betrayed feeling burning in her chest. "Mom . . . Mom wouldn't have . . ."

"She did," Piotr confirmed, hands open and beseeching at his sides. "After the deed was done Mary was filled with great fury. Such powerful emotions drew me to her like a . . . like a spirit to the Lightbringer. A moth to the flame, seeking and yearning the heat even as it burns."

Wendy turned her face away, flushing in anger and dismay. Her hands balled into fists on her knees and her entire body was trembling; Wendy felt pulled taut as piano wire—one poke and she'd vibrate to pieces. "Tell me."

Clyde shrugged, as if to say: *You asked for it.*

"Back then, Elise was brutal because she liked being on top. Forget the Good Work, forget giving up seconds of her own life to send others on—Elise reaped only when she had to in order to keep from burning up the way you folks do. Make no mistake, Elise was in it for the profit. The Never was just a way for her to make more moolah, to further the family cause. And she was good at it back then. Making money, making connections, hand over fist."

"Until?" Wendy asked.

"Until your grandma started thinking that maybe using the dead like that wasn't such a good idea. That maybe those old books they make the young'uns read were saying more than just the how of it, like some sort of instruction manual. That maybe there was a history, a purpose there."

"So Mary's momma got high-minded," Elle drawled. "I bet fancypants cousin Elise didn't like that one bit."

"No miss, Elise didn't. When it was suggested that maybe they needed more girls out there doing the Good Work, not fewer, that maybe they ought to be giving them the Good Cup to drink sooner rather than later . . . that they, as a family, had a job to do and that maybe they weren't doing it the way they were supposed to . . . well, Elise took to the idea of reaping for just reaping's sake, for no profit and no glory for the family, like a duck to lava."

Wendy frowned. "What about Nana Moses?" Clyde gave her a

funny look so she clarified, "I'm sorry, what about Elise's mom, Alonya? What did she have to say about Elise and my grandma getting into it? I know my grandma was her niece and Elise was her daughter but I've met Nana . . . Alonya and she didn't seem too thrilled with Elise in general. Whose side did she take?"

"Alonya? Neither. No time. She was back east, in New York, when the roosters came home to roost. Elise was running the show on this coast and Alonya was forever away. By time Alonya found out, the deed was long since done."

Wendy felt her stomach sink. "How'd Elise make it fly with the other Reapers? How'd she get them to go along with it? With flat out murder like that?"

Elle snorted. "What would you do if you were in Elise's shoes? Elise runs your clan like a gaggle of goodfellas. I bet she found out your grandma's biggest, closest secret and used it to beat her nosy cousin down."

"Mary told me once that her mother was a natural," Piotr said softly, suddenly, rubbing his temples and grimacing. Wendy didn't need to ask him what was going on; Piotr was remembering. "That talented blood all tangled and twisted together; her momma's parents—your great-grandparents—were third or fourth cousins, twice removed or some odd thing. They didn't know it when they got married since the families were far enough apart to not concern them—no deformed babies—but their blood was still close enough to make *interesting* connections."

Clyde grinned. "Got it in one, comrade. There are a lot of people in this town with a touch of Reaper blood in them, not even counting the entire families who were discarded from the main family tree for little reasons."

"Like you," Piotr said.

Clyde sneered. "My own grandma was the last Reaper in my line. When the family ran low on good Reapers they sure came around to check my ladies over. Eventually, when my girls turned

out to be duds, they dropped my branch from the family tree completely. There are a whole lot of people in this state with a drop or two of Reaper blood in 'em, most who never have a clue. Walking around, possibly spotting ghosts every now and then, when drunk or drugged but they pass it off as hallucinations. Nothing to see here but the rotting dead. Move along."

Jon hadn't gotten to see much of Wendy's fight with the creature before, so he was startled by how vivid the creature was up close. It was like something out of a horror movie, too ugly to be real, except for the fact that it crouched on the hood and roof of his dad's car, denting the metal with sharp pincer-like hands and drooling wet ropes of slimy substance that was flecked with pink foam and tiny, writhing bugs.

Once, he realized, it had been a gang member. The tattered remains of a shredded plaid shirt hovered somewhere near what Jon could only assume was the beast's waist. Torn jeans dragged behind.

Gagging, Jon staggered back a step, then another.

The creature, clicking, followed him.

"You're not real," Jon told it. His entire body was shaking, shivering like the last leaf clinging to its branch in the face of an oncoming storm. "You're . . . you're not supposed to exist in the real world."

The creature chuckled, dark and wet, as broken sounds wrenched from its throat. It took Jon several seconds to realize that it was trying to speak.

"Rrrreeee-prrr. Rrrreeeeeeeeee-prrrrr."

Reaper.

"Luuuuuddddeeeee Waaaaalllllhhhheeeerrr sssshhhpppeeeekkkk toooo uuuuuuu."

Lady Walker speak to you.

"The Lady Walker wants to talk to me? *The* Lady Walker?" Jon swallowed. "I don't have any say in the matter, huh?"

The creature slowly shook its head, slobber sloughing off its

shredded face and sinking into small pools in the parking lot. A hand dropped down on Jon's shoulder and he barely bit back a scream.

"Boo."

Wendy knew her mouth was hanging open. Clyde chuckled and gestured for her to close it.

"I don't know why you're surprised, girl. There might be a whole lot more naturals wandering around, like your grandma, if the Reapers kept a closer tab on them," Clyde explained gently. "But seeing death with your own eyes without being . . . altered . . . well, it doesn't happen that often. It takes a specific moment, a precise instant, when you have to be watching a soul leave the body for that natural instinct to be roused. And that just isn't that common unless you're planning for it, maybe working at a deathbed. Lotta Reaper girls worked as nurses in emergency wards back then."

"So my grandmother hid her natural status for years . . ." Wendy whispered, "but Elise still found out. And she made my mom do the deed. To kill her. Her own mother."

"Your *babushka* died raving in the hospital, burning with immense fever," Piotr said, reaching out and taking Wendy's hand. She shook it free and glared at him, not missing the tight, worried glance Lily and Elle shared at the exchange.

"Well that sounds familiar," Elle grunted, crossing her arms over her chest. "Wendy, baby, have I mentioned recently how much I do not love your family?"

"What I don't get is, *why* did Mom do it?" Wendy ground out after several seconds. "Why?"

"The choice was taken from her," Piotr reminded her gently. "It is the law of your kind to kill the natural. Mary was just following orders, *da*? Just doing her duty to her family. She was all tangled up inside—Mary trusted Elise, their *de facto* leader, and felt betrayed by her own mother."

"He's hit it on the head," Clyde agreed. "Just a kid trying to do an adult's job."

"That's utter and complete crap," Wendy said bitterly. "I'm the same age my mom was back then, right? I'd never, ever have turned her in. I'd have . . . I don't know, done something. Protected her or something! Found out why they thought she was such a danger, not just taken their word for it! You have to ask questions, you have to think for yourself! Because you don't do that to family! It's so important that you watch—"

Wendy faltered as her mother's words, words pounded into her year after year during their training sessions, hung on the edge of her tongue.

"You watch your back," she finished lamely, cheeks blazing, remembering all the times her mother had shoved those very words in her face. "You ask the right questions."

Clyde raised an eyebrow. "Well, I guess she raised you a touch smarter than her mother raised her then, huh?"

"How did Tracey die?" Wendy asked dully, not rising to Clyde's bait. The shame curled in her gut. She'd been so *angry* at her mother for all that time, so certain that her mom had no clue what it really was like to be this way. She had it easy, she had training, Wendy had thought at the time. She'd been irritated that no matter what she did, Mary never believed that Wendy understood where she was coming from, what lessons she was trying to impart.

Now, with the fact that Wendy really hadn't had a clue staring her in the face, Wendy felt small and tired and very, very sad. "How did my mother kill her?"

"Same way," Clyde said, almost offhandedly, though it was obvious that being so cavalier about the answer hurt him. "After their momma died, Tracey started talking with ghosts instead of reaping them, including reading old books and stories so she could hunt down the Lady Walker. Tracey had a plan to oust Elise."

"And Elise had spies galore. She found out."

"Indeed she did." Clyde snapped his fingers. "Pulled up the ol' rule book and waved it around at everyone who'd listen, talking about civil war among the family, about how Tracey was a traitor to their blood, to the Good Workers and the Good Work, yada yada yada, plotting with the Council to overthrow the Reapers, so on and so forth."

"But that was a lie."

"Oh no, it was God's honest truth," Clyde sighed. "After her mother was put down, Tracey had had enough of Elise and she didn't care who knew it. Feisty little thing. Mary tried her best to cover for her big sister but Tracey pissed off Elise one too many times. The second time around Mary fought the orders from up high tooth and nail, but Tracey demanded that Mary kill her."

"Why would she do that?" Elle asked, interested despite herself.

"It was either that or they both died, yeah? Her execution was one of the only times I ever left the mansion. I hitched a ride and I . . . I was there, hiding, watching it all. They had Reapers all around ready to force her but Tracey voluntarily knelt down in that circle of theirs, threw her arms wide, and bared her belly. Just waited for her little sister to rip her Light out whole. Kept her eyes open the entire time."

"This was up at Fort Funston?" Wendy whispered.

"Yes'm. They've got a shed out there, part of—"

"I know it," Wendy said sharply, forcing down the sick feeling in her gut, remembering how, only the day before, she'd been examining the faded circle on the floor and the gull excrement splattered on the walls. The fact that Wendy'd stripped down and trained in the same spot where her mother killed her aunt was disconcerting and sickening.

"But how . . . how, after all that, did Mom manage to convince them to let her take control of the Bay Area by herself?" Wendy wondered, shaking free the memory of Jane and Emma gauging her naked body, how they'd discussed her tattoos and what she'd need to become more like them. "I mean, it's ridiculous that after both her

mother and her sister were executed that Elise'd go for something like that."

Clyde looked at Piotr and smirking knowingly. "That truly is a question for the ages, huh comrade? How does such a black sheep get her way despite all the death that followed her like a plague?"

Piotr frowned. "I do not follow your meaning."

"Touched any living folk lately?" Clyde asked, holding up a hand and flexing his fingers. "Maybe went in a little deeper than you normally would? You do remember doing that, don't you, comrade?"

"What the hell!" Jon said, voice shaking roughly. He spun back to the beast. It was gone. "What the HELL, Chel!"

"Dreamscape, dummy," Chel said, patting Jon familiarly on the arm. "Wendy told us about 'em, remember? I'm sorry about the beastie, but I couldn't resist when I realized that we were sharing a dreamscape."

Jon frowned. "Wendy said it wasn't easy to build a dreamscape. How'd you manage it? Wait, are we still asleep?"

"Yeah, we are." Her voice dipped as Chel, glancing around, drew Jon closer and whispered. "But here's the thing . . . I didn't make this place. I woke up here just like you."

"That's because *I* made it," murmured a quiet voice from behind them. The twins turned as a woman, white-haired and slim, stepped out from behind the car. She was regal, playing with a thin strand of pearls, and the faded, intricate ink at her neck and wrists spoke louder than any words. *Reaper*.

"You two are quite difficult to trace, by the way," she added. "Your signatures are much more subtle than Winifred's. She . . . blazes."

"You're Elise," Jon said, fear nailing his feet to the earth. He knew that he ought to do something, spit in her face possibly, but the woman radiated self-assurance and poise. She held all the terrible sway of the unknown.

"You are correct," Elise said. "Look, my time with you is short. You two are barely napping, we must make this—"

Chel, unburdened with Jon's passive nature, punched Elise in the face.

Elise stumbled back, her hands pressed to her freely flowing nose, eyes wide with shock. "You . . . you hit me!"

"That is for putting my sister in the hospital, you bitch," Chel said, shaking her hand. "Come another step closer and I'll tack on chasing us away from San Ramon."

"She—and now you, apparently—must be kept aside, away from the machinations of the Lady Walker," Elise growled, her voice muffled from behind her hands. "You cannot expect me to leave souls of such unbridled power just *laying around* where anyone could access you!"

"Speaking as one of the, you know, *owners* of the souls, you can shove it, lady," Jon protested sharply. "People aren't *things*. You can't just put us where you want us and expect us to be there when you get back. We're not one of your bullied ghosts, Elise. We're—and I really hate saying this—supposed to be *family*. You don't do this to family."

"I am the matriarch of the Reapers!" Elise snapped, dropping her hands and exposing a clear and untouched face. "If you wish to learn to control your powers, to not begin burning yourself up from the inside, then you need us! You need our help. You need *my* help, to live a long and productive life! All you have to do is follow orders! Is it really that onerous, that difficult?"

"If those orders are coming from you," Chel pointed out dryly, "yeah, it really is that hard. We weren't raised in your little death-cult, lady. We want nothing from you."

Elise stilled. "Fine. You have a point. Perhaps you have no need of the Reapers yet. However—"

"However nothing," Chel growled, crossing her arms over her chest. Jon was startled to realize that the pavement at her feet was

starting to crackle and crack in ever widening circles. "You're in *our* dream, Elise. What do you want? Really want?"

"A trade," Elise said, pursing her lips as she regarded them steadily. "If your sister won't treat with me, perhaps you will. For all our sakes."

Chel's reply cracked, whip-like, across the space between them, setting up echoes that hurt Jon's ears. "No deal."

Elise scowled and Jon realized why Wendy shifted uneasily whenever she spoke of Elise's displeasure. Her expression promised terrible pain for any who would thwart her. "You haven't listened to—"

"Don't want to. If Wendy won't deal with you, then you need to get lost. And now. Before I try to rearrange your face for real." Chel turned her back on Elise.

"Not even if I will free your friend Edward from his bonds?" Her voice dipped low and Jon shivered at how the words seemed to ooze their way around them, pulling them close. "He's dying. I was at his body only an hour ago. He will not last the night. It's truly a miracle he's lasted this long, you know. Someone has obviously been helping him. Giving him their will."

"And whose fault is that?" Jon was surprised. He hadn't meant the words to blurt out like that but there they were, hanging in the air, accusing and pointed. *Oh well*, he thought, *in for a penny*. "Get out," he demanded. The world around them trembled and Jon remembered Wendy telling him that the original dreamer had the real power in a dreamscape. Jon raised his voice. "Get out." The pavement shook harder. "Get out, Elise! This is my dream! You're not welcome here! GET OUT!"

Jon shoved his hand forward, demanding the Light, cupping all his anger and pain in a ball between his hands. It filled his palms like hot putty before flaring into a blaze of flame so fierce it blinded him. Hands ablaze, Jon knew he had to get rid of the Light before it scarred him.

He blindly blasted at Elise's feet.

Or it would have. When the smoke cleared the pavement was a melted pile of tar and goo, but Elise . . .

Elise was gone.

None of them moved. Piotr's trick with the ER doctor was still too fresh in their memories, and the fact that Clyde apparently knew Piotr was capable of swaying the living with a touch was disconcerting for all of them. Wendy stared at Clyde, unblinking, wondering just why this man was here, at the Winchester, instead of on the Council and running the city. He seemed to have an innate understanding of the way the Reapers worked that Frank didn't. Why was he *here* instead of *there*?

Piotr cleared his throat. "You are suggesting that I—"

"Suggesting nothing. Stating a fact."

"Is that possible?" Lily asked, playing with the teacup, running the pads of her fingers along the rim. "For Piotr to sway a Reaper in that manner?"

"Sure it is!" Clyde said jovially. "Mary even bragged to me about it. She made sure that Elise was too busy to notice Piotr sneaking up on her. Afterward Elise had half the family packed and gone within the week, and the other half on their way by time the moon had waned. When a few decided to protest, Mary already had the city sewn up tight, didn't she?"

"Like a shroud," Piotr agreed, holding out his hands and frowning at his extended fingers. "I have lost so much," he murmured in a voice so low that Wendy had to strain to hear him. "So much that I am still recalling, relearning, layers and layers of memory that wash upon me in moments, unexpected and often unwanted but still . . . still needed. And I fear that I am running out of time to discover the rest."

"Always so impatient, Piotr! Your recollections will return," Lily assured Piotr firmly, reaching forward and brushing a hand

across his cheek, eyes warm and wise. The gesture was so comforting
and kind that Wendy wasn't jealous; her worries over Lily's friendship with Piotr seemed shallow and petty now in the face of that
instant, intimate understanding. "They will come in time. Abide
until then."

Clyde turned back to the filthy hole in the wall and reached
inside. "Mary left this here a few years back. She said I'd know when
it was time to let it go," Clyde said, drawing back. When he opened
his hand a thin chain tumbled from his palm, catching the dim light
and glittering in the faint security lights of the Never. A key dangled from the chain.

"What is it?" Wendy asked. For some reason the sight of the key
was setting warnings off in her head.

"Nothing much, just a key," Clyde said, but he was grinning. "I
hear tell it opens a door."

"Truly, for that is the nature of keys," Lily said dryly. Elle
snickered.

Clyde chuckled. "You know what, girl? I like you. You've got
spunk." He cleared his throat and spun the chain so the key swung
wildly on the end. "Fine, fine. This key opens up a door out on Russian
Hill. Kind of hard for you to make your way there now, I understand,
what with the spirit web forest and all, but if you can find the door it
goes to, well, there might be some sort of reward in it."

Piotr shook his head. "We care not for rewards. That is not our
goal."

"Depends on the reward, don't it?" Clyde said, winking, before
twisting back to the panel and rifling again in the hole. After a
moment he pulled out a plain, wood-handled knife. Wendy squinted
and could make out that the weapon existed both in the Never and
the living lands. "There's also this. Little knick-knack that found its
way down my branch of the family ages ago. I probably should've
passed it back to the current branch, but screw 'em. My grandma left
it to me. It was mine."

Lily straightened, cocking her head as he held the blade up, glinting in the security lights. Clyde caught the movement; he smirked at Lily and held out the knife. "Go on, girl. Take it. It's a funny little trinket, yeah? It'll be solid for you just as it's solid for me."

Frowning, Lily took the knife from him, holding it up and out as she examined it so that Wendy, leaning forward, could get a closer look. It looked like a basic knife, nothing more, a tarnished blade and wooden handle with no fancy carving or intricate knots to indicate its origin. When Wendy sat back, sharing a puzzled look with Lily, Lily then ran a finger along the dull edge and said, "Even though it can be wielded in the living lands, this knife is still worse than useless to us. What is the point? Please, elaborate."

"Who knows? The Reaper with the funny hair was sure interested in that key, though. Kind of demanding little thing. I don't cotton to little girls ordering me around, mind, but she knew her history right enough."

"Funny hair?" Wendy asked. It was the second time Clyde had mentioned the Reaper's hair. "What was funny about it?"

"The color." Chuckling, Clyde shook his head. "I see some strange ones come through this place ever day but her hair was bluer than berries and bonnets, m'dear. Bluer than a summer sky."

CHAPTER NINETEEN

"**J**ane," Wendy groaned, burying her face in her hands. "God, she gets around."

"God ain't got nothing to do with it, kid. I told her to go to hell." Clyde tossed the key and chain to Wendy, who reflexively caught it and stuffed the chain in a pocket.

"Did she?" Lily asked, grinning and rolling the handle of the knife in her palms. Wendy was glad Lily was testing its weight; if any of them could make magic with a blade it'd be Lily. It made her feel better to know Lily had Piotr's back with such a weapon. It eased Wendy's mind.

"She left pretty quickly, at that. And now, kiddies, our time is done. I have to make sure all the holes in the property are nice and closed. I don't want any Walkers wandering in. Especially now that the Lady Walker is out and about."

Elle patted her pincurls primly, sneering, "Well maybe if you rethought your 'not letting us stay' stance, you wouldn't have that problem, huh? Wendy here might be temporarily neutered, but her kid sister and brother are both as natural as blooming blossoms now. Her kid sister took out one of those creatures all by herself not two hours ago! Food for thought, old man. You should let them stay."

"Oh really? That *is* interesting news," Jane said, stepping from the hallway leading into the dining room with a dark, vicious smile. She sinuously strode forward, tilting her head forward so that her hair fell across her forehead, obscuring her eyes. "I didn't have proof before—just a hunch—and look, it paid off! A whole *family* of blood traitors! Goody!"

"Oh lovely," Elle said, sliding to her feet with the grace of a dancer, "the bitch returneth."

Wendy stood also, mimicking Elle's movements. Together they squared their shoulders and circled the Reaper, attempting to hem her in. If their positioning bothered her, Jane didn't let it show. Rolling her eyes at Wendy, Jane rested one fist on her hip, her artistically shredded shirt swaying with the motion. Wendy tried to ignore the way the motion exposed the intricate swirl of tattoos that swirled all the way to her navel. Some were puffy and fresh-inked, the new scabs cracking around the edges. "Such bravado! Such gall. Do you think that I'd bother with the likes of you people if I was worried that you could hurt me?"

"What the *hell* are you doing here, Jane?" Wendy demanded, glaring at Clyde.

"Don't look at me," he said, holding up his hands and frowning at Jane. "Last I checked, this piece of baggage was high-tailing it out of here."

"I had a feeling," Jane said to Clyde, "when I realized my timing was off and you genuinely hadn't seen Wendy. Well, I thought that maybe our fugitives here might come visit you after I'd left. Plus, how many chances does a girl get to tour this place at night? It's spooky as he—" Jane yelped and dodged backward as Lily, taking advantage of the lull in the conversation darted forward and slashed at Jane's throat.

"Oh, you skank," Jane cried, massaging her neck. "You scratched me! Barely but still . . ." Then she frowned deeply, probing her skin with the tips of her fingers. "Wait a sec . . . *how* did you—"

"Cutting you is the point," Lily said and spun left, kicking out and forcing Jane back a step.

Jane, scowling now, balled her fists and the Light began to gather in her palms. "Oh it's on like Donkey Kong. Come on, let's see what you got."

"Stab her, Lily!" Piotr ordered. "In the shoulder, in the arm . . . where doesn't matter, but cut her!"

Moving like liquid, Lily shot forward in a precisely timed roll and sliced across Jane's forearm as she came up and bounded to her feet. Jane yelped and the Light blazed for a brief moment before dying down.

"What the . . . oh you mother—"

The Light blazed again . . . and petered out, the normally brilliant glow only a faint ember at the tips of her fingers. Jane shook her arm as the Light sputtered, expression swerving from annoyed to frightened to pissed all in a split second.

"What's happening?" Wendy demanded and Jane's lips curled back from her teeth and her eyes darkened. She was *furious*. "Piotr?"

"I recognize the blade now," Piotr explained, loud and insistent, grinning at Jane like a shark as he spoke. His hand was pressed flat against his chest again; Wendy could see the pain in his eyes. "I recognize it and know it for what it is. The effect will not last long, Lily! Press your advantage!"

Piotr didn't need to tell her twice. Spinning the blade expertly in one hand, Lily darted forward again and Jane, unable to call on her Light to lull Lily with a siren song, was forced to dodge again. Elle, smirking, reached to her shoulder for her arrows to help, only to find them gone. Wendy groaned; now she remembered that they'd all left the rest of their weapons out front on Clyde's orders.

"What happened?" Elle demanded of Piotr, edging toward the door and her weaponry, but unwilling to not watch Lily's fight. "What'd that thing do to her?"

"It's cut her off from her Light," Wendy said. "But how? Why?"

"How is for another day," Piotr said. "It matters not, you have my word on this. Why? It is a cursed thing, taken from the world by the Reapers to protect their own skin. A murderer's blade, it only works for a short time. However brief though it may be, that time is often enough." His hand reached up and brushed his shoulder.

"Pete, you know more than you're letting on," Elle grumbled.

"According to the Reapers, he always has," Clyde said, scowling at the way Lily and Jane circled one another and the way Wendy and Elle had flanked to the edges of the room. Jane wasn't giving as good as she got but she was managing to keep Lily from cutting her again. "Part of being unending and all that."

Suddenly Jane smiled and straightened.

Wendy knew that look.

"LILY!" she shouted, sprinting forward, "GET DOWN!"

The blast of dark Light was like inhaling ice. Wendy tried to scream and failed, feeling the cold roll over her in a freezing wave, the sheer intensity of it drawing the air from her lungs and flinging her back.

Spun around, Wendy's head cracked against the doorway. She tumbled to the floor and Jane's foot clipped through her face as Jane fled through the doorway. Across the room Clyde shoved open the door and Piotr and Elle ran through—Elle shouting for Jon to fetch her bow and Piotr shouting for Chel.

Wendy, catching her breath, forced herself to stagger to her feet as Lily, running fleetly and brandishing the knife, slid around Wendy and ran after Jane past glassed in rooms and doors, sprinting all the way to the grand ballroom.

Clyde, chasing Lily, shoved Wendy aside and shouted, "Don't break anything! DON'T BREAK ANYTHING!"

The ballroom was better lit than the dining room. The glinting lights reflected off the fresh-polished wooden floors and walls and ceiling even in the Never. Wendy, limping after Clyde, stumbled aside as Lily kicked out and Jane staggered back, nearly elbowing Wendy in the face. Wendy made a belated grab for Jane, willing to risk both the burning heat of the girl and the freezing cold of the dark Light, but Jane was too quick and twisted out of reach.

Dark Light. Dark Light.

Wiping the back of her hand across her mouth and wincing in

pain as her bruised and battered ribs reminded her that she still had a living, breathing body somewhere, Wendy tried to remember what little she knew about the dark Light. Emma had used it to weave the barrier around Wendy's Light. It was cold to the touch—colder than Piotr's embrace had ever been—and slippery. Before, Wendy had been able to pry open only the thinnest sliver between a section of dark Light and the normal weave she kept over her soul to protect herself . . . but the darkness had expanded to fill the gap she'd left.

That was it. That was all she knew.

Crap.

Jane, at least, seemed to be having difficulty controlling the dark Light. Her hands, glowing fiercely, were shaking, her expression was grim and tight. She flung an arm out and a ball of dark Light separated from her hand and flew across the room, pounding into Lily's chest and downing the lithe girl with a heavy thud.

Coughing harshly, Lily bounced to her feet and, brandishing the knife, advanced again, strafing left to pin Jane between the organ and the wall. Jane pushed forward and Lily leaned in, grabbing Jane by the back of her head and shoving down, yanking her knee into Jane's gut and her elbow into the back of Jane's neck.

Jane, stunned, side-staggered and fell to one hand and a knee, breathing harshly, her blue hair hanging in her face and obscuring her expression. Lily kicked her under the ribs and Jane jerked to the side, shoulder banging against the organ and sending up a discordant crash as her flailing arm slapped the keys. The knife whipped down and Jane rolled forward, sliding through Lily's legs at last second. Lily hissed in pain.

"It's wearing off," Wendy realized aloud. "Whatever that knife did to Jane, it's wearing off. CRAP."

Jane either heard Wendy, or had come to her same conclusion. Popping up from her roll and staggering as if punch-drunk, Jane gathered the dark Light in her palms once again and flung the balls of energy at Lily.

Clyde yelled as Lily dodged and the balls scoured a large black hole in the far side of the room, setting the Never ablaze with chilling, freezing blue-white fire. Stripping off his shirt, Clyde rushed to the blaze and pounded on the edges of it with the cloth, cussing at the top of his lungs as the blue-white blaze burned his palms.

It looks like the hole in the horizon, Wendy thought, squinting at the purpling edges of the hole. Staring too closely made her eyes water and ache and the cold thrumming from the rip in the Never was teeth-achingly intense. *Is that what the hole in the horizon is made of? Dark Light?*

A harsh grunt behind her brought Wendy back to the fight in a vivid burst. She spun on her heel as Clyde, fire smothered, pushed past her, growling under his breath.

"LILY!" Wendy yelled when Clyde, cursing, strode over to Jane. He reached for the Reaper's upper arm, grabbed her and spun her around. So enraged was he over the damage to the mansion that he didn't see the white glow at Jane's chest or the grin spreading across her face.

"LILY, MOVE!"

"You! You Reapers! You don't care about nothing important! NONE of you! You keep this up, young lady, and I'm going to— *HURK!*"

Clyde staggered back, gripping his chest, as Jane slowly pulled her spear of Light from the gaping hole she had made. He frowned and looked at the wound, fell to his knees, and burned to ash before their eyes.

"Awesome," Jane said and wet her lips. She was shaking heavily. "You two . . . you almost had me there." She held up both hands. "I . . . I wonder . . ." Light glowed in each palm—normal, silvery-white Light in her left and the dark Light in her right. "Oh yeah," Jane laughed. "That's the ticket."

Lily, growling, dove at Jane, and the retaliation as Jane let go with both barrels was blindingly fierce. Wendy screamed as Lily

jerked and went down, essence pouring freely from the corners of her mouth and her battered nose. Her eyes were already bruising, the left-hand side of her jaw swelling and purpling.

Jane strode up and grabbed Lily by the back of her blouse, yanking the spirit to her feet one-handed. No sooner had Lily's feet touched the ground than she shoved forward, arms and knife outstretched. Jane pinwheeled her arms backward, flailing slightly, and Lily snatched Jane by her shifting shirt, yanking back until Jane was off balance and stumbled forward.

Once she was sure Jane was firmly caught, Lily fell backward, using her momentum to drop into a roll and jerking Jane with her, pinioning her legs outward to jam Jane in the gut, flinging the Reaper up and over her back as Lily rolled to a kneeling crouch. Jane, flying high over Lily's head, slammed above the fireplace, cracking the mirror in both the Never and the real world.

Lily strode to Jane and lifted the knife high, prepared to stab down, when Jane's hand shot out and wrapped around Lily's long, sagging braid, loosened in the battle. Lily began stabbing and kicking, but was lifted by her hair and flung against the far wall. The Never was so dense here; rather than flying through the brick and mortar, Lily slammed hard against it, her head cracking against the corner of the organ.

"Lily, hang on!" Wendy shouted, skidding across the slick ballroom floor. Her feet went out from under her and she slid into the wall. In the distance she heard Piotr shouting and Elle cursing.

"Wendy . . . Wendy . . . run," moaned Lily. She slid the knife toward Wendy; it skidded across the polished floor and landed at Wendy's feet.

"No, I can't!" Wendy protested. Without thinking she knelt down and snatched up the knife.

"WENDY! RUN!" screamed Lily as Jane slipped completely into the Never, the Light blazing from her core. Wendy knew that Lily had no chance now; the siren song was sweet and clear, the Light

fierce and burning. If she stayed, Jane would go after Piotr and Elle next. She might call in reinforcements to attack Chel and Jon.

As the tendrils of Light stabbed Lily through, Wendy, weeping, turned tail and ran.

CHAPTER TWENTY

Wendy ran for the back door, skidding to a halt as she realized that Clyde had let them in and now Clyde was gone. How the hell was she supposed to get out?

Pounding on the door, Wendy shot a glance over her shoulder. It was like she was trapped in the middle of a horror movie. Wendy could hear Jane strolling around the corner behind her like a serial killer on the prowl, hunting for cheerleaders to kill.

"HELP!" she screamed, slamming her fists so hard against the door they went momentarily numb. "HELP! LET ME OUT!"

"Wendy!" yelled Piotr from the other side of the door. "Back away!"

Without questioning him, Wendy stumbled back. Very faintly she heard a tinkling noise and then a loud crash. Seconds later Chel shoved through the door and Wendy sprinted past her into the gift shop and from there into the parking lot. Behind her she heard Jane curse and her steps sped up; Jane ran after Wendy, but Chel was faster.

The door slammed behind them.

"GOGOGO!" Wendy snarled, not bothering to see if the others were following. Chel had broken a window out to enter the gift shop—Wendy dove through the opening with Piotr and Elle at her heels, Chel hurrying behind.

"Where's Lily?" Elle demanded. She'd fetched her weapons and had her bow ready to fire but Wendy would be damned if she waited around long enough for Elle to try and use them. Thankfully, Jon had the car already running; he waited in the driver's seat like a 20s wheelman, hunched over the steering wheel and ready to peel out.

"Gone," Wendy threw over her shoulder, running for the idling car. "Into the Light. Jane reaped her and Clyde. Get in the car, we have to boogie."

"No. NO!" Elle snarled. She turned on her heel and started storming back toward the building, but was stopped as Piotr, a few steps behind, dropped his shoulder and barreled into her midsection, lifting Elle up and back, flinging her through the car door and into the back seat. Wendy, perched at the end of the backseat, grabbed Elle by the shoulder so she couldn't squirm free. Piotr jumped in the backseat and bracketed her in; Elle, cursing loudly, was stuck.

The passenger side door slammed. Chel pounded on the dashboard. "Go!"

Jon didn't ask twice. He put pedal to the floorboards and they were off, swerving onto the street and speeding toward the highway as lightning forked overhead.

Wendy sighed in relief. Unless she busted out a priceless window or found another exit, Jane was trapped inside the Winchester Mystery House. Elise might be able to break Jane out of jail, but she'd still have some mighty fast talking to do—so far as the security cameras were concerned, Jane was the only person in the house. Every other participant, except for Chel busting out the window in the gift shop, was a spirit. Chel was wearing a hoodie and their dad's car was splattered all over with mud from maneuvering around the holes in the highway and driving in the soggier sections of the breakdown lane.

"I hope that bitch gets arrested," Wendy muttered. Beside her Elle was simultaneously crying and cursing, punching Piotr repeatedly in the arm and shoulder for not letting her turn back and demanding Jon turn the car around. She lunged for Wendy's door but Wendy was ready; she'd wrapped her hand in Elle's quiver-strap and yanked the flapper back to the seat. When Elle glared at her, Wendy shook her head.

"Don't try going through the trunk or floor," she said evenly.

"My grip's strong enough to keep you here, especially with Piotr as backup. If you try and go back there I'll sit on you."

Sniffing, Elle twisted away and buried her face in her hands. Her shoulders shook with silent sobs and Wendy ached for her.

"What happened?" Piotr asked.

"Jane's power came back. Lily sacrificed herself to get me out." Wendy's eyes were leaking; she swiped at them and sniffed. "Clyde was dumb. He tried to tell Jane off, got too close. She speared him clean through."

Piotr scowled. "If Jane dared attack Clyde, then we are in a great deal of trouble. Clyde was untouchable."

"Well, Jane didn't feel that way," Wendy retorted darkly.

"That Reaper better watch her step," Elle muttered. Tears were streaming down her furious, ferocious face. "The next time I lay eyes on her, I'm going to kill her."

Jon, guiding them onto the highway, jerked as he tried to stifle a yawn, and failed. Both he and Chel seemed edgy but Wendy was too overwhelmed by what had just gone down to question the twins on what had them twisted up. "Where to now?" His expression was drawn.

Elle opened her mouth but before she could say anything, Wendy leaned forward and said, "We're heading back up to the city. Leave the highway and take the back roads. Just in case we're on camera from breaking that window, we don't want to leave a trail."

Rubbing his eyes, Jon swerved; the front right wheel momentarily kissed the breakdown lane. "We are?"

"Yeah," Wendy said, fingering the dull knife uneasily. "We're going up to the spirit web forest."

"Why the hell do we want to do that?" Chel asked. "I mean, I can handle monsters, but—"

"Fabulous!" Elle said, eyes fierce with hatred. "I'd love to get my mitts on this Elise dame. No more Miss Nice Ghost."

"You're staying in the car," Wendy said, her tone brooking no

argument. "Jon, put the pedal to the metal. We don't have a lot of time here." The clock on the dashboard had to be wrong—there was no way that they'd only been in the Winchester for fifteen minutes. It felt like hours had passed, but if the clock was right then dawn was still at least a couple hours off. It was barely four-thirty.

"We'll see," Elle replied. "You can't be everywhere at once, Wendy, and you're not exactly the Lightbringer anymore. Until you figure out how to get your Light unlocked you're as weak as a babe in the woods."

The road was sparsely populated, but there were still a few other sets of headlights gleaming as they passed. Jon swerved slightly from sheer exhaustion as they reached the speed limit and then sped even faster.

"Be careful," Chel yawned, poking the radar detector before reclining her seat. "There are still a ton of cops out."

"I've got this," Jon snapped, irritated and half-turning in his seat to glare at Chel. "I might not be facing down nasty, twisted oogies from the deep but I can manage a car just fine! And I *don't* need to take the back roads, Wendy! I can handle myself! Don't tell me how to drive!"

As if to prove his point he stabbed a finger at the console and flipped a switch, switching from the radio to the mp3 player. Heavy metal started low, then Jon angrily spun the dial, ratcheting the sound from one to eleven.

"TURN IT DOWN!" Chel screamed.

"NO!" Jon yelled back. "YOU CAN'T ALWAYS BOSS ME AROUND, CHEL!"

Wendy thought about interceding between the twins but something told her to butt out. Jon and Chel loved each other deeply . . . deeply enough to tear into one another when they needed a release.

Obscured by the darkness and the noise, Wendy eased over Elle, trading places. Elle slid into the spot by the window and pulled her knees up to her chin, resting her head on her knees while the land-

scape flew by. A tear tracked down her cheek; Wendy began to reach out, to comfort Elle, but was stopped by Piotr's hand on her wrist, by his head shaking slightly.

The music was so deafening that when Piotr tugged Wendy close to try to talk, she had to make him speak into the cup of her ear to be heard.

"Let her be, Wendy," Piotr said. "If you try to ease Elle's pain at this time, she will grow enraged. When Elle is angry, upset, it is imperative to leave her be, to let her calm and center herself. Without Lily . . . this will be harder."

Wendy, reluctant, nodded and curled into Piotr's side, resting her head on his shoulder. He wrapped an arm around her and kissed her temple, rubbing his chin against the edge of her jaw and squeezing her fingers.

"This moment is almost nicer for being stolen," Piotr admitted. "I have hardly had any time to hold you."

"But Lily—"

She felt his arm tighten around her shoulder, felt the fine trembling of his fingers as Piotr drew her closer. "Yesterday . . . or the day before—I've lost track of time, to be honest—Lily and I fought. About you." He buried his nose in her hair and inhaled. Untangling their fingers and gently cupping Piotr's face, Wendy could feel the wetness sliding down his cheek.

Though Wendy hated to ask, she could sense that Piotr wanted to get this off his chest. "Why did you fight over me, Piotr?"

"Lily . . . Lily . . . was . . . a good friend."

Piotr wrapped his other arm around Wendy and hugged her tightly, speaking rapidly, his face buried in her curls. "She knew that I was being stubborn about you, about contacting you. She did her best to make me see reason, to guide me to the proper path of contacting you. Lily knew that I did not want to leave you. It made me a selfish person, I thought, to stay with you when we could not be together. Just being close to me was . . . is . . . dangerous. When you

are in your body we draw energy and will from one another but Lily thought that we could control ourselves. She was . . . disappointed in my choices and the reasons I offered to back my decisions."

Wendy chuckled damply. "That sounds like Lily. Faith for miles."

"I already miss her," Piotr admitted, voice trembling. "Was it . . . was she . . . how did she . . ."

"She fought to the very end," Wendy replied. She bit her lip, troubled. "Are you sure you want to hear the details of how she died?"

"I owe this to Lily," Piotr said simply. "After so many centuries of friendship I must honor her by hearing the tale of her end."

"She and Jane were—"

The car swerved as Jon slammed on the breaks. Then it swerved again, left, right, left, the tires screaming on the interstate. Elle, beside the window, was yelling something that Wendy couldn't make out over the blaring music. Wendy shoved forward halfway through Jon's torso and halfway through the emergency brake, meaning to grab the steering wheel and help guide Jon, to keep him from overcorrecting, but her hand went right through it.

"WHERE IS IT?" Jon screamed, his voice cracking in Wendy's ear as he struggled with the wheel. "WHERE'D IT GO? SHIT SHIT SHIT SHIT FUUUUUCK!"

Next to them, Chel had grabbed the handle over the passenger door, her other hand jammed out and shoved against the glove compartment. The loose corner cracked open under the force of her fist, some of the change that had gathered at the bottom of the compartment spilling out and showering Chel's knees in a rain of silver and copper.

"NO! NO! NOT AGAIN!" Wendy screamed as the car swerved again, the front wheels hitting a patch of black ice and spinning out, flinging them into an uncontrolled spin on the 101. Wendy spied the twisted shape of the creature galloping down the highway beside them as the vehicle spun and spun. Then they hit the divider and the car was airborne. Grabbing Piotr, Wendy closed her eyes.

Silence.

CHAPTER TWENTY-ONE

The winter water was ice cold.

Wendy surfaced, gasping and treading water, as the waves slapped her harshly, the riptide sucking at her feet. On the beach a white figure stood bathed in light, holding a lantern high as the wind howled and screamed.

Above the hole in the sky was devouring the moon.

"I'm dreaming. I have to be," Wendy said and a wave slammed into her, cutting her off and shoving her roughly under the frothing chill. Wendy struggled to the surface and, keeping the shore to her left, set out parallel to the beach, swimming with all her might.

Wendy didn't know how long she swam but when she finally dragged herself, coughing and sputtering, onto the shore the moon was only a thin sliver in the sky, the stars were purple and bright, and being pulled into the gaping wound in the heavens. The stars were exploding like fireworks across the cup of night.

Spitting the filthy saltwater onto the rocky shore, Wendy lay on the damp sand and, for one brief moment, prayed. She wasn't a religious person—being the Lightbringer for so long had stripped her from all desires to follow any kind of deity—but she knew she needed the guidance, even if only for a few minutes.

"I know I'm not really into that whole 'creator' thing, but if you're really up there," she murmured to the dissolving sky, "a little help would be appreciated. Thanks. Amen or something."

There was a discreet little cough from behind Wendy as pale

white light washed across the rocks by her outstretched hand. Wendy sighed and, squelching, rolled over.

"Hello Elise. Long time no want to punch in the face."

"I am having a most productive nap, Winifred," Elise said, settling on a convenient piece of driftwood Wendy didn't recall being there moments before. "How about yourself?"

"I think I've been knocked unconscious," Wendy said conversationally. She wasn't sure why she did so, but she added, "Nasty beastie chasing us."

"Hmm," Elise said noncommittally. "I wonder, have you managed to catch up with my granddaughter yet?"

"Which one? The one who was hauled out on a stretcher or the one who's been trying to kill me for shits-n-giggles?"

"Jane, of course." Elise held out a hand and Wendy marveled at the shining rings that appeared and disappeared from the ether as Elise skillfully shaped the dreamscape around her body. Around her neck a lovely golden necklace appeared and reappeared, flickering in the light. "I am quite aware that you have nothing whatsoever to do with Emma's collapse. It was, however, a convenient excuse. I did warn you that I intended to bring you to heel, Winifred, in any way necessary."

"How generous of you to tell me of the screwing me over up front," Wendy replied snidely. "As for Jane, yeah I saw her. Of course the last time I saw her, I'm fairly sure several strong security systems did too. So she might be busy for a while."

Elise eyed her for a long time before nodding once, thoughtfully. "I do believe you're telling the truth."

"OF COURSE I'M TELLING THE TRUTH!" Wendy exploded. Then she spotted the slight quirk of Elise's lips and realized the woman was baiting her. "Jane's locked in a mansion, Elise, after trying to capture me. On the orders of the Lady Walker, I'm sure. If you want her, you're going to have to pull some of those strings you bullied ghosts for and go get her yourself. She can't pass through the walls on her own."

"A mansion? Oh, please, Winifred, any Reaper worth sipping from the Good Cup knows how to walk through dense walls in the Never," Elise sneered. "Just because you cannot—"

Wendy allowed herself a taunting smirk. "Not these walls. You might say this place is one hell of a tourist trap these days. Ghost trap, too."

Elise paused, uncertainty flickering in her eyes. "Surely you don't mean the Winchester—"

"I do, actually," Wendy said, laughing in Elise's face. "Locked her in."

"Please, dear," Elise said, relieved, the condensation practically dripping from her tone. "All she has to do is request that Clyde—"

"Clyde. Clyde," Wendy said. "Funny you should mention him. Guess who Jane reaped earlier tonight? I mean, yeah, he was getting irritated with her, threatening to throw her out on her blue-tinted ass but—"

Elise paled. "No."

"Yes."

"No! No-no-no!" Elise screamed, grabbing the hair at her temples and yanking hard. "Oh that stupid . . . idiotic . . . moronic little . . . *bitch*!"

Overwhelmed by Elise's unexpected reaction, Wendy took a step back. "Okay, officially weirded out now. That's a little overkill, don't you thi—"

"Oh shut up, you pitiful blood-traitor!" Elsie snapped, stalking off toward the surf. "You have no idea what we're dealing with!" she yelled over her shoulder.

Troubled, Wendy started to follow her. "I don't? Fine! So tell me then!"

"Jane will try to blast her way out of the Winchester House. She will use all the Light at her disposal to force a hole in the Never, to not be taken by the police! We are ruined! And you . . . you are clueless! Pointless, clueless, an albatross hanging round my neck, dragging me

down when I most need my wits to face . . . to face . . . oh, never mind! You're untrained, you're ignorant of the real dangers here. You're worse than useless. You're a babe in the goddamned dead woods."

Wendy, shrugging, began to run after her, digging her feet deeply into the sand. At first catching up with Elise was difficult, but then Wendy remembered that this was her dreamscape and suddenly the sand beneath her feet spread outward, becoming a flat, grassy plain. A nearby pier jutted out of the grass, a small rowboat tied to it resting atop a swell of water turned into feathery bushes. Gulls screamed in the distance, startled and loud. A fish-turned-snake slithered across Wendy's foot as she slowed, approaching Elise.

"You mean the hole in the horizon?" Wendy asked as she reached Elise's side. "That big ol' opening to the great deep? The grosser than hell creatures coming out of that thing who then take over souls and warp them into something *truly* nasty? Is that the big ol' nasty danger that has your panties in a twist, Elise?"

"Yes," Elise replied, nettled, glaring around at the lush greenery with a sour, puckered mouth. A gull, confused as to the change, hopped across the grass and hopefully poked its beak into a largish hole in the ground, jerking back as the crab within snapped at it with claws that shifted into tiny paws as the crab dropped, grew fur, and became a groundhog before their eyes. "Yes it is. How do you—"

"Does it matter how?" Wendy asked. Then she smiled, warmth spreading across her chest. "That's . . . that's the wrong question to ask."

"Fine," Elise growled. "What is the right question?"

Wendy was ready. "Why did you have my grandmother and my aunt killed?"

Elise raised an eyebrow, startled. "Clyde?"

"And Frank. Lots of people have been quite forthcoming tonight and we've put a crapton of miles on Dad's car getting alllll the answers. But maybe, in the interest of hearing all sides of the story, I want to hear it from your lips, Elise. Maybe I want to hear your side of things."

"Top of the Mark to the Winchester House. You have been get-

ting around," Elise murmured. "I assume they were the ones that
told you about the—"

"Who doesn't matter. Why did you do it?"

Elise didn't roll her eyes, but Wendy could sense that she desperately wanted to and only refrained out of some sense of superi-
ority. "Why? Think, you silly girl! Your grandmother was a natural—a *secret* natural—who was questioning everything about how
we'd done our jobs for centuries. At the time we could not allow naturals to live, specifically one who was comfortable lying to us for so
long! She was too much of a danger—"

"She was a danger?" Wendy interrupted, abruptly furious.
"Really? Because, the way I hear tell it, she had kept herself hidden
long enough to have a nearly thirty-year-old daughter. Remember
her? Tracey? So that doesn't seem like a lot of danger there. Seems
like my grandma wasn't struggling that badly, possibly because she,
oh, I don't know, actually had her powers under control?"

Elise narrowed her eyes at Wendy. "She reaped a soul every night like
clockwork, true. Specifically a Shade, usually the weakest Shade we were
aware of. Never more, never less. Honestly, I thought her a coward, too
afraid to challenge herself with a normal spirit or a Walker. But then—"

"But then—?"

"But then she was forced to reap a Walker one night, and the
subsequent blowout of unbridled energy killed the cousin patrolling
with her in the process. She lied about that too, or didn't Clyde pass
that little tidbit of information along? A family killer. Blamed it on
a strong Walker. We believed her. At first."

Wendy flushed. "I didn't know that part."

"As you just said, there are two sides to every story, girl," Elise
said. "I have many, many faults, I'll admit. I do not like reaping. I
don't wish to give up my life to send on the ungrateful dead. Furthermore, I feel that if we are going to be such unnatural abominations of nature then we ought to be compensated well as such. What
we do is a curse, it goes against the will of God."

"Seriously?" Wendy asked. "You really believe—"

"What I believe is of no concern to you," Elise said sharply. "All that matters is that your precious 'right' questions are answered. Speaking of—your aunt, Tracey? She was condemned to death because she was dealing with the dead."

"So what? You made deals with them all the time. In fact you, what, actively threatened them? So, not so much making deals as bullying them around."

"That is quite different. I deal with normal spirits. Tracey dealt with the Lady Walker," Elise said coldly. "Frequently, over and over again, after her mother's demise. It was brought to my attention that the Lady Walker and Tracey had plans beyond simply getting me out of town the way your mother did—though I'm still uncertain how exactly she managed to get us to all agree to leave so readily."

Wendy stilled, sighing. "I knew that. I was hoping it wasn't true. The one thing I don't get is why. What could Tracey have to share with the Lady Walker? That's the only part that still makes no sense to me."

"Is that all?" Elise asked. She threw her head back and laughed, clapping her hands. "All your work, all your sleuthing and you still don't know what this is all about? What the core boils down to? For shame, Winifred! I thought you were smart!"

"Enlighten me then," Wendy said dryly, ignoring Elise's derisive laughter.

"Tracey and the Lady Walker wanted to end the world, Winifred," Elise said flatly, waving an arm to encompass the dreamspace. "The lovely little limbo your beloved Rider friends are wandering around in? They wanted to destroy it. Rip it end from end. That is what I was trying to stop by killing your aunt, Winifred. I wanted to stop the utter destruction of the Never and every soul in it."

Elise looked up to the darkening sky above them; the clouds were back, flashing lightning and booming thunder rolled across the pristine blue, crashing so loudly the grass shook.

"Not that it matters now." Her lips twisted. "As we all shall

suffer for Jane's misdeeds tonight. Surely even you've felt the earth-quakes by now. The hole between the worlds is gaping, and if Jane has done the damage I believe she has—"

"Damage? You mean reaping Clyde?" Wendy began covertly looking for a seashell door. She knew there had to be one somewhere close, even if the dreamscape beach was nothing but grass now. Her mind flicked briefly to the dream of earlier, she and not-Mary walking along the beach, Mary explaining how to build a shell door out of only the best pieces . . .

"I mean that by reaping Clyde, Jane has made the hole in the sky that much worse," Elise growled. "Clyde was allowed to remain the gatekeeper of the Winchester Mansion for a reason. He was an impor-tant piece holding together the tide surging behind a dangerous dam."

"But . . . Clyde said it was because you couldn't catch him. He had too many hiding spots—"

Elise snorted. "Nonsense. Do you really believe that enough money passing the right hands couldn't get a large group of Reapers into the mansion for a private tour? That if we walked those halls, Light shining, that Clyde wouldn't be easily drawn from whatever pathetic hidey-hole he'd settled into, to beg for the Light? No, girl, hardly. We left him untouched because Clyde happened to be sitting on one of the thinnest spot in the Never for a thousand mile radius. We—the Reapers—built the original farmhouse that stupid old woman turned into the Winchester Mansion. We needed a soul with Reaper blood, with special abilities, to maintain the property."

Wendy couldn't help but be simultaneously impressed and surprised.

"We did it to plug a hole, and the result is that everything above it grew solid in response. The Winchester place, like Alcatraz, like several other locations around the City, is a spiritual sponge. All of them are, due to the holes at their core, the ridge—the surrounding buildings near them—are particularly strong."

Wendy swallowed. "Like the Palace Hotel?"

"Exactly," Elise said, startled. "Yes, the Palace Hotel is one such location, though none are as strong as the Winchester."

"And what happens if Light . . . goes off . . . in one of those places . . . ?" Wendy swallowed heavily.

"At first? Nothing. But depending on the force of the Light, the quality of the Light . . . the edges of the cork would crumble, allowing a hole to open from the darkest, coldest places into the Never and subsequently into our world."

Wendy blanched, remembering the powerful pulse of Light that had blasted out of her as Piotr shoved her soul-orb back into her body. She'd destroyed the White Lady and all her henchman, not to mention one of the Riders and all thirteen Lost in the room . . . but she'd also caused an earthquake and blasted out the power in the living lands for a very large radius.

Carefully examining a small pile of rocks, Wendy reached down and picked the top one off the pile. It crumbled in her hand. No. No good. The quality of the sediment here was terrible.

"A blast of Light in a sensitive location would open a hole," Wendy whispered, heart thudding hard in her chest. "A hole between the worlds."

"Originally Tracey had planned, with Mary, to gain access to Alcatraz," Elise said sharply. "They'd planned on becoming bosom buddies with the spirit who'd taken up residence there, and to set off a blast of Light that would crack a hole in reality itself." She was talking about Ada, Wendy realized.

"But Mom wasn't a natural. How could they have set off a big enough blast?" Wendy wondered, examining a tree nearby. The branches were thick but crooked. They felt off, wrong. Not strong enough, the material wasn't good enough. She moved on. "That's an awful lot of power."

Elise smirked. "There are times you show such spiritual savvy that I forget you have barely cracked the first of our books. Winifred, dear girl, you've heard of Seers, correct?"

Like yesterday, the memory swam over her. Piotr, sitting on the edge of her bed during the short, sweet time they'd spent getting to know everything they could about one another, holding her hand, telling her that he was impressed a Seer of her capacity was willing to deal with him.

"*Most Seers,*" he'd said, caressing a circle in her palm, "*they are . . . how do you say . . . they are cynical. They are jaded and angry at the world, da? They do not like to deal with spirits. We ask far too much of them. We make them tired.*"

And Wendy, who hadn't had the heart yet to tell him that she was more than just a simple Seer, had let Piotr cling to this notion, that all she was a girl who could speak and see the dead, a girl who knew of the Never and was not flustered by it. She'd lied to him so that he wouldn't hate her. That time, albeit wonderful, had lasted far too briefly.

Wendy swallowed deeply. "Yeah," she said, poking a nearby stick with a toe. It snapped beneath the pressure of her foot. Not good enough. "I've heard of them."

"Seers are our kind," Elise said. "Simply that. They are simply Good Workers who have lost the thread of our family, pruned from the main trunk for the good of us all. Frequently they are naturals who have never seen a soul pass on—completely harmless to us, for all they can do is listen to the moaning of the dead. They cannot interact with the Never, they can touch nothing, can do nothing. So we allow them to live their simple, basic little lives, unmolested. Seeing but not touching. Harmless. Mostly."

Wendy rubbed her hands up her arms. There, next to the pier and boat-on-a-bush, was a stack of bricks. Wendy concentrated on them and, one at a time, the bricks vanished from their current location and reappeared in the flat ground next to the pier, settling firmly in the grass, end to end. She quickly shaped the door's initial rectangle, amazed at the feeling of *power* simply arranging the dreamscape bricks had given her. "I'm sensing a big 'but' coming."

"Indeed. These Seers, especially those who are unnoted naturals,

still have the capability to become naturals. They have a great power slumbering deep within themselves. In the right hands, they could be a weapon. I used to think your mother was planning on finding a Seer and using them to blast the hole open. Then I learned about your inborn skills. And that you have a sister, an—as yet, so far as I knew at the time—unawakened sister."

Wendy thought of her mother; the way Mary's lips always pinched when she spoke of Chel and the opportunity for Chel to possibly become a Reaper like Wendy. The lingering circles beneath her eyes, the worry lines bracketing Mary's mouth.

"You think my mom was considering using Chel like some kind of bomb?"

For the first time Wendy had known her, Elise's expression grew pitying. "I think she was planning on using you both. Mary would have been a fool, given her family line, to not take into consideration the possibility that you or your sister was a natural. Mary was a smart woman; no, she doubtlessly knew. And she was biding her time."

Wendy felt sick. Everything Elise told her twisted in her gut, like the snakes wriggling in the grass, sliding sinuously across her toes, all going in the same direction, all the snakes slithering toward her freshly constructed door.

"I'm done," Wendy whispered. She pushed past Elise, yelling, "You can rot here for all I care!" and dove for the door, praying that she'd constructed it correctly, that she'd felt her way around the problem the way she was supposed to. Nothing would be worse than slamming face first into a brick door in front of Elise while the Reaper laughed and judged her from behind.

Luck was with her; Wendy had shaped the door well. Her hand wrapped around the handle and it shifted in her grip, transforming from a ragged, broken brick to a smooth handle against her palm. Wendy pressed down, the door opened, and she stepped through.

CHAPTER TWENTY-TWO

Wendy knew she hadn't hit her head, but when she opened her eyes she sensed that time had jumped forward. Minutes had passed. The shared memory was done, the dreamscape was complete; Wendy was back in the shattered remains of the car, her siblings were in the front seat and Piotr was beside her, gripping her hand, his body mostly turned away, half in and half out of the car. Wendy couldn't tell if he was awake or unconscious.

Slowly she reached out and rested her free hand on the concrete block—once part of the divider separating the highway—that was broken in large chunks and littering the ceiling of the car, on which she rested. The concrete pieces sat alongside the shattered remains of the side window, the blasted bits of the rearview mirror and the jagged curls of metal and plastic from the side door.

In the front seat Chel was crumpled, hanging upside down, arms and legs dangling limply. The airbag had gone off, pinning Jon's bulk in place, but he didn't look okay either; blood poured from his ears and the corners of his mouth, his obviously broken nose gushing through the tear in his face over the bridge of his nose and dripping down his forehead into his hair. In his delirium, Jon coughed raspily and spat. The first result was bright, crimson red, the second chunky and dark. The third, he spit out a tooth and moaned.

"The car's upside down," Wendy said dumbly, not entirely sure what was going on, how this could happen to her again? Hadn't she been in enough car accidents in her life?

Except . . . this wasn't exactly life anymore, was it?

Wendy turned her head and found herself face to face with Elle

. . . or what had once been Elle. Twisted limbs were close enough to touch but Wendy desperately hoped the thing stayed far, far away. She thought that if she brushed up against it, she might die screaming.

"Wendy," Piotr whispered beside her, his low, even voice startling Wendy painfully and nearly surprising a yell out of her, "back away. Back away slowly. Go through the thin spot in the door."

Easing backward, Wendy tried to only look at what had been Elle out of the corner of her eye. The creature inhabiting her had turned Elle's face into something resembling a pincushion, all splintered bones and long, jagged tusks poking ragged holes in her cheeks. "What . . . what happened?"

"It took her over right after the wreck, while you were out. It ambushed us, caused the wreck, probably for this very reason," Piotr said, barely breathing the words.

"Piotr . . . Elle . . ." Wendy whimpered. "Elle's . . . face . . ."

"Shhh," Piotr hushed her, eerily calm as he eased the rest of the way out of the car. "Slow and steady. Back away."

Wendy, knees grating across the rubble on the ceiling of the car, eased backward out of the vehicle. Elle's ruined face stretched after her, the cartilage in her neck popping and rippling as her body remained crouched just outside the car and her head followed Wendy.

"Chel's unconscious," Wendy hissed to Piotr, who helped her stand outside the car. They could hear the wails of the ambulance very dimly in the distance. "I don't know what to do! I can't reap it, as I am . . ."

Piotr, who'd never taken his eyes off his old friend, shook his head. He was still backing up, one hand on Wendy's elbow guiding her over the detritus strewn across the highway as the Elle-creature pulled its twisted, torn body after them.

"If you can't reap it," Piotr hissed, "then we have to destroy her."

"What? But it's Elle . . ."

"Walkers eat the Lost. Shades lose all will to live. Wendy, the Never is just as complex an ecosystem as the living lands. You can destroy that thing. Elle would rather die than let herself be perverted like this."

He was right, Wendy knew that, but the idea of trying to fight and kill this creature that had once been the sardonic, quick-witted flapper seemed incomprehensible.

Wendy scrabbled inwardly against the bindings around her Light. She'd make do with anything—Light, dark Light, anything, anything at all, that would keep her from having to go hand-to-hand with this spiny, sharp creature who stood where Elle once had.

The Elle-creature stalked toward them, blond hair hanging limply against its torn and tenderized cheeks. It snarled low, deep in its throat and paced back and forth, like a stalking cat. The thorny spines thrust from Elle's spine quivered with a terrible life of their own, throbbing and bobbing to the beat of her steps.

Wendy cringed, expecting the pounce any moment . . .

It never came.

The Elle-creature—horrible to look on, growling like a trapped wildcat—snarled at them and paced, blocking off any avenue for escape that wouldn't leave Chel and Jon—both glowing faintly—completely helpless against the Elle-creature's frenzy.

"Wendy," Piotr said after several long seconds of tense standoff. "Is it me . . . or is Elle . . . not going to attack us? She seems *lovushke* . . . she is trapped, she is torn."

"You noticed that, too? She's not even playing with us, like a cat might, or like that other thing did . . . she's just . . . pacing."

Piotr frowned and held out a hand. The Elle-creature snarled and snapped forward, swiping her elongated, razor-sharp fingers at him. Piotr yanked away at last second, but not before a cut opened up on his hand, the essence dripping over the back of his hand and pattering on the ground. The Elle-creature made a noise Wendy could only describe as a cross between a chuckle, a growl, and a soft, desperate moan.

It stretched its impossibly long and lithe neck forward, pressing Piotr out of the way as it leaned down and lapped up the spilled essence from the ground. When it pulled back, it licked its chops. For a brief moment it gazed longingly at Piotr's hand and the essence still

welling there, before the neck shortened again and the Elle-creature curled on the ground, tucking its paws beneath its body.

"This isn't the same as with Ada," Wendy whispered. "I think . . . I think Elle sometimes has a kind of control over the creature. Not much, but enough for now."

"I believe you may be correct," Piotr replied and knelt down. "Elle . . . are you in there? Elle?"

The creature shook, head lashing from side to side, droplets of stinging hot and freezing cold drool splattering Wendy's arm. She yelped and used her skirt to wipe off the liquid; the smear quickly ate a hole in her skirt.

It's like the poison Ada was making, Wendy thought to herself. *Dime-sized acid holes, eating through essence.*

"Elle," Piotr began again when the creature's flailings had stilled. "Elle? Elle, can you be separated from this beast? Do you know? What do you wish us to do? Elle?"

The Elle-creature snarled at Piotr and leapt up, charging. Piotr danced back, darting out of the path of the swipes, spinning side to side like a berserk matador as he dodged her razor-claws.

"Elle!" Wendy yelled trying to move like Piotr did, but failing and nearly being swept off her feet by Elle's enormous, slashing tail. "Elle! Stop this! STOP! You can stop, Elle, you can . . ."

Wendy stopped and backed away. This was no use. Elle—if she really had control and it wasn't some figment of their wishful imaginations—had already lost it. The beast was in charge now and it seemed intent on ripping Piotr apart. The Elle-creature stood on two legs and used its immense reach to swipe and claw at Piotr. Her belly—its belly—was exposed.

"I can do this," Wendy muttered under her breath, striding to the car. There, in the back, were Lily's bandolier of bone knives and Elle's arrows, bow, and quiver. Wendy gathered up both sets of weapons and strode to the edge of the fight. She'd only ever shot a bow and arrow once, during Girl Scouts when she was nine, and she'd been dismal at

it then. Wendy was fairly sure she could remember the basics of archery if it came to that, but she was hoping that it wouldn't.

Instead, Wendy drew two of the bone blades, slipped the bandolier over her head, took a deep breath, and dove into the fray. Elle, concentrating on Piotr, didn't notice Wendy at first. The bone knives were wicked sharp but dulled quickly against whatever Elle's skin had become. Still, Wendy was persistent and she had an idea.

Wendy angled her body so that Elle's belly was always exposed; she directed the blades into Elle's gut, hacking and slicing in a loose perforated circle at Elle's core. Elle's claws opened up holes in Wendy's shoulders, her hips, her arms. None of the damage Elle inflicted was too severe though. Wendy got the sense that the beast was holding back or, rather, that some nearly-gone part of Elle was *holding* the beast back.

When the last, nearly dull knife plunged through the hole Wendy hacked around Elle's cord, Wendy yelled in triumph. Her hand shot forward and she grabbed the end, drawing the diseased remains of Elle's cord forward, pulling it taut and firm.

Then she sliced Elle's cord off.

The resulting explosion was rainbows and Light.

When the paramedics arrived minutes later, Wendy and Piotr were ready to jump into the back of the truck as they trundled first Chel and then Jon's stretcher on board the ambulance. Wendy had so much she wanted to ask Piotr but now was not the time.

"Hang in there," Wendy whispered, dodging around the paramedic to lean over her sister. "Hang in there!"

Jon moaned around the tube jammed down his throat. Piotr, kneeling behind Jon's head, brushed his hand over Jon's forehead, cooling him. Neither Piotr nor Wendy looked out the back of the truck at the ruined remains of the car or the black smear of ash where the Light had blazed from the sky above and burned Elle to nothing right before their eyes.

Piotr and Wendy remained silent as the ambulance wailed all the way to UCSF. There they jumped off as Chel and Jon were wheeled past the ER doctor who, on seeing them, cursed loudly.

"I know these kids," he snapped at the EMT as they rushed Chel past him. "What happened?"

Wendy didn't get a chance to hear the EMT describe her sibling's condition; Eddie hesitated on the far side of the ER. Gasping in mingled joy and horror, Wendy rushed across the floor. When she approached him, he flinched back, taking in the damage she'd sustained in one angry, helpless glare.

"Eddie?! You're here! Why are you here?! What are you—"

"I don't know why you're surprised," he said, giving Wendy a quizzical look. "You told me to find someplace safe to hide. What better place than next to my own body, right? So I caught a ride up here and have just been wandering Neurology for the past several hours. It's been a madhouse though. You will never guess who wandered in not an hour ago!"

"Jane?" Wendy asked hopefully. "Tell me that she blew herself up messing with the Never at the Winchester. Make my day, Eddie. I'll kiss you if you can."

Piotr rolled his eyes at her declaration and Eddie looked wistful. "Um, alas, but no, our mystery guest is not, in fact, Jane. I'm guessing you had another run-in?"

Piotr and Wendy shared a look. "You could say that," Wendy said, deciding not to tell Eddie about Lily just yet. "Coming here wasn't exactly in tonight's plan. So what do we do now?"

"You should visit your room first," Eddie suggested. "We'll check in on your body and then figure out where to go from here. No offense, Wendy, but I'm not leaving you guys again. Things have gotten way too creepy and weird around here for my peace of my mind."

"Creepy?" Wendy said, perplexed. "What's going on?"

He shook his head. "One thing at a time. Let's go check up on you first."

CHAPTER
TWENTY-THREE

"You have no idea how glad I am to see you two," Eddie said as he peered around Wendy's doorway into the hall. "I felt like I was gonna go crazy here by myself."

Piotr was resting a moment, hand pressed to his chest as Wendy stood over her still body, amazed at how emaciated she looked. Her skin was paper-pale and dehydrated, showing the thin blue veins snaking just beneath the skin. Four fans were blowing full-blast at her, and someone had piled up gel-packs all around her entire body.

"I'm dying," Wendy said, reaching out and touching the big toe on her right foot. Her flesh felt dull and distant, not like something she should feel at home crawling back into. "I don't know how to feel about that."

"Don't feel anything about it for now. So far you're safe," Eddie said, frowning. "That's all that matters for the moment. So you're not looking your best, true, and you're still burning up but I'm sure . . ." he drifted off and then frowned, looking quickly between Piotr and Wendy. "Hey . . . wait a second. Where are the others?"

"Chel and Jon both were in that car accident we came in on," Wendy said flatly, examining how fast the saline was dripping into her veins. They had it turned all the way up but her body seemed to be sucking up the moisture like a desert. It wasn't making a difference. "The crash . . . it was terrible, Eds. Neither of them might survive. They can't help us right now. They can't even help themselves."

"Oh no," Eddie whispered. "Like my dad?"

"Yeah," Wendy said, turning away from her body and taking his hand. Eddie drew her close and they hugged a brief moment, his chin resting on her shoulder as Wendy trembled in his arms. "Are you okay?" he asked. "It still freaking you out?"

"I'll be fine," Wendy sighed, taking Eddie's hand in her left hand and Piotr's in her right as he stood and joined them in the doorway of her room. "I'll be better once I know how they're doing. On the way to your weirdo thing, let's go see if there's any word on Chel or Jo— wait . . . hang on a minute . . ."

Dr. Kensington, the pushy doctor from before, slipped past them, rushing silently down the empty hallway of the Neurology floor. In one hand he held a pair of faded bunny slippers. In the other, he had a pair of glasses.

"Oh look," Eddie said. "Hey, question, kind of important actually: that's the guy from before, right? The guy that wanted to call CPS on your dad?"

"Oh me, oh my, yes," Wendy said, "it's Dr. Asshole. Going off duty, Dr. Asshole? I never expected you to be the type to wear bunny slip—" Wendy broke off as the memory came to her.

The EMT team pushed through the emergency doors, shoving a stretcher between them as a crying robe-clad woman in bunny slippers and glasses hurried behind.

The injured woman gasping on the gurney lifted her arm and pointed to Wendy as she passed, twisting her head to keep Wendy in sight as the EMTs passed. Dr. Kensington was going to be the doctor on this case; Wendy shuddered. The whites of her eyes were red, the pupils blacked out her irises and her mouth was bright red, dripping down her chin and neck. Her malformed face stretched oddly, angularly, out of place and the bones in her forearms punched through the skin, spiky and white and pulsing.

Despite all that, it was obvious that the two women could see them. The robed woman dodged around Eddie as she hurried through the swinging doors, dropping her left bunny slipper in the process. Wendy attempted to pick

it up to return it to the robed woman. Wendy'd forgotten she was a spirit; her
hand went right through it.

"Wait. Wait a second. I know that slipper," Wendy muttered and
raced out the door, hot on Dr. Kensington's heels. Eddie and Piotr
followed. The doctor sped through the Neurology wing and down a
narrow hallway, stopping at last at the Psychiatry ward. There he
tapped on the glass and a bored-looking orderly pushed a buzzer.

Dr. Kensington and his three ghostly tails stepped into a tiny room
where the orderly examined the doctor "Is this strictly necessary?" the
doctor demanded. "I'm not going to smuggle her any weapons."

"Who?" Wendy asked, wishing the doctor could hear her. "The
bunny slipper lady didn't look crazy to *me*. Frazzled, yes, crazy, no.
She could see us, though . . . they both could." Thinking about the
woman on the gurney, the one who'd pointed at her, Wendy mused,
"Maybe it's her friend?"

"Orders, sir," the orderly said casually, lifting up the gigantic doctor's
lab coat and patting down his hips. "Are those glasses yours, sir?"

Dr. Kensington, startled, flushed. "No. These belong to my
nurse. She handed them to me and—"

Ignoring Dr. Kensington's flustered excuse, the orderly reached
over to his station and grabbed a plastic basket. "In the basket, sir.
You'd be surprised what some of these folks can do with a little bit
of wire like that. And those lenses don't look like no safety glass, neither. In the basket."

Dr. Kensington, gritting his teeth, dropped the glasses in the
basket, his sleeves shifting enough that Wendy could see the edge of
the tattoo circling his wrist. "Will that be all, son?"

"Go ahead. I'll buzz you in." The orderly waved him on.

"Why are we on the psych ward, do you wonder?" Eddie asked
and Piotr shrugged. Wendy, however, had an idea. It was a dis-
turbing, impossible idea, but one that wouldn't let go.

"Piotr," she said slowly as they followed Dr. Kensington

through two more buzzing doors and into a great, empty tiled room with folding chairs and tables lining the far wall, "what do you think would happen if one of those creatures tried inhabiting a human? A living human, not just a spirit?"

"I . . . I don't know." Piotr paused, blinking in surprise. "Living flesh is not malleable the way essence is. If I want, I can change my clothing at will. I could, with enough energy and time, could even change my face itself. But the living are not loosely put together the ways souls are. Would that not kill a living person?"

"It probably would," Eddie agreed uneasily. "I mean, what that crazy thing did to Ada was just—"

"What if it didn't?" Wendy demanded, moving quickly to keep up with Dr. Kensington. He left the vast tiled room and took a left, gesturing for the nurse at the desk to buzz him into a room across from their station. "What if it found a way to—oh, holy shit!" Wendy backpedaled and slammed into Piotr, sending him skidding to the floor.

The room was covered in shit and vomit and blood. The woman who had pointed at Wendy was no more; her discarded flesh lay on the floor of the room like a snakeskin.

What remained of the woman clung to the ceiling by her teeth and her nails—muscles glistening, tendons hardening in the air, veins pulsing, desperately trying to bring blood to an envelope of skin that was simply no longer there.

"*A chorbn*," Eddie cursed behind her, dismay and disgust coloring the Yiddish.

"Dawn's coming," the creature crowed happily. "I can taste it!"

Dr. Kensington, snarling a warning, slammed the door behind him—closing it, *locking* it—and flung the slipper to the ground beneath the creature. The thing turned its head 180 to examine it but, thankfully, didn't stretch its neck the way Elle had to get a closer look.

"Your girlfriend—pardon me, ex-girlfriend—was so desperate

to have you back to normal that she would have tried to *swim* to Alcatraz if I'd asked her to," he said proudly. "I had her take a row-boat. But here's the proof. She's dead."

The creature chuckled and dropped to the ground in front of the doctor with a wet, meaty thump. Blood sprayed him in the face but Dr. Kensington didn't flinch. He smiled.

"Never her mind. Gone. Good. Now you brought some friends with you," growled the creature. "Tasty meat in you, soft life-in-death from them. Dessert!"

"Friends? Do you mean ghosts?" The doctor looked around the room, then slapped himself in the forehead. "Silly me. You've got me thinking *I* can see them, too. There are some in the room, you say?" He laughed and shook his head. "No worries, Kara. Shades are always wandering these halls. Pay them no mind."

The Kara-creature tilted its head at the doctor like an owl, nearly upside down, but then shrugged and rose to its feet. "I tire of this room. Let me out. I want to eat!"

"No," Dr. Kensington snarled. "We've punched another couple holes in the Never, but it's not enough yet. I wish you'd kept the skin on . . . you are a mess! It will have to be sheer chaos out there before I dare let you go free. You'll be noticed like this for sure." He prodded the bunny slipper with his foot. Wendy could see the blood speckling the top and suddenly, as if a switch flipped in her head, she sensed where the owner of the slipper had gone and knew without question what had happened to her.

"Less than a day," the creature moaned, clicking its teeth at Dr. Kensington. "The hole is opening . . . opening so wide!"

"Be patient," the doctor urged it. "Now. Are you sure you don't know where Laurie kept the spare keys? I must—*must*—get into the vault under Russian Hill. There are other methods, but your house is the most direct. We *need* that vault."

"Reapers had a key," the creature hummed. "Had a key and lost-lost-lost it."

"Not to the front door, they didn't," Dr. Kensington growled, unamused. "Think! Probe that meaty brain you're sucking dry and come up with the answer!"

The creature paused in its swaying, puddles of clear saliva dripping down its grisly chin and then, after a long, drooling moment, shook its head. "She blocks me, what little there is of her left. She blocks me."

"Keep trying," Dr. Kensington urged but without passion or force. "Just . . . keep trying. Every memory. She has to know where another key is. She has to." He gestured for the creature to ascend to the ceiling once more, and waited until it hung like a bat before he turned his back on the creature and tapped on the slit in the door. A loud buzz made the handle vibrate; Dr. Kensington eased out of the room.

"Oh doctor!" the nurse cried. "You've got blood all over your face!"

"She bit her tongue and spat at me," he said, the lie flowing so smoothly off his lips that Wendy actually believed him for a split second.

"Do I need to call—"

"It's already healing, she'd saved some in her cheek for me," he insisted, waving a hand at the nurse. "She's on lockdown in there, though. No one is to go in under any circumstances until I can get her regular doctor in on Monday. She knows her food is coming in under the door. Keep it that way. No. Contact. She's too dangerous. Do you understand me?"

"Yes, sir," the nurse said, flustered. "You've got . . ." she made a circling motion around her face. "A little . . . um . . . everywhere."

"I'll see to it," he said dryly and headed for the men's room, leaving Piotr, Eddie, and Wendy staring at one another, dumbfounded.

Slowly Wendy dug in her pocket, pulling out the knife and the necklace Clyde gave her. The key still gleamed at the end of the chain.

"I think," she said softly, "we're going to have to brave the forest

again to get to Russian Hill. Because if that dude wants something there so desperately that he fed those chicks to the creatures . . . well . . . we'd better get to it first. Clyde gave us this key. Everyone's looking for it. We should go soon."

"Well," Eddie said, "we could start by—"

"No," Wendy snapped. "No, no, no. I need you here."

"Excuse me? I'm not some baggage that you can just—"

"Eddie!" Wendy said, grabbing her best friend by the shoulders and shaking him. "I know you're freaked out. I get that! But did you just see what I saw? I. Need. You. Here. I need you here to make sure that asshole doesn't try to shove a creature down my throat—literally."

"I just—"

"Edward," Piotr said sharply. "Tonight I have lost my two oldest friends. Lily and Elle are gone. They are in the Light. Please do not make Wendy suffer the same as I suffer. *Puzhalsta*."

Eddie swallowed and looked around, realizing for the first time that Lily and Elle were not tagging along. "They're . . . dead? Lily's dead? Like dead-dead? Really?"

"Yeah," Wendy said dully, reaching forward and drawing Eddie into a tight hug. Eddie smelled like his leather motorcycle jacket and wood smoke and the coconut oil he used to keep his silvery-dyed hair smooth. She inhaled his scent deeply and stood on tiptoes to kiss the corner of his mouth. "I'm sorry. It . . . it was Jane. She got Lily. And one of the creatures got Elle. I . . . I couldn't stop it, Eds. I tried but I couldn't."

Eddie began to cry and Wendy pulled him closer.

"I can see that this . . . this is personal. I will go," Piotr said abruptly. "Please excuse me." He turned and strode down the hall, his shoes clicking loudly in the silence.

Wendy clung to Eddie like a drowning swimmer cast upon a buoy. Eddie just held Wendy and stroked her hair as she shivered with rage and sorrow in the circle of his arms.

"Come on," Eddie said, roughly clearing his throat after a few min-

utes. "Before you go there's someone you'll want to see." He led the way down the hall. Wendy realized they were heading to his room.

"Did you get a roomie?" she asked, wiping her eyes and feeling the need to lighten the mood with a little teasing.

"In a matter of speaking," Eddie said. He stepped aside and let Wendy be the first to enter.

Emma looked up from her spot beside Eddie's bed.

CHAPTER
TWENTY-FOUR

"Emma!" Wendy cried, rushing across the room and dropping to her knees beside the doctor. Emma's face was drawn, the circles under her eyes heavily shadowed and purple, but she was firm in the Never. Wendy flung herself at the slim doctor and hugged her tightly.

"Emma, I thought you were dead!" Wendy exclaimed, shaking with suppressed emotion as she drew back. Her mouth was dry, her palms sweaty. "They hauled your body out and the Lady Walker said . . . they said that she'd dragged some Reaper's soul into the forest . . . I thought it was you!"

"I'm not dead," Emma said, hands clenching her skirt taut between her knees. She forced herself to relax, visibly straightening and taking deep, even breaths. "Close, but not there yet."

"What happened?"

Emma raised an eyebrow. "Wendy, please. You're certainly smarter than that. By now you have to have the lay of the land. What do you think happened?"

"You were going to help me," Wendy sighed. "Undo all of Jane's sneaky work. Jane and Elise couldn't have that."

Emma touched a finger to her nose. "Bingo. Grandmother was . . . most displeased to learn that I intended to aid you in unbinding yourself. She had Jane . . . waylay me. One splitting headache and a high fever later, I find myself here."

Wendy cocked an eyebrow. "Speaking of . . . how are you here like this? Is your Light sealed away like mine?"

"My Light is safe. Jane merely administered a poison we normally use to wake Reapers to the Light. It's called drinking from the Good Cup. It brings you quite close to death if dosed properly. Jane was less than careful. I have faith, however. I'll be feverish for several days, but I've beaten this before, when I was initiated into the Reapers. I will beat it again."

"Oh. I thought maybe that you were like Eddie, like they wrapped your cord up the same way they did his."

"They wrapped your cord? That's it?" Emma gaped at Eddie; she grabbed him by the shoulder and shook in frustration. "I can fix that! That is simple to undo! Why didn't you say anything, Eddie?! Do you like risking your life?"

"I didn't think about it," Eddie said, flushing. "I was just so glad to see you still . . . well, sort of alive. It didn't even cross my mind to tell you that we figured out what the problem with my body was." He held up a nearly translucent hand. "Though I guess I should've, huh?"

Emma, laughing, shook her head. "I'm impressed, Wendy, I really am. Now that I look at him closely, I'm amazed that I didn't see the wrapping of his soul before. Come here, Eddie." She held out her hands.

Eddie hesitated. "What are you going to do?"

"I'm going to do what should have been done days ago, Eddie. I'm going to fix you." Emma cracked her knuckles and shook her hands to loosen them. "Come here."

He hesitated. "But what if Wendy needs—"

"Eddie," Wendy said sharply. "Do it. I can't . . . it kills me to say this, but I can't help you. Not like this. Not with everything going on. Please, Eddie. Please."

Eddie remained unconvinced. "Will it hurt?"

"No, Eddie, it won't," Emma said kindly. "It's a matter of finding the edge of your cord and spinning. Unraveling. Cords are

stretchy and flexible; they hold an immense amount of personal power in them—which is why a Walker's cord, their connection to the Light, rots away as they take in the essence of others."

Wendy frowned. That explained why Elle's body had virtually exploded when her cord was severed.

Emma, noting Wendy's angry expression, interpreted her concern incorrectly.

"I assure you, Eddie will be fine—nice and solid and waking up in no time at all. If I'd only known this before . . . so much misery could have been avoided!"

Frowning, Wendy sat back and held up a hand as Emma had held up Eddie's, wiggling her fingers in the pre-dawn light filtering in through the window. Her fingers were thinner along the edges, her hand losing substance. She wrapped one hand around the other wrist and squeezed, feeling the strange sensation of her not-flesh giving beneath her grip.

"Speaking of the spirit getting thin," Emma said, grimacing and examining her own hands. They were growing paler. "I'm running out of time. I must be waking up. Come here, Eddie."

Eddie stepped forward. "Okay," he whispered. "Do it. I'll hold down the fort. But you . . . don't you go getting yourself taken over, okay? No creature feature for you. Please?"

"Scout's honor," Wendy promised, tears in her eyes. "I love you, you know that, right? You big lug."

"Yeah, yeah," Eddie said. He wasn't crying but his voice was thick and tight. He pressed a sweet kiss to Wendy's temple and she inhaled the scent of him, trying to imprint his essence on her very soul. "I bet you say that to all your dead sexy best friends."

"Just you," Wendy said, playfully chucking him under the chin, attempting to shake off the overwhelming feeling that she would never see Eddie again. She stepped back to put distance between them, to give herself a moment to be separate before she lost yet another friend in the Never. "Just you, I promise."

"Hey, Wendy?" Eddie asked. When Wendy looked him in the eye Eddie winked and blew her a kiss. "All that stuff I said before, in my letter? I still mean it. I love you."

"I know, Eds." Then she moved aside as Emma knelt down and began to unravel the mess the Reapers had made of Eddie's cord.

"About Pete. If he treats you badly——"

"You'll be the first person I'll call," Wendy assured him. "Scout's honor."

"Amateurs," Emma muttered under her breath, her fingers darting in and out of Eddie's gut with remarkable speed. Beneath her hands the silver unwound from his center, whole but thin.

"What now?" Eddie asked. He cleared his throat nervously. Wendy crossed her arms over her chest. Part of her ached and wanted to run to him, to hold him one last time just in case . . . in case . . .

She held off.

"Sit in your body, Eddie," Emma instructed. "Lay back and try to line yourself up right. If anything feels like it's hanging out, it probably is."

Eddie chuckled as he edged onto the hospital bed. "No peeking at my insides, ladies, or under the sheet. A guy needs some privacy, you know."

"Be good, Eds," Wendy said.

"Always," he replied and laid back. Emma's hands flew over his midsection and, just like that, the loop of silver cord in her hands was gone.

"That's it?" Wendy said, amazed.

"That's it," Emma said and sighed. She sagged a little and Wendy rushed forward, catching her.

"You're a dumbass," Wendy said baldly. "You used some of yourself to link him back to his body, didn't you?"

"Had to," Emma said, wiping the back of her wrist against her forehead. "Whoever tied him up blocked him very well . . . on purpose."

"Elise," Wendy said.

"Most likely. Or Jane." Emma coughed roughly and held up a pale hand. "I'm cold. My body is, rather. They must be trying something new with me to keep my temperature down. How do you feel?"

"Thin," Wendy admitted. With Eddie gone and Piotr out of the room, she felt free to just be herself for once. "I don't know how much longer I can keep going, to be honest."

"I'm surprised you've held on this long," Emma agreed and winced. "You truly are very strong, Wendy."

"Just don't give up, okay? I'll try and sort this all out as fast as I can."

"You too," Emma said. She was so pale and thin now that the dawn light streaming through her glossy red hair shone rainbows briefly against the floor before clouding . . . and vanishing.

Heavy-hearted, Wendy left her best friend's stirring body behind and caught up with Piotr at the stairs. Behind her the machines in Eddie's room began beeping wildly as Wendy slid through the door.

"Where is Eddie? Did you say goodbye?" Piotr asked, glancing over her shoulder at the doctors rushing toward Eddie's room.

"Yeah," Wendy whispered, scrubbing a hand across her face. "I did. Come on."

"Russian Hill?" Wendy held up the key that Clyde had given her. An address had been finely etched into the bow of the key. Wendy scowled. It was almost too easy, it felt like a trap.

"Russian Hill," Piotr agreed. He surreptitiously pressed a hand against his side, but Wendy noticed. It pained her, but she said nothing, asked nothing. After their long and turbulent day, Wendy had learned the value of silence.

CHAPTER TWENTY-FIVE

The earthquakes were playing havoc with the highways so traveling to Russian Hill took longer than Wendy expected. She breathed a sigh of relief when they finally stepped off the bus. It had that wound its way drunkenly through the massive spirit web forest up Hyde Street and left them near the Norwegian Seamans Church, only a block away from the Francisco Street town home address listed on the key. Wendy was sore from head to toe from dodging the dangling webs and her essence felt weak, drained from just the proximity of the rent in the sky. She was definitely growing thinner.

The house was tan and set on the hill, the garage huddled below. During the ride over had Wendy thought that they would just pass through the garage but on reaching the house was surprised to find that it was solid in the Never.

Very, very solid.

"There's nothing important here," Wendy said to Piotr, both of them gazing up at the town home. "This isn't like Alcatraz or the Winchester house, it can't be a node of power or whatever, it's not special. It's just a home, right? So why is it so solid? It's like the Palace Hotel. I could kick that wall down before I'd go through it."

Piotr shrugged. "This is a mystery. Is it important?"

"Who knows? I'm just trying to figure out the right questions to ask these days." Wendy turned and began mounting the stairs. "Well, here's hoping someone left the door open, otherwise we're not getting in."

The owners of the home had locked the door behind them but luck was smiling on Wendy for once. She and Piotr stood on the

stoop debating how to find a way inside when a white van pulled into the driveway below. A skinny white girl with dreads and an intricate cross scarred into her collarbone mounted the stairs to the front door; she was carrying a bucket jammed with cleaning supplies and a mop and humming a jaunty tune under her breath.

On the front stoop, she pulled out a ring of keys and, pausing to yawn, picked one.

"Hello?" the maid called, sliding the key into the lock and tapping the door as she slowly entered. "Laurie? Kara? It's Seri! I know you two are probably sleeping off New Years so I'll just . . . oh my . . . oh shit . . . shitshitshit!"

Seri dropped her cleaning supplies and fled, leaving the door open just enough for Wendy and Piotr to squeeze inside. Once in the house, Wendy realized exactly why Seri had run. In addition to several long, brown hand-shaped splotches on the walls, there were large muddy footprints in the foyer, and several puddles of dried blood on the floor. The entire foyer stank of death and decay; exactly like the hospital room they'd just left.

Wincing and holding her breath, Wendy followed the filthy trail deeper into the house. It led past several mirrors, all busted into a spider web of cracks. Shards littered the floor. "Piotr," Wendy whispered, "I've got a really bad feeling about this."

The door to the basement was open.

"I believe that woman—Kara was her name?—lived here," Piotr said. "I think that she and the bunny-slipper woman lived here together."

"Yeah, I'm starting to get that vibe as well," Wendy said. "Should we . . . should we go down there?"

"We have come this far," Piotr said. "I have lost Elle and Lily and Dora and Tubs and Specs and James. All this . . . no, Wendy, we cannot hesitate."

"Right," Wendy said. She took a deep breath. "Okay. Let's . . . let's go."

Together, holding hands, they followed the horrible splotches down two levels to the basement. The lights were still on, dim and flickering and still in the clammy chill. The hearth across the room was in pieces; there were shattered remains of a mirror jumbled against the far wall.

"Piotr," Wendy said. "Is that my imagination or is there a door back there?"

"I see it, too," he said and drifted forward as if entranced. Wendy felt the chilly tug of the air moving around them as she squeezed Piotr's hand.

"It's a door only in the Never," Piotr said, bending down and examining the destroyed ruins of the fireplace. They were a frame for the heavy, solid wooden door set in the middle of the stone in the Never alone.

Dazed, Piotr reached for the handle. The door didn't budge. Wendy's hand dipped into her pocket; she pulled out the key Clyde had given her. The one Tracey had given him.

Wendy swallowed, turning the key over in her hand. Was she ready for whatever was behind that door? She had no clue but sensed that the answers were there, waiting.

"I think this is what we need," she suggested at last and handed the key to Piotr. He slid the key into the lock and turned.

Click. Click. Click.

THUD.

The door opened when he pulled the handle this time.

"Oh," Wendy sighed. The light that lit this tiny room was nothing more than reflected sunlight. There was a hole in the ceiling, cunningly cut and covered with thin mesh and thinner panes of glass, that allowed the natural dawn light to filter down, illuminating the great mounds of dust that had accumulated over everything. Shelves lined the narrow room and the items on them were neatly stacked and sorted: books, piles of linen, rolls of parchment, and small statues, totems, and intricate, delicate woodcarvings.

Wendy, holding her elbow over her nose to protect her face, blew on the closest pile of filthy items. The dust rose up in a huge puff and Wendy coughed despite herself, inhaling great quantities of the filthy air.

"I know these things," Piotr murmured as the dust settled and Wendy's mighty blow had cleared the first tangled bundle. They were base tan tunics, embroidered with fine black and golden red thread. Piotr ran a hand over the fabric and smiled.

"I cannot believe these are here," he said quietly. "I cannot believe they have traveled so far. I'd forgotten . . . so much. I didn't know that they brought these, too. I would have thought that they'd have mildewed to dust by now. I suppose in the living lands that they must have." He squinted around in that strange way Wendy recognized as Piotr looking into the living world. "I cannot tell," he said at last. "The Never is simultaneously too thin and too strong here."

"Piotr?" Wendy asked, recalling something from the last memory he'd shown her, the girls playing by the river. "This stuff. This is the stuff made by your mother?"

He nodded absently. "Yes. I think . . . I think these are the treasures of the Reapers. I think . . ." he reached into the next pile and then froze.

"Oh, Wendy," Piotr whispered.

"What is it?" she asked. "What did you find?"

Slowly Piotr took the length of fabric in both hands and pulled it from the shelf. It flapped out, longer than he was, and puddled on the ground.

"My mother's cloak," he whispered, aghast.

"Shut up!" Wendy gasped, startled. "How'd that get here? Why doesn't your mom have it?"

"You don't know? No, no, of course not. We've been so, so very busy, running like rabbits through the night. Now it is dawn and we are here, together. Come close, Wendy," Piotr said, setting aside the cloak and taking her hand, "and I will show you."

Wendy licked her lips. "You mean like another memory? Like before?"

"*Da*," he said. "The last one, I think. We have had no time for me to finish the tale, but now . . ." His hand surreptitiously grazed his side. "Now I think I must."

That decided it. "I'm in," Wendy said. "Shove me down the rabbit hole, Alice."

Piotr smiled and drew her close amid the filth and dust, wrapping his arms around her waist and leaning Wendy backward. Wendy wrapped her arms around his neck and let him support the bulk of her weight as Piotr pulled her closer.

He kissed her.

The memory fell around them like gentle rain, a halo of muffled mist pouring along the ground as Piotr's recollections rose from the mist.

"My mother," Piotr said, pulling back from their kiss and frowning at the web now entirely encasing his chest, "knew that the Reapers would never give up. She'd offended them. They would return."

"How long did the Reapers leave her alone before they came again?" Wendy asked. It killed her to know that this was what Piotr had been carrying for centuries, locked in the back of his skull but unable to access the knowledge. Piotr had sworn he'd protect the cloak and the necklace—and she knew Piotr was not one to give his word lightly—to him, knowing that he'd sworn to uphold some duty but had shirked it . . . it must be so maddening.

"To Sanngriðr, it was as if she'd stepped out of the room a moment, as if she'd given my mother just enough time to think things over and come to the most obvious solution. For the rest of us, the Reapers . . . the three Riders on shining horses . . . came once more as the year died."

"That's enough time . . . you all could have bailed. Why were you still there?"

"Death cannot be outrun, Wendy. Sanngriðr had my mother's scent—she could have found her anywhere in the world. Furthermore, where were we to go? This was our home. Though, granted, the villagers would no longer do business with us. My mother's wares went unsold for the first time ever. We spent the entire autumn putting away my father's extra harvest, for no one would dare trade with the tainted children of the red-witch."

"Your mother?"

"*Da*. And no one cursed more loudly than Uncle Kirill, who now knew that my father had lied to him all those years before. Kirill wanted nothing to do with my mother after that—he'd spent two decades believing that it was not his failing that allowed his brothers to die, but simple bad luck. Now he was faced with the truth—he had not been good enough a swordsman to save them and the only reason he was alive was due to a *woman*."

Piotr spat. "It infuriated him; *she* infuriated him. Kirill was wrongheaded in many ways. His wife had died birthing his son Yuri, and Kirill never remarried. When he found out what she was, he blamed her loss on Mother. Kirill thought Mother ought to have stepped in and saved her despite the fact that Mother never even learned of my aunt's bleeding before my aunt was a day dead."

"Ouch. That's . . . that's just rough," Wendy said. She couldn't imagine the grief Kirill must have carried around with him every day, the anger that must have blazed into being on learning that one of Death's handmaidens had been so close at hand all along. "I kinda get that. So was Kirill around when Sanngriðr and the others showed up again?"

"In the dead of winter, as the dawn broke the horizon, I sat with my father and Uncle Kirill in the trees of the forest as, far below us, a large boar foraged. It had found good pickings over the autumn, the swine was still fat and jolly, snuffling beneath the snow for lunch."

Piotr grimaced as, around them, the memory unfolded, growing

brighter and firmer as he relived it. Past-Piotr was on the highest branch, arrow notched as Kirill, on an opposing branch, silently lifted one hand. Wendy spied Borys in the bushes, a large spear at hand, a notched sword by his feet.

Kirill dropped his arm and the arrows flew, one after another, embedding themselves in the boar's neck.

Jerk or not, Wendy thought, the man was talented with a bow; Kirill's first arrow speared through the boar's eye, the second impaled the other, and the third embedded itself in the neck so that a large spurt of blood gushed across the thick snow.

Grinning, Borys jumped from the bushes, spear and hand, and approached the boar. "Tonight, my family, we feast well! Kirill, I give you my thanks. We have not had meat in weeks. My girls are getting scrawny!"

"You needn't thank me but be careful," Kirill ordered Borys, unstringing his bow. "She is not yet dead. Let her bleed a bit before you get within biting range."

"Which is why I lead with the spear," Borys replied cheerfully, stepping past the bushes. He had hardly gotten a foot closer when, from the trail, they heard a sharp, furious squeal. A second boar charged forward, her head up, mouth open, and bit Borys sharply on the leg.

"Papa!" Piotr cried from his vantage point in the tree as his father toppled to the snow. The second boar, scenting his blood, bit again and again, her sharp tusks and teeth rending the flesh of his leg apart in seconds.

"Piotr!" his uncle ordered, rapidly restringing his bow. "I'll stay with your father. Run and get Yuri! Be quick! Watch for boars!"

Past-Piotr scrambled down the tree.

"Piotr!" His father cried. "Forget Yuri! Get your mother!"

"No!" demanded Kirill. "Borys, be still you stubborn fool and let me help you for just once! Eir cannot help here—you are only wounded, not dying. Get Yuri, Piotr. Hurry!"

Past-Piotr sprinted off, leaving his uncle and father behind.

"I took the fastest route to find him, but my cousin was not in the fields or the village," Piotr said as the world pulsed around them, short snippets of Piotr stopping to check each location flashing around them and fading rapidly. "He was not even at the cabin at the edge of the woods. So I headed for home. If I could not find Yuri, then my mother would have to do."

Wendy shook her head. She knew how this had to go. "The Valkyrie were there, waiting."

"Correct. My mother had taught my sisters all she knew about the Reapers—how to fight them long enough to escape, how to run to earth and hide in flowing water to disperse their scent—but Eir didn't expect Sanngriðr to return so quickly. She thought that Sanngriðr's Riders would wait at least until the spring to come again."

Wendy felt her stomach sink as the large center room of Piotr's home coalesced into being around them—his sisters were all there, some spinning and weaving together a safe distance from the fire, the elder girls rubbing salt into flats of fresh-caught fish as Þrima and Róta, sitting together on the hearth, taught the tiny, red-haired toddler how to sort hewn wooden blocks into a basket. Eir alone was missing from the scene though Wendy could hear light, pleasant humming from a back room.

"They're all here," Wendy whispered as Piotr's deaf sister passed through her on her way toward the back of the hearth room. Wendy closed her eyes, expecting that the touch of the girl would burn the same way the touch of the living did, but there was nothing, not even the faintest pressure.

"Save for my father, my uncle, and my cousin Yuri, yes, my entire family was in this house," Piotr said. "They were taken by surprise."

The drama had built so that Wendy expected Sanngriðr to fling open the door to the cottage. The polite knock and sudden silence that followed were startling. Wendy jumped in surprise.

In the stillness Róta rose and, carrying her toddler on her hip, opened the door.

Sanngriðr attacked.

Only Piotr's arm wrapped around Wendy's waist kept Wendy from trying to uselessly thrust herself between Róta and Sanngriðr.

Róta did her best to dodge the spear of Light that flicked forward and stabbed her through the gut—she was still holding her daughter, after all—but Sanngriðr had the element of surprise and, unlike Róta, Sanngriðr had no one to protect.

The sound came rushing back and with it the sharp, sudden scream as Róta hit the ground.

As one the sisters leapt up, some going for Sanngriðr and others fleeing toward the room in the back where the humming originated, shouting, "Momma! Momma!"

Sanngriðr's Light caught the runners first—a series of stabs and they lay twitching on the ground, blocking the doorway. Summoned by the noise, Eir came running from the back room but by time she reached the hearth room all her daughters were dying, bleeding sluggishly across the previously clean floors.

"Sanngriðr!" Eir spit, dropping to her knees beside her closest daughter and glaring at the Reaper. "What have you done?!"

Sanngriðr raised one eyebrow. "I should think it would be obvious, Eir. You were given three chances to bring your husband to Freyja's door. Instead you spread your legs and bore him children. Thankfully none were boys or you'd be in a true mess."

"Freyja sent you? Freyja wanted you to do this?"

Sighing, Sanngriðr rolled her eyes. "No, sister. This was my doing alone. Now will you come? Your children are dead, and the wind whispers to me that your beloved farmer is dying in the woods. All that you love is on Death's door. Come with me now and guide them into the Light."

Tears sliding down her cheeks, Eir licked her lips. "Borys is . . . no. NO! He's fine. He is far away from here. You're lying!"

"I don't need to," Sanngriðr said simply, examining a spot of blood on her hand and wiping it off with a thumb. Frowning, she checked the hem of her cloak, relaxing visibly when it proved fresh and clean of blood. "One of his companions comes here now, running at top speed to fetch you."

"No," Róta said, pulling herself to a standing position using the doorway. "You will not—"

"You are wasting your last minutes alive rebuking me," Sanngriðr said, "when you could be using them to try and soothe your dying daughter."

Immediately Róta paled and dropped to her knees, crawling quickly toward red-haired child, leaving a long, dripping trail on the floor behind her. Wendy ached for her—it was obvious that her little girl was probably not going to make it.

"I will destroy you," Eir said, rising to her feet, the hem of her skirt dripping the blood of her daughters.

"Hardly," Sanngriðr sighed. "Now that the distractions have been taken care of, come with me."

The room blinked—went dark for a brief instant and then flashed back—as past-Piotr barreled through the door and slid on the pools of blood, going to a knee beside Róta's head. Piotr cracked his temple on the edge of the table falling down; a long, jagged gash welled open and began to drip down his face.

Eir and Sanngriðr were gone.

"What happened?" Piotr demanded, shaking Róta's shoulder. "Where's Momma? Róta? Róta?!"

"One of the Riders," Wendy heard and she turned. There, in the far corner, Þrima sat, covered in blood from head to toe, her hand pressed against the gaping wound in her side. She was exhausted, pale and worn, blood dripping from the corner of her mouth but Þrima was somehow, miraculously, still alive. "The ladies who're like Momma."

"The Reapers," past-Piotr and Piotr both said simultaneously.

Piotr's face was wet with tears, his flesh was curdled-milk pale; the scar on his face stood out in stark, twisted relief. Wendy hugged him and he held her close, burying his face in her hair. She felt the drip of his tears as, beside them, his past self hugged Þrima and demanded details.

"I'm tired, Piotr," Þrima whispered at last when she'd described the day. "I'm so tired."

"I'll get help," past-Piotr promised. "Just . . . just don't . . ."

Þrima took his hand in hers and edged over, resting her head in his lap, her fingers loosely grasping his clean left knee, leaving a small bloodied handprint clearly against the leather. "I wish Róta were here," she said, eyes fluttering closed. "My head feels so heavy . . . I wish she could brush my hair. Róta is the only one who can always get the tangles . . ."

Þrima stilled, her breathing hitching once, twice . . . and no more.

CHAPTER TWENTY-SIX

Piotr yanked Wendy so close she could hardly draw breath. He shook in her embrace—heavy trembling that nearly knocked Wendy to her knees. She braced herself and held Piotr, saying nothing, only rubbing his back and letting him weep into her hair until the ends of her front curls hung lank and damp from the tears.

At long last, the shaking slowed. Piotr pulled from her arms, wiping the wetness away with a forearm. "My sisters were dead," he said as his past self very carefully, very slowly, eased his littlest sister's head off his lap, resting her red curls in the clear spot on the floor where he'd sat.

"You took the cloak," Wendy said. She could sense where the rest of this story was going.

"I fetched the cloak," he agreed. "And the necklace. I put the cloak on—I was wet and cold and struck numb from the horrible moment—but I did not put on the necklace. I could not find Yuri. My mother was gone and when I asked for help in the village it was as if they couldn't see me. At the time I was too stupid from what I'd just witnessed to realize that the cloak was hiding me from them. All I knew was that it was time to return to my father and my uncle in the woods."

Wendy swallowed thickly. "What happened next?"

Piotr smiled bitterly. "Watch."

The walk from the homestead into the forest took longer than Wendy had imagined it might. Piotr's past-self trudged through thigh-high snow in places, the cloak the only thing keeping him warm, the blood dripping from the gash in his forehead down his face, staining the cloak even further. Birds silently lined the canopy

of trees above him; the air was filled with feathers and snow as he forced himself to keep going, to keep shoving on, until he could reach his father.

When Piotr reached the clearing where Kirill and Borys rested, Wendy wanted to rush forward and stop him. Kirill was clearly on edge, his hand trembling on his bow, an arrow already notched and ready to fly. Beside him Borys was white and feverish, pouring sweat and moaning. His leg was a ruin; she could spot the obliterated bone poking through his skin in several places.

The boar's powerful jaws had snapped his leg like kindling. Kirill had somehow managed to mostly dress the pigs by himself— they both hung by their heels from the trees he and Piotr had been resting in—but the blood beneath the bodies had long since stopped steaming and now puddled in a congealed mess.

"Kirill knew the blood-scent would attract predators, like wolves or bears, but meat was too precious to waste, especially in the dead of winter," Piotr said beside her.

"He looks nervy," Wendy said.

"I was a fool to approach him so close to the camp. The smart thing to do would have been to make noise long before I drew close, but I was so wrapped up in . . . everything, really . . . that I didn't see how crazed Kirill was."

"You took off the cloak," Wendy said as, before them, past-Piotr did just that. He'd hardly loosened the clasp at the throat, becoming only faintly visible, when Kirill screamed and let the arrow fly.

Past-Piotr jerked back as the scream ripped from his uncle's throat. The arrow, had it flown true, would have embedded itself in his face. Instead it furrowed a large gash across his cheekbone.

Kirill, still screaming, notched another arrow and let fly, then another, then another. Piotr, hunched over, took the second arrow from temple to jaw, the third in his right shoulder, driving him to the ground, and the fourth, due to his fall, missed him completely. It would have nailed directly into his heart.

"Oh Piotr," Wendy whispered.

Piotr shook his head. "It gets worse."

His body lay twitching on the ground, mostly covered by the cloak. The arrow in his shoulder had been shoved all the way through due to his fall and the arrowhead gleamed wetly, dripping on the back of the cloak; Kirill, scowling, set aside his quiver.

"You," he whispered, glancing briefly over his shoulder at Borys, sleeping uneasily and breathing harshly beside him. "Always you, like your sisters in your feathered finery! Did they convince you to come home this time, to do your job right as you were supposed to in the woods that day? Borys is old now, yeah? Are his words no longer pretty enough to save him? Is it finally his time?"

Kirill spat on the ground. "I'm sorry, Eir. I can't let you take him. *This* time I will save him, the way he saved me. If I have to kill you myself, I will."

Kirill drew the knife strapped to his leg and, moving slowly, approached Piotr's bloody body. The cloak twitched as Piotr struggled to rise to his hands and knees, the hood of the cloak hiding his face, blood dripping freely onto the snow beneath him.

"You don't have to watch this if you don't wish," Piotr told Wendy. "It is not pretty."

"I've hung on this long," Wendy whispered through numb lips. Her heart was pounding in her chest, her gut twisting in horror and anticipation. Piotr pulled her closer; Wendy realized that he was prepared to grab her again.

Kirill kicked the body on the ground and stabbed down. Piotr, wounded, bleeding freely, pushed up, exposing his face in the last moment, startling Kirill into faltering. The knife slid down Piotr's cheek, flaying the side of his face from temple to jaw.

Piotr, expression twisting into a furious snarl, still had enough strength to grab his uncle's wrists and yank hard, jerking the knife and Kirill's wrists downward. Kirill's knife turned in his grip; Piotr surged forward and *shoved*.

The sound of the knife punching into his heart was first a sharp crack as Piotr broke Kirill's ribs, followed by a wet squish as the knife slid in.

Wendy closed her eyes but quickly forced herself to open them again. Piotr was asking her to act as witness; she didn't dare hide behind squeamishness now. "You killed him."

"I killed him," Piotr said as his past-self yanked the knife free and threw it to the snow. Kirill, hand pressed against his chest, shook his head. "My uncle would have killed my mother in an instant—had *planned* on killing her, in fact. I killed him first."

"Piotr?" Kirill asked, wheezing. "You . . . you were not supposed to be . . . where . . . where is Eir? That cloak . . . the other bird-women wore . . . where is your mother, Piotr?"

"Dead, for all I know," Piotr said, grabbing his uncle by the front of his leather vest. "But you would have killed her, Uncle. You would have hurt her, my mother, your married-sister, instead of me. Why, Uncle? Why?"

"Her death-sister, the one who rode the steed across the sky," whispered Kirill, blood flecking his lips now. He hugged Piotr close and the blood poured from his chest, pulsing all over Piotr with every heartbeat until the entire cloak of feathers was sodden with blood.

"While I waited . . . for you, she came to me. She . . . she said that Eir would . . . come to take Borys, and that she would allow him to die because this was their way. She said that . . . he was . . . her responsibility. If Eir didn't . . . take him, he wouldn't . . . die only . . . suffer. She said Eir would . . . would wear her cloak of fine feathers . . . to get here faster . . ."

Piotr turned his face away and took the knife in his hand. "But I came instead." He dropped Kirill and his uncle collapsed to the ground.

Wendy's stomach lurched. She turned her face away and realized that Piotr—her Piotr—was supporting her the same way he'd once supported his uncle, before allowing Kirill's dead weight to crumble to the snow.

CHAPTER
TWENTY-SEVEN

"**D**o you love me so much now, knowing this?" Piotr asked quietly. He wouldn't look at her—he could not tear his gaze from his past-self who leaned down and cleaned his uncle's knife on the clean shoulder of Kirill's tunic. It was a colder gesture than Wendy would have expected out of him. "You think so highly of me but this is who I am. I am a blood-killer, Wendy. I am a murderer."

Then, startling her, past-Piotr strode to a nearby tree, took a deep breath, and flung himself backward at the trunk. The arrow head caught; the shaft of the arrow shoved back through his body, punching a second hole in his shoulder. Piotr twisted, snapping off the arrowhead and then reached up.

"What are you doi— OH MY GOD," Wendy cried, covering her eyes. She'd seen so much at this point—had hardly blinked as some of the foulest and most disgusting things had pawed all over her, had touched her with their rotten tongues and fingers and breathed their death-stench in her face—and yet it was the sight of Piotr, screaming as he yanked the arrow fletching first through the second hole that made her sick.

Wendy turned her face away and fought with her gorge.

"Wendy?" Piotr's arm curled around her shoulder. "Are you . . . how do you feel?"

She shook her head. Slowly her stomach settled. When she straightened, the world was white around them once more; Piotr's father and the woods were gone.

"Did he die?" Wendy asked.

"Yes," Piotr said. "When I left that Kirill in that clearing, I never saw either of them again. I thought I would be right back but I was wrong."

Wendy wiped her mouth with the back of her hand. "What happened?" She then paused, examining past-Piotr closely. "That knife . . ." she dug in her pocket and came up with the dull blade that Lily had been wielding against Jane. "This knife . . . they're the same thing. This is the knife that killed your uncle." She felt sick again.

"*Da.* It is. Drenched in the blood of a would-be kin-killer and wielded by a killer of kin. I put that knife away, just as you had, and I put my hand in my pocket," Piotr said. "And there was the necklace. I remembered . . . I remembered promising Mother that I'd keep both the cloak and the necklace safe. But the cloak was in ruin, you see, so I was at a loss. I knew there was no way I could clean it properly so it would fly."

"Did you put on the necklace?" Wendy asked. She put the knife away once more, hoping that she'd never have to look at it again. The thing creeped her out now.

Expression grim, Piotr nodded. "I was dying, though I didn't know it. I just thought I was uncomfortable—Kirill's arrow had damaged a few important nerves." He touched the twisting scar on his cheek. "Mostly I was annoyed by my head wound. It bled a great deal."

"I always wondered where you got that," Wendy whispered. "Why didn't the other wounds leave a mark in the Never?"

Laughing, Piotr looked over her shoulder. Wendy turned as a large, bright field bloomed into being around them. The sun was bright, the air warm, and nameless, impossibly beautiful flowers bloomed underfoot. Just behind her a simple sling-backed chair sat in a clearing. All around were men and women—attractive, healthy, strong-armed, and stern-faced—went about their daily business. They were all armed.

Wendy blinked in surprise. "Wait . . . is this . . . is this Valhalla?"

"Fólkvangr," Piotr said as past-Piotr appeared a few feet away from them, stepping from nothing the way Eir had on the day she'd met Borys. "These are the host-fields, the waiting fields where Freyja's Valkyrie bring half the honorable dead and all the women who die a noble death."

"All the women come here, huh?" Wendy raised an eyebrow. "Is it sexist that only half the warriors hang out amid the flowers, but all the ladies do?"

"Nobly-dead ladies," Piotr corrected. "And I didn't create the worlds, Wendy, I only know of their existence."

"So this is the Heaven I've been sending people to?" Wendy asked. "I guess this isn't so bad."

"Heaven? *Net*, Wendy, you misunderstand me. Fólkvangr is not where the Light leads. No one knows that, not even Freyja. This is but one possible afterlife. Mother once told me that there were more paths from the Light than stars in the sky."

"But isn't Freyja a god? Goddess? Whatever?"

"Even gods can die, Wendy," Piotr murmured as a woman, slim and lovely and familiar, sprinted across the field and caught past-Piotr as he dropped to his knees amid the fragrant flowers. "Even goddesses can pass into the Light."

"Momma," he whispered as Eir caught him. "Momma, I found you . . ."

"Hush, Piotr," Eir demanded, laying him on the ground in front of her. Hurrying, Eir yanked a long hair from her own head and a blade of grass from the earth. In her hand the grass became a needle, the hair a thread.

Eir set to work on Piotr's face, stitching up the gushing gash in seconds as two more women approached at a more leisurely pace. As they drew nearer, Wendy heard Piotr grumble beside her. The taller of the women was Sanngriðr.

The smaller woman, red-haired and lovely, clad in a plain white tunic and a simple silver hairband, settled herself in the sling-back chair a few feet away and politely waited for Eir to finish stitching Piotr's face.

"I see that you have brought Brísingamen back to me," the woman said. Her voice was quiet and stern. "Though the cloak I made for you is worse for wear, Eir."

Eir flinched. "I am sorry, my lady."

"It stinks of living blood, Eir," Sanngriðr sneered. "It is rife with it."

"Sanngriðr is not wrong," the smaller woman said and Wendy realized that this lady, barely more than a girl, must be Freyja. "Though she is crude and cruel." Her voice lilted strangely and Wendy shivered. Freyja's voice was so familiar . . .

"My apologies, my lady," Eir said.

"You should be sorry," Sanngriðr snapped. "You've caused us nothing but trouble, Eir! And for what? The affection of some human male? I hope spreading your legs was worth it, because—"

Freyja slashed the air with one hand, cutting the fierce woman off. "Sanngriðr, enough!"

Eir smoothed hanks of Piotr's bloody hair off his temple and cheeks, her face hidden behind her long hair. Wendy saw three drops patter down on Piotr's cheeks—she looked up at the sky and noted that it was clear before Wendy realized that Eir was silently crying over her wounded son.

"Eir," Freyja said, "we have not finished our conversation. You have not explained your actions."

"There is nothing to explain, Lady," snarled Sanngriðr. "Eir is a traitor! She allowed herself to become flesh . . . she not only gave birth to a *male*, but Eir did not bash his brains out when he slithered from her! Look at her cloak. Look at your precious golden Brísingamen! You granted her use of it so she could travel instantly to Miðgarðr and do your bidding quickly, and yet there it is, upon

the neck of her filthy son! He used it—*HE* used it—a living man . . .
he came here, with his beating heart, flying on Reaper wings!"

"I know why I gave Eir my Brísingamen, Sanngriðr," Freyja said
and her tone was sharp and strange. "Stop speaking. Your voice is
drilling in my temples."

"My Lady—"

"Sanngriðr . . . *stop speaking*!"

Scowling, Sanngriðr fell silent, but her expression was as elo-
quent as her words wanted to be.

"Eir," Freyja said, flicking a warning glance in Sanngriðr's direction, "insistent though she might be, Sanngriðr has a point. You
have disobeyed me. Several times. And I would have to be blind to
not see the resemblance between you and the boy lying there, to
smell the scent of Reaper in his very blood mingled with the human
stench—yet, again, Sanngriðr is not incorrect. He is alive. Dying,
true, but his heart still beats."

Freyja waited, but Eir did not defend herself. "Have you nothing
to say for yourself, for him?"

"His name is Piotr," Eir said, stroking his face. "He is my son—
the only one, though I bore eight other children from the seed of the
farmer you desired—and Piotr is the only of my nine babes still
drawing breath. What else is there to say? I am a mother and I was
meat and now I mourn, for Sanngriðr has killed every member of my
family. Do with me what you will, Freyja, for I am already dead inside."

"Sanngriðr, is this the truth?" Freyja straightened on her sling-
back chair, her heels bracketing the legs of the makeshift throne, and
plucked the silver band from her head. Freyja's long red hair tumbled
over her shoulder, pooling in her lap; her fingers played with the ends.

"Of course it is," Sanngriðr said, waving a hand dismissively at
Eir and Piotr. "Eir said that she would not leave her family, Lady, so
I made sure she would heed your call. I slaughtered them before
their hearthfire to show Eir what it means to be a Reaper, what it
means to disobey the word of the great Lady and our Reaper vows."

"Oh Sanngriðr," Eir sighed, shaking her head. "You utter fool."

"Silence, human-whore!" Sanngriðr snarled, pulling back a leg to kick Eir. Sanngriðr had hardly begun to swing when Freyja, standing so fast Wendy couldn't follow the movement, strode forward and yanked Sanngriðr backwards, flinging her to the flowers beneath their feet.

"Sanngriðr," Freyja said softly, dangerously, "*you* are the one who has forsaken your vows. Or have you forgotten them already?"

"What? I have done nothing of the sort!" Sanngriðr declared, rolling to her feet and wiping away the dirt smudging her tunic. "I have been true to you!"

"Reapers do not take life unbidden, Sanngriðr," Eir said, still caressing Piotr's face, still crying quiet tears between her words. "A life that ends before its time is energy, Light, wasted. Only when the soul is at the end of its days, only when the book of its days is about to close, may we step forward and collect it. Only then, if their flesh is stubborn, may we help cut them from the coil, slicing away the caul of their flesh. Only then."

"I didn't collect their souls, stupid Eir," Sanngriðr sneered. "I left their spirits in their flesh to rot."

Eir jerked, rocking back on her heels and letting out a great, long moan, nearly a howl of pain. She flung herself forward over Piotr's body, sobbing uncontrollably.

Freyja frowned. "Sanngriðr. Stand before me."

Sanngriðr strode past Eir, rolling her eyes at the woman's agony, and stood before Freyja, head held back, chest outthrust.

"Sanngriðr," Freyja said, "I tire of this matter and I tire of you. So I have decided it—I am done. I am done with you, Sanngriðr. I am done with Eir, and I am done with Miðgarðr. The host-fields are filled with an uncountable number of warriors. Valhalla is, as well. We have no need of Miðgarðr's feeble offerings—greater warriors are to be found elsewhere, in other realms, in other, stronger worlds."

Sanngriðr scowled. "I do not understand, Lady. What—"

"Henceforth, Eir, for your crime of dallying with a living human—for not only bearing him children, but for bearing him a boy and allowing your blood to be diluted in a male form—for this crime Miðgarðr is cut off from the Rainbow Bridge. No Reaper shall be allowed entrance or exit, unless they travel with my blessing, with my necklace. So cut off, Miðgarðr shall hang in the space without, at the mercy of the deep creatures, the dark ones, the Jötnar and Dvergar and Álfar. And worse. But, to prove I am not completely heartless, I will not leave the souls born to Miðgarðr bereft."

Eir lifted her face, tracked dirty with tears and blood, to Freyja. "My Lady?"

"I leave the handling of the spirits of Miðgarðr in your family's capable hands, Eir," Freyja said quietly, kneeling down and brushing a lock of hair off Eir's face.

"It is both my blessing and your curse: every year, for every drop of blood that has soiled your cloak, a hundred spirits must suffer in the not-realm born of your folly. Your children and your children's children and their spawn ever after must henceforth guide and guard these damned souls, ferrying them to the Light and the afterlife that even one such as I cannot reach."

"But my Lady . . . my children are . . ."

"What mother, who bled to bring her babies into the world, would not bleed to bring them to life once more?" Freyja asked in a whisper. "Will you give up your flesh—your human life—for your children, knowing that you are condemning them and their children and all generations hence, to an existence of being the only Light in a great and vast plain of darkness? They will suffer for your transgressions, just as you suffered to bring them into the world."

"How?" Eir demanded, wiping her face, expression cautious but growing lighter with hope. "How would they suffer? What is this curse?"

"They will live a short, painful life, Eir, burning up from the inside if they do not guide souls into the Light. Or they will live a longer life

spent in the good work of guiding souls . . . but one that could cut off with no warning, their books closing early, for without the Rainbow Bridge to follow, it shall require a bit of their life force to send a spirit across the vast nothingness and into the Light. If they do neither, if they turn their face from their duty, if they allow too many spirits to gather, then the spirit realm will overrun the living world. Miðgarðr will be laid open for the Dark Ones to plunder and feast."

"And if I do not?" Eir whispered. "If I do not give myself to you, if I do not wake my children from their death-sleep, what then?"

"Then their souls rot in their bodies," Freyja said simply. "Miðgarðr is still cut off and shall soon fall prey to the Dark Ones between the worlds. And you go on living happily here. I will, of course, hang your son's body by his heels for all of Fólkvangr to see and bear witness to. I shall not have a Reaper of mine dallying with a creature from a lesser realm, Eir. It cannot be."

"I choose your mercy, I gladly give my life." Eir shook her head. "But what of my son, Lady? I thank you for my daughters . . . but what of Piotr?"

Freyja sighed. "I am giving you eight of your children back and you quibble over the ninth?"

"I am a mother, Lady," Eir whispered. "I could not call myself such if I did not."

"Fine! Fine, foolish, greedy girl!" Freyja raged. "He has been here, has bled upon my sacred earth and been healed by your hair. You are spirit here, Eir, not flesh. His wound is closed, his heart still beats. He is now part spirit, part flesh, and all damned. Piotr cannot return to Miðgarðr now. Not as he is."

"But Lady—" Eir protested.

"I am not done!" Freyja growled, holding up a hand. "Bestill my heart; you Reapers do like to interrupt today!" She scowled between Eir and Sanngriðr.

"Piotr cannot return to Miðgarðr, but he can aid his sisters. I shall create a space, a place, where he can watch over the souls that

need yet to be gathered and sent across the deep, dark spaces into the Light. Those souls that shine brightest shall call to him; he will know your descendents and they can make use of him until such a time as I call them home. And this I shall not do, until every spirit has been sent on. Every single one and not before! I have said my piece. My word is my bond!"

"This is madness!" snarled Sanngriðr. "What sort of punishment is that? You bring her dead children back to life? You create a special place for her son to frolic about, where he can play with the dead as if he'd done nothing wrong? What sort of pain is this? What sort of suffering?"

"Hush, Sanngriðr," Eir hissed. "For your own sake if not my own!"

"Let her words dig her grave," Freyja said mildly. "She is doing splendidly."

"Have done with me then!" demanded Sanngriðr. "If this is what you call *punishment*, then punish me, my Lady. Let me hear your decree for my 'misdeeds.'"

"So be it. Sanngriðr," Freyja said sternly. "For your crime of not only cutting short the lives of eight children, but of leaving their souls lost within their shells to rot, I condemn you to rot as well. May your flesh show the degradation in your heart. Only the forgiveness of Eir's brood will give you back your flesh, but even then . . . even then, it will rot again in due time. Your face will be the mirror of your soul, Sanngriðr. This is your punishment."

CHAPTER
TWENTY-EIGHT

The white drew down and filled the world once more.

Wendy blinked and just like that they were back in the basement of the Russian Hill home, the stained and ruined cloak puddle at their feet, and the draft moving through the open door. No time had passed, she could sense it. That entire interlude, as before, had happened between breaths.

"So . . ." Wendy said, "that's it? That's all?"

"That is all," Piotr agreed, bending down and gathering up the cloak. He folded it reverently and set it back on its dusty shelf. "My mother gave up her life for my sisters. My sisters woke from their temporary death to find the house in shambles, blood on the floor and the hearthstone pried open. I was gone, and when Róta found villagers willing to venture with her into the woods, they discovered Kirill's body and my father breathing his last breaths."

"So your sisters never found out what happened?" Wendy was confused. "Then how did they know to become Reapers?"

"Life ends, life goes on. Róta held my father's hand as he passed and when she opened her eyes, Light filled the clearing. He stepped into the Light . . . and I stepped out of nothing. Freyja herself had come to leave Sanngriðr's soul and my own in the Never after she had cut Miðgarðr off from Fólkvangr and the other realms."

"How did Róta take it?"

"She begged Freyja to take her instead. Sanngriðr murdered

277

Róta's daughter, my niece, in the fray, as well. With no husband and no child, Róta felt that she had nothing to live for. She wanted to be dead too, to join them in the Light."

"Oh . . . Piotr, I'm sorry, I'd forgotten about your niece," Wendy said, reaching forward and fingering the silky cloth at hand. It was a small gown, just the right size for an infant, and slippery-smooth to the touch. She felt a tightness in her throat. "Freyja wouldn't help her too?"

"Freyja couldn't," Piotr corrected her, gripping his side and grimacing. "Mother was dead by then—her life forfeit. Freyja could not go back and undo what had been done—she could not stretch Mother's life further than had already been spent to bring back my sisters. And since Miðgarðr was cut off at that point . . . little Katusha's soul was lost. Or, as the case may be, *Lost*."

Wendy, driven by whim, kissed the silky fabric, inhaled its musty, dusty scent. "Did you find her?"

"*Da*," Piotr said, taking the tiny gown from Wendy and folding it, setting it back on the table of tunics.

"We found her in the room she died in, trying to get the attention of my other sisters. I took her under my wing and we found a safe spot to rest our heads while Róta took it upon herself to organize our sisters into . . . well, the Reapers. Freyja is stern but not heartless. She felt badly over missing Katusha; Freyja gave Róta our mother's cloak and Brísingamen as . . . a sort of penance, I suppose."

Wendy was startled. "She gave away her fancy necklace again? Why?"

"Freyja knew it was safest here, locked away on Miðgarðr away from the antics of the other gods who liked to steal it from her. Who would think to look for it amid the humans? It was worse than useless to my sisters. The necklace could only be used once—to call Freyja to Miðgarðr, to tell her that we had sent every soul in the Never into the Light. A single use—Róta knew the cloak and necklace had to be protected. This she took upon herself and handed down the duty to every matriarch since."

Wendy frowned. "Nana Moses didn't have a necklace on when I met her. She was just in a nightgown. Do you think she has it? Had it?"

Piotr stilled. "No. The necklace went missing many years ago. In fact . . . Wendy, now that I think of it, Brísingamen may be here, among these artifacts. We should look—your Dr. Kensington may be after Brísingamen. He demanded the key from the ruined woman-creature in the hospital; only Brísingamen and the cloak are worth risking everything over."

"Good point," Wendy said, turning around and eyeing the closest shelf. It was covered in rings of all shapes and sizes and small chests of overflowing chains. She sighed and set to work sorting through the tangled links. "So your sister built the Reapers . . . and you built the Riders? Were you trying to be sarcastic?"

Beside her, hands deep in his own box, Piotr grinned. "*Da.* I decided to steal the name before Sanngriðr could take it again. Over the years, we gathered souls to us. I found teenagers and children, she sought out the furious, the disenfranchised, and the truly evil. Sanngriðr was bound and determined to ruin everything as frequently as she could. She wanted to make us suffer for our transgressions."

"That makes a sick sort of sense, I guess."

"Eventually our family grew so large that the Light became a nuisance—we were beckoning the creatures from between the worlds and they gnawed on the thinner edges of reality around us. We had to spread out; we had to thin our ranks. Instead of every child being taken to deathbeds as an aid, a washer of limbs and listener of prayers, only the chosen children, the strongest and smartest and quickest were taken. And then, in time, only the chosen girls."

"Why only girls?"

Piotr shrugged. "That I do not know. It happened in the space of only a few generations—around the time many of the main branch of the family had traveled on longships to a little green island amid a choppy sea."

He smirked and moved on to the next box in the line. "The

spirits were so many and so strong there that the Never had long since begun to weaken. The living could see the dead in spots and had found certain patterns could confuse the weak Shades, could turn away the Walker's bite. They'd taken to working the patterns into their very skins, to keep the Walkers from reaching through the thin spaces and feasting upon them." He reached forward and tapped Wendy on the collarbone. "They are quite useful, *da?*"

"The Celtic knots," Wendy said, impressed as she paused to finger her wrist tattoos. Her skin was so thin beneath her fingertips, Wendy worried that if she pressed too hard she might poke a hole in her essence. Her body must be nearly brain dead by now, burning up with the fever. Strangely, despite her promise to Eddie, Wendy found that she didn't care about the possibility of dying as much as she should. Some perverted part of her rejoiced at the idea of staying in the Never with Piotr. "You really did get around."

"The Reapers got around," Piotr corrected. His search through the jewelry done, he picked up a book off a stack near the door. He blew the dust off it and paged through the chapters, shaking his head when he found nothing.

"I was only along for the ride—training spirits as I went in the art of keeping souls safe. The keeper of the cloak and necklace, usually the next in line to become the matriarch, would travel, and I generally would travel with her. Instinctively, I followed the main line of descendents, those who kept the necklace."

"Which eventually led you here, to protecting the Lost and training the Riders how to survive and scavenge," Wendy said, following his example and beginning to clean and examine the items around her. The jewelry boxes had been a bust for Brísingamen, but that didn't mean some savvy Reaper hadn't hidden it between layers of tunics or rolls of parchment. "How?"

"I found many different dead warriors on my travels and trained with them, promising to pass their secrets along to my Riders. I spent only a generation here, a generation there, before the longships

came again and I boarded. I traveled the world this way, catching rides with the fierce sailors until eventually I found myself on unfamiliar shores, surrounded by leather-clad natives."

"America . . . or what would become America?" Wendy guessed. This shelf offered nothing that seemed to scream "special" to her. "Wow, Piotr. Just . . . wow."

"And now, I am here, in this burial chamber of my past, looking at the detritus of my life." Piotr ran his hand along the table by the door. "The space is so thin here, so tattered. If you wave an arm you could nearly poke through."

"I think . . . I think there was a creature here," Wendy said. "I think this place was where that thing that took over the lady in the hospital punched through."

"This is not a surprise to me," Piotr said. He blinked, startled, and picked up a necklace off the same section he'd found the cloak. Wendy didn't need to ask if it was Brísingamen—it glowed with a faint silvery aura that sent shivers down her spine.

"The puzzle pieces fit now," Piotr continued, pocketing the necklace as he gave Wendy a long, meaningful look. "Sanngriðr has been stalking the naturals she could locate, mostly Seers, finding ways to lure them to spaces in the Never both powerful and thin."

"Then she uses one of her Walkers or her own abilities to off the Seer," Wendy continued grimly, blowing the dust off the second shelf as she walked along and pausing to examine the artifacts lined like soldiers in neat rows, "punching a big ol' hole in the Never and the spaces between."

"Or, in this case, the living lands and the space between," Piotr replied, rubbing under his ribs and stepping away from the shelf. "A creature slips through and seeks out a ghost, or a living person, to inhabit. They . . ." he broke off, clutching his chest and cursing.

"I'm tired of being quiet about this," Wendy snapped, furiously sorting through the totems in front of her. "We need to deal with your . . . web issue." Nothing stood out. She moved to the next pile.

"It hurts, Wendy, this is no lie," Piotr said, forcing himself to straighten and continue dusting off the shelf, examining the items beneath each mound of dust, "but I have said nothing because there is nothing to be said. The web, the seed, it will not kill me. I know this now; my memories have only confirmed this. I will ache and suffer, yes, but I cannot be destroyed. So long as the Never exists, so shall I walk on. In a way it is a terrible blessing—the webs . . . I can feel their connection. I can feel how they are gathering life from all over the city, how they are gathering will. All they need is to release it."

"Great. Lots of power there," Wendy grumbled, "like a spirit nuke just hanging out over the city, dangling over our heads, waiting to bust an even bigger hole between the worlds. Fabulous. Just. Frickin. Fabulous."

"Come," Piotr said, stumbling to his feet but refusing Wendy's offer of aid. He reached out and took his mother's cloak in his arms, holding the crusted, dusty thing to his nose and inhaling deeply.

"Come, Wendy. We have what they want . . . at least, what Sanngriðr desires. It is time we took this battle to her."

CHAPTER TWENTY-NINE

In the hallway of the townhome, Wendy paused, grabbing Piotr's arm. "Wait. I don't . . . I don't know if I can do this."

"Do what, Wendy? Battle Sanngriðr? Remember, for all her fierceness, the Lady Walker is simply Sanngriðr showing her true face—rotten and mealy, falling apart. We will force her to stop her sabotage. We will bribe her with the cloak if we must. She doesn't want to be here. If she is gone we can do the Good Work in peace, as we were supposed to."

"No . . . I mean . . . I don't think that . . . wait. Stop, okay, just . . . stop." Wendy sank to the floor and, finding a clear spot to rest her face, laid her forehead against the cool wooden floor of the entryway.

Don't just barge ahead. Think things through, Wendy, she urged herself. *Ask the right questions.* Slowly, she straightened.

"Piotr. If we . . . if we chose a side, which one would you pick?"

He raised an eyebrow and knelt beside her, laying the cloak on the floor. "A side? What do you mean? What sides are there?"

"Think about it," Wendy urged. "The Reapers, right? They're not . . . well, they're not what they were initially supposed to be anymore. They haven't been for quite some time. The whole point was to reap as many ghosts as they could so a backlog didn't start to build up. But then they started narrowing down the field of who could reap, and then they started killing off the most powerful Reapers, the naturals, because they were scared of them. It's like . . . it's like a game of telephone!"

Piotr gave her a quizzical look and Wendy sighed. She loved

him a great deal but he missed so *much* sometimes. "It's not important, okay? My point is that the original message, the original *point* of the Reapers, has been hugely garbled. And Elise, who tries to keep from reaping at all and instead just uses the spirits, is making it way, way worse!"

"I understand," Piotr said, leaning against the wall, "but I do not understand why you speak of choosing sides."

"Think about it . . . *why* is Sanngriðr poking holes in the Never? There's got to be a reason for it—she's even got Reaper-ish people on her side, like Dr. Kensington. He was working closely with the creature and . . . oh. OH!" Wendy's hand flew to her mouth. "That son of a bitch!"

Piotr gave her the quizzical look again. "What is it?"

"Chel and Jon are naturals. We know they took a Seer up to Alcatraz and fed her to one of those weird holes in the Never to start up the earthquakes . . . And Dr. Kensington was trying to make Chel and Jon stay at the hospital where he could keep an eye on them. I bet he was planning on . . ." Wendy stopped, shivering with fear and rage. "I bet he was planning on feeding them to one of those nasty holes, as well. To start a quake or be a body for a creature or something."

"They're in the hospital now," Piotr reminded her, voice tight. "Unconscious."

"And easily transferable," Wendy moaned. "He's already proven that he's okay with giving the go-ahead to fake paperwork! He'd have to be an idiot to miss a chance like that. Sign a few sheets, doll up a couple family members like EMT's . . . hell, lie and get actual EMT Reapers in on it . . . and whisk Jon and Chel away on a 'hospital transfer' that never reaches the next hospital." She pressed a hand over her mouth. "They've been in the hospital for over an hour! What if he's doing that right now?"

"We must hurry faster," Piotr said grimly, stumbling to his feet and gathering the cloak. "I am with you, whatever you decide, Wendy."

Wendy nodded and stood quickly. "Then let's cut him off at the pass. Let's hunt down Sanngriðr and find out from the horse's mouth why she's doing all this, what she wants to stop this madness." They stepped outside the townhome door. The spirit web forest waved in front of them, thick and full and brimming with stolen life. Beside her, Piotr hugged the cloak to his gut and groaned.

"She's in the city somewhere," Wendy said, wrapping an arm around Piotr to help support him. "But where?"

"I think there," Piotr said, lifting his head and pointing to a thin spot in the forest canopy. Through the hole in the webs they could see the huge purple-lipped mouth of the hole pulsing and moving, almost as if it would speak. Wendy didn't have to see above the canopy to sense that the hole now filled the sky.

A sharp Light burst up and outward like a firework. The earth shivered wildly beneath their feet.

"That," Wendy said when the tremors had subsided, "is not a good sign."

"What, like the end of the world?" Piotr whispered as the sky above the flash of Light peeled open. Creatures from the deepest parts of the space between worlds began falling like hail from the mouth in the sky.

"We have to close the hole," Wendy insisted. "How long do we have before those things can start inhabiting normal people?"

"I do not know."

An ambulance careened around the corner in front of them; Wendy jumped back, barely avoiding being flattened.

"That hole is big enough it's near Nob Hill now," Wendy muttered, orienting herself on the stoop. "Come on, Piotr. Let's go!"

CHAPTER THIRTY

They ran. They ran as fast as they could, as far as they could, dodging the zombie-like living who shambled up and down the sidewalks. Spirit webs clung to the living like twisted wires, sucking their life with audible gulps. Wendy and Piotr dodged swerving cars as the drivers, succumbing to the low-hanging webs, spun out and crashed, slamming into walls and trees and nearly running over passersby. The ghosts of the living shouted at one another in tinny voices that hardly penetrated the strange thick-thinness of the Never. Wendy and Piotr moved from healthy spot to weak spot, from solid to the shreds of once what was.

They ran and ran and ran, Piotr clutching the cloak and his side but never complaining, never asking to stop. Finally, at long last, they caught a taxi heading in the right direction. Wendy shoved Piotr into the passenger seat as the taxi idled, waiting as a speeding trolley zipped past. Wendy flung herself after Piotr into the taxi and crouched in the passenger side as the family of four in the backseat sat perfectly still, the spirit webs clinging to their faces sucking all the joy and life out of them through their eyes. Wendy worried that if she moved the webs would sense her feeble energy and attack her.

"Hang on," Wendy whispered to Piotr. "Hang on."

Wendy arrived at the foot of the Mark Hopkins to find over a half-dozen Reaper bodies lying on the ground like litter—many of them women she'd spotted earlier in the evening waiting outside as Nana Moses' body was loaded into the hearse. Several Walkers hovered nearby—more than one had given themselves up to the beasts, as well, and were twice as twisted and vile as before. But some, thankfully,

seemed to be merely their normal, rotting selves. Wendy wondered what they thought of the mess their Lady had gotten them all into.

Knowing Walkers, they didn't care.

Elise and Sanngriðr were face to face only feet away from one another. Sanngriðr's hands were curled into fists; Elise wiped blood from her mouth with the back of her hand. They'd obviously been having words.

Elise coughed, blood flecking her lips. "I won't let you do this. The Never isn't yours to play with!"

"You have no say, old woman," Sanngriðr sneered. "Your years of torturing the dead for your own gain are almost done. I can see your remaining hours. They hang above your head pendulously, dipping lower and lower as your time runs out."

Wendy and Piotr approached. Wendy, feeling as if her gut were burning up, realized that her flesh was as thin as paper, her hair brittle as glass.

"Piotr," she whispered. "I'm almost done. I'm dying."

"I know," he said. "I can nearly taste your death approaching. You do not have much time left."

"Very poetic," Elise snapped at Sanngriðr. "Futile, though. You have been the bane of my family for too long. This ends now, you rotten old hag."

Elise smiled; her teeth were lined with red. "Go into the—*hurk!*"

Elise dropped to her knees, hands going to her gut. There was a fist through her side that flexed open and closed, blood dripping from the creature's fingers and splattering on the floor. The hand wiggled its fingers as if to say hello, and then, suddenly, yanked back through Elise's body with a loud, wet *squelch*.

"Damn it!" Wendy cried as Elise, no longer supported by the arm thrust through her belly, slumped to the floor. "Why the hell do you have to be so damn *evil*, lady? You are *not* making this decision easy on me, either of you!"

Sanngriðr ignored Wendy's outburst. "What were you saying, dear?" she asked Elise politely, kneeling down and tilting her head so that they were on the same eye level. "You seem to be at a loss for words. Cat got your tongue? Or just your spleen?"

The twisted-Walker nearest Wendy chuckled, as did the one who'd impaled Elise on its fist. It shook its claw, blood droplets flying and coating Elise in a fine spray.

"I don't care what you had planned for your family, for this age," Sanngriðr said, wiping a few of the red droplets off the slightly more intact side of her face. "I have long since tired of this hideous gray land. If I can't escape it, then I will simply have to bring the Never down, and Miðgarðr along with it. Freyja will know her folly soon enough."

Sanngriðr reached forward and casually yanked the golden necklace free from Elise's neck. "I'll take that, thank you."

"Don't . . ." Elise moaned. "You don't know what you're doing . . . that's been in my family for . . . must protect it . . ."

"She thinks Elise was wearing—" Piotr began.

"I know," Wendy hissed, hushing him. "I'll talk to her. You . . . you just stay back, okay?"

The creature nearest them sniffed and turned their way. It howled, low and long, and Sanngriðr turned, spying Wendy.

"My, my, my," she purred, finally acknowledging Wendy. "Look what the cat dragged in. Hello, Wendy. Or should I call you Light-bringer? I prefer Reaper's Bane to be honest—you've done such a good job keeping them busy and on their toes for me while I accomplished my business about town. You've even gone so far as to donate your own kind to the cause."

Sanngriðr tilted her head up at the gaping wound in the sky and laughed. "Your sister must be on her way to Alcatraz by now, did you know? Your brother, too. The little Seer we used earlier hardly did anything at all—only let one or two beasties through—but two naturals . . . well, they'll make *such* a bang! Maybe one even loud enough to wake the gods."

The Lady Walker shook Elise's necklace. "And if not, well, I'll set the alarm. But you don't know what I'm talking about, do you? Oh no, no history or books for the lovely Lightbringer . . . this girl reaps not by rote but by vote," she sneered. "You *ask* the ghosties if they want to go away. How . . . progressive of you."

"Sanngriðr, you're making a big mistake," Wendy said, trying to appease her, to slow her down enough to get the Lady Walker to drop her guard. "A huge mistake. You don't want to do this."

"Did I give you permission to use my name, girl?" sneered the Lady Walker, Sanngriðr, bridling, all lazy humor vanished as she narrowed her eyes at Wendy. "I think you ought to shut your mouth while you still have one to shut. How did you even learn . . . no. No matter. Perhaps you're not as dumb as you look, after all. Anything is possible, I suppose."

"Making with the grandiose threats, huh? Have we reached that part of the fight already?" Wendy said, rolling her eyes. Her hands thrust into her pockets and her fingers brushed the haft of Lily's dull knife. It worked on Reapers . . . maybe, with luck, it would work on the Lady Walker or the other creatures as well.

"Listen, lady, I think you're nasty," Wendy said baldly. "I mean, seriously, seriously gross inside and out. But the fact of the matter is that you're not going to accomplish anything by opening up that wormhole or whatever you've got hanging in the sky. All you're going to do is get every soul in the Never devoured."

"That is the whole point, is it not? Isn't that what your Reapers are really supposed to be about? Sending every single soul on? I'm simply speeding up the process by ripping a hole between the worlds."

"*Every* soul," Wendy stressed. "*Including* yours. Or do you think all the creatures that come crawling from the depths of nothingness are going to sit pretty and beg for treats the way these two are?" She flicked a glance at the two twisted-Walkers and noticed the discomfiture briefly cross their faces. The creatures inhabiting them were

beginning to understand what Wendy was getting at, and they didn't like it.

Smiling, Sanngriðr jiggled Elise's necklace in front of Wendy's face. "That is why Brísingamen is key to my ambitions. This bauble is my pass from this place, girl. When I use it, when I call Freyja to this gray hellhole that she created, a rift shall open into Fólkvangr and I can slip through. I have spent two millennia here, cut off from my divinity, living as a human might, suffering as a human does . . . no! No more. It has driven me mad with grief for the host-fields! No, girl, I will go home and nothing you or your pitiful little family can do will stop it."

"Sanngriðr," Wendy said, trying to calm the terrible rage building within the Lady Walker, "then why have you done the things you've done? Why have you stalked the Reapers all these years, hindering them instead of helping them?"

"Hindering? HINDERING? I WAS HELPING! Every single soul in this place is one soul too many, girl! And you call yourselves Reapers!" Furious, Sanngriðr pounded a fist against her thigh.

"You don't deserve the name," she sneered at Wendy. "If a single one of you had done your job, your mandated duty, correctly in the first place, then all of us would have long since entered the Light! But no, oh no. NO! *You*, little girl, get the idea that a soul must have a choice, that they have to be ready to move on. And that one—" Sanngriðr spat at Elise, "uses the souls for her own selfish gains, to advance her pathetic *living* existence. That is not the way of the Reaper! You cleave the soul, you set them free. You do not sit down with them and have a drink of vodka!"

Wendy thought of Frank, most likely waiting at the bar in the Top of the Mark, tossing back shots and watching the bleeding sky with dead, tired eyes. Wendy winced.

"I tire of this. I tire of all of you," Sanngriðr said softly, gripping Elise's necklace so that the tendons of her hand creaked and popped. "Your grandmother, your aunt . . . I hated them and they hated me,

but once they understood the history, there was no question of not doing their duty. This one, this *would-be matriarch*, had them killed for daring question the status quo!"

"My mother—"

"Ah, yes, let us speak of Mary, shall we?" Sanngriðr shook her head, glaring at Wendy. "How *you* of all people managed to topple the White Lady is beyond me. She alone of your cursed clan was able to adequately work the weave and weft of a spiritual connection. Such talent and skill . . . snipped close by her pathetic excuse for a daughter."

Wendy flinched. She'd stopped her mother from destroying the thirteen kidnapped Lost and then accidentally sent them into the Light herself. The White Lady and all her attending Walkers had vanished in a flash of Light, a blaze so hot it had sent everyone in the room on . . . except for Piotr.

Wait a moment.

Overwhelmed, Wendy slumped to the ground. How could she have been so stupid? The problem had been staring her in the face for hours now and it wasn't until now—now, watching Elise bleed out—that the answer had come.

"You are . . . were . . . a Reaper," Wendy said, pondering her words carefully. "Are you still? Can you still, uh, separate a soul from its body? Can you still, um, 'work the weave and weft' of a spirit's connection to its shell?"

"Are you really flame-haired beneath that terrible dye?" mocked Sanngriðr coldly. "Are you truly female? Manipulating the mysteries of the spirit is not what I do, idiot girl, it is what I *am*. I could no more turn off the inner workings of my very nature than this pathetic woman," Sanngriðr kicked Elise, "could smother her greed."

Wendy licked her lips nervously. She couldn't believe that she was going to ask this.

"I think . . . I think maybe you don't have to . . ." Wendy

cringed, "maybe you don't have to be this extreme. Destroying both worlds, I mean. Putting the living lands at risk so you can go home. I know you're angry, I know you want everyone . . . *everyone* to suffer the way you have but . . . I think we can help one another."

"I sincerely doubt that," Sanngriðr said. "I can't imagine what you could offer that I need."

Wendy swallowed thickly. "Well, for starters . . . how about I end the world?"

CHAPTER THIRTY-ONE

Sanngriðr blinked in surprise. Wendy was mollified to realize that she'd startled the Lady Walker into speechlessness.

"Let me explain," Wendy rushed to say. Her best chance of getting Sanngriðr to go along with the half-reasoned plan—she was still working it out—was to keep talking before Sanngriðr could get a word in edgewise. "This isn't a trick."

She sneered. "An auspicious beginning, for certain."

"Look . . . I'm not . . ." Wendy glanced at her feet. "I'm not Elise, okay? We have to see eye to eye on that before we can go any further. Yeah, I want spirits to *want* to go into the Light, rather than just shoving them in without the go-ahead, but I'm not withholding the Light from them if they ask. I'm not making them do stuff for me. I'm just . . . I'm just putting myself in their shoes. There's no penance to it."

"You understand so little about the Light, girl," Sanngriðr sighed. "Once they get close enough to the Light, any fears or trepidations a soul has melts away. They are eager to enter the Light. It is where they are *supposed* to go."

"I know that now," Wendy said, nettled at Sanngriðr's tone. "Even the most sane of spirits has a self-destructive streak, Sanngriðr."

"Again, you use my name," she said and there was steel beneath the words. Sharp steel. "I warn you, girl, such careless words will—"

"Yeah, yeah, you'll be pissed at me," Wendy said, making a zip-it motion to Sanngriðr. "My plan's simple, okay? I want to blow up the Never."

Sanngriðr groaned. "I should have known that you were speaking nothing but lies, girl. Either that or you are a naïve fool.

The Never cannot be 'blown up.' It is as eternal as blasted Freyja. It is endless and heartless as the Lady herself!"

"Oh really?" Wendy said. "Because not a month ago I destroyed every spirit in Palace Hotel in one fell swoop. There's nothing of the Palace left in the Never. It's all gone. Just a blank space the webs have taken over."

Sanngriðr raised an eyebrow. "I beg your pardon? How—"

"I'm a natural, you know that," Wendy said. "One who, as you yourself noted, is burning up." She held up a nearly transparent hand. "There's not much of me left, to be honest. I'm crispy fried."

The pause that followed Wendy's declaration was long and measured. After several minutes Sanngriðr rose to her full height. "Come closer."

"Wendy," Piotr murmured, his voice carrying no further than her ears, "be cautious." He squeezed her hand.

"Always," Wendy said and crossed the distance between Piotr and Sanngriðr. It felt as if she were traversing some vast gulf of space—the Lady Walker now emitted a tangible cold, an icy aura that shocked the system the closer Wendy approached. She shivered and forced her legs to keep going, passing Elise, passing the assembled creatures and Walkers, and finally reaching the Lady Walker.

Sanngriðr tilted her head and examined Wendy closely. "You are not lying. You have a great deal of spiritual energy built up within. This should have burned you to a crisp by now; how have you not burned up? How are you holding on? It should be impossible."

"I don't know. Maybe I'm just stubborn. Maybe I'm just lucky."

Narrowing her eyes, Sanngriðr tilted her head. "No. I think not. I think this is a ruse to stall me. I think you believe you can save both the worlds. No, girl, no. I have suffered too long to allow you to stroll in here and try and sway me!"

"Sanngriðr!" Piotr snapped. He straightened to his full height, his arm wrapped around his gut, fingers splayed against his ribs. "Sanngriðr, you know who I am."

She laughed. "Of course I do."

Piotr leaned down and gathered up his mother's cloak. Then he flung it at her feet. "You know what this is."

Sanngriðr paled; her expression grew greedy and covetous. "How did . . . yes. Yes, boy," she said slyly, "I know what that is."

"I give it to you," Piotr said. "In exchange for Wendy to do as she will with no interference from you or yours. She wishes to attempt to destroy the Never and *only* the Never. You will help her. For this."

"No, Piotr—" Wendy protested but was cut off as Piotr jerked a hand sharply, lips tightening. She quieted.

"I give this to you, the cloak of my mother, so that you may return home," Piotr said. "So that you may face your Lady and spit in her face if you wish. I care not. But this ends. Now."

Sanngriðr snorted. "Deal, boy. But how do I know that this little natural has the power to even—"

"The last time my soul was released," Wendy hurried to point out, "it caused an earthquake in the living lands." She looked up at the hole in the sky. "Sound familiar?"

"Your energy wasn't concentrated properly in the Never then," Sanngriðr sneered, plucking at the ruins of her face. "Such sloppy handling of your power, allowing it to spill over into the living lands."

"I did the best I could, given the circumstances," Piotr replied dryly. "Since my goal was to return Wendy's soul to her body, not harm anyone."

"*You* had access to this Reaper's powers? Outside her body? How . . ." Sanngriðr paused and looked between the two of them, confused, before comprehension dawned. "Oh, my. Your mother really *was* very good at what she did, girl. If she were still kicking I'd give her my compliments."

Sanngriðr laughed, not bothering to hide the cruel glee. "Had the White Lady succeeded in her endeavors, she would have returned

to the living lands, riding the wave of your power. She pulled it out whole, yes? A ball of fiercely burning Light?" Sanngriðr shook her head. "Using the power of a natural's soul as a conduit. Brilliant. If she had succeeded—"

"Well, she didn't," Wendy said flatly, "which is lucky for you, isn't it? If my mother had killed me returning her soul back to her body, you wouldn't have me to play this stupid cat and mouse game with. She wasn't a natural; she couldn't have offered you what I'm about to. So what will it be? Will you help me?"

"Don't," moaned Elise from the ground at their feet. She wiped one ringed hand against her torn mouth, smearing the blood further across her cheek. "Don't do this, Winifred. Please."

"No one is talking to you," Sanngriðr sneered, kicking Elise in the gut. The older woman doubled over but Wendy, ignoring Sanngriðr's snide expression, knelt down by Elise.

"What would you have me do, Elise?" Wendy asked softly. "I've seen the beginning of what we are. I know what we were supposed to be."

"You don't have to listen to our ancestors or whatever ridiculous nonsense you think you found," Elise whispered. "Tracey and Mary thought they found it, too. I knew that they were wrong. Just as you're wrong. We are what we make of ourselves. We are *Reapers*! We make the rules here!"

"And if making your own way hurts everyone else? If making my own way leaves countless souls to suffer?"

"They chose this suffering," Elise reminded her. "They must toil through their penance! Many souls turn from the Light on their own. Many are frightened of the lives they've led, the sins they've committed. The Never may not be perfect, but it's a safe place for them to recoup themselves, for the spirits to find their own way. Limbo, Winifred. A respite from Heaven and Hell. Don't you think they've earned the right to decide on their own?"

She had a point.

"If I unweave the fabric of your soul, you may not survive the explosion," Sanngriðr interrupted idly, fingering Elise's chain, dangling around her neck. "Have you thought that far, girl? Once done it cannot be undone. If your Light does not obliterate all the souls, you will have failed and the Never will still exist."

"Yeah, I got that part," Wendy growled.

"If I take your Light but this fails, you will still stink of Reaper. You will still taste of the Light but be unable to protect yourself. You will most likely die a painful death at the hands of Walkers or Lost or even creatures from between the worlds. Not that you will last much longer, as it is. Your body is nearly done."

Wendy flicked a nervous glance at Piotr. He nodded; Sanngriðr was telling the truth. Wendy squared her shoulders and put on her most haughty expression. Her heart was racing. "I can handle myself, Sanngriðr."

Though she knew it would most likely bother the older woman, Wendy knelt and smoothed Elise's tangled hair. She just didn't look like *Elise*, lying there bloodied and beaten. Elise shook her head and wordlessly lay her cheek to the ground, beaten and done.

"Wendy," Piotr said in an undertone, "you do not have to do this. You can let them fight among themselves."

Rising to her feet, Wendy was tempted. So, so tempted. The Lady Walker and the Reapers had been at one another's throats for centuries—why should it fall on her to change it all?

And then she remembered Kara, hanging from the ceiling, bloodied and crazed, corrupted by the creature and torn asunder yet still having enough strength to keep the location of the hearth, the door to the Never in the basement of her own home, locked away from Dr. Kensington. He'd killed her girlfriend, the worried woman who wore bunny slippers to the ER, sacrificed her to open up the hole to the darkest realms, and still Kara fought with the beast and kept her cool.

What about Chel and Jon? What about Eddie?

Decision made, Wendy sniffled. "The dead have made their choices. The living deserve to be given that chance. I'm going to do it. I'm going to destroy the Never."

At her feet Elise moaned and Sanngriðr laughed.

"Is it enough? Will it be enough? My Light . . . powers . . . whatever? Are they going to be enough to get the job done? Is there any way I can . . . I don't know . . . any way I can up my powers so I don't burn out the way you think I will? Enhance them or something?"

"Short of allowing yourself to burn to a crisp and releasing your Light seconds before your body gives out, no," Sanngriðr said shortly, crossing her ravaged arms over her chest. "We can, of course, do this if you so desire, but it will ensure that you cannot return to your human body when this is all done. The act of destroying the Never by yourself will kill you. You won't even be able to go into the Light. You'll merely burn out."

"*Net!*" Piotr snapped. "This is not to be allowed."

"Excuse me?" Wendy said, irritated. She tried not to think of the promise she'd made Eddie. "*Allowed?* Who do you think you are, Piotr, my dad? You aren't the boss of me. You can't just tell me what I can and cannot—"

"Wendy," Piotr said, grabbing her hand. "*Solnyshko moyo*, look at me. *Net, lyublyu tebya vsem sertsem, vsey dushoyu* . . . I love you . . . *puzhalsta* . . . please, please, were anything to happen to you then I could not bear it." Piotr drew her close, resting his chin on her shoulder and pressing small, feather-light kisses against her jaw as Piotr whispered his explanation fast and low.

"Wendy, you have so much to live for . . ."

"What, and your mom didn't? My mom didn't?"

"This is not about them," he said urgently. "They are both dead, Wendy. This is about you and this world. You do not belong here. You are still alive. *Puzhalsta*, Wendy, please, please . . . please do not do this thing."

Sanngriðr stepped close to them. "I can appreciate your tender

moment, children, but I am a woman on a schedule. Wendy, make up your mind. You can sacrifice yourself and burn out, or—"

"Wait," Wendy said, pounding Piotr once on the chest and bouncing on the tips of her toes, overwhelmed with excitement. "Wait! The spirit webs!"

Piotr's hand brushed his chest. "What?"

"The spirit webs. They're full. *They're full*!"

Nodding, Piotr glanced at Sanngriðr; both he and the Lady Walker gave Wendy a quizzical look. "*Da*. Brimming."

"We can tap that, right? Tap their . . . juice? All that living willpower? All the Shades the webs devoured? Use the power to—"

Sanngriðr's laughter, long and cruel and overjoyed, cut Wendy off. "I was wrong, girl! You are *every bit* as smart as your mother was! YES! Yes, yes, if you let me infect you with a spirit web, you will be connected with the forest. Of course, again, you are so weak that the web itself may kill you."

"She doesn't have to," Piotr said. He rested a hand on his chest. "I already have a seed inside me."

Sanngriðr raised one ruined eyebrow. "Indeed? I see."

"How . . ." Wendy swallowed deeply, "how do we . . . how do we do this?"

Sanngriðr lifted the necklace. "Wearing this, Piotr takes your orb of Light and flings himself into the mouth between the worlds. That is all. It will destroy the—"

"NO!" screamed Elise, shoving to her feet and striding forward. Light bloomed in her hands—fierce and sharp and blazing—and Piotr dropped to his knees beside Wendy, dazzled.

"Everything you do is poison! The Never must *not* be destroyed! I will destroy her first!" Elise screamed and, just like that, she was writhing with Light, a fiery figure with ribbons alight, flinging herself at Wendy. Sanngriðr moved too slowly, Piotr was down . . .

And, falling back, Wendy's hand scrabbled in her pocket. The dull knife ripped through the side of her jeans . . .

. . . jutting out . . .

. . . stabbing Elise between the breasts, punching through the ribs and burning Wendy's hands. Elise, grunting, sliced jaggedly at Wendy's face and temple as she writhed on the blade.

"Kill . . . you . . . abom . . . ab . . ." Elise whispered, the Light fading from around her body as she became nothing more than a run-ragged old woman once more, the Reaper's power leaving her body in a rush of heat and one final blast of Light. Above them the hole rumbled and blazed. The earth trembled beneath them.

Then, just like that, Elise sagged . . . and was done.

Kin-killer.

The knife blazed.

Wendy dropped the knife frantically, but her palm had been embossed with marks of the blade. Struggling out from beneath Elise proved difficult—her fingers spasmed and ached; she clutched her hand to her chest as Elise fell to her knees and fell forward, truly dead this time.

"Oh, Wendy," Piotr moaned beside her. "Oh, Wendy."

"Enough of this. No more distractions! You! Boy! Go to the roof," Sanngriðr ordered, passing Piotr Elise's necklace. "Wear this. You know what it is."

Piotr didn't smirk as he took the forgery. His expression was properly grim, but Wendy could sense the lightness in his body as he took the links from Sanngriðr's hand. Sanngriðr knelt down beside Wendy. "Are you prepared, girl? This will hurt."

"Wait," Wendy said. "I . . . I want to be there."

"On the roof?"

"Yes. I need to . . ." Wendy licked her lips. "Let me say goodbye. Please."

For an instant she thought Sanngriðr would deny her, but instead the Lady Walker laughed. "Love. All my misery stems from

love. Fine. Go. I will follow in five minutes and not a second more."
She waved a hand at the hotel. "Do not make me regret trusting you,
girl."

Leaving Sanngriðr, Wendy and Piotr approached the hotel. A
gauntlet of Walkers, both inhabited and not, stood beside the path.
As they passed, Wendy paused to speak to the first Walker. "Am I
making the right decision?" she asked. "Would you . . . would you
want to go into the Light if you could?"

The Walkers shifted uneasily, and then the one Wendy picked
to speak with nodded. "Once, scared of death." It raised its hooded
face to the blackness boiling above. Creatures were pouring from the
hole now, directly above the city.

Wendy, distantly, could hear the living screams.

"Now . . . scared of this." The Walker chuckled raspily. "Is this
truth? Can flesh, can you, end the Never? Make there be no more
pain? No more death?"

Nervously, Wendy glanced over at Piotr and Sanngriðr. "I don't
know. They think I can. We'll see."

The Walker indicated the blackness. "Then try. Be quick. Stop
you, we will wait. We tire. We wish sleep."

Wendy glanced around the gathered Walkers. "After all this
time . . . you all really feel this way? You're done fighting?
Honestly?"

"Flesh chatty-chatty too much," warned the Walker. "Time
ticking. Go. Finish this."

Hurriedly, Wendy moved to join Piotr and they both hurried
into the hotel, rushing past guests and speeding to the roof.

They had to cut across the Top of the Mark to get to the roof.
Frank and the Council watched them pass silently. The mysterious
greaser was there, Wendy noted, lounging in the far corner by the
piano. He winked at Wendy as she passed and, pulling a comb out
of his pocket, began to comb his ducktail. Where the comb ran, the
black turned to red . . .

Startled, Wendy spun on her heel. Surely she hadn't seen that right?

The greaser was gone as if he'd never been, nowhere to be seen. Wendy frowned. Something about the way he moved . . .

Once they were on the roof, together in glorious privacy, Piotr turned to Wendy and drew her into a loose embrace. He brushed her matted, crooked bangs off her forehead and tenderly kissed the ragged, clotted cut zig-zagging at her temple. "This will scar, I think. We will be a matched set."

"Let it. I don't care."

Shaking his head, Piotr sighed and dropped his arms. The normal Walkers below had all retreated from the twisted creatures. More than a few of them were watching the distant skies, the endless ebony expanding beyond the mist, shifting uneasily as the growing mass sucked at the edges of their tattered cloaks, sending the ragged edges fluttering in the wind.

In the distance twisted creatures were dropping, free-falling, from the rent in the sky. Their numbers were small now but the dead were many, the spirit webs expanding rapidly, trapping souls as they flourished and flowered.

"It's time," he whispered.

CHAPTER THIRTY-TWO

To die will be an awfully big adventure.
—J.M. Barrie, *Peter Pan*

Wendy shook her head. "No! I'm not ready. We're not ready. I just found you. I just . . . Piotr, please. Please. Sanngriðr can give us ten more minutes. Twenty!"

"Wendy." Piotr repeated gently, "It's time."

"But it's not fair," she said, tired now, sagging and feeling the hot tears leak out of the corners of her eyes. Piotr, unashamed, was crying as well, taking both her hands in his and rubbing her knuckles with the pads of his thumbs. Wendy sobbed as Piotr pulled her hands to his lips and kissed her fingers, her wrists, even turning her hands over and placing tender kisses in the cups of her palms.

"Wendy," he said, whispering the words between kisses, "I waited for you in the breath between moments, in the space between worlds. I waited and I hoped and eventually, after I forgot that I was waiting for you, you finally came. It's been a very long time, Wendy. And I have suffered every day."

Blinking the tears rapidly away, Wendy nodded once. "I know."

"Don't you think . . ." Piotr looked over at the Walkers, some who'd drawn closer to the hotel, edging surreptitiously away from the shadow cast across the sea. "Don't you think that I—we—have earned our rest? Even Sanngriðr has suffered, Wendy. Evil as she is, she deserves to go home."

Sanngriðr, approaching from the stairs, heard this last bit. Joining them, she rolled what remained of her eyes and laughed

darkly. "Seeing as you never should have been born in the first place, hearing that you believe your time to be nigh amuses me."

"It isn't?" he asked, cocking an eyebrow.

"Oh it is," she smirked. "But this is far too graceful an end than you deserve. If it were up to me."

"Yeah, yeah, Sanngriðr," Wendy said, shaking her head and forcing a tired, sad smile. She hated the woman but her tears were done. It was time. "And if pigs could fly we'd all have bacon on the wing. Beat it for a minute."

"Only because the souls are done . . . only for this reason will I leave," Sanngriðr said, tilting her head back, smiling at the ever-darkening sky. "But hurry, boy. Our time draws close." She left, leaving Piotr and Wendy alone again. As she stalked away Wendy spotted the figure hiding around the corner. The red hair. The white cloak. It was a brief glimpse, nothing more, and Wendy *knew* this time that she hadn't imagined it. She thought of going after the figure but decided that, in the end, the spy watching them didn't matter.

Piotr did.

"I am sorry that I said you were being foolish," Piotr apologized, dragging Wendy's attention back to the moment at hand. "It was unfair of me. You have every—"

"No, you're right, I'm . . . I'm being selfish." Then, without warning, Wendy flung herself into Piotr's arms. He caught her just as she pressed her lips to the cup of his ear and whispered, "I'm going to miss you."

"I'll miss you too, Curly," he whispered back, wrapping a finger in an errant curl and tugging. "More than you will ever know."

Resting his forehead against Wendy's, Piotr threaded his hands in hers, took a deep breath and asked, "Are you prepared?"

She wasn't, and she never would be, but Wendy sniffled and nodded just the same. "What happens to you now?"

"I've been a teenager for two thousand years . . . now . . ." Piotr broke off and chuckled, shaking his head. Wendy felt the wetness of

his tears as he drew her close again, pressing a damp, warm kiss against her cheek. "I think it's time that I grow up." He hugged her again. "Thank you, Wendy. For everything."

Stepping back, Wendy reached into his pocket and grasped the real Brísingamen. It was surprisingly heavy and slippery from Elise's blood still on Wendy's hands, thrumming in her palm. Hands trembling, Wendy slipped the necklace over Piotr's head, hiding it beneath the collar of his shirt, noting the pitch change as the somnolent siren hum at the edges of the purple-white ring of Light ratcheted up several notches. In her periphery, standing at the edge of the roof, Wendy noticed that several of the Walkers had dropped to their knees, and were shaking and rocking back and forth, what remained of their hands pressed flush against the sides of their head, uselessly trying to drown out the song.

"This will hurt," Sanngriðr warned Wendy, drawing out the knife that Wendy had just used to kill Elise. Sanngriðr had wiped it clean of blood but Elise's Light had warped the blade into a waving shape.

"Do it," Wendy said.

She held her arms wide at her sides, palms up and open. Piotr's fingertips brushed her wrist. His touch was cool and comforting.

Wrapping her fist around the end of Wendy's cord, Sanngriðr pulled it taut and slashed down, severing the cord from her navel in a stroke and slapping the silver coil into Wendy's palm. Wendy jerked as Sanngriðr jammed her fist into the hole she'd created and sliced the bindings free, gathering up the edges of Wendy's Light and rolling it together. The sensation hurt but was also cleansing, like lancing something inflamed inside her. Wendy felt the heat that always traveled with her stretched and pulled from her veins, from behind her eyes, from deep within her heart. Wendy squeezed her cord to concentrate on holding off the pain and breathed deeply. Sanngriðr was taking longer than the White Lady had, but Sanngriðr knew exactly what she was doing.

She felt it the instant the Light was gone.

"Done," Sanngriðr said triumphantly, snatching Wendy's cord from her hand and smoothing it between her palms, encasing the Light in the glossy, satiny length.

The silver length was cool and soft to the touch, like slippery satin in her palm. Wendy rolled it in her hand; she felt hollowed out.

"Now, boy," Sanngriðr said. "It's your turn. End this. End our suffering."

The hair on the back of Wendy's neck rose as, in the distance, the wail of the hole in the sky lengthened and rose to a high-pitched scream. The Walkers and creatures on the ground were writhing now, shaking and twisting on the stone. The noise was deafening.

"Are there words?! Some spell or something?!" Wendy shouted, trying not to stare at the jittering Walkers. The blackness was close now, maybe only a few miles out to sea, the heavy space between the worlds teeming with shrieking, screaming faces and watching, filmy red eyes.

"As was done," Sanngriðr yelled, "let be undone. The stipulations of my penance, of Piotr's penance, have been met. The Never is no more! WE ARE FREE!"

"Are you ready, Piotr?" Wendy yelled, straining to be heard over the cacophony. The creatures within the hole could see what was happening. The noise from beyond the Never was so loud it filled the world, setting even her teeth to aching.

Standing at the edge of the roof, Piotr grabbed Wendy and kissed her. "Time to fly," he said and shoved Wendy's Light into his own chest.

The blast of Light drew the fracturing sea up, a reverse rainstorm pattering against the underside of the bubbling, frothing clouds. The raging sea whirled up and up, huge waves crashing up and out. The creatures of the dark shrieked and screamed, furious to be losing their prey, and were thrown back, the space between worlds flung far, far away once again.

"Freyja, you bitch," Sanngriðr snarled. "I'm coming for you!" She ran at the hole and jumped, her body twisting in midair, becoming a dirty-winged gull and vanishing into the darkness.

Cupping her cheek one last time, Piotr winked at Wendy and ran at the edge of the hotel, flinging himself over the rim, and falling through the hole stretching across the sky.

The moment he vanished the Never began to crack apart in earnest, huge silver cracks spreading from beneath the hotel and swallowing the writhing Walkers whole. The distant darkness at the very edges of Wendy's vision were swallowed by the wash of Light, the world, the universe, everything cradled in a sudden siren song.

Uncaring, Wendy stood alone at the edge of the abyss, numb as the Never broke like glass and shattered around her. Across the water a brilliant beam of Light streaked across the sky, spearing the city and cracking across the Top of the Mark, stabbing down in one sharp burst.

At last, everything was Light. She stood upon the last shreds of Never as the cracks neared.

"I never said goodbye," Wendy realized, laughing as the ground peeled away.

Arms encircled her from behind. They were pale and thin, but strong, and the perfume was familiar.

"Mom," Wendy whispered. She felt a brief pressure against her cheek, the barest touch, and felt more than heard her mother's throaty chuckle against her cheek.

It was good. *She* was good. But the illusion was not quite good enough.

"You're not my mom," Wendy said and could not stop the tears from burning her eyes, pooling and spilling down her cheeks. "It's been you this whole time, hasn't it? I saw you earlier, hiding around the corner. I . . . I kind of had an idea. You were the greaser at the Westglen, weren't you? You were the White Lady. You were in my dreams."

"I have been with you since your birth," the woman using Mary's voice murmured as, all around, the Never crumbled. "My touch alone kept your soul from burning you alive. I have walked with you through the darkest nights looking for your mother. I marked you; you are my redemption. Even gods can err . . . I needed a living soul to undo what I have done."

"That's it? That's all you have to say for yourself?" Wendy asked bitterly. "That's everything?"

The arms tightened for an instant and Mary's smell filled Wendy's nose; the sweet, silky scent of curling in her mother's lap when she was sad, the scent of sharing a midnight box of Oreos after a good reap, the scent of popcorn and movies, of Christmas and funerals, of hot summer nights and chill February fevers.

The scent of home.

Wendy swallowed thickly. The cracks were nearly at her feet. "What do I do now?"

"Close your eyes," Freyja whispered in Mary's voice, her breath feathering the hair at Wendy's temple. "Close your eyes and dream."

Obediently, Wendy closed her eyes . . .

EPILOGUE

...And opened them again.

Wendy recognized those ceiling tiles.

Hospital. Again. Long-term ward.

Typical.

Dad's insurance, Wendy thought, must really love her. Shifting, she glanced around the room. Eddie was sprawled half-across the foot of her bed, snoring and covered in his leather jacket. He held her hand, even in sleep, and Wendy marveled how even now, even after everything they'd been through, Eddie was unwilling to let her go.

Jon, stitched up and sporting a large cast on his left leg, overflowed the recliner under the window, head hanging off one arm and his good leg dangling off the other. Her dad wasn't in the room, but his briefcase was on the floor next to Jon. Wendy smiled to see it.

Only Chel, both eyes blackened and beautiful face covered with a multitude of tiny scratches and stitches, was awake. She looked up from texting when Wendy shifted.

"Hi," Wendy whispered. Eddie immediately stirred, lifting his head and smiling. He sat up and wordlessly hugged her, his strong arms pulling her close, the smell of him as familiar as sweet summer rain. Wendy felt him trembling and, for the first time in a long, long time, realized how much Eddie cared.

"I'm sorry," she said. The words caught in her throat, choking her, coming out rough.

Chel, sensing they needed a moment, went to the bathroom, locking the door behind.

Eddie held her face in his hands and shook his head. "No need to be." Then he kissed her. "I missed you."

"Piotr's dead. The Never is . . . the Never is gone."

Eddie nodded. "I know." Then he hugged her again and Wendy realized that it was over. She squinted but could make out nothing. If there were any spirits around, Wendy couldn't see them. The Never really was no more.

"I love you," she said. "You're my best friend, Eds."

He smiled and wrapped an arm around her shoulder. "I know that, too." He kissed her temple and relaxed back, and Wendy, tired, curled into his side. She'd slept so much lately, had drifted in and out of dreamscapes and the nightmares of the Never. Now, just for a little bit, all she wanted was a guaranteed . . .

Dreamless . . .

    Sleep . . .

Safe in her best friend's arms,
    Wendy closed her eyes.
        And didn't dream.

"You know that place between sleeping and awake,
that place where you can still remember dreaming?
That's where I'll always think of you."

—J. M. Barrie

ABOUT THE AUTHOR

K.D. MCENTIRE, author of *Lightbringer*, *Reaper*, and the short story "Heels" (which can be found in the anthology *When the Villain Comes Home*), lives just outside of Kansas City with her husband, children, and various pets. She spends her miniscule free time reading, writing, and battling her Sims 3 addiction (when reddit hasn't swallowed her soul whole) and is on the web at http://www.kdmcentire.com.